BENEDICT HALL

BENEDICT HALL

CATE CAMPBELL

KENSINGTON BOOKS
www.kensingtonbooks.com

KENSINGTON BOOKS are published by

Kensington Publishing Corp.
119 West 40th Street
New York, NY 10018

All Kensington titles, imprints, and distributed lines are available at
special quantity discounts for bulk purchases for sales promotion, pre-
miums, fund-raising, and educational or institutional use.

Special book excerpts or customized printings can also be created to fit
specific needs. For details, write or phone the office of the Kensington
Special Sales Manager: Kensington Publishing Corp., 119 West 40th
Street, New York, NY 10018. Attn. Special Sales Department. Phone:
1-800-221-2647.

Kensington and the K logo Reg. U.S. Pat. & TM Off.

ISBN-13: 978-0-7582-8759-5
ISBN-10: 0-7582-8759-3
First Kensington Trade Paperback Printing: June 2013

eISBN-13: 978-0-7582-8760-1
eISBN-10: 0-7582-8760-7
First Kensington Electronic Edition: June 2013

10 9 8 7 6 5 4 3 2 1

Printed in the United States of America

For my father,
F. M. Campbell, M.D.
In memoriam

CHAPTER 1

Frank Parrish went down the steps of the Alexis Hotel and turned toward the Public Market just as the shopkeepers were opening their shutters for the day. He walked with deliberate steps, trying not to hurry, though his need was urgent. Thin sunlight glistened on the gray waters of Elliott Bay. A sharp breeze chilled his face. He turned up the collar of his greatcoat, but he drew deep lungfuls of salt-scented air, wishing he could cool the fire burning in his arm. His shoes clicked on the Market's wooden walkway as he passed the high stalls, where fishmongers would soon shout their wares, and the day stalls, where farmers were setting out potatoes and squashes and onions. Following directions from one of the hotel's bellboys, he climbed a short set of stairs that led to the café on the upper level. The café jutted over the pier, an establishment of one room, with ironwork tables and chairs and a zinc counter stretching along one side. White cotton curtains filtered the morning glare from the bay.

The café was open, but empty of customers. A woman in a long bib apron looked up with an automatic smile when Frank stepped through the door. "Good morning, sir."

He took off his hat, and nodded to her. He saw her glance, first at the major's insignia sewn into the cuff of his coat, and then, inexorably, at the empty sleeve folded into the opposite pocket. Her smile softened into one of pity, an expression he had come to dread. She put down the glass she was polishing. She said in a gentle voice, as if he were as fragile as a child, "Get you something, sir? Coffee?"

He fiddled with the brim of his hat, hesitating. He hadn't come for coffee.

The army doctors had told him some pain was to be expected. In the hospital in Virginia they dosed him alternately with laudanum and morphine, but both made him feel slow and stupid, and did little to quell his pain. The kindest of his doctors prescribed whisky. It was corn whisky, shipped in from Canada, the only legal stuff they could get, and the nurses measured it out in careful doses. It was harsh and sour, the way medicine should be, but it was strong. It was the only thing that worked.

Frank was damned glad to be away from the hospital, but he still craved whisky. The bellboy had whispered that everyone in Seattle knew how to get around Prohibition because they'd had four extra years to figure it out. He had recommended this place. Frank could only hope what they sold here wouldn't make him go blind, or give him jake foot.

He avoided the barmaid's eyes as he dropped his hat on a table by the window. The humiliation of his need was nearly as bad as the pain. But not quite. He muttered, "Do you have—uh—anything stronger, ma'am?"

She didn't hesitate. "Wait just one moment, sir," she told him and disappeared through the swinging door behind her.

Frank sat down, stretching his long legs beneath the little table. He fought the urge to knead his arm with his fingers. That only made it worse. In fact, any touch—fingers or towels or bedsheets—further inflamed the knobby ends of his amputation. Even the sleeve of his shirt, gently folded over it and tucked into his pocket, chafed against the rough red skin.

The barmaid returned with a thick white mug in her hand.

She plucked a cotton napkin from the zinc counter, and crossed to Frank, the long hem of her apron fluttering around her ankles. "Here you go, sir." She set the napkin on the table, the mug on the napkin.

The liquid in the mug was most definitely not coffee. The pungent smell of peat rose from it, and Frank's mouth watered in anticipation. He nodded his thanks, and made himself wait till she had gone back behind the counter before he took his first swallow.

The whisky burned in his throat, a welcome fire that nearly made him groan. His second swallow sent warmth radiating into what remained of his left arm. The third flowed on, like a river running to the sea, washing away the pain of mutilated flesh, shattered bone, severed nerves. It went farther, to that space where there was no flesh or bone, where it soothed the phantom pain that had tortured him half the night.

He couldn't help himself, though he knew the barmaid was watching. He closed his eyes, and sighed his relief.

Frank had spent the previous night pacing his hotel room, gritting his teeth against the agony in his arm. It was a small room, the least expensive the Alexis had to offer. There were six steps to the door, three to the window, four more to the bed. He had walked those steps over and over again, counting the hours until the slow winter dawn lightened the sky beyond the window. Now, three fingers of whisky in his belly brought respite at last. He could have wept with gratitude.

The barmaid reappeared at his elbow. She picked up the empty mug, and set another in its place.

He kept his gaze on the slice of glassy bay he could see through the drawn curtains. "Thanks," he said, his voice rough with the bite of the whisky.

She lingered beside his table. "Beautiful morning for January, isn't it?"

"Yes, ma'am." He forced himself to lean back, lift his chin, and look into her face.

She was plain, and no longer young, with tired eyes and a sad mouth. She said, in a tentative way, "Lost your arm over there, sir?"

He hated saying the words. He lifted the mug, and drained half of its contents in a gulp.

She persisted. "Was it France?"

Frank set the cup down, and said in a flat tone, "Jerusalem."

Her expression of sympathy turned to one of confusion. "Jerusalem?"

"Yes." Most Americans knew little of the war with the Turks, Frank knew.

She twisted her apron. "I guess it was awful."

Frank shrugged. The movement loosened the sleeve from his pocket, and he shoved it back with his right hand. The barmaid turned from him to pull the curtains back, giving him a view of the bay. A black freighter with angled stacks was steaming out to sea, trailing twin clouds of smoke. Seabirds dipped and soared above the fishing boats docked at the pier, and Chinamen in shapeless pants trotted to and fro, carrying tin buckets of shell-fish and wicker baskets of salmon.

The barmaid came back to the table. "Can I bring you some food?"

"No." Frank drained his cup and handed it to her. He came to his feet, reaching for his hat. "I'll take my check, please."

She took two steps backward, a mug in each hand. "I'm sorry. I guess I talk too much," she said, her homely face flushing. "Don't go, sir. I'll leave you be."

Frank said, "It's all right," but he knew his voice sounded angry. He reached into his pocket for his money.

She took another step, shaking her head. "No charge for our men in uniform, sir. My boss says, any man who went to fight the Huns deserves his drink."

"Kind of him." Frank dug for a quarter, and dropped it on the table. "For you, then."

He jammed his hat on his head and hurried away before she could thank him. His boots clattered down the stairs and echoed on the wooden planks of the walkway.

People were beginning to gather in the Market. At the fish-mongers', two women in long winter coats haggled over pink slabs of salmon. Housewives straggled past the vegetable stands, fingering turnips and spuds. The morning air rang with the sounds of gulls crying into the wind, of the clopping of horses' hooves on pavement, and the harsh whine of an automobile motor. Frank left it all behind, and wandered up First Avenue in search of breakfast.

The scent of frying bacon enticed him into a short lane called Post Street. It was too narrow for much traffic. The buildings were small, and a bit dilapidated, jumbled together like a set of bad wooden teeth. He passed an Italian grocer setting out trays of greens, a barbershop with a striped pole, a shoe repairman with blackened fingers who tipped his grimy cap as Frank went by. He found a tiny diner with a chalked sign in its window pro-claiming BREAKFAST, 75¢. He stepped around an iron rooster doorstop and into the smoky haze of the interior. He had to duck his head to clear the lintel.

There were just two tables, and the cook and the waiter were the same man, but the food was hot and filling. Frank tucked into scrambled eggs and thick sausages and potatoes fried with onions. He sat on when he was replete, drinking black coffee, gazing at passersby through the greasy window.

He leaned forward to watch a tall woman stride up the street toward the diner. She carried a black leather satchel in her gloved hand. Her coat, something short with a drooping fur collar, fell away to show a low-waisted, loose-fitting dress. It reached only to the middle of her calves, showing strong, slim ankles. Her hat was some sort of bucket-shaped thing, and her hair was bobbed in the new style, leaving her neck bare. Her small breasts, unfet-tered by corset or stays, moved with her purposeful steps.

Frank tried to imagine Elizabeth dressed like that, but he couldn't do it. When he had seen her last, her skirts brushed the high tops of her boots, and her shirtwaist buttoned to her chin. Her hat had been wide-brimmed, with a posy of flowers at the crown.

The cook appeared beside Frank to lift his empty plate. He nodded toward the woman as she passed by. "These modern girls," he growled. "Bare legs, cropped hair. Smoking. And that one's a doctor. It's indecent. Makes you wonder what you fought for, don't it?"

Frank looked up at the man, a big-bellied, whiskered fellow in a stained apron. He wanted to speak a denial, but in some obscure way, the cook was right. The changes Frank found in his country, and in himself, disturbed him. He had gone off to war in search of glory and honor, but had found only filth and waste. The lifeless corpses of the enemy gave him no more joy than did the bloody bodies of his own men lying in the dirt of the hills. Somehow, out there, he had lost more than his arm. Some other part of himself had gone missing.

It wasn't just the war. He had mustered out of the army into a society he barely recognized. The Eighteenth and Nineteenth amendments passed while he was in the Virginia hospital. His new job had evaporated without a word of warning. And Elizabeth—well, perhaps it was asking too much to expect her not to have changed. Nothing was as it had been.

These thoughts stole his tongue. The cook turned back to his kitchen, and Frank knew that he had, again, failed to say what was expected of him. In the past year this had happened too many times. The high-spirited Montana boy he had once been had vanished. The Great War was over, but it had left Frank to wage a new war, with himself as the enemy.

He groped in his pocket for the money to pay for his breakfast, and the cook came back to scoop it up without a word. Frank spoke a monosyllabic thanks, and ducked out of the diner, turning back toward his hotel.

Just three days before, Frank Parrish had stepped down into the broad expanse of Seattle's King Street Station after a long train journey from Virginia. He stood in the terminal for an hour, his valise in his hand, while the bustle of a thriving city swirled around him. He saw faces of every color, bodies of every shape, clothing from a janitor's overalls to a mink stole with bright dead eyes that glinted at him under the brilliant lights. He put down his valise for a time to rest his fingers, then picked it up again, worried someone would steal it.

All he had in the world was in that valise. His discharge papers, his medical records, his old uniform, his medal in its little black box. A packet of letters from Elizabeth.

His mouth twisted at the thought of those letters. Nurse Gregorio had offered to burn them. He couldn't think, now, why he hadn't allowed her to do it. It was stubbornness, he supposed, or perhaps simple disbelief. Elizabeth had been part of his future since he was seventeen.

The ranch in the Bitterroot Valley had also been part of his future, but that was pointless now. What could a one-armed man do on a cattle ranch? It might have been different if he had been able to tolerate the prosthesis, but every attempt to fit it caused such ghastly pain that both he and the army doctors had given up.

After waiting another hour, and watching two more trains deposit their travelers, Frank had to accept that no one from the Alaska Steamship Company was coming to meet him. It would be all right, he told himself. He had Eccles's letter in his pocket, assuring him of his new position and suggesting a hotel to stay in. No doubt someone had mixed up the dates of his arrival, or gotten the train number wrong. His arm hurt, as always, but it would feel better if he walked for a bit, got himself moving after days of being cooped up. He stopped a porter and asked directions, then forded the crowd to make his way out of the station.

Frank's first impression of Seattle was of grayness. Sky, streets, mist-shrouded buildings, all were painted in drab shades. Automobiles mingled with horse-drawn carriages and slow-moving oxcarts. Walkers carried umbrellas and wore boots against the dampness of the streets. As Frank turned down Yesler, a streetcar clanged by, its scarlet paint the sole spot of color.

Ahead, Frank could see the dull gleam of the bay. Behind him, the hills were thickly forested. A spatter of rain freshened the air as he walked, and all of it worked together to create a kind of frigid charm. He was cheered by a spurt of optimism. He found the Alexis Hotel at the corner of First and Madison. He set down his valise for a moment so he could straighten his collar and wipe raindrops from his hair, then picked it up and went inside to secure a room.

By ten o'clock the next day, Frank's good mood had evaporated. At the Alaska Steamship Company, Eccles blustered an apology for his broken promise. He blamed the general strike of the year before, the influx of returning soldiers, the depression that had sucked the energy out of the wartime boom. He didn't offer to pay for Frank's travel expenses, and Frank was too proud to admit he had spent most of his savings on his train ticket. Eccles, avoiding his eyes, shook his hand, wished him luck, and said good-bye. Frank spoke no more than a dozen words throughout the whole encounter.

He took the streetcar back to the hotel, and spent the rest of that day in his room, trying to think what to do next. A letter from his mother had been waiting for him when he checked in, and it still lay, unopened, on the marble-topped washstand. He cradled the aching stump of his arm gingerly in his right hand, gazed out his window into a gloomy drizzle, and tried very hard not to wish he had died of his wound in the field hospital outside Jerusalem.

Now, his third day in Seattle, Frank Parrish spread the contents of his wallet on the bedside table and contemplated them. It was a bit like looking over your ammunition and wondering if you had enough to make the run up the hill. He had grown to hate loading his clip, checking the bolt-action on his rifle. The Lee-Enfield was supposed to be his pride; but the sight of the rounds, cold and hard and lethal, called up images of torn flesh, staring eyes, slack lips, the tortured postures of the dead. Sometimes it had been all he could do to swallow his reluctance, to put those rounds into the clip, to accept that he was, when ordered to do it, going to fire his rifle at living human beings.

He made an impatient sound in his throat. He had to stop thinking of all that. The issue this morning was money.

Frank had left college to join the war, too impatient to wait for his own country to declare. At the time it had seemed a grand and adventurous thing to do. The British uniforms, the clipped accents of the officers, the romance of the cavalry had drawn him away from classrooms and lectures and boyish pursuits. The King's army had been pleased to commission a man who knew both engineering and horses. He did real engineering in the King's army, building bridges and throwing down roads. He had loved the work until he saw an actual battle.

Nothing like blood and guts—literally—to dim the glories of war.

He tossed his emptied wallet aside, and picked up his mother's letter. He pictured her bent over the kitchen table, writing by the light of a kerosene lamp while his father tamped his pipe and stared into the fireplace. He had postponed writing to them, hoping to send them good news of his fine new job. Now he had nothing to say.

Frank felt a wave of sorrow for his parents, but he couldn't go home jobless and broke. He couldn't face seeing Elizabeth, meeting his old friends. He gazed down at what remained of his left arm. The worst of it all was knowing that it was his own fault. A stupid waste. With a shudder of loathing, he drew his sleeve down and tucked it into his waistband.

He scooped up his money, poured it back into his wallet, and went to stand beside the window. The morning sun had retreated behind a layer of clouds, and the city streets looked cold and unfriendly. They had barely dried from the day before, and now it looked as if there would be more rain. Frank turned back to the bureau for the list of potential employers he had written out. His arm began to ache again, despite the generous shots of whisky the sad-faced barmaid had served him.

A diffident knock on the door came just as he reached for the list. He called, "Come," and the door opened, barely enough for him to see the apologetic face of the Chinese maid.

"Oh, sorry, sir." Her voice was high and thin, birdlike. "I thought you were out. I'll come back later."

"No," he said, more sharply than he intended. The pain always made him snappish. He drew himself up, and tried to speak more gently. "No, it's all right. Come in."

She was a pitiful thing, with a child's body and huge eyes with dark circles beneath them. She came in, carrying folded sheets over her arm, and it seemed to Frank her step was unsteady. He dipped a quarter out of his wallet and laid it on his pillow before he sidled past her into the hall, shouldering into his coat as he went.

He was halfway down the corridor before he realized he had left his list on the bureau. He muttered, "Hell," but he didn't turn back. The list was more or less arbitrary in any case. He had simply written down every possibility he could find in the slender Seattle city directory.

He strode out of the hotel and turned toward the port. If Alaska Steamship had no job for him, perhaps Pacific Coast would, or the Shipping Board. Failing those, he would just knock on the doors of likely places and see what turned up.

At the Good Eats Cafeteria at First and Cherry, Frank spent a dollar on a lunch of chowder and bread. As he ate, he cast his eye over a copy of the *Seattle Daily Times* someone had left on the table. The headline blared, in two-inch type, that unemployment was higher than ever. Frank turned the paper over and shoved it away.

As he paid his bill, the cashier smiled at him. She was rather pretty, in that way very young girls are, with pink skin and clear eyes, but her hands were familiar to him, broad and work-hardened, like those of the country girls of Montana. He touched his cap to her, and she blushed. He stepped out of the café and turned left.

"Hey!" came a voice somewhere behind him.

Frank started off down the street, assuming the call was for someone else.

"Hey!" There was a laugh in the voice this time, and it seemed vaguely familiar. "Cowboy! Is that really you?"

Frank stopped, and turned slowly. Cowboy was his army nickname. He hadn't expected to hear it ever again.

A young man bounded easily across the street toward him, dodging a truck farmer pushing a wheelbarrow full of vegetables. "Cowboy!" he exclaimed again.

Frank, repressing an urge to slip away into the crowd, waited where he was on the sidewalk. When his old comrade reached him, he drawled, "Benedict. Completely forgot you were from Seattle."

Preston Benedict thrust out his hand, exclaiming, "I'll be damned!" They shook, and Benedict said gaily, "I was sure those quacks had killed you!"

"Not quite." Frank took back his hand, and gazed, narrow-eyed, at Preston Benedict. He didn't look like any other veteran of his acquaintance. His color was high, his eyes clear and untroubled. His fair hair sprang vigorously from his forehead. He made Frank feel old and used-up.

"Come on," Benedict said, with a wave of his hand. "Let's have a drink. You can tell me all about it." He put his left hand on Frank's back, as if to guide him. The hand slid across the back of his greatcoat and encountered the empty left sleeve.

Benedict dropped his arm and stared at the empty sleeve tucked into Frank's pocket. "Damn, Cowboy! Lousy luck. You lost it after all."

Frank's jaw ached, and he realized he had ground his teeth together. He said only, "Yes," but hot, sudden pain flared through him.

Benedict gripped his good arm. "Come on. We need a drink. I know a place."

A drink sounded better than ever to Frank, but he shook his head. "Can't," he said. With care, he disengaged his arm from

Benedict's hand. It wasn't easy. Preston Benedict's fingers were strong.

"Why not?" Benedict demanded.

Frank took a half step away, making a space between them. "Appointment," he said. "I'm looking for work."

Benedict's smile widened, and he clapped Frank's good shoulder. "As am I, old man! As am I. We can compare notes. What kind of work are you hoping to do?"

Frank made a vague gesture. "Engineering," he said. "Came out to work with Alaska Steamship, but the strike . . . Position is gone."

Benedict clicked his tongue. "That's rotten, Cowboy."

Frank shrugged.

Benedict chuckled. "Talkative as always, I see," he said. His blue eyes sparkled, and his smile was easy and confident. Frank wondered why he disliked this man. He always had, even when they were both under fire out in the East.

"Listen, old man," Benedict said. "I'll let you get on with it, if you insist. But you must come up to the house, have dinner. Where are you staying?"

"Alexis. A couple more days, anyway."

"Good hotel! Excellent. I'll send the car. Six o'clock?"

"Thanks, but I don't think—"

Benedict clapped his shoulder again. "No arguments, now! You must meet the mater and pater, tell them what heroes we both are." His grin was as guileless as a boy's. "Car at six!" He was gone, dashing back across the busy street, before Frank could think of a way to refuse.

He chided himself as he walked on. It was nice of Benedict to pretend they were friends. By the time they met, Frank was already disillusioned, soured on the war. He had made a few friends in Allenby's army, but most of those fellows had died in Turkey. He was disinclined to become attached to anyone else, and he didn't share Benedict's enthusiasm for all of it—the shooting and the bloody charges and the vanquishing of the enemy.

He'd been in the field hospital when Benedict came back from Jerusalem, and by the time his first, brutal surgery was over, Benedict had shipped out.

Frank remembered now hearing that Preston Benedict was the youngest son of a wealthy Seattle family. He wished he had found a way to escape the dinner invitation, kind though it might be. He didn't look forward to suffering through a formal dinner, trying to be polite to well-bred strangers. Small talk was, as Preston had reminded him, not one of his skills.

Preston congratulated himself as he strolled up Western Avenue, where coolies and Indians labored on the slippery wooden docks, hauling who-knew-what back and forth, gibbering their weird languages at one another. Mother would be pleased when he brought home a war buddy, and a superior officer at that. Father would like Parrish. Everyone did. His brother Dick should be glad to meet another man who had been in the show. Too bad about the arm, but there was something glamorous about a wounded war hero. It felt like a lucky day. Maybe Margot would be stuck at the hospital and miss dinner entirely. That would be a bonus.

The sapphire, hanging on its silver chain beneath his shirt, felt cool and heavy against his chest. He touched it with his palm, thinking he should decide soon where he wanted to work, some office where his war record and the Benedict name would command respect. He would choose the right firm, sit down with the owner, settle his future.

He came to a bench facing the bay, and threw himself down with his legs outstretched. The clouds had cleared, and the wintry sun shone on the Olympics rising in their snowy majesty beyond the water. Relaxing was pleasant, but, he reminded himself, he'd been idle for an entire month. That was long enough, surely, for a man to recover from his war experience.

The Near East had been a nasty place to spend his war at first. Allenby's people acted like snobs, looking down their noses at the Yanks, making officers like him do the scut work. He'd had to run back and forth along the supply lines, carrying other people's gear as if he was no better than a coolie.

But then, when the battle ebbed in the hills of Judea, he and Carter had marched into Jerusalem with Allenby's forces, and everything changed.

He closed his eyes for a moment against the weak sunshine. A scuffle of feet on the sidewalk made him open them again.

A little gaggle of boys had gathered around him. There were three of them, the usual street urchins with ragged hair, short pants showing dirty ankles and scuffed boots. Their noses ran, and their faces were dirty. Preston straightened.

Two of the boys backed away, but one held his ground, pointing to the insignia on Preston's collar. "You're an officer." One of his front teeth was missing, and the other was broken, making him lisp.

Preston smiled. "Of course."

The brat gave him a gap-toothed grin. "Didja kill anybody?"

Another boy, from a safe distance, said, "Yeah, didja? Kill some Huns?"

"I did." Preston leaned forward, and the boys' eyes widened. He said, still smiling, "Do you want me to show you how?"

Three open mouths greeted this question. Preston laughed. He put out his left hand and caught the broken-toothed boy by the arm. He spun him around to hold him tightly around the chest, while with his other hand he grasped the kid's skinny neck. The boy cried out, then choked as Preston's thumb and forefinger constricted his throat. Preston lifted him off his feet, bending his neck backward. The urchin reeked of mud and grease. He kicked, and pulled at Preston's arm with desperate hands.

One of the other boys said, "Hey, mister! Don't hurt Jackie, he's—"

"That's captain," Preston said. He squeezed the boy harder. Jackie's grimy hands clawed at his sleeve. His kicks grew weaker, his tattered boots flailing harmlessly around Preston's knees. "This is how you do it, boys."

"Let him go!" one of the urchins shrieked. Both of them began to cry. Their weeping was openmouthed and ugly, intensifying the mess of dirt and mucus on their faces.

Jackie's feet twitched, and his fingers scrabbled uselessly against Preston's arm. He made thick gasping noises that died away when Preston tightened his fingers.

Preston felt the curious attention of the nearest dockworkers turn to him, drawn by the boys' wailing. He gave the hapless Jackie one last little squeeze, and released him. The boy fell to his knees, scrambling away over the pavement as he sucked in air with noisy gulps. His companions reached for him, and pulled him up between them. Jackie leaned on them, his lips white, his face pinched with panic.

"Hey!" one of the brats sobbed. "Whatcha think you're doing?"

Preston chuckled as he came to his feet. The boys backed away, clinging to one another in that endearing way of the powerless. The familiarity of it, even with these unworthy adversaries, warmed Preston's groin.

"Scary, isn't it?" he said.

One of them cried, "What is?"

Preston let his grin fade and his voice harden. "Killing people. It's no joke."

"We wasn't joking!"

Jackie sniffled, "You hurt me, mister."

One of the others said, "Captain, Jackie. He's a captain."

Preston nodded. "Right you are, lad. Captain." He touched two fingers to his cap. "You learned something here, boys. See you remember." He spun on his toes, feeling full of life. Yes, this was a lucky day. A good day to decide what to do next.

CHAPTER 2

Dressed in the same suit he had worn all day, Frank stood on the steps of the Alexis, awaiting the car Benedict had promised, and dreading the evening ahead.

It had not been a good day. The managers of two firms had offered sympathy, but nothing more. With the contraction of the economy, they said, they were letting people go, not hiring. He had to screw up his courage to call upon three more businesses. Two were polite, but not interested. At the third, a company that fabricated boilers and other steel products, the proprietor took one look at his empty sleeve and said, "Major, you're wasting your time and mine. You'd better take your disability pay and go home."

Frank stiffened. It was possible that one day a pension from the British Army might reach him. There had been no sign of it yet, but he wasn't going to say so. It was none of this man's business. "Sir," he said, "I can be an engineer with one arm."

The man looked angry, as if Frank had done something to affront him. "Have you done any drafting since you got out?"

"Happy to demonstrate," Frank said. "Do you have a drafting table?"

The man blew out a breath. "Look, Major." His mouth drew down, creasing his heavy cheeks. "I went at this all wrong." Frank watched his eyes drop once more to the empty sleeve, then rise to Frank's face. Something flickered in those eyes, some complex emotion, quickly repressed. "I should have just said we're not hiring."

Frank looked past the proprietor's shoulder at the shop beyond. A few men in coveralls were working there. Several wore metal hard hats that looked very much like the helmet Frank had laid down for the last time when he mustered out. In a distant corner, the flare of a soldering iron cast yellow sparks over the cement floor, and in a small office to his right, a woman in a shirtwaist sat typing on a massive Underwood. The struck keys made heavy clanking sounds. Beyond her was an empty desk, holding nothing but a lamp.

"Looks to me, sir," Frank said stubbornly, "as if you could use some help."

The man gave him a mulish look, and didn't answer for a long moment. At first Frank thought he was going to point to the door and ask him to leave, but then he saw the slight tremble of the man's lip and a mist in his eyes that must have blurred his vision. Frank took a step back. Something was wrong here.

The man started to speak, but his voice cracked, failing him. He cleared his throat, and stared past Frank's shoulder. Frank knew there was nothing there but the blank stucco wall of the next building. He took another step toward the door. The man was right about one thing—he was wasting time.

The older man finally forced his throat to work. "My son—" he began. He hung his head suddenly, and his fingers clutched the battered wooden counter in front of him, knuckles going white as he struggled to control himself.

Frank stopped where he was. The muscles of his belly tightened.

More than a hundred thousand American soldiers had died over there, from battle injuries, influenza, infections. Twice that many came home gravely injured, hopelessly shell-shocked, or maimed for life. The numbers were even worse for the Brits, who had been in the war three years longer.

Frank could guess at what had caused this man's misery. The business was supposed to go to a son who had fallen and would never return. Or his position was being held for him in the hope he would one day recover enough to take it. Or the general strike of '19 had set the business back so far that this man, in the face of his loss, had no more heart for it.

Frank couldn't bear to hear it. He had no solace to offer. He growled, "Sorry to trouble you," and turned sharply away. He let the door swing shut behind him. He didn't look back to see if the man had recovered himself or had buried his face in his hands to weep.

And now, after a day of such disappointments, Frank stood on the steps of the Alexis waiting for a strange car to take him to have dinner with people he didn't know, and would never meet in the normal run of things. What kind of family would produce a man like Preston Benedict? People of privilege, certainly. Money, advantages, history, good fortune. He would simply have to endure it, tolerate the careful questions and the looks of pity. He would be polite, as he was brought up to be, and he would make his escape as early as he decently could, to go in search of more whisky.

The Essex was a sleek black vehicle, and the driver who stepped out of it, courteously inquiring as to Frank's name, was every bit as sleek and nearly as black. When he had ascertained that Frank was, in fact, Major Frank Parrish, the driver bowed, very much like one of the British officers' batmen.

The car was one of the new enclosed sedans, with burgundy velvet upholstery and polished windows shining like crystal under the electric streetlights. The driver introduced himself as "Blake, sir. Mr. Benedict's butler." He asked in cultured accents about the suitability of the Alexis, and Frank's liking for Seattle, as he adjusted dials and choke and headlamps. He pressed the electric starter, engaged the clutch, and began the climb up Madison and away from the city center, driving with the same dignity he displayed in his speech.

Frank settled back on the wide seat to watch the town spin slowly by. The car took a left turn, and he craned his neck to find a street sign. Broadway. They drove for another five minutes, making way for the occasional cart, and once for a streetcar clanging its way along the road, then turned right and wound even higher onto a tree-lined hill.

"Aloha Street, Major," Blake said as the car followed the twisting road. He turned left at the top of the hill. "Fourteenth Avenue. The Benedicts built their home here thirty years ago." He pulled to a stop in front of an enormous white building with elegant pillars and a broad porch that wrapped around the three sides Frank could see. For a painful moment Frank simply stared at it. Benedict had called it "the house," but this was like no house Frank had ever set foot in.

Cupolas decorated every wall. Lights shone from three floors. A tall tree of a type Frank didn't recognize stretched dark, leafless branches across the façade, and a wide, manicured lawn surrounded it.

The butler said, "Here we are, sir. Benedict Hall." Frank suddenly longed to change his mind, refuse the invitation after all, but Blake was already out of the automobile, holding the door.

As Frank climbed out, Blake bowed again. "I'll announce you, Major."

Frank followed him up the walk, feeling utterly out of place. Such formality belonged, it seemed to him, to a different age. His Montana roots had taught him nothing about such things, though he had seen it in the British forces. The aristocrats, the officers, found it natural that some other man should clean their shoes and oil their rifles, even serve tea in a dirty trench while bullets flew overhead. Frank had never become accustomed to it.

Blake took off his driving cap as he opened the front door, revealing hair curled close to his scalp like gray wool. He left Frank standing in the hall, and disappeared.

Frank unbuttoned his greatcoat and slipped out of it, careful to tuck the empty sleeve of his jacket securely into his pocket. When Blake returned with an attractive woman of middle age, Frank had already hung the coat on a mahogany coatrack and scuffled the dirt off his shoes onto the coir mat inside the door.

"Mrs. Edith," Blake said. He held his cap in his hands, and nodded toward Frank. "This is Mr. Preston's guest for the evening. Major Frank Parrish. Major, Mrs. Benedict. Mr. Preston's mother."

The woman came forward, holding out a very slim, very white hand. Frank took it. He felt as if he was expected to bow over it, but he couldn't imagine such an action. He shook it gingerly.

Edith Benedict put her other hand over his and squeezed. "Major Parrish! We are so glad Preston happened to run into you. We're simply delighted to have you, someone who knew Preston over there, who fought by his side. . . ." Her voice faltered as she caught sight of Frank's sleeve, flattened into his jacket pocket.

He said hastily, "Thank you, Mrs. Benedict. Kind of you to—"

Her pale cheeks turned rosy. She released his hand, then passed her own over her eyes as if to erase what she had just seen. "It's just lovely to have one of Preston's friends here," she said in a breathy tone. "Just—just so lovely. Come and meet my husband, won't you?"

Blake walked back out the front door, closing it behind him. Mrs. Benedict led Frank into a room to the left of the hall. "The small parlor," she said.

Frank supposed there must be a big parlor, or this room could never be called small. There was a fireplace with a fire crackling in it, and an abundance of dark wooden furniture and upholstered chairs arranged on a plush carpet woven in deep colors. He shook the thick-fingered hand of Mr. Dickson Benedict, and the even bigger one of his son, Mr. Dick Benedict. Another Mrs. Benedict, young and very pretty, with painted eyebrows and short hair waved in rows like a washboard, rose from a chair beside a cabinet radio, and came forward to be introduced. Soon they were all seated around a little cocktail table, and the elder Mr. Benedict was offering a bottle of what looked like real, pre-Prohibition whisky. As he poured two fingers into a tumbler and handed it across, saliva flooded Frank's mouth.

He waited until everyone was settled before he lifted the glass to his lips and tasted it.

He had been right. It was the real thing. His eyelids dropped at the pleasure of its smooth fire caressing his tongue, slipping easily down his throat.

Dickson Benedict, a ruddy, thickset man, smiled across the table. "I see you appreciate good liquor, Major," he said. "It's still legal in our own homes, of course. I saw the way the wind was blowing five years ago, and I laid in a supply."

"Sir," Frank said, lifting his glass to his host.

Mr. Benedict lifted his glass in return, and took a generous sip. Dick Benedict leaned forward as if to say something, but at that moment Preston burst into the room.

It was the only word Frank could have used to describe his entrance. All conversation halted, and every face turned as he flung himself through the door and strode across the carpet, an energetic figure with shining blond hair, bright blue eyes, and a loud voice. "Parrish!" he exclaimed. "Glad you could make it!" His arrival seemed to diminish every other person in the room. Certainly Frank felt diminished by it, overshadowed and dull, even as he stood to shake his hand.

"Did you meet everyone?" Preston poured himself a drink, then dropped into the chair closest to his mother's. "Mater, you're a regular cover girl tonight!" he said. "And Ramona—been to the hairdresser's? You look like a picture. Dick, you're a lucky dog."

Both women bridled with pleasure, and it seemed to Frank that Ramona's eyes shifted from Preston to her husband and back again, measuring. Mrs. Benedict could hardly take her eyes from her younger son. Frank thought this affection must be the source of the warm welcome she had lavished on him at the front door.

Frank took a draught of whisky while Preston commanded center stage as if a spotlight had been turned on him. "I might have landed a job today," he announced. "At the *Times*."

Ramona smiled at her brother-in-law, and when he winked at her, her powdered cheeks colored. She touched her hair in that self-conscious way some women had, as if they were preening birds. Dick, the older brother, stood a little apart, watching his wife and his mother bask in Preston's glow.

Frank glanced sideways to see how the senior Benedict was taking it all, and was startled to find Dickson Benedict watching him instead of his son. There was something canny in the older Benedict's dark eyes, a knowing arch to his bristling gray eyebrows. He looked away immediately, reaching for the decanter, but Frank felt as if Dickson Benedict was assessing his reaction to Preston.

Frank put his glass down, and let his empty right hand rest on his knee.

Blake came in a moment later. He had replaced his driving gloves with white cotton ones. He wore a different coat, and he carried a small tray in one hand. He stood in the doorway to announce dinner, and everyone rose.

Dick said, "What about Margot?"

"I've just brought her, Mr. Dick," Blake said. "She went up to change her frock."

Preston took Frank's arm. "Come on, Cowboy. We'll go find our chairs. My sister is always late."

Dickson Benedict said, "Our daughter is a doctor, you know, Major. She has a private practice downtown."

Preston caroled, "No practice without patients. Or hadn't anyone noticed?"

Frank caught the dark look Dick flashed on his younger brother, and a little quiver of intuition vibrated in his belly.

Edith Benedict said mildly, "Now, now, Preston darling. We have to let her try. I'm sure she'll settle down soon enough."

There was a slight bustle and press as everyone left the parlor. The dining room was elongated, high-ceilinged, charmingly illuminated by small lamps and a little forest of candles in a silver candelabra. Crystal decanters waited on two immense sideboards. A long oval table covered in white linen was liberally set with silver and china. Stemware and silver sparkled with candlelight. Edith showed Frank to a chair beside Preston's, and took her own opposite her husband.

They had just settled into their chairs when the sister made her appearance.

Dickson Benedict greeted her with, "At last. Late again, Margot."

"Sorry, Father. I did my best."

"Never mind, dear. We're just glad you're here," Edith Benedict said. "Margot, this is Preston's friend from the army, Major Parrish. Major, our daughter, Miss—that is, Dr. Benedict."

Margot Benedict was a tall woman with straight, short dark hair and bright brown eyes. She crossed the room with a decisive step, and put out a long, narrow hand. "Major Parrish. How do you do." Her voice was rather deep, and her gaze was as direct as a man's.

Frank stood up, bumping his leg against the table, his napkin dangling awkwardly from his only hand. "Dr. Benedict." As he reached to shake her hand, his napkin fell to the floor, and he felt his neck burn when Blake hurried forward to retrieve it and bring him a fresh one.

The doctor's hand was cool and firm. Her eyes assessed him, measuring the emptiness of his sleeve, coming back to his face without a hint of embarrassment.

Relieved by this, Frank found himself smiling. "I saw you," he said. "On—what's it called?—Post Street, I think."

"I must have been on the way to my clinic. I often walk down from the hospital. It's awfully nice you've found your way here, Major."

"Yes," he said, and for the first time he felt it might be true. "Thank you."

Dinner began. Two freckled, redheaded maids in frilly aprons appeared with the first course. They distributed bowls around the table, and ladled out a clear soup, peppered with croutons. It was too salty, but Frank drank it all anyway, to offset the buzz of whisky. He was careful with his spoon, hoping for no more embarrassing incidents. While he ate, he watched the Benedict family.

The elder son and daughter looked like their father, dark-haired, dark-eyed, and tall. Preston resembled his mother. Even now, when she must be nearing fifty, Edith Benedict's upswept hair was a soft blond, only lightly touched with gray. Her skin was smooth, her eyes the same blue as Preston's. The resemblance ended there, though. She was soft-spoken, gentle, even diffident. Preston spoke loudly. His laugh rattled the crystal, and his grin flashed at everyone and everything in the dining room, including the twin maids, who blushed and curtsied whenever he addressed them.

When a plump black woman in a long apron came in, bearing a platter of meat and roast potatoes, Preston jumped up to hold the door open as she passed through. She gave him a huge smile, showing uneven teeth like yellowing ivory in her round, perspiring face. "Mr. Preston, y'all get yourself right back to your chair. Old Hattie can manage a platter of roast beef!"

"It smells wonderful, Hattie," he said as he sat down again.

"I bin savin' this good roast just for you!"

She set the platter in front of Dickson Benedict, and brought an enormous carving knife and fork from a sideboard. Dickson stood to carve the joint. Frank saw the thick slices fall away from the roast, black at the edges and brown all the way through, and thought how his father would complain to see a good loin of beef ruined that way.

The maids set fresh plates, and Hattie dished up potatoes on each one while Dickson laid on slabs of the beef. When everyone had a plate, Hattie stood smiling at Preston. He took a bite of the dry meat, and bowed to her. "You've done it again, Hattie! You're a genius!"

Satisfied, the cook bustled out of the dining room, the little maids in tow.

Dick cut into a slice of beef, and scowled over it. "It's practically charcoal," he muttered. "Mother, can't you talk to her?"

"I have tried, dear," Edith said faintly. "Poor Hattie. She does her best."

"Overdoes it," Dickson said. "Sorry, Major. Old retainers, you know."

Frank said, "It's delicious, sir."

Preston laughed. "Beats that boiled leather they served in Allenby's army, right, old chap?"

Frank chewed the bite of meat in his mouth. When he could swallow, he said, "A great deal better than hospital food."

At that, Margot Benedict leaned forward. "Where were you, Major?"

"Hampton, Virginia."

"Oh, yes. The Soldiers' Home. Were you there long?"

"Felt like it."

"I'm sure it did." She mashed a roasted potato with her fork. "I saw a lot of combat veterans in my residency. Such a sad business. Smashed to bits, some of them."

"Please, Margot, dear," Edith said.

The younger Mrs. Benedict leaned forward. "The thing is," Ramona said brightly, "it's over now, isn't it? It's all finished, and Preston is home safe and sound."

An awkward silence followed this statement, and Ramona Benedict turned as pink as the georgette of her frock. "Oh. Major Parrish, you, too, of course. Safe and—"

He wanted to say something to put her at her ease, but he couldn't think of what it might be. He set his fork down, and cleared his throat.

Margot Benedict said in an even, unhurried way, "Don't worry, Ramona. I'm sure the major is glad to be home, injured or not."

Frank managed to say, "Right," and cursed himself for being tongue-tied.

Preston said cheerfully, "You'll have noticed Cowboy's not much of a chatterbox."

Dick said, "Cowboy. You'll have to tell us about your nickname, Major."

Frank said, "I'm from Montana, Mr. Benedict. Ranch country. Someone started calling me Cowboy, out in the East, and it stuck."

Edith Benedict rang the bell, and the two maids returned. They jostled each other, each vying to be the one to take Preston's plate. The winner was too hasty, and spilled gravy on the tablecloth. She fussed, making little curtsies even as she dabbed at the mess with a napkin. Margot Benedict said, "For heaven's sake, Leona! Leave it." The girl jumped, and fled, the gravy-stained napkin in her hand and the other maid close at her heels.

When they were gone, Edith said, "Margot, really. You terrify the poor girls."

"I do?"

"You scowl at them so!"

"And that was Loena," Preston added, chuckling. "Not that it matters which is which."

"Now, now," Edith said. "What will the major think of us?" She turned to Frank with a polite smile. "Tell us about your family, Major Parrish. Where is your ranch?"

Frank managed a few words about Missoula, about the beauty of the Montana landscape, and in response to a question from Dick Benedict, the price of beef on the hoof. To his relief, dessert was soon served by an abashed Loena—or Leona—and for a few minutes there was no need to talk. From beneath his brows, Frank watched the doctor push with her spoon at the unfortunate rubbery skin covering the pudding, then give it up. He managed to scoop out a bite or two from the cut-glass dish before he also put down his spoon. She winked at him, and he smiled back.

They all trooped back to the small parlor for their coffee. Someone had built up the fire, and it blazed merrily in the fireplace. Dickson Benedict sat near it in a chintz armchair. With a pair of tiny silver scissors, he snipped the end off a thick cigar. He put a match to it, and drew until the end glowed cherry red. With a satisfied grunt, he blew a gout of smoke, then leaned back with one hand resting on his modest paunch, the other holding the cigar between thumb and forefinger.

Preston stood by the fire, one elbow on the mantelpiece, smiling down at everyone. Dick and his wife settled on a short divan, and Frank, feeling long-legged and awkward, found a chair opposite them. The doctor pulled a chair close to the circle for her mother, then perched on the arm of the divan.

Dick looked up at her. "So, Margot. How's the doctor business today?"

Her expression was rueful. "A little slow, I'm afraid."

Preston said, "See any actual patients, doc? Or did you spend your day dusting the furniture?"

She turned to face her younger brother. "Actually, Preston," she said in a deliberate way, "I saw a nice case of alcohol poisoning today. It was classic—cyanotic, blurred vision, impaired motor skills."

Preston gave a mock shiver. "Nasty! So what did you do for him?"

She sighed, and let her gaze drop to the flames. "Nothing, I'm afraid. He was not eager—in his own words—to have me 'look inside his drawers.' "

Ramona Benedict burst out, "Margot, for heaven's sake!" Frank's startled glance found her glaring up at her sister-in-law, her rouged lips pouting. "Spare us the details!"

"Oh, sorry, Ramona," the doctor said lightly.

Preston said, "Did you need to look inside his drawers?"

At this, Ramona gave a musical laugh. Her husband snapped, "Preston can say it, but Margot can't, Ramona?"

Ramona gave a delicate shiver. "It's just so—so unladylike."

Preston chuckled. "What do you expect from a suffragette? Cowboy, you'll soon learn my sister doesn't concern herself with femininity."

Frank, managing a cup and saucer on his knee, glanced up at Margot Benedict. Her eyes met his, and there was a challenge in them. "Do you object to women's suffrage, Major?" she said with asperity.

"No." He shifted the cup and saucer to the little piecrust table in front of the divan. Every eye turned to him, and feeling self-conscious, he smoothed his pant leg over his thigh. They were waiting for him to say more. In the silence, filled only by the crackling of the fire, he searched for words. "My mother," he began. "The other ranch women—they work hard. Physical work."

Ramona said, "Really? Do they—what do you call it—punch cows, and everything?"

Dick Benedict said, "Oh, for God's sake, Ramona."

"Sodbusters," Preston said.

Margot put down her own coffee cup and fixed Frank with her dark gaze. "You're saying they've earned the right to vote, aren't you, Major? Did they march?"

"Didn't need to, Dr. Benedict. Montana gave women the vote in 1914."

"That's right! I'd forgotten. You have that congresswoman—Jeannette Rankin, isn't it? That must have been an exciting election."

"I don't really know. I shipped out in '15."

"Ah. You were gone a long time," Dickson Benedict said. He puffed on his cigar, and a wreath of blue smoke circled his head. "Different world you came back to, isn't it, Major?"

Frank nodded.

"You see the headline in the paper today?" Dickson said. "Six thousand men out of work in Seattle. It's a shame."

Margot said crisply, "How many women, Father?"

It had the feeling of an old argument. Considering himself safely out of it, Frank picked up his coffee cup again, leaving the saucer on the table. Dickson Benedict growled, "It's our service boys who can't find work, Margot. It's a disgrace."

"Come now, Father. It's been more than two years. Some servicemen are working, and some aren't, just as in the rest of the population. It's a depression."

Dickson began a response, but Edith forestalled him, saying, "And you, Major? Where are you going to work now that you're out of the service?"

* * *

He didn't look like the sort of man Preston would befriend. Or perhaps, Margot thought, as she finished her coffee, it was the other way around, and Preston was not the sort of man this Frank Parrish would normally associate with. The major was painfully lean, and she guessed he had not been out of the hospital very long. She wondered if his war experiences were what had begun the premature graying of his black hair. His eyes were a startling clear blue, with sooty lashes, the coloring some people called Black Irish. The Irishmen she knew, though, were talkative to a fault. Frank Parrish was nearly wordless.

In answer to her mother's question, he said, "I came out for a job with the Alaska Steamship Company."

Her father arched a thick eyebrow. "I heard they weren't hiring."

"So I found out, sir. When I arrived."

"Damn shame," Dickson said.

"That's terrible," Edith said in her soft voice. "I'm so sorry, Major."

Dickson gestured with the cigar. "What sort of work are you planning to do?"

"Hoping to do some engineering, sir."

"The strike hit us all hard."

"Not you, Father," Preston said. "You were way ahead of those unionists, weren't you?"

"He paid them a living wage," Margot snapped. "And promised them their jobs would be safe if they felt they had to walk out in sympathy."

Preston said, "Is that what you did?"

"I look ahead, son," Dickson said. He stubbed his cigar out in a wide cut-glass ashtray. "Best advice I can give you—any of you—is to look ahead five years."

"I don't know if we can, Father," Margot said. "You have that sort of vision. It's your special gift, I suspect. I'm not sure I can see to the end of 1920, much less all the way to 1925."

Their guest's eyes turned to her. Blue lights flickered in them, reflections from the fire. He gave a measured nod of agreement.

"I'll put in a word for you, Major Parrish," her father said. "I know pretty much everyone here. Allen's the highway designer. Bill Boeing's little company is building seaplanes, and he might need an engineer. I'll ask around."

"Thank you, sir. Kind of you."

"Not at all, not at all," Dickson said. He patted his rounded stomach in a complacent gesture. "Servicemen are a special concern of mine. I let three women go last month so our veterans could get back to work."

"Father!" Margot exclaimed. "You didn't!"

Dickson grinned, and leaned back, crossing his legs. "No, daughter, I didn't. But I knew I'd get a rise out of you."

Dick said, "It happens, though, Margot. You know that."

"It's appalling."

Ramona gave a theatrical sigh. "What's appalling, Margot, is a married woman working when she doesn't have to, and a man going without a job because she's taken it!"

Margot tapped her coffee spoon in an irritated rhythm against her saucer. "Who are you to judge a married woman's need to work, Ramona?"

Preston laughed. Dick said, "Now, now, you two." Margot threw him an icy glance, and Ramona glared at her husband as if daring him to say anything further.

When Margot rose from her chair, Frank Parrish stood up. "Please don't get up, Major," she said. "I have to see a patient at the hospital."

"Oh, Margot," her mother said. "Can't it wait until morning?"

"No. Major Parrish, I hope you'll forgive me."

"I'll call Blake," her father said.

"No, don't," Margot said as she pushed in her chair. "Blake's day has been long enough. I'll take the streetcar."

"That's what Blake is for, Margot."

Margot shook her head. "I'm not having an elderly Negro on

his feet twenty hours a day just because you think I can't take care of myself."

Frank Parrish cleared his throat. "Uh, sir," he began. "I can—I mean, I would be happy to escort Dr. Benedict."

Margot said, "No, please. You stay and enjoy the company. I'm perfectly fine."

Her father said, "That's an excellent idea, Major."

Margot said firmly, "It's chivalrous, but unnecessary." She started out of the dining room, saying, "Have a nice evening, everyone." She hurried away before anyone could offer a new argument.

She still had to persuade Blake before she could escape unhindered. When this was accomplished, she retrieved her medical bag, put on her hat, and buttoned herself into her coat as she strode down the street. She glanced over her shoulder once or twice to be certain her father had not won out in the end, and sent Blake after her.

She swung up into the streetcar and settled near the front. As it clicked along Broadway she contemplated Major Frank Parrish. She wished she could get the shirt off him and have a look at his arm. There had to be a reason he hadn't been fitted with a prosthetic. It looked as if he had lost the elbow, but there were contraptions for that. She had seen a few in her residency, and they were being improved all the time.

He had seemed a nice enough sort at dinner, someone she might like to know better. But he was Preston's friend, and that wasn't a good recommendation. There must be some hidden darkness behind those vivid eyes.

After the doctor left, the war talk Frank had expected commenced. With his arm soothed by whisky and wine, Frank stretched his legs out to the fire and relaxed a bit in one of the upholstered armchairs. Dickson Benedict poured snifters of brandy for each of the men. Preston began an embellished account of the skirmish that cost Frank his arm but won him his medal, while Frank, embarrassed, stared into the flames. Preston's tale had little to do with what had actually happened.

He didn't say so. Dick and his father were enjoying the story, as far as he could tell. Frank took a sip of brandy and rolled it in his mouth, savoring its sharp sweetness.

Of course, he hadn't been the hero Preston was describing. He had been a man in the wrong place at the wrong time. He had obeyed his orders, and done his duty, but he felt no pride. What he felt was disgust. Humiliation.

Preston was saying, "So Cowboy threw himself in front of one of the colonel's troops, and took the round in his left hand."

It hadn't been like that.

There had been a little knot of Turks hunkered down in a fold of the hills, trying to halt the British march on Jerusalem. They wore the traditional scarves called *kafya*, and their kerchiefed heads popped up from time to time as they took potshots at the advancing army. The main battle was already accomplished. The colonel Preston spoke of was mounted, and so was Frank. He didn't like the English saddle, with its bars and stitching in all the wrong places, but the horse had been a fine big gelding with an Arab cut to his head and his ears. He had an Arab's temperament, too, tolerating the *thwump-thwump* of the guns all right, but dancing with impatience at any delay, as when one of the mobile field guns, the small wheeled cannon that were so effective in driving the enemy out of their bunkers, blocked the way.

One of the iron wheels of the gun carriage jammed into a crevice none of the soldiers towing it had seen. They had been moving fast, and momentum drove the mounting into the ground with a great thud. Two of the infantry lost their balance and fell to the ground, with a third struggling to keep the barrel from going over. He couldn't do it. It overbalanced, freezing the cradle trunnion, sticking the mouth of the cannon straight into the rocky ground. The soldiers sprang up, but though they struggled valiantly, neither their efforts nor the cursing of the colonel did any good.

They should have left it. They should have finished their climb up the hill, routed out the nest of Turks, then sent a detail back to recover the gun when it was all over. But Colonel Beardsley had another vision, all of his forces driving smoothly up the hill, pouring over the height so that Allenby's right flank marched, unimpeded and triumphant, into the old city. Beardsley, like Frank's gelding, had no patience. He had his eye on a promotion, and on that curious ceremony in which King George would whack his shoulder with a ceremonial sword so that Mrs. Beardsley could be called Lady. None of that made any sense to Frank. But Beardsley ordered him to see what was wrong with the mobile cannon, to help the soldiers get it free, drag it forward into position, and put an end to the intermittent fire from the bunker.

Other officers called orders and queries, fired rifles, ducked when the Turks jumped out of cover to shoot at the approaching force. Dust swirled up from the ground in yellow clouds. Only the men on horseback could see both their troops and the target.

Frank reined his horse to the right, to circle the gun carriage and assess the position of the wheels. It was bad. The weight of the cannon had driven the whole engine into the hillside, one wheel spinning slowly in the air, the other wedged into a crevice of granite. Frank scowled at it as the soldiers gazed helplessly at him.

"Don't see how you managed that," he shouted over the noise of the battle.

One of the Brits, a stocky fellow with sandy whiskers and a snub nose, tugged at the cannon's cradle without effect. Another, a skinny boy who looked to Frank like he should still be in short pants, pushed back his cap and squinted up through the dust. "It was too steep, sir," he shouted back. His eyes were a painfully bright blue against the red rims of his eyes, inflamed by the dust. "We was at the back of 'er, and we couldn't see 'er nose for the dust. Gave 'er a shove, and over she goes!"

"Have to dig it out," Frank told him.

"We know," the boy called back. "But the rocks—"

"Need a lever!" Frank's nervy gelding threw his head, and danced through the dust, nearly stepping on the soldier.

"Yes, sir," the boy began. "But—"

Impatiently, Frank pulled the horse's head to his knee to stop his curvetting. The gelding spun in a tight circle, and stood still, blowing, shivering with tension. The colonel shouted something, and Frank signaled with his hand that he heard him. He secured the gelding's rein in his right hand, and threw his right leg over the cantle to dismount.

His memories of the moments that followed remained painfully clear, despite the nearly two years that had passed. The seconds that changed his life stretched and slowed, illuminating each speck of the whorls of yellow dust, every freckle on the face of the lad from the Cotswolds. The boy straightened, stepping up out of the crevice where the cannon was lodged. Frank saw his head emerge from the dust, his cap pushed back, his pale face lifted, mouth open to explain to the major why he couldn't get a lever under the mouth of the gun. It seemed, in Frank's crystal memory, that he could also see the bullets spinning toward the hapless boy, just as he put his own left foot on the ground.

There were two shooters, triangulating the infantryman in their sights. Their shots lifted him, turned him. One ruined his face. Another pierced his throat just below his beardless jaw.

Frank heard his own hoarse cry, knew his mistake even as he made it. Though it was too late for the boy, Frank lurched forward, left hand out to catch him as he fell, bloody and broken, back into the dust cloud.

But the Turks weren't finished. The gelding reared and backed away, throwing Frank off balance as he found himself stretched between his hold on the reins and the lad collapsing against him. Three shots sounded a dull staccato through the tumult. One missed. Another, with a sickening sound of breaking bone, took the gelding down, shot straight through his pretty forehead.

The third caught Frank's left arm, shattering the radioulnar joint, ripping the radial artery. Blood spurted in a scarlet fountain, mixing with the blood of the dead boy and the dust of the field, its flow turning sluggish and ugly.

Frank Parrish had stared down at the ruin of his arm, knowing, with a cold certainty in the midst of the heat of battle, that he was going to lose it.

Both of the elder Benedicts were nodding, murmuring admiration. Frank shook his head, but Preston said, in his smooth way, "Nonsense, Cowboy. You tried to save that poor bugger. Not your fault you couldn't do it."

Dick Benedict said, "It's a pity about your arm, Major."

Frank never knew what to say about the arm.

Preston said, "That's right, old son. We all felt terrible about what happened."

Frank stared into his brandy snifter, wordless. Dickson Benedict came to his rescue, saying, "Come now, Preston. Tell us about Jerusalem. Did you see the sights?"

Preston began a travelogue of the wonders of Jerusalem. Frank watched him above the rim of his glass.

Preston seemed larger, somehow, than he had in the East. He was better looking, more confident. His smile, though it seemed too easy to Frank, was full of charm, and bestowed evenly on everyone, even the freckled maids who slipped in and out from time to time. His conversation was quick and clever.

When there was a pause, Edith turned to Frank, saying, "Were you there, Major Parrish? When Preston led the charge against the Turks?"

Frank put down his glass, gaining a moment to frame an answer to Preston's mother. Her gaze was innocent, vulnerable, as she waited to hear grand things of her son. Preston's eyebrows lifted slightly as if to encourage Frank to say whatever was on his mind. He wouldn't do that, of course. He knew well that his own views of war weren't shared by everyone, not even those who had fought it.

The truth of Preston's "charge against the Turks" was that it had been a rout. Two dozen mounted officers had crushed a little knot of foot soldiers beneath their horses' hooves, and slashed them with their bayonets. Frank had heard Preston say afterward that the whole encounter gave him a chance to use his bayonet for something other than toasting bread. In truth, the enemy had already been decimated by a grenade tossed by a foot soldier. The officers had cut down the remaining handful of Turks.

Frank's principal memory of the event was the acrid smell of smoke peppered with the coppery tang of blood. He had held his gelding back, disgusted by the carnage.

But he had to answer Edith's question. He leaned back against the brocade of his chair, and answered cautiously, "I was. Good horseman, Benedict. Tricky mare they gave him."

Preston laughed. "Wasn't she, though, Cowboy? Too much thoroughbred in her, I always thought. Still, too bad she didn't make it."

Frank stared into the candle flames. The memory of the mare, screaming when a machine-gun round shattered her slender foreleg, was one he wished he could wipe from his mind.

Dickson Benedict said, "Explain something for me. I thought the machine guns made the cavalry obsolete over there."

Dick put in, "Trench warfare is the new thing, right?"

Preston nodded to Frank. "What do you think, Cowboy? You're the real horseman. Is the cavalry old-fashioned now?"

Frank said, "Afraid so." They watched him, waiting for him to expand on the subject. He shifted a little in his chair, wondering if he could politely get away soon. "Horses are no defense against artillery. And they're expensive to transport. Feed, water."

Preston nodded. "Cowboy's right, though the Brits don't want to believe it. They find the cavalry romantic, you know."

"It is." Ramona set her coffee cup aside, and leaned forward, her eyes brightening. "There were pictures in the *Times*. Soldiers on horseback, officers with their medals and swords, the horses prancing. They look so—so proud. Don't you agree, Major Parrish?"

It was a question Frank couldn't answer. His jaw twitched with tension, and he took another sip of brandy to cover it. He had spent months trying to forget. These curious questions, asked with such naïveté, made it all new again. Twinges ran through his arm, despite the alcohol the Benedicts had lavished on him.

Dickson, again, seemed to understand. He harrumphed, and pushed the brandy decanter forward. "Nasty subject, isn't it, Major? I don't blame you for not wanting to talk about it."

Dick said, "But, Father, the Great War! The war to end all wars. It's a wonderful thing."

Preston smiled at Frank. "Come on, Cowboy. We won, after all!"

Frank met his clear-eyed gaze, and gave a slight, one-shouldered shrug.

"More coffee, Major?" Edith Benedict asked. It was, after all, just dinner conversation.

"No, thank you, ma'am. Think I'd better—that is, in the morning, I need to—"

Dickson stood up. "Yes, of course, Major. I almost forgot." He walked to a cherrywood writing desk against one wall, lifted its slanted lid, and rummaged through cubbyholes until he found a slim leather-bound book. He came back to his chair, settling his weight into it with a grunt, and began to riffle the pages of the book. "Let's see, let's see," he muttered. "I have it here somewhere."

In no time after that, it seemed, Frank found himself in the Essex being carried back through the moist, cool night to the Alexis. His arm had ceased to hurt the moment he left Benedict Hall. He had names in his pocket, with addresses, and permission to mention Dickson Benedict's patronage. Blake had assured him he would be taking the car out again in any case to pick up Dr. Benedict from the hospital, so Frank gave himself up to the brief comfort of the ride.

As they pulled up before the Alexis, Frank asked, "Blake, do you know of a rooming house?"

Blake set the brake, and turned in his seat. His eyes gleamed white in the darkness of the car's interior. "You don't care for the Alexis, Major Parrish?"

"It's fine. Too expensive."

Blake opened his door, and came around the car to open Frank's. "I'll ask around for you, sir. I'm sure I can find something. I'll leave a message with the desk."

"Thanks. And thanks for the lift." Frank put out his hand, and Blake stared at it in something like horror. He took off his cap instead, and bowed.

Frank withdrew his hand, and shoved it in the pocket of his

greatcoat. He could have felt chagrin at his *faux pas*. But somehow, the mistake made him want to laugh. He hid this with a nod of his own. "Good night, Blake."

"Good night, sir. I'll call the hotel tomorrow."

Margot Benedict felt sure the smell of ether still clung to her as she stepped out onto the sidewalk on Fifth Avenue. The sky was already gray, and morning was no more than an hour away. It had been a long and frustrating night.

Her patient, Sister Therese of the Holy Names, had presented with fever and poorly localized pain in her abdomen. She had been vomiting, and the sister who came with her told Margot she hadn't eaten for two days. Palpating, Margot found rebound tenderness at the McBurney's point. Straightforward appendicitis, of course. She gave the little nun an injection of morphine, and called for the surgeon.

When Dr. Whitely arrived, he reeked of alcohol, and his step was unsteady. Margot remonstrated with him, but he swore he was capable, and he did seem to settle down as they scrubbed up. The anaesthesia went well, and the initial incision had been made steadily, with moderate bleeding. The peritoneum was inflamed, but there was no pus to drain, and she anticipated a swift surgery and closure.

It was after midnight, and there was no one in the operating theater but Margot, Whitely, and a night nurse. The observation level was empty, and their voices echoed under the high ceiling. Under normal circumstances, Margot would have been gratified to be here, allowed to assist the surgeon and gain some credits toward her own surgical privileges.

But Dr. Whitely maintained a steady, irritating chatter throughout the procedure, making jokes and then laughing at them. Even through his mask she smelled brandy, so she kept a close eye on his hands as he prepared to separate the mesenteric attachment. It was a damned good thing, she thought now, breathing the predawn air, that she had. He had almost perforated the appendix with his scalpel. Only her snapped "Watch it, Doctor!" had caught his attention, and refocused him on his task.

Whitely was angry with her, of course. Easier for an older doctor to be angry at a younger one, and a female at that, than to admit he had endangered a patient. She could complain to the board of the hospital, but that would draw negative attention, lodge a black mark against her name, and do little to chastise an established physician. It was more likely Whitely would complain about her, claim insubordination or something. She would have to let it go.

When she had first come to this hospital as an intern, there had been two other women physicians, but they had both left to take up rural practices. In fact, the number of women physicians nationwide was diminishing rather than increasing. Margot worried over that.

The click of a car door brought her back to herself. Blake was waiting for her at the curb, holding the door of the Essex open.

"Blake, for heaven's sake," she said. "You haven't waited here all night?"

His teeth flashed white in his dark face. "Dr. Margot," he said sleepily. "You know I couldn't let you find your way home alone in the dark."

"You should be home in your bed."

She settled herself on the backseat. There was a pillow cast aside in the front. He had been dozing here, no doubt, but right in front of the entrance so he wouldn't miss her when she came out. As he fired the ignition and turned on the headlamps, she said, "This is nice, Blake. It's been a difficult night. Thank you for waiting."

He turned in his seat to smile at her. "It's an honor."

Despite the hour, Blake insisted on dropping her in front of the house before he drove around back to garage the car. Margot let herself in through the front door. She hung her coat on the mahogany rack, and trudged up the stairs, suddenly so weary she could hardly keep her head up. She would give herself four hours to sleep before going to the office. If she was a few minutes late, Thea could manage.

She had just slipped inside her bedroom, and was trying to close the door without making any noise, when she heard a sound from the hall. She paused. It could be someone on the way to the bathroom, but her parents had their own bath, as did Dick and Ramona. She and Preston shared the front bath. Her bedroom was on the north side, where the old camellia towered over the portico of the porch. When it was in bloom in the spring, it almost completely blocked her view of the brick water tower of Volunteer Park, just opposite. Preston's room faced west, toward downtown, offering a nice view of the Olympics in good weather.

The sound came again. Someone, Margot thought, was weeping in the hallway. Curious, she let her door swing open a few inches.

Leona—or perhaps Loena—had just passed on her way to the back stairs. Her white shirtwaist was untucked, hanging outside her black skirt. Her arms were wrapped around her slight form, as if she were cold. She wore no shoes, and was creeping along the hall on her bare tiptoes. She sniffled, and released one hand to swipe at her nose.

Margot stepped out into the hall. "Loena," she whispered, hoping she had the right name. The girl seemed not to hear. Margot hurried to catch up with her. She put a hand on the girl's shoulder, and Loena—or Leona—whirled. When she saw Margot, she covered her mouth with both hands. Her pupils dilated, nearly covering the pale blue of her irises. Her skin was dead white behind her freckles, and her lips looked swollen, even bruised. Her hair, usually pinned up in a roll, fell in reddish hanks to her shoulders.

Margot said sharply, "Are you ill? What's wrong?" She reached for the girl's wrist, and wrapped her hand around it to feel her pulse.

The maid whimpered some protest, and tore her hand away. She turned, and broke into an uneven run toward the back stairs. Margot didn't want to shout, with everyone sleeping. She called in an urgent undertone, "Wait! I'm not angry with you—but it's late, and—" She started down the corridor, but the girl reached the end of it before Margot finished her sentence. The door to the back stairs opened and shut with a hasty click, and she was gone.

Margot stopped where she was, staring at the closed door. She could hardly chase the girl up into the servants' quarters. Still, she felt she should have done something more. Her tired brain was barely functioning. Something—but what could it have been? She might have held on to the silly thing, ordered her to stop, but that seemed awfully harsh.

Uneasy, frowning, Margot went into her own bedroom and closed the door. Obviously, the maid had come from Preston's room. Was that any of her business? The twins weren't children. She supposed she would just have to let it pass.

Margot stripped off her blouse and skirt, and threw them over a chair to deal with in the morning. She drew on her nightdress, and fell into bed with a sigh of pure exhaustion. A moment later she got up again to draw the curtain against the rising morning light. She lay back down, and pulled a pillow over her face.

She couldn't help worrying about the weeping girl, about Preston, about what Father would say if he knew Preston was seducing the maids. And about what Dr. Whitely would say about her. It took a long time for her to push all of it out of her mind. Eventually, she slept, but it was the hot, restless sort of sleep that comes at the wrong time of day, and she found herself awake again no more than an hour later.

She thrust the covers off and got up. She could get by one day with no sleep, she reminded herself. She had done it often enough in her internship.

She dashed water on her face in the bathroom, then pulled on a dressing gown and woolen socks to protect her feet from the cold floors. She crept downstairs, trying not to wake anyone who had the good fortune to be still sleeping. She would have a cup of coffee, then dress for the office. Sometimes, she had learned, if she behaved as if she had actually slept, she could convince herself she felt rested.

She turned on the lights in the kitchen and had to squint against their reflection in Hattie's gleaming appliances. The enamel and nickel of the gas range had been polished till they sparkled. The Colonial Electric Percolator was filled and ready on the tile counter. Margot plugged it in, and leaned her hip against the counter as she waited for it to brew. It made a cheerful noise, the water bubbling up through the central tube to sing against the glass top. The kitchen filled with the aroma of fresh coffee. Margot let her head drop back against a cupboard, and her eyes drooped despite her best intentions.

"Dr. Margot?"

Margot's eyes flew open, a little guiltily. "Oh! Blake! What are you doing up?"

His face crinkled into a dozen lines as he smiled at her. "Me?"

She managed to laugh. "I know, I know. Both of us. I couldn't sleep, though. I hope you didn't get up on my account."

"No, no. These old bones don't take much to lying in bed." He crossed to a cabinet and took down two pottery mugs. He held them up to show her. "You'd like a big cup, I imagine?"

She grinned at him. At Edith's breakfast table, the coffee cups were tiny china things with gold rims that had to be refilled a half-dozen times before the meal was over. "Yes, indeed," she said. "I do want a big cup. Maybe two."

The percolator ceased its tune, and Blake brought the cups to the counter. Margot poured for them both as Blake went to the icebox for a bottle of cream. They sat opposite each other, and sipped in friendly silence for a few moments.

"Is your back bothering you again?" Margot asked after a while.

Blake shook his head. "I'm just old," he said. "Don't you worry about me."

"Blake, of course I worry about you. You should let me have a look."

"No," he said, shaking his head. "You have your own patients."

She put one hand over the top of her coffee mug, enjoying the warm steam on her palm. "I remember when you hurt it, you know, Blake."

"Now, how could you remember that? You were only three."

Margot pushed her hair back from her face with both hands, and yawned. "Still. I do."

He propped his elbows on the white enamel tabletop. "That was a bad horse."

"Daddy should have sold it before that. Before he kicked you."

"Probably. But he didn't know, and neither did I." Blake took a long drink of coffee, and rose to refill his mug. "I like driving the Essex a whole lot more than I did that buggy."

Margot accepted a refill in her own cup, and smiled at Blake as he sat down again. "Some changes are good, then."

He lifted his gray eyebrows. "Lots of changes are good, Dr. Margot. Automobiles." He nodded toward the percolator. "Electric coffeemakers." And with a wink, "Lady doctors."

"Lady doctors aren't so new, you know."

"New enough to this old man," he said. "Especially the little lady I've known since she was born."

Impulsively, though she knew it made him uncomfortable, Margot reached across the table to cover his cold dark hand with her warm one. "What would I have done without you, Blake?"

He gently slipped his hand from beneath hers. "Why, you had your mama and your daddy."

Her smile faded. "But it was you who saved me, Blake. Over and over."

He pursed his lips, and sipped his coffee without answering.

In fact, she reflected, as she went upstairs to shower and dress, they never spoke of it. They never had. Not even when it was all going on, when she and Dick were fighting the battle every day, did any of them talk about it. Edith wouldn't listen. Dickson was never at home. But Blake—steady, faithful Blake—was always there, a tall dark figure to intervene, to pick up the fallen, to repair the broken.

She might have survived in any case, Margot thought. But it had been bad. She might not have.

CHAPTER 3

Preston came into the Beaux Arts building of the Seattle Carnegie Library from the paved courtyard on Fifth Avenue. He had never been a library patron in his youth, but he supposed, as a new employee of the *Daily Times*, he could be expected to spend time there. He strolled past the bindery and the mendery, on into the vaulted lobby. A skylight far above his head shed winter sunlight on the marble floor. Steel and chrome and stone glittered with it, dazzling his eyes, matching his mood.

He would start at the *Times* on Monday. He would be a surprise to the managing editor, of course, but the man could hardly object to someone hired by C. B. Blethen himself. It had been easy. The Benedict name wielded a lot of influence. And with the stone caressing his chest, the talisman that had so changed his life, Preston had felt relaxed and confident. He had never spoken so persuasively, he thought, or exerted his charm more effectively. Securing a position had required almost no effort.

He spied a woman with an old-fashioned, high-piled hairstyle and pince-nez hanging from a cord around her neck. He had no doubt she was a librarian, indeed almost a caricature of one. He asked her for the classics, and she led him to a cavernous space where long tables stretched between the stacks. "Can I help you find something?" she asked in disinterested fashion.

"I don't want to trouble you," he said. He flashed her his best smile, but she only nodded, and started to turn away.

Her remote demeanor challenged him. He touched the sapphire beneath his shirtfront, and leaned a little forward, to make her look into his face. "If you could," he said, affecting a diffident air, "just point me toward Near Eastern history."

This caught her attention. She pinched the pince-nez and placed them on her nose before she turned, with a brush of long skirts against a pair of high-buttoned boots, and led the way to a bookcase with deep shelves. Thick tomes leaned this way and that, looking as if they had not been disturbed for years. "These," the librarian said, in a voice now vibrating slightly with interest, "have been here since the building was dedicated." She peered at Preston through the pince-nez. "Mr. Carnegie himself sent them after our old building—you'll remember, of course, the Yesler mansion—burned down."

"Ah," Preston said in noncommittal fashion. He had been six at the time.

"A wonderful gift. The bequest was the grand thing, but these books are priceless."

"Ah," he said again.

"Something in particular?" She looked at him more closely, and a light of understanding came into her eyes. Her voice warmed a little. "Were you over there, sir?"

He dropped his gaze, implying the experience was too painful to talk about. "I was."

"I see. Piqued your curiosity about its history, no doubt."

"A bit. Thanks." Preston could see she was more interested in books than people. He released his hold on the stone. Why waste his energies on this dried-up old maid? There were more tasty tidbits, and very near at hand. Under his nose, as it were.

The librarian hesitated, her curiosity engaged now. "You're sure I can't—"

A rush of impatience sharpened his tongue. "Excuse me," he said, and liked the pink of embarrassment that touched her sallow cheeks. She removed her pince-nez, glanced around the room as if looking for someone to scold, then tripped away, her archaic boots tapping angrily on the bare oak floor.

Preston soon remembered why he had so rarely frequented libraries. There were so many books, all seeming to say the same thing in the same way, drowning the reader in torrents of words, making him wade through dull pages and obfuscating chapters in search of what he wanted. Only his real interest in learning about the woman who had first owned his talisman kept him working.

He flipped pages, tossed books aside, picked up others to scan them and then reject them. Obviously, most historians were more interested in Suleiman than in his bride. In some sources, the remarkable woman who had bent a sultan to her will merited no more than a paragraph. In others, the writers dismissed her as little more than a romantic fable. In his irritation, Preston ripped a page, then glanced over his shoulder. That ice witch of a librarian could probably hear a torn page from three rooms away.

He tried more of the histories, but each was more tedious than the last. They utterly misunderstood the glory of Roxelana's power. Their ponderous voices drowned her drama in floods of facts and citations only the most dedicated academic could care about.

He found one letter, in a volume of a compilation immodestly called *The World's Story*, that purported to be an eyewitness account, written by someone who claimed to have met the sultana. Preston didn't believe a word of it. The writer described her as "stout," but that was preposterous. The Roxelana he saw in his dreams, the enchanting creature known as Khourrem Sultan, the Laughing One, had won a crown with only her wits and beauty. She could not have been stout. It was not possible. He wished he could punish the writer for daring to say such a thing—but of course, the offender was long dead and gone.

So was Roxelana, for that matter, but she had left her secret behind.

Preston shoved the book away. He propped his chin on his fist, and closed his eyes to see her in his mind, to savor the image he had held of her since he first heard her story in his dusty billet in Jerusalem. She had been lean, he was sure, with slanting dark eyes and a slender bosom. Her fingers were long, the nails filed to curving points. Her hair would have been her glory, dark and Slavic, curling around a pronounced jaw, a sign of her strength.

He opened his eyes, and leaned back in the hard wooden chair. Why could these fools, these pretenders to wisdom, not see what he did? Roxelana, the slave bride of Suleiman the Magnificent, had been a diamond of a woman, hard and brilliant and many-faceted.

He left the pile of books where they were, and walked out of the classics room, through the foyer, now gloomy with sudden rain, to the double glass doors. He adjusted his fedora to a jaunty angle as he trotted down the grand staircase to Fourth Avenue. He was about to become a man of letters. If he cared to, he could write her story properly, with all its intrigue and excitement.

He wouldn't do it, though. Her secret was his. It had come into his possession when he—let us say, *acquired*—the sapphire. As he turned west on Madison to wander toward the water, he wished he could bury his face in that thick black hair, trail his fingertips across her lean shoulders. Roxelana had been a woman worthy of him. Probably the *only* woman worthy of him. She could have matched his determination, his clarity of purpose—and his ruthlessness. The world demanded ruthlessness. How else could a man—or a woman—achieve his or her rightful place?

Preston found himself in the Public Market, his swift steps ringing hollowly on the wooden walkway. He smiled at a Chinese vendor hawking some sort of silk slippers, and grinned at the fish vendors in the high stalls, who offered shining silver salmon and baskets of oysters dripping salt water. He bought a paper from a newsboy, and tucked it under his arm. He walked past the day stalls to climb the narrow stair to the café. He took one of the metal tables in the window and ordered coffee.

With a mug of coffee in his hand, he opened the paper, but he didn't read it. His eye was caught by the gleam of rain-blurred light on gray water, the slant of a fishing boat's sails silhouetted against the cloudbank. Everything in Seattle was cool, with muted colors and soft sounds. Jerusalem had been very different. And Jerusalem had changed everything.

The strange thing about that day in Jerusalem was that he hadn't wanted to go into the Old City at all. The crowds made him uneasy, those throngs of dark-skinned people with their sly glances and jabbering languages no one could understand. It was Carter's idea. He had only gone along with it to show he wasn't afraid.

The truth was that he was terrified. He was frightened of everything—the other officers, the horses, the bayonets, the guns, and the cannon with their great thumping blasts that shook the ground and knocked the gunners right off their feet. Preston felt as if things were exploding all around him, at meals, at teatime, even when he tried to sleep. He felt inadequate and inept, and he suspected the other officers of sniggering at him behind his back. More than once he woke up whimpering with fear, and Carter, who had been out in the East for months, would make some joke and bring him tea to calm his nerves.

But, as it turned out, fate had him in its hand. His destiny had drawn him into the Old City and guided him to the sapphire. It hadn't really been Carter at all.

Benjamin Carter was a big, noisy Brit. He had the grossest tastes, in food and women and war, but not the slightest bit of embarrassment about them. And until that day in the Old City, though Preston was the officer and Carter his servant—his batman, as they said in Allenby's army—Preston mostly did what Carter wanted.

Their relationship looked like a friendship, but Preston didn't trust it. He feared that Carter secretly despised him, that he, too, was laughing at him with his mates. Carter didn't give away his true feelings, naturally, but that was part of the system. He was as obsequious as all the other batmen, but when they were on their own, he dropped the "Yes, sir" and "No, sir" altogether. Preston didn't know if he was supposed to order him to speak properly or assume that all the batmen did the same. Half the time Carter seemed to be hiding a smile, as if Preston were a child to be humored. Preston hated that, but he had no idea how to go about replacing him, and he was afraid that, if he tried to get rid of him, Carter would tell everyone his Captain Benedict was a coward who woke sobbing in the night like a frightened baby.

But all of that was before their day in the Old City.

They left their billet in the late afternoon to ford the bustle of the Damascus Gate and take a stroll in the Muslim Quarter. In the squares, crowds of veiled women and turbaned men mixed with uniformed soldiers and bearded Jews. Carter loved a sort of kebab he could buy straight from smoking grills, handed over with dirty fingers by men who bowed and nodded, then sneered at the fat Brit behind his back. Preston wouldn't touch the kebabs, but Carter was always hungry. Soldier-Servant rations were never enough for him. He ate the meat as he walked, dripping grease over his cuffs as he led the way through noisome alleys lined with tiny dark shops. Preston felt anxious, and nauseated by the smells of unwashed people and suspicious foreign foods, but he followed. He wasn't sure he could find his way out of the quarter on his own.

They came upon the antiquities dealer seemingly by accident. His windows were stacked with painted boxes, dusty amphorae, hookahs with long, twisting tubes, ropes of beads, flat cloth shoes with embroidered toes. Preston paused at the open doorway. It was dim in the shop, but it was quiet, and it smelled pleasantly of some sort of spice. Carter's messy meal stank of rancid fat and made Preston's nostrils twitch. He said, "Carter—I want to go in here."

Carter, chewing, waved his thick hand. Preston stepped in through the door, and his glance fell on a short curved sword in a brocade scabbard.

The dealer, a small man with dark eyes gone rheumy with age, emerged from the back of his shop through a curtain of beaded fabric. He wore a fez, and he smiled at Preston with lips so dark they were nearly purple. "Many fine thing," he said, bowing, clasping his hands before him. "Many fine thing, special for you. For your lady."

His accent was thick, but he spoke decent English for a Turk. Preston pointed to the sword, and the shopkeeper scurried to take it down from the wall display. He carried it to Preston, and presented it on both palms. Preston took it in his hands, and slid the blade slowly out of the scabbard.

Just then Carter appeared at his shoulder. He gave a low whistle when he saw the sword. "Have a care, guv. That looks bloody sharp."

Preston ran a finger down the flat of the blade. The edge of it, with its cruel arch and pointed tip, had the shiny look of steel recently sharpened, though the flat was pitted and stained with age.

The shopkeeper murmured, "Very nice. Very old, sir."

Preston glanced up. "How old?"

The dealer shrugged, and spread his hands. "Who knows? Very nice."

Preston slid the blade back into the scabbard and laid it on the counter. Carter said, "Gonna buy it, guv? Snappy souvenir of our glorious victory." He drew out the word *glorious*, laughing, then fell to scrubbing at the spots on his sleeve with the heel of his hand.

"I don't know," Preston said. He tapped the scabbard with his fingers. "How much?"

The little man's eyes brightened. "For you, very nice, very nice. Five pounds."

Preston turned to Carter. "Five pounds is about twenty dollars, right?"

Carter nodded, and laughed. "Way too much, old son," he said gleefully. "Make him come down."

Preston, heartened by Carter's approval, turned back to the dealer. "I'll give you ten shillings."

The shopkeeper pressed his right hand to his heart. "Sir, you pain me."

Carter chortled, and Preston said, "His English is improving, don't you think?"

The man dropped his hand to sweep it over the scabbard, brushing the raised stitching, the old stained velvet. "You see, very old." His dark lips pursed. "Four pounds."

Carter was fingering a scarf draped over an enameled mirror, but he left it, and came back to the counter. The dealer leaned closer to Preston, making him want to step back. "Very rare, sir," the man said. "Very old."

Preston said, "One pound, then. I don't even know if it's genuine."

"Likely not," Carter said. The dealer threw him a glance full of venom.

Preston pushed the scabbard away from him, across the counter. "Last time. One."

The shopkeeper's look of pain was genuine this time. He opened his hands and held them up. "Sorry, sir. Not possible. Three pounds, possible. One, not possible."

"No good, old son," Carter said cheerfully. "Too much."

Preston thought he might have paid it, if Carter hadn't been so sure. He gave the sword a final glance, rapped once on the counter with his knuckles, and turned away. Carter grinned, and the two of them started out of the cramped shop. The door was too narrow for them to pass through together, and for once, Carter stepped back to let Preston go ahead.

As he stepped into the shaft of hot sunlight falling through the open doorway, Preston looked up, distracted by a gleam of something blue. He stopped, and Carter's heavy stomach bumped his elbow.

It shone beyond a barrier of smoky glass, its suspending chain draped over a tiny, discolored mirror. It was as long as the first knuckle of Preston's thumb, and nearly as wide. The facets were irregular, and poorly cut, but the color—violet with tinges of purple—was vivid, alive with light. It seemed to flicker, as if a blue flame burned in its depths. Preston's fingers curled, yearning to touch it, to feel its weight in his palm, to *have* it.

Carter shifted behind him, eager to be on his way again, but Preston saw nothing but the sapphire tempting him, calling to him from its crowded cabinet.

"What's this?" he barked over his shoulder, pointing at it.

The shopkeeper, sensing a sale after all, hurried from behind his counter, a ring of brass keys jangling in his hand. He brushed past Carter with a murmured apology, and stood at Preston's shoulder to see what had caught his eye. His indrawn breath was one of pure regret. "Oh, no, sir," he said. He stepped back, making no move to unlock the cabinet. "Oh, no, so sorry. Is not possible."

"What d'you mean, not possible?" Carter thundered. His voice, in the cramped space, made Preston wince. "What's it doing there if it's not for sale?"

The shopkeeper said, "So sorry. So sorry." He turned away in a swirl of his cotton robe, and retreated to his counter.

Preston could not take his eyes from the sapphire. "What is it?"

Carter said, "Just some old necklace, Preston."

The dealer spoke in the firmest voice he had used thus far. "No. Is from Khourrem Sultan, sir. Very old. Very valuable."

"Name a price," Preston said softly. Suddenly, strangely, nothing in the world mattered but the possession of that jewel, that dully gleaming sapphire. Carter made some movement, but Preston held up his hand, forestalling him. The jewel glittered at him from its tarnished silver chain, its crude facets reflected in the ancient mirror, and he knew he couldn't leave the shop without it.

"No," the shopkeeper answered. There was both regret and pride in his voice. "Is not for sale, sir." He nodded toward another cabinet, where lesser pieces jumbled together in piles of dull stones and broken chains. He gestured to it with both of his slender, nervous hands. "Please," he said. "Many others. Please."

Preston forced himself to look away from the sapphire. His chest tightened with the old, familiar pressure as he fixed his gaze on the dark shopkeeper. "Tell me why the necklace is not for sale."

The man folded his hands in front of him. "Is not mine."

Preston stared at him, assessing the probability that the man was lying to him, deliberately standing between him and this thing of beauty. "Whose, then?"

"Khourrem Sultan," the man said again. "Is very bad, sir."

"What d'you mean?" Carter began, but Preston silenced him with a flick of his fingers. He crossed the creaking wooden floor, and laid his hands on the counter to gaze across it into the shopkeeper's face. The sword in its scabbard still lay between them.

Preston pointed back at the cabinet. "For that, you can have your five pounds."

At that moment the dark little man, dealer in antiquities, made a fatal error. His last mistake. He laughed.

The sword made a slight snicking sound as Preston pulled it free of its scabbard. It made a louder sound, like that of a boot sucking free of a mud puddle, when it slashed the shopkeeper's folded arms. It sounded like the crack of a whip against stirrup leather when Preston struck through the man's throat, nearly severing his head from his neck.

The shopkeeper's body crashed backward through the beaded curtain. Instantly a scream began, the long, winding shriek of a woman. The ululation set Preston's bones to tingling.

Behind him, Carter swore. Preston snapped, "Break the glass, man, and be quick!"

In moments, the cabinet lay in shards, and the sapphire—the jewel of Khourrem Sultan, whoever that was—lay deep in Preston's pocket.

There was blood on his uniform, but that was hardly unusual. He threw the sword to the floor, and left it there. He and Carter melted into the crowds in the street just as a knot of men dashed toward the shop in answer to the panicked wails. Preston's heart thudded with pleasure, as much for the thrill of exacting justice as for the delight of the sapphire's weight in his pocket.

And that was before he knew the nature of his prize.

* * *

One of the British officers, a lieutenant called Mather, had been raised in Africa and could read Arabic. It was from him that Preston learned the story of the sapphire. The theft of the jewel was apparently much bigger news than the death of a minor dealer of antiquities. There had been many deaths in the war, but, according to the account in *el-Carmel*, there was only one jewel of Khourrem Sultan, a woman of the sixteenth century popularly known as Roxelana.

The great mystery, according to *el-Carmel*, was how the sapphire came to be in an obscure shop inside the Damascus Gate. Mather read the account, translating as he went, sometimes struggling for the English word, sometimes puzzling over an Arabic construction.

"Roxelana, born Aleksandra Lisowska in about 1510, was captured by Turkish slavers from her Ukrainian village and sold in Constantinople to the *harem* of the Turkish sultan, Suleiman the Magnificent. One of three hundred young women belonging to Suleiman, she distinguished herself through wit and personality, becoming known as Khourrem, the—let's see, the Laughing One, I think.

"Legend says that Roxelana possessed a single jewel, a gift from the young sultan. She called it her only estate, all a poor harem girl was allowed. It never left—" Mather stumbled, searching for a word. "Her person, I suppose. Or her body, I'm not sure.

"Her rivals claimed the jewel, a large blue sapphire, had—" Another hesitation. "Powers of magic—" Mather shook his head. "That's not quite right, I'm afraid. The word means evil power, but I don't know how to translate it."

Mather took off his spectacles and rubbed his eyes. "There's more, but it's hard to read. She built things, apparently, and sponsored some charities, things an Ottoman woman hadn't done before."

He laid the paper aside. The others in the unit relaxed in camp chairs and sipped their tea. The sapphire nestled deep in Preston's vest pocket, cool and heavy and sweet.

"So how did the jewel get to Jerusalem?" Carter asked. Preston threw him a warning glance, and his face paled quite satisfactorily. Everything between them had been different since that day in the antiquities shop.

Preston said, "How can they be sure the one that was stolen was hers?"

Mather tapped the paper. "The dealer was a Turk. The report says he acquired it himself during repairs to her mausoleum."

"Acquired," Preston said smoothly. "He stole it. And now someone stole it from him."

"The paper says he was a respected dealer."

"Don't mean he ain't a thief," Carter said.

Preston cleared his throat, and tapped the fingers of his right hand on the arm of his camp chair. Carter subsided, and brought the teapot to refill Preston's cup. Preston said, "Tell me, Mather. How did you come to grow up in Africa?" He sipped his tea, and listened politely as Mather related his childhood as the son of a British Army officer.

In the days following, Carter argued that Preston should sell the jewel. "Then we can split the money." His eyes fixed on Preston's vest, where the sapphire was hidden.

"Split it?" Preston drawled. "Why should we split it? You didn't do anything."

Carter frowned, searching for an argument. "Smashed the glass," he said after a moment.

"I did all the dirty work," Preston said. "The hard work."

Carter was polishing Preston's riding boots. He spat on the toe of one, and rubbed it fiercely with a blackened cloth. "It was dirty, all right," he said to the boot. "But I didn't tell."

Preston, leaning indolently against a cupboard, laughed. "No, Carter, you didn't tell. That's worth something, and I'll see you're compensated." Carter looked up, a hopeful gleam in his small eyes. "I won't sell it, though," Preston finished. "It goes home to America with me."

Carter grinned. "I'd love to come to America, guv. Just say the word."

"We'll see." Preston caressed his vest pocket to feel the shape and solidity of Roxelana's jewel. The image of her was taking shape in his mind, Roxelana the laughing one, the daring one. The slave girl who owned nothing but her courage and a powerful sapphire. Her slanting dark eyes seemed to shine over the centuries, to cast their seductive glance onto him. Thinking of her made his loins stir.

He dropped his hand, and nodded to his batman. "We'll see. And that's Captain Benedict, Carter. See you remember."

The look in Carter's small eyes was one of surprise and discomfort. It gratified Preston to see it, and he touched the jewel once again through the fabric of his vest.

Frank went to call on William Boeing in his office in the Hoge Building, on Second. The Hoge was modern, eighteen stories, with an exterior of terra-cotta and tan brick and elaborate cartouches. Boeing's office was full of heavy furniture, which would have made it look old-fashioned were it not for the pictures on the walls. These were photographs and illustrations of sea sleds, of flying boats, of soaring triplanes, every one of them manufactured by the Boeing Airplane Company. The receptionist who welcomed Frank was a trim young woman in a gleaming white shirtwaist and navy-blue ankle-length skirt. She led him into the inner office, held the door for him with a professional smile, then disappeared.

Frank took a seat across from a tall, well-built man in early middle age. Boeing wore owlish spectacles and a pencil mustache. He had thinning brown hair, which he brushed back with his hand every few minutes. His gaze, through the round glasses, was intense, nearly unblinking.

Boeing shook his hand, eyed Frank's empty sleeve, and said merely, "Rotten luck, Major."

"Yes, sir." Frank took off his hat and shrugged out of his greatcoat. He could see his resume laid open on the broad mahogany desk, his slender portfolio of vellum drawings beside it.

Boeing tapped the resume with a finger. "I was in the navy, myself."

"Yes, sir. Navy Reserve, I believe."

"That's right. You wouldn't mind working for a navy man?"

Frank hesitated, then allowed himself a contained smile. "I'm sure you would have joined the army if you could, sir."

This won a laugh from Bill Boeing, and he leaned back in his chair, still smiling. "The Boeing Airplane Company means to prove that commercial aviation is the future, Major."

"Seaplanes?"

Boeing nodded. "Seaplanes, yes. But more than that. We've been hit hard by war-surplus biplanes, but we can't let that stop us. I intend to build better airplanes that can carry more weight and travel farther—in other words, commercial air travel." He reached for a model that rested on the corner of his desk, and set it down in front of Frank. "This is going to change the way people think of flying."

The model was made of balsa wood and paper, neatly painted with the company name and the letters C742K on the tail. Frank picked it up in his hand, and turned it to see how the propeller was attached. He lifted it to look at the angle of the wings and the proportion of the tail to the body. He itched to take the propeller off to get a look at the pitch of the blades. He peered at them, bringing the model close to his eyes. "Is this a scale model?"

"More or less. This is based on one of the mail planes, but I'm working on a prototype. You can see we're trying the Stearman wings."

"I do. What degree of pitch do you use? This looks a lot like a boat propeller."

"You're right. Our sea sled uses it, too." Boeing leaned forward, and pointed to the propeller housing. "We're trying to reduce vibration. Some of our contracts aren't our own design—there's the de Havilland, and the army wants an armored triplane—but we think we can do better starting from the ground up."

"How thick is the skin?" Frank rotated the model. "And the payload? The range?"

For half an hour they discussed the pros and cons of two wings over three. When the receptionist knocked on the door and came in with a coffee service, Frank looked up in surprise. He had all but forgotten where he was and why he was here.

The young woman laid the tray on the corner of the desk and left the office. Boeing poured coffee, and handed Frank a cup. He shoved the creamer forward so Frank could reach it. "So, Major. I gather you're available now? I can offer you a hundred a month. I know it's not much, but if things go well with the B-1, things will look up."

Frank's fingers suddenly began to tremble. With care, he set the coffee cup down. "Sir—don't you want to interview me?"

Boeing gave a cheery grin. "Why, son, we just had an interview!"

"Oh, but I—we were just—"

Boeing took a great slurp of hot coffee, and banged his cup down with a rush of boyish enthusiasm that belied his professorial appearance. "Major, all that matters to me in the world are airplanes! We've had to build furniture and flat-bottomed boats and God knows what-all since the war ended. But what I want to do is this!" He pointed to the model again. "I believe you're the man to help me, and I think my chief engineer will agree." He picked up his cup again, and rose to walk to the window. He pointed his thumb at the city beyond the glass. "We're going to put Seattle on the map, Major, and not just for boats. When people around the country—no, around the world—think of Seattle, I want them to think of airplanes. *Boeing* airplanes."

Frank rose, too, and went to stand beside the older man to look down on the street below. "As many automobiles as wagons down there now," he said.

Boeing chuckled. "Exactly. Good man." He clapped Frank's shoulder, then pointed to a framed clipping on the wall above his desk. "That article is from *Scientific American*. Ten years ago. It says that 'to affirm that the airplane is going to revolutionize the future is to be guilty of the wildest exaggeration.'"

"The revolution of the future already started," Frank said. "With warfare."

"Right you are," Boeing said. He polished off his coffee with a toss of his head, then shook one long forefinger at Frank. "Mark my words, son. One day no one will think anything of buying passage on an airplane when they want to travel."

He sat down again behind his desk, and leaned back so he could look into Frank's face. "So. Are you going to join the Boeing Airplane Company, Major?"

Frank's heart beat so hard he thought it must show through his coat. He managed to say, with reasonable calm, "Yes, sir. Yes. I would be pleased to join you, if you'll have me. Your vision of the future—that's exciting."

Boeing grinned again, and reached for the candlestick telephone on his desk. "I have to call Dickson Benedict and thank him for recommending you. I think you'll be a great fit." He spoke to the telephone operator, then cradled the earpiece against his chest while he waited for the connection. "How long have you known the Benedict family?"

The sidewalk felt like air beneath Frank's feet as he walked back to his hotel. He could hardly believe the swift change in his fortunes.

Dickson Benedict's name had opened three doors for him. Only one of the businesses had asked if he made his drawings before or after the war, a polite way of asking if he could draw one-handed. He assured the man he had prepared his portfolio while he was at the hospital in Virginia, but there had been no job offer. The second business had shown interest, but the salary they mentioned was substantially lower than the one Bill Boeing had tossed off so casually.

More than that, Frank knew in his bones that Boeing was right. Roads needed to be built, and ships, too. But air transport would outshine them all one day. It would be faster, more efficient. A man could soon reach New York from Seattle in a couple of days, instead of the week it took to get there by train. Frank was willing to bet someone would fly across the Atlantic before long, and maybe even, one day, across the mighty Pacific. The thought of being part of that movement, of contributing to that progress, made him feel youthful again, filled with hope. A swell of returning confidence enlivened his step.

Now, at last, he could write to his mother and father. He would telephone Dickson Benedict to thank him. Or better yet, go to his office, and shake his hand in person.

Then he would search out the rooming house Blake had found for him. He had a week to get himself settled before his employment would start. Seattle was to be his new home.

He felt better than he had for nearly two years. As he walked briskly back to the Alexis, the gray sky above his head felt cozy rather than forbidding. The cool, damp air was soft in his lungs, and the clang of the trolley as it clattered down Madison charmed him. He had a job. He would soon have a place to live. He felt like a man again.

He should, he thought, shop for a new overcoat. His war was over.

The doorbell of Benedict Hall sounded its three-tone chime just after one o'clock. All the family was out, and Blake and Hattie and the twins were at lunch in the kitchen. Leona said, "Shall I go, Mr. Blake?"

Blake laid down his soupspoon, and pushed away from the table. "No, Leona. Thank you, but I'll get it." Leona nodded.

Her sister didn't lift her eyes from her soup bowl, and Blake frowned to himself as he thrust his arms into his coat sleeves and adjusted his collar. Loena had been glum of late. Usually the sound of the twins chattering filled the kitchen at mealtimes. They tended to do their chores side by side, and their light voices could be heard gossiping as they were cleaning the upper hall, dusting the front room, polishing the long table in the dining room. Blake wondered if they had had a falling out. Or perhaps Loena was ill. He could ask Miss Margot to have a look at her. Dr. Margot, that was.

He indulged in a private smile of pride as he smoothed the lapels of his jacket. He had always known that girl would be something special.

The doorbell chimed again, but Blake did not hurry. Whoever this caller was should learn that in a proper house, it took time to answer the door. This was not, after all, a hotel. He paused behind the closed door and cleared his throat before he turned the handle.

A rather large person stood on the step, thick-featured, with a pendulous belly and big, scarred hands holding the lapels of a well-worn service coat. Blake bent a haughty eye on him, and the man, evidently recovering his manners, snatched off his cap to reveal pale thinning hair. His eyebrows and eyelashes were pale, too, giving him a bleached look.

"May I help you?" Blake asked.

"I'm looking for Preston Benedict," the man said, in the slurred accents of the English working class.

"Oh, yes?" Blake answered in his most remote tone. "And who is calling, please?"

The man grinned, showing discolored teeth. "I'm Carter, mate," he said. "Benjamin Carter. Sergeant, I was. Preston's batman."

Blake drew a slow breath through his nostrils. Carter didn't exactly smell bad, but there was something distasteful about him, just the same. He said, with emphasis, "*Captain* Benedict is not at home. He's working."

Carter gave a crude snort of amusement. "Working! Preston? That's a good laugh."

Blake stiffened. "Pardon me," he said. This time he sniffed audibly, and he directed his gaze above the man's head, no longer caring to meet his faded eyes. "Perhaps, Mr. Carter, you will allow me to give Captain Benedict a message?"

Carter's laughter died. "No need to turn up your nose at me, mate. I think I know how I should be treated! You may be standing there like a lord, but you're still a nigger."

Blake took a deliberate step back, and shut the door firmly in Benjamin Carter's face.

He stood still for a moment, listening to the gutter curses beyond the door, waiting until the angry footfalls fading down the steps of the porch told him the man had given up and left. Then, straightening his jacket and holding his head high, Blake went back to the kitchen. Automatically, he glanced into the rooms he passed, to assure himself everything was in order.

Hattie looked up when he came back into the kitchen. "Oh," she breathed. "Lost your temper?" Leona turned a curious gaze on him, too, and even Loena raised her drooping head.

Hattie knew him too well. Blake tried to relax his rigid face. He took his time removing his jacket, shaking it out, hanging it on its peg beneath the big Sessions clock. He crossed to the counter to pour himself a cup of coffee, then carried it back to the table, pulled out his chair, and sat down.

"Who was it, Blake?" Hattie asked.

He blew out a breath, and looked at her with affection. He had known Hattie a long time. She had come to work for the Benedicts more than twenty years ago, and she hadn't changed much in all that time. Even as a young woman, she had those cushiony cheeks, generous hips, and deep bosom. Her chin was fuller now, her shoulders more rounded, but she had the same broad South Carolina accent she had the first day he met her at King Street Station.

He wouldn't tell her what Benjamin Carter had said. There was no need to wound her. This had not been an easy house, but he and Hattie had always been treated with respect. They were as much a part of the family as two Negro retainers could be. Hattie deserved better than to hear the casual insult of an ill-bred limey.

He sipped from his coffee cup. The brew had gone bitter from sitting in the pot since breakfast. "It was another soldier," he told Hattie. "An Englishman who was in the war with Mr. Preston."

Hearing Preston's name, Hattie brightened, as she always did. "Lordie, is that right? Is he coming back, then?" She braced herself on the table as she hefted herself out of her chair. "I should make some cookies. Maybe a pie."

"I expect he'll be back," Blake said. It was probably true. That sort didn't give up easily.

Loena and Leona rose, too, and began clearing away the soup bowls and water glasses. Blake sat a moment longer, finishing his coffee, as the twins clattered dishes in the big sink. Hattie took butter and milk from the icebox, and set the range to heat. Blake watched, postponing going out to the garage to try to scrub a spot of oil from the concrete floor.

He shouldn't take offense, he knew, at the word Carter had used. Everyone—that is, everyone except the Benedicts—used it. He should accept it as a reminder that, despite everything, he had come to a good position in his life. He was the only one of his family to be born a free man, free to choose his own work, free to tread his own path. His mother had hoped for him to be a businessman or a teacher. But he had worked for Dickson Benedict for more than thirty years, made a good salary, tucked a bit away for his old age. He had a right to be proud.

Hattie began to cream butter in a pottery bowl, her wide hips swinging as she worked the spoon. The twins put on their aprons and disappeared upstairs with a mop and a bucket of cleaning rags. Blake sat on for a moment, staring at a slice of his own reflection in the nickel finish of the range. At this distance, the bit of his face he could see looked as smooth and unmarked as it had been the day he first met Mr. Dickson.

He had been twenty-six years old, as old as Mr. Preston was now, but infinitely older than his years. He hadn't fought the sort of war Preston and Carter and Frank Parrish had fought. His battle had been of a different sort. And it had lasted a lot longer.

Blake was born in 1866, and his newly freed parents, in gratitude to the President, had named him Abraham. The owner of the plantation—their owner—was one Franklin Blake, of Columbia, South Carolina, and all his slaves bore his name. He was neither worse nor better than other slave owners, as far as Abraham Blake knew. His mother and father were allowed to live together. Their one-room shack stood in a row of such dwellings.

None of them had lighting or plumbing or even a window. Abraham's parents couldn't read, but they pinned the Emancipation Proclamation on the inner wall of their shack just the same.

It was after the battle of Antietam that Franklin Blake had come around to give a copy of the Proclamation to each of his slaves. He explained that this was the reason the South was going to war. He said that if such a proclamation was enforced, his "people," as he called them, would have no work and no place to live. They would have no one to take care of them. He told them to pray for President Davis and General Lee and the Confederacy, so their way of life could be preserved.

Abraham's parents told him they said nothing to the master, only accepted the paper and went about their labors. At Hilton Head and Port Royal, Negroes celebrated their freedom with dancing in the streets, but for the Blake slaves, little changed. They were technically free, but as that paper yellowed and curled on their wall, the war raged around them, and they waited in cautious silence to see what would happen.

Franklin Blake's only son, fighting for the Confederacy, was killed at far-off Baton Rouge. The master nearly went mad with grief. News trickled into the slave quarters, little by little, stories of battles won and lost, rumors of Negro soldiers fighting for the North, tales of destruction told in horrified whispers.

When the war reached the Blake plantation, Abraham's mother was already pregnant with him. She and his father watched the fire rise above the city of Columbia, reddening the horizon, blotting out the stars with smoke and flames. The next day Master Blake, walking like an old and broken man, toured the slave quarters. In a voice that cracked with weary grief, he told everyone they were free to leave whenever they liked.

Abraham's parents had no idea where to go or what to do. They owned nothing. They had no skills. All they had was each other and that faded, crackling piece of paper. They unpinned the Emancipation Proclamation from their wall, and set out for the burned city. Abraham Blake, their only child, was born in the ruins of Columbia, in a hut behind a gray clapboard house that had escaped the firestorm.

By the time he was ten, the sheer weight of poverty had nearly broken his parents. His father walked six miles every day to work for a small cotton farm, whose white yeoman owner had never been able to afford hired help before. He thought having colored workers made him one of the nobility, that aristocracy he had envied and hated before the war. Abraham's mother, desperate for her son to take advantage of his free status, cleaned floors and windows in the local Baptist church so Abraham could attend the school there. No one had much to eat those years, and the Blakes had less than most. Their health failed, bit by bit. One morning, when Abraham was thirteen, his father failed to wake up. Later that same year, his mother contracted lobar pneumonia. She was gone in a week, leaving Abraham alone in the world.

He stayed in the hut behind the gray house. He kept going to the Baptist school, because he had promised his mother on her deathbed. He spent his evenings begging odd jobs, or just begging. One or two eating places, now owned by free Negroes, fed him their leftovers. When the school closed, the Freedmen's Bureau helped Abraham find work on an indigo plantation.

Not until he arrived at it did Blake realize it was old Franklin Blake's place. The master was still there, stooped and white-haired, resentful now of the Negroes who worked for him. When he learned Abraham's name, the boy became a special target.

Franklin Blake often withheld Abraham's pay on the basis of some complaint. He gave the boy the worst jobs, the dirtiest jobs, and he criticized everything he did. No one intervened when the old man took his cane, Carolina pine with a marble lion's head on its top, to Abraham's back. Abraham tried getting help from the Freedmen's Bureau, but it was a loose organization, and there was no one to counsel him. He grew into a lanky, bone-thin young man, solitary and silent.

He went on working for Franklin Blake because he didn't know what else to do. As the old man weakened, his temper grew less and less stable. What was left of his family had dispersed, leaving him alone to descend into despair and madness. He spent his nights drinking. His cook and housekeeper locked themselves in their rooms at night to avoid his rages. One clear, star-filled night, he came looking for someone on whom to vent his ire, and he found eighteen-year-old Abraham and Old Billy, a middle-aged former slave, stirring the work vats. Abraham wore a bandanna around his face against the stench of the indigo.

Franklin thundered at them, "Whatcha all think you're doin'? There's too much lime in that vat!"

Old Billy knew Franklin Blake's ways. He dropped his paddle without a word, and fled into the darkness. The paddle spun once in the noisome brew, and started to sink. Abraham tried to catch it with his own, but it slipped away, disappearing below the surface. Franklin strode toward him, shouting, "Now see what y'all done! Now see! Ya Goddamn nigras can't do anything right without an overseer, and I can't be ever-place at once!"

Abraham lodged his paddle in a holder, so it wouldn't join the other one at the bottom of the vat. He turned slowly to face Franklin, hoping the old man would calm down. "Suh, we wasn't the ones measured the lime." He ducked his head, but kept an eye on the lion's head cane in Franklin's right hand.

Franklin was right in front of him now, his left hand like a blue-veined claw on the edge of the vat, his right hand brandishing the cane above Abraham's head. "Fish it out! Fish it out!" the old man shrieked in a voice as high and thin as an old woman's. He snatched the bandanna from Abraham's face, scratching his cheek with his ragged nails, washing him in bourbon-laced breath.

Abraham reached for his paddle to comply, but Franklin gave him no chance. His arm trembled with rage as he lifted the cane, ready to bring it down on Abraham's head.

There was nothing new in the scene. Abraham had lost count of the times Franklin Blake had struck him, or whipped him, or shoved him to the ground in a fit of temper.

But Abraham was eighteen now. He wasn't a boy anymore. He was a man, a hungry, friendless man. He was a head taller than Franklin, and forty years younger.

He seized the cane with his left hand, stopping its downward trajectory. Franklin struggled to take it back, cursing and spitting. He staggered, and his face purpled as he gripped the cane with both hands and pulled.

With a nearly casual tug, Abraham yanked the cane from the older man's hands. He didn't threaten Franklin, didn't try to hit back or push him with it. He only held it high above his head, out of Franklin's reach. Franklin choked, "Goddamn it, boy, give—" but he never finished the sentence. His eyes bulged, and his mouth opened and closed spasmodically, like a gasping fish.

Abraham staggered back in horror as Franklin reeled and fell. The old man collapsed on his back, sightless eyes staring upward. The boy didn't need to touch him to know he was dead. He stood over him, shocked into stillness, the cane still in his hands, his own mouth hanging open.

When he looked up, dry mouthed and stunned, he found Old Billy standing in the door of the shed. Two men were with him, white men. Old Billy had gone to the next farm for help.

No one cared that Abraham swore he hadn't touched Franklin Blake. No one wanted to hear how many times that cane had bruised his back and shoulders, had brought bumps to his skull and contusions to his wrists. The old plantation owner was dead, and though everyone knew it was his own mean nature that killed him, it looked better to have someone to blame. They blamed Abraham.

Blake sighed, and pushed aside his empty coffee cup. It did no good to think about the old times, the bad times. He should know better. He got up, straightening carefully around the twinge in his back.

When he looked up, he found Hattie watching him. She gestured with her buttery spoon. "Ain't no use havin' a doctor in the house if you won't let her help you."

"I don't like to trouble Dr. Margot."

"That girl loves you, Blake," Hattie said, turning back to her counter to pour sugar into the bowl. "She'd swear it ain't no trouble."

"I know." He crossed the kitchen to the little porch that served as a back entrance. He kicked off his house shoes, and put on a pair of work boots. He pulled on a worn canvas coat. "I'll be in the garage, Hattie."

"Got your gloves?" she called from the kitchen.

He smiled to himself. Hattie had the instincts of a mother goose, and no chick was too old or too big to be sheltered under her wing. She was a bad cook, as Blake and the whole family knew, but she was a good woman. "I've got them, Hattie. Thank you."

Hattie had scolded him, in the early years, for changing his accent. She said he was being uppity. Pretending to be something he was not. Blake never explained to her the real reason he shed his Southern drawl and prison slang. He had one, though, a good one. He spent a great deal of time with the Benedict children, Dick and Margot and Preston. He didn't want the children—only in the privacy of his own thoughts did he call them *his* children—to speak like slaves, or like inmates of the Chatham County Convict Camp. He wanted them to speak like their parents, in neutral Pacific Northwest accents.

He pushed through the swinging screen door and walked outside with a little rush of satisfaction at his place in life. A man never forgot, he supposed, what it was like to lose his freedom. Six years in Chatham County Convict Camp had taught him to appreciate going in and out of doors at will.

They had also taught him how to use the lion-headed cane to defend himself. He had managed to keep the cane by hiding it in his trouser leg, and it was the only stroke of fortune he was to experience for some years. The camp was a brutal place where only the toughest and meanest survived. Abraham had gone in as a young man, still tender with hope. He came out a hardened warrior who knew how to fight for his life. He was tall and strong and tough. He killed twice during his years in prison, without pleasure, but also without regret. It had been necessary.

Released at last from Chatham County, aided by a kindly lawyer, Abraham needed work. There were plenty who wouldn't even interview an ex-convict, but Dickson Benedict had looked at his record, asked one or two questions, and never mentioned it again. He also never asked about the lion-headed cane Abraham carried along with his cardboard valise.

Abraham cherished a deep hope, when Mr. Benedict hired him, that he would have no need ever again to fight for his life, but he kept the cane just the same. It was part of his past. He had held it through his years in the camp, and he carried it with him to Seattle, never letting it out of his sight on the long train ride, when he slept in a baggage car with other black men moving north. The cane was a symbol and a reminder of who and what he was.

As he collected bleach and a scrub brush and bucket from the storage closet in the garage, Blake remembered those first weeks in his apartment over the garage of Benedict Hall, weeks in which he would wake in the middle of the night, sweating, shaking with anxiety, only to remember that the real nightmare was over. No more work gangs, lice-ridden cells, meals of rice and bad meat, prison bosses wielding whips from horseback. No more fellow convicts sneaking up on him to steal what little he had, food or clothes or the cane he kept hidden under his mattress.

He was free. And he was grateful to his very soul for Mr. Benedict's trust.

If a man committed himself to a life of service, he thought, he might as well be the best servant he could. His life may not have fulfilled his mother's hopes, but it was a good life, and the affection of the Benedict children—two of them, in any case—had been an unexpected grace. A blessing for which he was humbly thankful. He was happy enough. Too happy to let a nasty-mouthed Brit ruin his day.

He poured bleach on the grease spot on the cement, and began to scrub.

CHAPTER 4

Margot found Sister Therese drowsing in her whitewashed iron bed, with another of the Holy Names sisters perched on a stool beside her. The visitor's black robes pooled around her on the tiled floor, and the white of her wimple gleamed under the bare electric light of the ward. The patient, bereft of her habit, wore a white scarf wrapped around her head that made her look round eyed and vulnerable, like an infant. She roused to give Margot a wan smile. "Dr. Benedict," she said faintly. "You're so kind to come and see me every day."

"Good morning, Sister Therese." Margot set her bag down at the end of the bed, and nodded to the other nun. She cast a quick look over the ward. There were eight beds, but only half were occupied. The radiator clanked quietly to one side, but otherwise the room was quiet. She bent over her patient, and folded back the bleached chenille coverlet. "How do you feel? Any pain?"

"Oh, no, no pain."

The other nun scowled. "She was in pain. They gave her an injection, but it made her awful sleepy."

Margot nodded. "It was scopolamine. Being sleepy is fine.

Rest is what she needs now." She loosened the bandage over the surgical site, and pulled it away to reveal a nicely healing incision, the edges well matched, the skin pink and cool. "Did the injection help?"

"Oh, yes."

Margot pressed lightly with her fingers, finding the belly soft to the touch.

"Dr. Whitely did such a good job, didn't he?" Sister Therese said. She craned her neck a little to see the incision. "Such neat stitches."

Margot smoothed the bandage back over the incision. "Actually, these stitches are mine. But yes, your surgeon did a good job."

"Your stitches?" the visitor said suspiciously. "We understood the doctor would do the operation."

"Sister!" Sister Therese hissed. "Dr. Benedict *is* a doctor."

"Well, I know, but—"

"Sister!" the patient said again. Drops of anxious perspiration appeared on her forehead.

"Never mind, Sister Therese." Margot replaced the chenille blanket over her patient, and took her wrist to feel the steadiness of her pulse. "Your incision looks good. I'll take these stitches out tomorrow, and as long as your appetite is good and you have no problems with your bowels, you can go home next week."

Sister Therese caught Margot's hand in her own small ones, and held it. "I felt so much braver knowing you were there with me, Dr. Benedict. God bless you."

Margot's heart gave a little leap of pleasure. It was for moments like this she had wanted to be a physician. Even if Sister Therese had no idea how close she had come to disaster, it gave Margot a rush of satisfaction to feel the pressure of those cool little hands, to see the spark of life shining in her patient's eyes. She gently released herself, and straightened, smiling down at the little nun. "If you have any more pain, tell Matron to call me."

"I will. And I'll pray for you."

Margot paused in the act of picking up her bag from the foot of the bed. "Thank you, Sister Therese. I appreciate that."

As she left the ward to go upstairs to see another patient, she wondered if Whitely had bothered to see Sister Therese postoperatively. She doubted it. She had heard him boast more than once that a surgeon should avoid close involvement with his patients. In this case, Margot was more than happy to have him keep his distance.

She had just put her hand on the latch of the door to the children's ward when someone called her name. "Dr. Benedict! Wait a moment."

Margot dropped her hand, and turned. "Good morning, Matron."

"Good morning, Doctor." The surgical matron for Seattle General was an old-fashioned nurse with strict ideas about comportment of both nurses and physicians. She still wore the voluminous apron and long skirts of an earlier day. Her gray hair was rigidly controlled in a tight chignon beneath her starched cap. The student nurses in her charge trembled at the sound of her step coming through the wards, and even a doctor or two had been known to duck into a closet or stairwell to avoid being collared by the stiff-necked Nurse Cardwell.

Margot herself, during her internship, had received a sound scolding from Matron for having dropped a surgical glove outside the operating theater and failed to pick it up and properly dispose of it. Nurse Cardwell's steely eye still caused a quiver in her belly. "Is there a problem?" Margot asked, striving for a confident tone, but fearing that her voice quivered, too.

Alice Cardwell, lips pursed, rustled toward her, carrying a sheaf of papers. Margot couldn't recall ever seeing the nurse without something in her hands—instruments, files, blankets, an emesis basin. The pockets of her apron bulged with cotton, a stethoscope, a pair of bandage scissors. She reached Margot, and looked up into her face with a grim expression. "A warning, Doctor."

"A—a warning?" Margot hated feeling as if she were a student again, struggling to satisfy patients and supervising physicians and senior nurses who knew far more than she did. She recalled Nurse Cardwell's skeptical tone when she'd addressed Margot as "Doctor" for the first time.

She folded her arms, and stiffened her own neck, reminding herself she was a fully qualified physician with her own practice. She really shouldn't be cowed by a nurse, no matter how competent.

The older woman took her arm, and pulled her a step or two away from the door. Her fingers were strong and warm. "I wasn't in the operating theater the other night," she said. "But I heard about it from my nurses."

"Sister Therese's appendectomy," Margot said.

"That's the one."

"And what's the trouble, Matron?"

Nurse Cardwell's eyes were like flint. "Dr. Whitely was impaired during surgery, I'm told. Your patient could have been seriously harmed."

"She could indeed. It was a very good thing I was present."

"Yes. But that's not good enough, Dr. Benedict. You should have filed a complaint with the board of directors."

Margot's heart sank like a stone settling to a riverbed. "Oh, Matron." She sighed, and her neck bent as she rubbed her forehead with her fingers. "I didn't think it would do any good. And the directors would be furious with me."

Nurse Cardwell raised one gray eyebrow. "This isn't about you, Dr. Benedict. This is about your patient."

Margot dropped her hand, turning the palm up in a gesture of conciliation. "You're right, of course. I know that. The board wouldn't listen to me, though, Matron. And they would very likely revoke my hospital privileges."

"It's not the first time Dr. Whitely has come into my operating theater under the influence." Margot's lips twitched at the words "my theater," but she pressed them together. "You were able to protect your patient this time, Doctor, but what if you or some other physician isn't able to do that next time?" Cardwell dropped her hand from Margot's arm, and riffled the files she held with an impatient finger.

"Why has no one else complained, Matron?"

Cardwell sniffed, and looked away. "Like you, they're afraid of Dr. Whitely's influence with the board."

Margot said, an edge creeping into her voice, "So, Matron. You're saying that I—the newest physician on staff, and a woman to boot—should be the one to take the plunge?"

Cardwell brought her eyes back to Margot's, and Margot thought she detected a glimmer of sympathy in them. "Well, Doctor. Sister Therese is your patient. From what I'm told, Dr. Whitely very nearly killed her."

"I won't argue with you about that. But I will have other patients, and they will also need surgeons. I tried to choose a prudent course."

She received a brief nod. "I take your point," Cardwell said. "But I hope I can count on you—if someone else lodges a complaint—to support me if I ask for censure for Dr. Whitely."

Margot expelled her breath. "Yes, Matron. I will. Although I won't like having to explain why I didn't complain myself."

"No." Nurse Cardwell ordered her files, and tucked them under her arm. "No, my nurse said precisely the same thing." She smoothed her already-sleek hair. "I do wonder, Dr. Benedict, if we women shouldn't try to help one another more."

Margot couldn't help a short, rather bitter laugh. "Matron! You were harder on me than any of the other interns. I assumed that was *because* I'm a woman!"

Nurse Cardwell pursed her lips before she said, "Exactly so. You and the other women physicians carry the future of all of us on your shoulders." She stepped back, and nodded toward the door to the children's ward. "Well, Doctor. I believe you have a patient to see. Thank you for speaking with me, and good morning." She turned, her back straight as a ramrod, and swished efficiently down the corridor, leaving Margot to go into the children's ward in a fog of bemusement.

Once she finished her rounds, she walked down Madison to Post Street. It was raining, or rather it was misting, the sort of falling damp that left hair and eyelashes coated with moisture, but wasn't really heavy enough for her to unfurl her umbrella. She unlocked the door to her office, and stood just inside, brushing the fine wet film from the fox collar of her coat. Next time she had a surgical case, she promised herself, she would insist on a different surgeon. But Alice Cardwell had given her something to think about.

The six stories of the Times Square Building soared above Fifth Avenue, a cliff of rose-buff terra-cotta dominating the urban plaza beneath. Preston passed the typographers working at long lines of linotype machines, and climbed the stairs to the newsroom. The carts called turtles rattled down the aisles, and the pneumatic tube system hissed and clicked above his head. People shouted at one another across the room or over the telephone. Preston wound his way through the bustle to his desk, freshly outfitted with a telephone and a typewriter and a fresh new blotter.

Blethen had given him *carte blanche*, more or less, to write his column the way he wanted to, and he had a year's trial to build his readership. He had decided to call it "Seattle Razz." It would be full of gossip, society news, theater reviews, all reported in a jaunty and slightly snide tone. He meant it to be breezy and gay, very modern.

PRESTON BENEDICT
SEATTLE RAZZ
THE SEATTLE DAILY TIMES
CAPITAL 3795

He liked the way it looked, printed in blue ink on ivory card stock. It would be his entrée to every society event in the city. It would give him access to the best parties, the most exclusive homes, and the prettiest women. Everyone would want to speak with him, to be mentioned in his column, to be singled out. He would be sardonic, like Dorothy Parker in *Vanity Fair*. He would make fun of some people, and flatter others when it suited him. "Seattle Razz" would be the place everyone looked first to know what was in and what was not. The whole idea was brilliant.

He spent the morning looking up telephone numbers and making a list of contacts. At lunchtime, he took his umbrella from beneath his desk, and strolled through a light rain to his father's office in the Smith Tower. He nodded to one or two men he recognized in the onyx-paneled lobby, then rode up to the eighteenth floor in the steel-cage elevator. As he stepped out, nodding his thanks to the operator, he wondered why his father couldn't have taken offices in the tower itself. Surely those were the spaces with the most cachet. But Dickson Benedict was never one for ostentation. Except for the sprawling Edwardian mansion he had built in the first flush of his success, he liked to live quietly.

Preston let himself into the office, and smiled at the receptionist in her fashionable drop-waist dress. "Hullo, Eleanor," he said. "Is the old man in?"

Eleanor gave him a cool upward glance, and pushed herself away from the Underwood typewriter. "I'll see if he's free," she said, her voice and face glacial.

Ah, Preston thought. A challenge.

"I would appreciate it," he said. "Lovely dress you're wearing, by the way. You couldn't have bought that in Seattle."

Her eyes flicked down over her dress as if she had forgotten what she was wearing. "I do all my shopping here, as it happens, Mr. Benedict. Frederick & Nelson has an excellent businesswoman's department."

He opened his mouth to compliment her on her taste, but she was already gone, her heels clicking across the marble lobby. As the door shut behind her, he thought, Just wait, sweetheart. Wait until you have a chance to be mentioned in "Seattle Razz." You'll talk to me then.

Eleanor was back a moment later. "Mr. Benedict can see you," she said. "This way, please." She turned and walked back toward his father's office, and Preston followed. He could have found his own way across the lobby, of course, but it was nice walking behind her, admiring the sway of her hips in the thin wool crepe.

The chill of his reception evaporated when he stepped into his father's domain. Dickson rose and came around his desk, smiling, his hand out. "Preston, good to see you, son. How's your first day?"

"Good, good," Preston said. He shook hands with his father, and sat down in the wide leather chair opposite him. Dickson took his chair behind the desk, and pushed a stack of papers to one side. Preston leaned forward, and placed one of his new cards in the cleared space. "Here's what I'll be doing, Father. A pulse-of-the-city column. News, gossip, society reports."

Dickson picked up the card and read it. " 'Seattle Razz'? I don't think I know what that means, son."

"It's slang," Preston said, with a breezy wave. "You know, jazzy, up-to-date. That's the sort of column it will be." He tried to hold his smile as he watched his father's brow furrow. He couldn't help seeing that Dickson was slow to look up at him, that he laid the card down with a little snick of the corner, as if he didn't mean to pick it up again.

"Well, Preston," Dickson said. He leaned back in his chair and steepled his fingers. "I'm sure C. B. knows what he's doing. It just all seems a little—frivolous—doesn't it?"

A nasty sensation swept down Preston's neck to settle in his belly, tightening the muscles. "Frivolous?"

"I don't mean—I think it's wonderful you have the position, and that they want you to be a columnist. Most enterprising of you. I just thought it might be—" He cleared his throat, dropped his hands, shifted uncomfortably in his chair. "I thought you might be writing news, you know."

"It *is* news, Father," Preston said. His voice quivered slightly, and he leaned back, crossing his legs. The old, familiar tension intensified. "It's society news."

"Oh, yes, I see," Dickson said. His eyes wandered past Preston's head to the rain beading the windows, dripping down the glass to pool in the bronze window frames. "You have to understand, son, to me, news is about—oh, money, politics, business. Things that matter."

The sensation swelled inside Preston's skin, rising from his gut to kindle a flame deep in his chest. He swallowed, trying to control it, and he spoke with exaggerated evenness. "In my opinion, Father, society matters a great deal. What people wear, where they go, what entertainment they enjoy. It's important."

Dickson brought his gaze back to his son's face. He smoothed his tie with his hand. "I have no doubt your mother and your sister-in-law would agree."

Preston raised his brows. "But not my brother?" And with a tinge of bitterness he could not quite disguise, "Or my sister?"

There was something distinctly unfatherly in Dickson's expression. "Your sister is different, Preston. You know that."

Preston forced himself to laugh. "Not really a woman, you mean?"

"I don't mean that at all. She's always been her own person, even when she was small."

"Believe me, Pater, Dick and I both know that!"

"Dick seems to understand better than you do. Of course your mother laments Margot's disinterest in the things you're talking about, but I applaud it. She's devoted to her calling."

Preston gave a light clap of his palms together, and stood. He needed to get out of his father's presence before the fire in his chest burst into something ugly. "So nice chatting with you, Pater," he said lightly. "I really must get back to the old grindstone. I just wanted to share my good news."

Dickson stood up, too, and put out his hand again. "Congratulations, son," he said. A stiff smile curled his lips. "Your mother will be pleased. Tell C. B. he should come for dinner soon."

"I will. I'm sure Hattie would be delighted to spoil a salmon filet for him."

Dickson gave a halfhearted chuckle, and Preston saluted him with two fingers to the forehead, pretending jauntiness. He let himself out of the office, closing the door behind him rather more firmly than he had intended. As he walked past Eleanor's desk, she looked up with a professional smile.

"Good to see you again, Mr. Benedict," she said.

On an impulse, he pulled another card from his pocket. "I'll just leave you my card, Eleanor." He flashed his teeth. "You might hear some news I don't."

He laid the card on her desk, and she picked it up with manicured fingers. "A column? How interesting."

"You know," he said. "Cultural events, society news . . ." He looked her up and down, with deliberation. "Fashion. I can see, Eleanor, that you understand fashion."

She put a hand to her Peter Pan collar. "Why—why, thank you, Mr. Benedict. I do—take an interest—actually."

He nodded, and turned swiftly on the toe of his well-polished wingtip. The heat building inside him was threatening to explode, and he needed an outlet before it did. He pushed the call button for the elevator, then tapped his foot impatiently as he waited for it to arrive.

He didn't realize until he was back on the street that he had forgotten his umbrella. He pulled his fedora down over his forehead as he turned up Yesler, walking with a quick, irritable step through the rain, cursing steadily under his breath. It was much harder to find an outlet here. And now, with his new position, he had to be careful. His reputation mattered more than ever.

But fury simmered behind his breastbone. Other people walked by, ordinary people who would never understand, any more than his father did. He had made a special effort to share his success with his parent, and had ended up—again—listening to a lecture about his unnatural sister. It had been going on all his life, and he was sick to death of it. His fists throbbed with the need to strike something.

She must have felt this way often. Roxelana. Khourrem Sultan.

For such a person to live as a slave, even for a few short years, must have been agony. Before she acquired her great sapphire— how she must have suffered under the yoke of authority! But she came into her power, in time. And he would, too. She had risen to her rightful place in the world because she had not shrunk from doing what was necessary. It was too bad, really, that there was no kingship for him to win, no throne to ascend in this pallid latter day. He had to make do with lesser achievements.

Frustration made him grind his teeth until his jaw ached. He stopped abruptly, and another pedestrian nearly collided with him. Too angry even to apologize, Preston gave the man a hard look before he glanced around to see where he was.

They called it the Tenderloin, a neighborhood bounded by Yesler and Jackson. It was hardly the right beat for "Seattle Razz"— but it was the perfect beat for Preston Benedict in the throes of temper. He spun to his right, and walked purposefully toward the brothels and saloons that lined the muddy street. His hands trembled with the need to feel flesh beneath them. His stomach roiled with the craving for violence.

Margot had seen two patients by midafternoon. One was a child with a boil to be lanced, whose mother paid Margot's fee without demur. The second was a woman with a mild case of cystitis. Margot sent her off to the apothecary with a prescription for uva ursi and a referral to a urologist at Seattle General. She warned her of the dangers of using the herb too long, and made her promise to call back in a week. This patient, too, paid her bill before she left. Margot saw her to the door, and when it closed, she turned to Thea with a grin. "We made actual money today!"

Thea looked up from her ledger. "Why so surprised, Doctor? I believe that's the idea."

"That *was* the idea," Margot said. She strolled back to her tiny office, tapping Thea's ledger with her fingers as she passed. "But I can hardly remember the last time a private patient actually paid a fee!"

Thea chuckled, a little palely. Margot stopped in the doorway and looked back. "Thea? Are you all right?"

The nurse looked up. She tended to look tired all the time, but today her eyes were bloodshot, the lids swollen. Her skin was pale as milk, making the tiny moles on her forehead stand out like flyspecks. She said, with a breathy sigh, "No sleep. Norman had a bad night."

"The scopolamine isn't helping?"

Thea shook her head, and then, suddenly, pressed both hands to her mouth. Her eyes filled and overflowed, and she began, with an uncharacteristic loss of dignity, to sob.

"Oh, Thea!" Margot strode to the desk to crouch beside the weeping woman. She put her arms around Thea's shaking shoulders, and waited for the storm to subside.

When Thea's tears eased, she lifted her head, pressing her eyes with the heels of her hands. "Oh, blast, Margot. I'm sorry."

"There's no need for that. Shall I send Norman to the hospital?"

Thea sniffed one more time, and wiped her nose with a handkerchief. She drew a shaky breath. "Norman's terrified of the hospital. He saw such awful things there, after France."

"Go home to him, then, Thea. It's late anyway. See if you can both get some rest."

Thea hesitated for a moment, then nodded. "Thank you. I think I will." She reached beneath the desk for her pocketbook, and was on her way to the coatrack for her hat and coat when the front door of the office burst open. Margot, standing beside the desk, turned.

A plump little woman stood in the doorway, hatless, wearing a battered cloth coat pulled around what looked like a nightgown. Her hair, the harsh yellow achieved only with peroxide, was wet with rain. She was crying, big tears making white rivulets in the thick layer of powder that covered her cheeks.

A day for tears. Margot said, "I'm Dr. Benedict. What's the trouble?"

The woman sobbed, "Please come, Doctor. Come quickly! He's hurt her awful bad."

Margot eyed her for only a moment, then said, "Yes, I'll come. Thea, you'd better lock up." She reached for her coat and hat, and picked up her bag. As she strode to the door, Thea thrust an umbrella into her hand.

It was a walk of fifteen minutes. Margot tried to keep the other woman under the shelter of the umbrella, but it wasn't big enough to cover both of them. The rain had intensified, and it dripped onto their shoulders, the drops gathering and swelling on the surface of the umbrella, then splashing off the ribs at odd angles so Margot felt her face and hair were as wet as if she had no umbrella at all. Her guide set a brutal pace, sobbing steadily as she walked. Margot was hard put to keep up, though her legs were much longer.

As they hurried up Yesler, she said breathlessly, "What's your name?"

"Carola," the woman said. She was puffing, too, but showed no sign of slackening her pace. "It's my friend Anna's been hurt. Beat up bad. I'm afraid she's going to bleed to death."

"Where are we going?" Margot panted.

Carola pointed at the spire of the depot on Third Avenue. "Just past that. Anna's a crib girl, like me." She gave Margot a sidelong glance. "But the other girls said you wouldn't care."

"Nor do I."

"She's Chinese," Carola said. "You don't mind about that, either?"

"Of course not."

The cribs were houses broken into single rooms, mostly with little or no furniture, rented out by the owners for the sole purpose of prostitution. The city fathers had relegated all such business to Skid Road, also known as the Tenderloin. Parlor houses mixed with flophouses in the district that extended from Yesler and Fifth to Railroad Avenue. Margot had never actually walked into the area, but she had seen it from the safety of the Essex, with Blake at the wheel. And of course she, like the other interns at the hospital, had treated countless cases of syphilis among the soiled doves of Seattle. She had met crib girls before, and no few of their clients.

She followed Carola up a short flight of rickety wooden steps. They went into the ramshackle house without knocking, and straight down a short dark hallway to a room at the back. Carola pushed through a splintered door. Margot steeled herself, and followed.

Even before she walked into the tiny, low-ceilinged room, she smelled the blood. The walls were splashed with it, the floor was sticky with it, and the bed—little more than a cot—was soaked in it. The injured girl lay on the bare ticking of a thin mattress. More blood matted her long black hair. Her face was so swollen Margot couldn't see her eyes, and her labored breathing filled the room.

Carola stood to one side. Tears and rain had dissolved most of her face paint, and Margot saw that beneath the mask of cosmetics she was terribly young. She whispered, with a hiccup of a sob, "Can you help her, doc? Please?"

Margot had learned that people coped better if they had something to do. She said in a low tone, "I'll do all I can, Carola. I need you to go somewhere where there's a telephone. I have a friend with an automobile."

"I could go down to the depot. If they'll let me use it."

"Tell them I sent you. Call this number, and ask for Mr. Blake. Explain to him where we are, and that I need the motorcar."

Carola nodded, and was gone before she could see the doubtful look on Margot's face as she bent over the girl on the cot.

Whoever had beaten this girl had held nothing back. At a guess, he had used a bludgeon of some kind, probably to avoid injury to his hands. It was obvious the girl's jaw was broken, and perhaps her cheekbone. From the shallowness of her breathing, Margot feared several ribs were also fractured. She worried that a lung might be punctured, or the spleen ruptured. The girl had defensive wounds on her hands and her arms, and her back was bruised, as if she had curled herself into a ball, trying to protect herself. It was terrible to see.

Rage at the perpetrator made Margot's heart pound, but there was no time for her own feelings at the moment. She would report it all to the police once the girl was stable, for all the good that would do. There weren't many who cared what happened to crib girls.

She started with a morphine tincture from her bag, slipping it under the girl's tongue. Her patient was clammy with sweat, and when Margot managed to lift her swollen eyelids, her pupils were dilated. Margot brushed the girl's distended abdomen with her fingers, and the girl—Anna, she remembered—protested in mumbled Chinese. Her lips were dusky, and her fingers, when Margot lifted them, were the same.

There was little she could do until she reached the hospital. Margot set about making the girl as comfortable as she could, and waited for Blake to arrive.

* * *

When Margot left the operating theater and trudged out to the street, the Essex was still there. Blake got out, moving stiffly, and opened the rear door for her. Margot gave him a grateful nod, and collapsed on the backseat with a groan.

When Blake had maneuvered himself back into the driver's seat, she said, "You need to stop driving for a few days. Give your back a rest."

As he adjusted his cap, he met her eyes in the mirror. "You're one to talk about rest, Dr. Margot."

She gave a short laugh. "Maybe we should make a pact."

"Are you all right?" he asked as he fired the engine.

"I am. My patient's not."

"I'm sorry about that."

"Thank you. And thank you for coming to get us. I know it wasn't pleasant." She pulled off her hat and tossed it on the seat beside her, then laid her head back on the burgundy velvet. She remembered Thea, and Norman, but it was too late to go there now. It would have to wait. She didn't close her eyes, because she didn't want images of little Anna, broken and bleeding, floating up behind her eyelids. She watched the streetlights slide by instead, and the warm rectangles of light in the houses they passed. She should have asked Matron to speak to Sister Therese. If anyone needed prayers, it was Anna the crib girl.

She felt stickiness against her knees, and she knew her dress was ruined. She would have to slip it out to the burn barrel. Her mother would have a fit if she saw it. She had knelt on that bloody floor without thinking—not that there had been anything else she could have done. Anna's crib was as bare as a barn—more so, perhaps. There had been nothing, no coverlet or towel or blanket, to kneel on. At least barns had straw in them.

She let herself in through the front door and dropped her bag on the mat. She kept her coat on, in case she encountered her mother, but she didn't expect to. She had missed dinner by hours. She slipped off her shoes, and climbed the stairs in her stocking feet.

When she had shed the stained dress and ruined stockings,

and bundled it all up to dispose of later, she pulled on her house-coat and went back downstairs in her bare feet. Hattie would have left something on the stove or in the oven. She felt almost too tired to eat, but she knew if she didn't try, Hattie would make a fuss. She was grateful to find the kitchen empty, lit only by the glow of a single bulb over the range. She opened the oven, and found a plate covered with a clean dish towel.

She poured a glass of water, then settled herself at the table with the plate and a knife and fork. She was chewing a bite of rather gluey shepherd's pie when Preston came in.

He raised his eyebrows at the sight of her. "Margot! Gosh. You've had a long day."

She swallowed, and reached for her water glass. "I didn't think it would ever end." She put her fork in the shepherd's pie again, but she didn't raise it to her lips. Her throat went suddenly tight, and her eyes stung. She gripped the fork with her fingers, willing away the threatening tears of fatigue and fury. She was not, surely, going to cry. Not in front of Preston.

He bent over the table to see her face. "Oh, Margot. You've really had it, haven't you? What you need is a drink."

She took a shaky breath, and looked up at him. He grinned down at her. "Come on, old girl. Let your little brother doctor you for a change."

"Preston," she said in a tremulous voice. "A drink sounds wonderful."

She sat taking deep breaths while he fetched the decanter and two tumblers. He poured two fingers of whisky and handed the glass to her, and she took a good mouthful. Now she did close her eyes, feeling the hot comfort of good blended whisky settle in her stomach. "Thank God," she muttered.

Preston pulled his chair a little closer. "You want to talk about it?"

"You don't want to hear it," she said. She took another sip of Father's whisky, and pushed the dinner plate away.

Preston laughed. "That shepherd's pie wasn't any good the first time," he said. "I can imagine what it's like now."

Out of loyalty to Hattie, Margot said, "Oh, it's fine. I'm just too tired to eat. And it really was an awful day."

"You should tell me all about it," he said. "I'm a newspaper-man now, after all."

She looked at him over the rim of her glass. "Really not your kind of story, Preston."

He put his hand on his chest in mock hurt, and flashed his white smile. "They're all my kind of story." He held out the de-canter, and she allowed him to refill her glass. "Come on, doc. You'll feel better if you get it out."

She took another sip, and set her glass down. It seemed he really was trying to help. The war had changed him, she could see that. It wasn't just that he looked different—that was natural, of course, after more than four years—but he seemed more confi-dent than he had as a boy. He seemed less—*desperate*, was the word that came to mind.

She drew a tremulous breath. "There's a girl in the hospital," she said, gazing at the caramel swirl of whisky in her glass. "Some-one beat her so badly that I—" She broke off. The Sessions clock ticked loudly in the quiet, reminding her that she would soon have to be up again.

He prompted her. "A girl? Who is it?"

"One of the crib girls, from down past the depot. I don't know her real name. Chinese. They bring them in, you know, by promising work. They don't tell them what kind."

Preston leaned back in his chair, and sipped his own drink. She glanced up, and found his blue eyes fixed on her intently. "Well," he said. "Just a hooker, then."

"She's little more than a child."

"You can't tear yourself up about that sort of—about all your patients, Margot."

She sighed again, and finished the whisky in her glass. "I know. It's just that this was so vicious. The worst I've seen." She stood up to carry her plate to the sink. "Maybe you can get someone to write about it, Preston. Get some attention."

"No one will care, Margot. Not about a whore." His voice had gone hard, and it made her turn to look at him. He waved a negligent hand. "Put it out of your mind, doc. I'm sure you did all you could."

She felt her temper flicker, but it was a weak flame. She was just too tired. Others would react the same way as Preston, dismissing the young Chinese prostitute, refusing to waste police hours trying to find who had hurt her. "I'm going to bed. Thanks for the drink."

Just as he stood and picked up the decanter, the candlestick telephone in the hall rang. Margot said, "Damn," and hurried to the instrument before the ringing could disturb the rest of the house. She said, "Yes? Yes, this is Dr. Benedict." As she listened to Matron Cardwell, the cold crept up from the floor into her bare legs. When she replaced the earpiece and set the telephone down, she found herself shivering from head to toe.

Preston was standing in the doorway to the kitchen. "You're not going out again?"

"No," Margot said. She pulled her dressing gown close around her and started for the stairs on her icy feet. "There's no point in going back to the hospital. My patient expired."

It seemed, as winter wore away, that Preston's new job agreed with him. He was cheerful at breakfast and dinner. Ramona and Edith glowed in his presence. He called Margot "doc" most of the time, but refrained from making jokes about her struggling practice. He and Dick were cordial, and Dickson made a point of asking him, when they were all together at dinner, how the job was going. If he didn't go so far as to actually read "Seattle Razz" himself, he reported comments he heard from his secretary, who was, it developed, a faithful reader.

"So, doc," Preston said, grinning up at Margot as she came into the dining room one April morning. "You have your picture in the paper!"

Ramona and Dick were already seated, and Ramona was smiling at Preston as he folded back the page of the newspaper. Margot pulled out her chair. "What are you talking about?"

One of the twins poured her coffee as she unfolded her napkin. Preston held out the paper. "There you are! It pays to have a brother in the biz."

Margot laid the folded newspaper beside her plate and gazed down at it. She hardly recognized herself in the picture at the head of Preston's column. "My God, Preston. This is awful. Couldn't you have stopped them running it?"

He snatched the paper back. "I thought you'd be glad to get some attention for doing good works, Margot! I pulled some strings to have that picture taken." His handsome face reddened, and when Leona tried to take his plate away, he snarled at her, "Not yet, damn it. You can't see I'm not finished?"

Margot said, "Preston, there's nothing left on your plate."

He snared another piece of toast from the rack and slapped it onto the empty plate as Leona shrank back from the table.

Margot said, "I suppose no one likes their newspaper photos." Her voice sounded nearly as hard as Preston's, but it wasn't just the ugly photograph that was bothering her. She dreaded going to the office today. She and Thea were going to sit down with a pile of bills, and she didn't know how she was going to pay them. "I'm sorry if I didn't show proper gratitude, but don't take it out on Loena."

"Leona, doc," her brother said. He took a huge bite of the toast she was sure he didn't want, and leaned back in his chair. "I don't know why you can't tell the poor girls apart. Loena is the one getting fat."

"She is?"

"You haven't noticed?" Preston laughed, and crammed the rest of the toast in his mouth. He jumped up, still chewing. Margot watched him warily. He swallowed, then pointed a mocking finger at her. "You should look around you, doc. See what's happening in the world."

"Speaking of photos," Ramona said brightly, "did you see those pictures from England? From some village called Cottingley? These two little girls took pictures of fairies! Actual photographs! Everyone's talking about it!"

"What nonsense," Margot said snappishly, then immediately wished she had let it be.

Dick laughed. "Of course it's nonsense. Ramona, fairies? Really."

"They have *photos*," Ramona insisted. "And all these spiritualists are traipsing all over that tiny town."

Margot put her coffee cup to her lips to keep herself from saying anything else. Preston winked at Ramona, and said, "More things in heaven and earth, right?"

She nodded, though Margot doubted she got the reference.

Leona came back into the dining room with Margot's eggs. Preston touched his forelock, good mood evidently restored as swiftly as it had dissipated, and tripped gaily out of the dining room. Margot picked up her fork with one hand, and with the other pulled the paper back across the table. The picture was really ghastly. She looked as tall as the Smith Tower, and that dress—the one her mother had ordered from Frederick's—was a horror. She should have taken the time to go down and be fitted, but it had seemed such a bore. She wondered if Preston might have chosen the least flattering picture he could find, just to spite her.

Reluctantly, as she ate her breakfast, she read the opening paragraphs.

> The gala evening held to benefit the Good Shepherd Home took place at the palatial home of Mr. and Mrs. Albert Ryan. The cream of Seattle society attended, from Mayor Caldwell to entrepreneur Mr. William E. Boeing of the Boeing Airplane Company. The guests danced to the lively music of the Harry Harrison Band, and dined on caviar and French champagne as an ice sculpture of Mount Rainier gently melted beneath the chandelier.
>
> The Misses Blackburn sported the latest in evening wear, backless dresses imported from Gump's in San Francisco. None of the young blades

could take their eyes from the young ladies. Mrs. Nellie Cornish and Mrs. Robert King were resplendent in sweeping chiffon gowns, based on a French design. Both ladies swore to this writer they purchased their dresses right here in Seattle, but they had the look of Paris about them. The male guests, to a man, sported fish-and-soup, which—to you uninitiated—means black tie and tails.

Pictured above, with the Matron of the Good Shepherd Home, is the young woman physician, Dr. Margot Benedict, who recently opened a private office in Post Street. Dr. Benedict—yes, your columnist's own elder sister—avows that the Good Shepherd Home is a favored project of hers. She lent gravitas to what was otherwise an evening of light hearts and bubbling laughter.

Margot groaned, and shoved the paper away. "Gravitas, indeed," she muttered.

"Excuse me, Miss Margot?"

Margot glanced up. "Oh, Leona. Nothing. I was just talking to myself."

The girl poured her more coffee, and Margot gave her a quizzical glance. "Where's your sister this morning?"

Leona's cheeks flamed, drowning her freckles in pink. "She—" she faltered. "She—Loena's not feeling well."

Margot set down her cup with a click. "Why didn't someone call me?"

The flush of the girl's cheeks subsided in a wave, leaving her pale face sprinkled with cinnamon freckles. "She don't want to see anybody, miss," Leona faltered.

"Nonsense." Margot stood up, pushing back her chair. "Let's go and see her right now." She marched out of the dining room, with Leona skittering nervously behind her.

As they walked into the hall, Edith appeared on the stairs. "Where are you going, dear?"

"Loena's ill, apparently," Margot said. "But no one saw fit to let me know."

Leona made a small noise, like a trapped mouse. Edith said, "Margot, please. It doesn't help if the servants are frightened of you."

Margot turned to Leona. "I'm sorry," she said. "I have things on my mind this morning. I didn't mean to be—to be harsh."

Leona dropped a curtsy, which only irritated Margot more, but she repressed the sniff she longed to make. "Come now. I really do have to get to the office, but I'll see your sister first."

She gave her mother a brief nod, and pressed on toward the back stairs. There she waited for Leona to precede her, and followed the girl up the staircase.

The twins shared a long, narrow room on the third floor, with a slanted ceiling. A gable-fronted dormer looked down into the tall camellia, abloom now with white, waxy flowers. The morning light shone on the spotless white coverlets of two single beds and reflected from the mirrored tops of the matching bureaus. A rocking chair was drawn into the dormer, and in it sat Loena with some needlework in her lap. Her hair was fiery in the sunlight, but when she turned her surprised face to the visitors, Margot was shocked by the pallor behind her freckles.

"Loena?" Margot made an effort to speak gently. "Leona says you're not feeling well. You should have sent for me."

"Oh, no, Miss Margot," Loena said in a trembling voice. "It was just a little stomach upset. I wouldn't want to bother you."

Margot started across the room toward her, but Leona, in a gesture Margot was sure took all her courage, stepped into her path. "I can take care of her," she said.

Margot stopped. "I'm sure you can. But why not let me have a look, now that I've climbed the stairs?"

Leona started to demur, but Loena said softly, "Never mind, Leona." The rocker's runners clacked as she stood up. She laid her sewing on the window seat and turned to face Margot with the air of one facing an executioner. She wore a loose cotton dress, and no apron. "They're all going to know soon enough."

CHAPTER 5

Spring in Seattle, Frank found, was a fragile season. It crept shyly on the heels of winter, opening tentative buds, uncurling reluctant leaves, offering its flowers one by one—pale hellebore, vivid tulips, yellow and white daffodils. At last, as if the season were gaining confidence, azaleas blazed forth in white and pink and red. The flower beds bloomed with color around Building 105, a structure everyone fondly referred to as the Red Barn, where Frank worked at one of the long drafting tables beneath tall mullioned windows. The rains of spring were warmer and softer, though still frequent. Frank acquired an umbrella to protect his new camel's hair overcoat and the Stetson dress hat he had carefully chosen at Frederick's.

He felt a little like the spring himself, beginning to bloom in his new life. His mother had asked if he couldn't take a few days to come home, and he had responded by inviting his parents to Seattle instead. He explained that he didn't want to take time off from work so early in his new position. What he didn't tell them was that he knew, if he went home to Missoula, he would be sure to meet Elizabeth. He didn't want to see her. Didn't want to remember.

His rooming house, recommended by the Benedicts' butler, was on Cherry Street, just down the hill from the twin bell towers of St. James Cathedral. His room was modest but comfortable, a bedroom and a little sitting room, where he could lay his papers out on a round table and sit in an aged but comfortable chintz-covered chair. He shared a bath, an odd space tiled in mauve and brown with a door at either end, with another tenant. His landlady, a widow of about sixty, was pleasant enough, if a bit strict about things like visitors and alcohol on the premises.

Luckily, Frank thought wryly, he was a quiet drunk. He had found his source. He never bought more than he needed, and he smuggled his supply into his room under his coat. Mrs. Volger never needed to know.

It had become a ritual. Every evening, when he got off the streetcar, he walked to the diner where he had a bowl of chowder or a sandwich, and the proprietor slipped him a little tin flask under his bill. Frank walked up Cherry, greeted Mrs. Volger if she was there, and went up to his room to drink until the pain in his arm subsided. The pain seemed to lie in wait, dormant through the workday, coming to life once he left the Red Barn and started into the city. It would flicker during his supper, as if to make sure he didn't forget its existence. By the time he started his walk up First Avenue to Cherry, it began to burn in earnest, making him hurry his steps.

On this night, when the azaleas lining Mrs. Volger's front walk were in full bloom, he had a copy of the *Times* under his arm, and his flask secure in the inner pocket of his coat. He climbed the stairs two at a time. He spread the newspaper on the table and fetched his tooth glass from the bathroom before he locked his door, kicked off his brogues, and sat back in the chair.

The first sip was bliss, promising relief in the next few moments. He savored the bitter taste of the liquor, knowing it was going to quench the fire in his arm. A second sip, and a third, and the pain began to die down, to flicker out as if it, too, were done for the day. He poured a bit more whisky into the tooth glass, re-capped the flask, and began to turn the pages of the paper.

He stopped when he saw the picture at the head of "Seattle Razz," Preston Benedict's weekly column.

Frank had read Benedict's column once or twice, but he had no interest in the latest fashions or who was marrying whom in Seattle society. It seemed strange that a man like Preston would be writing about such things, but he supposed even a Benedict scion needed to work.

The picture was of Margot Benedict, Dr. Benedict, posing for a photographer at a benefit. He had not seen her for months, but he remembered her as a tall woman with a commanding pres-ence. She had, as his mother would have said, a face that would age well, being strong featured and finely cut, a face he had liked. The *Times* photograph made her look merely plain. Even to his untutored eye, the gown she wore didn't suit her, hanging too loosely about her narrow waist and hips. Its hem drooped to the toes of her shoes, hiding what he recalled were excellent ankles. She looked like someone's image of a lady doctor. He wondered if she cared.

He leafed through the rest of the paper as he finished his whisky. When the glass was empty, he was ready to take off his vest and shirt. He hung them carefully in the wardrobe before he went to stand before the small oval mirror above his bureau, and face the ruin of his arm.

Would he ever, he wondered, be able to look at that red, swollen flesh without remembering Elizabeth's horrified face?

He had tried to warn her in a letter. He didn't know how he could have explained it any better. In the event, it was obvious he had failed to prepare her.

When Elizabeth first arrived at the hospital in Virginia, she met him in the lounge, where other wounded soldiers were receiving friends and family. He spotted her from across the room, and made his way through little knots of people, soldiers in hospital-issue dressing gowns, women in straw hats and long, drifting summer dresses, men in boaters standing awkwardly beside them. Elizabeth, her cheeks very pink, came in through the door, led by one of the nurses. Her clothes looked too warm for the Virginia summer, a long skirt and pleated shirtwaist with a high-collared jacket. Her fair hair was gathered into a thick twist at the nape of her neck beneath her wide-brimmed hat. Even from across the room, she looked apprehensive.

He hurried to her, wishing they had let him dress. The dressing gown was embarrassing, with its empty sleeve dangling. People gave him sympathetic glances as he passed them, the same ones they gave the one-legged men hobbling on crutches, slightly less grieved than the sorrowful looks bent on the men who had no legs at all, being pushed in wheeled chairs. He tried not to notice, mustering his most cheerful smile for his boyhood sweetheart.

Four years had changed her face. He remembered it round cheeked and full lipped, soft with youth. Now, at twenty-four, there were faint lines around her mouth and under her chin. Her cheeks were thinner, her mouth harder.

She kissed him gingerly, avoiding his left side. They sat in the lounge and talked, or tried to. He asked after her family, and the wheat crop, and the grazing. She asked him about the hospital food, and the voyage home. After a painfully short time, they ran out of things to say. He had never been much of a conversationalist, but they had been sweethearts. They needed time, he thought, to recapture the feeling between them, but he couldn't deny that it was a relief when she said good-bye, and went back to her hotel with a promise to return in the morning.

Rosa Gregorio came to him early the next day. She was his favorite among the nurses at the Soldiers' Home. He liked her direct manner, her Brooklyn accent, her unflinching way with his dressings.

She helped him sit up against his pillow. She poured out his whisky, watched as he drank it, queried him matter-of-factly about the level of his pain. She wrote in his chart, then hung it from the iron frame of the bed. When everything was done, she pulled a chair up beside him, sat in it, and gave him a level glance from beneath her starched cap.

"Looks like you have something to say, Nurse Gregorio."

"You're getting out next week, Major."

"Hope so." He shifted a little in the bed, pinned by her gaze.

"I saw your young lady in the lounge yesterday."

"Yes?"

"Nice-looking girl."

"Yes. Elizabeth."

"She come to get you, then?"

"My family sent her to keep me company."

"You're engaged."

He shrugged. "I think they call it an understanding."

The nurse folded her hands together in her lap. "Major Parrish, I seen a lot of you boys come through here. I been here two years already."

He waited. Rosa Gregorio, of everyone here, had been the most honest with him. It was from her he learned the surgeons had given up trying to repair the neuroma that caused him such anguish. It was she who tried to fit him with a prosthetic while he writhed in agony. She had told him, with a few straightforward words spoken in her Eastern twang, that there was nothing more the hospital could do.

She said, "You gotta show her now, Major. Don't wait till you're married."

"It's that bad?"

"Yes. It's gonna be a shock. It don't bother me, but I'm a nurse. I seen it all." She leaned back and folded her arms. "Be glad it's just your arm, Major. Some got it worse."

"I know." A heaviness settled around his heart then, and he had to look away from her kind, homely face.

"Want me to talk to her first?"

He set his teeth, thinking. After a moment, he shook his head. "I'll do it."

Her work-chapped hand gripped his shoulder briefly before

she walked out of the ward and on to her other duties. He was glad she hadn't said any more. He had the same feeling of premonition he had experienced that day on the battlefield of Megiddo.

Elizabeth returned just after breakfast. She looked pretty and old-fashioned, there among the other visitors in the lounge. He didn't think she had changed her hairstyle at all during his absence. She sat on his right side, and he took her left hand in his right one. Her eyes were wary, and her tentative smile trembled on her lips.

"Are you feeling well today, Frank?"

He nodded. "Fine." Her fingers were hot and restless in his, and he swallowed. No point in putting it off.

"They'll let you go soon," she said.

"Listen, Lizzie," he began.

Her eyes skittered away. "No one calls me that anymore."

"No?" He released her hand, pretending to adjust the collar of his dressing gown.

"Everyone calls me Elizabeth now."

"Elizabeth, then. Listen to me."

She raised her eyes to his. He had fallen in love with those eyes, blue as the wide Montana sky, perfect with her fair hair and rosy cheeks. "What is it?" she asked.

In as few words as he could manage, he told her what Nurse Gregorio had said.

She was silent for a long minute. Then, faintly, "I don't want to look at it."

For answer, he stood, taking her hand again to pull her to her feet. He led her out of the lounge, down the corridor to the ward where he had spent the last weeks. She protested once, weakly, but he gave a faint shake of his head, and pressed her into a chair beside the neatly made hospital bed. He sat down on the edge of it, and shrugged out of his dressing gown. He didn't look at her as he peeled away the dressing.

He felt, as the gauze and tape fell away, that this time he was seeing his disfigured arm through Elizabeth's eyes. He had grown used to its red, ragged appearance, the seeping scars left by the field surgeon, the raw skin where the stateside doctors tried, and failed, to repair the nerves. He had not quite become accustomed to the swellings at the end of it. He only hoped they wouldn't grow larger.

Now, with Elizabeth staring at the ruined flesh, he saw how ghastly it really was, how ugly and offensive. She made a slight sound in her throat, and turned her head away.

He bound his arm up again, as best he could with one hand. He pulled the sleeve of his dressing gown over it, wincing as the fabric caught on the bandages. She didn't watch any of this. "I've covered it," he said. Despair made his voice hard. "It's over."

Slowly, she turned her head again to face him. Her eyes had darkened, and her cheeks were mottled pink and white, the color of grief. She smoothed her hair with trembling hands, and fidgeted with the placket of her shirtwaist. "Frank," she began, and stopped.

"Nurse Gregorio was right," he grated. He made his neck stiff and his jaw hard. He didn't want to hurt Elizabeth, but if he broke down, if he showed his weakness, shed a single tear in her presence, he would never get over the shame of it. He glared at her, taking refuge in anger. "It's better you know, Liz—Elizabeth."

"It's so—" Her eyes filled suddenly with tears that gleamed in the bright light of the ward.

"Yes. It is."

"Frank, I don't know if I can—I just—"

"Stop. It's perfectly clear."

Her tears spilled over her cheeks, and she pressed a hand to her mouth. "I'm sorry," she said, her voice breaking on a sob. "I'm so sorry." She buried her face in her hands, her shoulders shaking as she wept. Frank sat in stony silence, willing himself to endure until she was gone.

Rosa Gregorio appeared as if from nowhere. She put an arm around Elizabeth's shoulders, urged her up from her chair, and guided her out of the ward. Frank watched them go, then kicked off his slippers and leaned back against the frame of the bed, the iron cold and hard against his neck. He gazed out the window at the sunny Virginia day, but in his mind he saw it again, Elizabeth's mouth crumpling, her face mottled by shock and disgust. He told himself he would forget it, in time. He would get used to it, as he was getting used to working with just one hand. But it hardly seemed possible just now.

Nurse Gregorio came back a few minutes later, carrying a tray with an extra shot of whisky on it. "Good job, Major," she said bracingly. "Got that out of the way. Now drink up."

He drank the shot, and set the glass down on his bed stand. "She left?"

"Yes." The nurse pulled the chair closer, and sat down. She put her fingers on his wrist, but he knew that taking his pulse was a pretext. She was steadying him. "There will be someone else, Frank."

"Sure."

"You don't believe me, but I seen that, too. There will be someone."

He didn't answer. The likelihood that another woman could tolerate his disfigurement seemed as remote as the chance of his growing a new arm.

"It's a shame." Rosa gave a click of her tongue as she released his wrist. "Country girl like that. She oughtta know better."

He couldn't answer. He wished it were dark, so he could stop controlling his features, stop hiding behind the mask his face had become. He put his head back and closed his eyes.

"I'll check on you later, Major," Nurse Gregorio said. Her voice had grown gentle, its usual sharpness smoothed and softened. He had never heard her speak like that, and it occurred to him that she was angry, too. Angry on his behalf. She touched his wrist, and murmured, "You have a bit of a rest now, Frank. This was a tough day."

He couldn't speak past the fierce ache in his throat. He kept his eyes closed, and listened to the whisper of Rosa's shoes on the linoleum floor as she carried his empty glass away.

* * *

Frank shook the *Times*, hard, as if the rattle of its pages could force him back to the present. He folded the paper and set it aside, to finish reading at the breakfast table.

It was not yet dark, the days lengthening as the season wore on. On such an evening in Montana, he would often saddle one of the quarter horses and ride out on some pretext or other—fences or cattle or irrigation—just to enjoy the smell of tamaracks greening, the twitter of birds flitting through the huckleberry bushes. He closed his eyes, picturing the blue outlines of the mountains against the darkening sky, the musical rush of the Bitterroot River tumbling over stones and deadfall.

He opened his eyes, and put his right arm back into the sleeve of his shirt, then tugged the left sleeve up over his stump. Suddenly, he couldn't bear to be within doors. He wanted to stretch his legs, to climb a hill, to breathe spring air, to see the peaks of mountains rise against the evening sky.

He left the house without meeting anyone, and walked swiftly down Cherry. His long legs covered the distance to the waterfront in twenty minutes. In the big buildings to his right, offices had closed for the evening. On his left, the bawdy houses and taverns were doing a lively business, light and laughter and fragrant cigar smoke spilling from their open doorways. A pale sliver of moon ghosted over the city as the sun set beyond the crystalline peaks of the Olympics. Other walkers nodded to Frank as he passed them. A horse-drawn cart clattered across First, and Frank followed it, meaning to cut through the Public Market and stroll onto the pier beyond.

Idly, he glanced to his right as he was crossing Post Street, and saw her just leaving her office. Margot Benedict. She was locking the door, adjusting her hat, pulling on her gloves as she turned away from the little clapboard building.

She looked much more herself than she had in the unflattering newspaper picture. She was slim, well dressed, confident. She turned toward him, striding along the narrow street, her medical bag in one gloved hand, a modest handbag in the other. He saw her tip her head up to glance at the moon from beneath the brim of her hat, and a faint smile lifted the corners of her lips.

Frank paused, thinking he would say hello, but just as he lifted his hand in greeting, the horrible thought crossed his mind that he might smell of whisky. Hastily, he dropped his hand, but it was too late. She had caught sight of him.

She quickened her step, her long legs flashing beneath her skirt. Her ankles looked slender and strong above her heeled pumps, and her bobbed hair swung energetically around her chin. He wondered why the photo in the *Times* had looked so awful. She was not a pretty girl, he supposed. She didn't have Elizabeth's soft features and full bosom. But Margot Benedict was a striking woman.

He sighed, resigning himself. If he smelled of whisky, he couldn't help it now. And it was damned nice to meet a friend on the street, even one he had met only once.

She reached him, and thrust out her hand to shake his. "Major Parrish," she said. "Good to see you."

He had forgotten how deep her voice was. He took her hand and shook it. Her fingers, through the smooth leather of her glove, were strong, and her handshake was firm. "Dr. Benedict," he said. "It's late. Long day for you."

She nodded, and her direct gaze gleamed at him through the gathering dusk. "I had actual patients today," she said, smiling. "Some of them have to come after work."

He couldn't think of a response. He released her hand, and put his own into his pocket.

She was, he thought, one of the most unselfconscious people he had ever met. She held his gaze directly, without embarrassment, as if they had been friends for years. "How's the job going, Major? Father tells me Bill Boeing was awfully glad to have you."

"It's good," he said.

"It's a fine company, Father says."

"Yes."

"Very good." She smiled at him. "Well. I'm afraid I have to be off. I have to go to the hospital and see a couple of patients. Awfully nice to run into you, though."

"Yes," he said. He wished he could think of something interesting to say. "Good night."

She gave him another nod, and turned to her left. He watched her moving purposefully up the hill toward Fifth. Too late, it occurred to him he should have offered to walk with her to the hospital. Escort her. It would have been the gentlemanly thing to do.

"Hell," he muttered, as he continued his lonely stroll toward the pier. "Parrish, you're a lost cause."

He was at his drafting table the next morning, analyzing stress points on airplane wings, when one of the stenographers came up from the workroom to lay a message on his desk. He murmured his thanks without looking up, and for long minutes, absorbed as he was in his problem, he didn't glance at it. When he finally picked it up, he caught his lower lip between his teeth and leaned back in his chair, holding the slip of paper between two fingers.

One of the other engineers looked across at him and laughed. "What's up there, Parrish? You're holding that thing as if it's about to catch fire!"

Frank hastily laid the paper on his desk, facedown. It was a silly gesture. Harry wouldn't know who she was, anyway.

Harry was watching him. "Must be a lady!" Frank felt his ears redden. Harry chortled again. "I was wondering when you were going to start meeting some of these Seattle girls, Parrish. Handsome devil like you!"

The rest of the room erupted in laughter. Frank felt like a schoolboy caught passing notes in class. He wished the stenographer had let him pick up the damned message on his way to lunch, but he forced himself to meet the curious gazes of his colleagues. "Just a friend," he said.

It wasn't enough for the ebullient Harry. He leaped from his chair and crossed the room to Frank's desk. "Come on, Parrish. Girl friend or man friend? You hiding something?"

Frank pushed the message beneath the blueprint he had been working on. He liked Harry. He liked them all, really. But he didn't know how to respond to her message, nor how to explain such a thing to these men. They all seemed so easy in their friendships. They often spoke of their wives or their young ladies in comfortable terms. Harry's wife had given up her teaching post when they were married, and now sent him off to work each day with elaborate lunches. Paul was walking out with a switchboard operator from the telephone company. One or two declared they would never settle down, but it was clear to Frank no one believed them. Frank's bachelor state had been remarked upon more than once.

The thing no one ever mentioned, of course, was his missing arm. No one asked about his war experience, a circumstance for which he was grateful. They knew he had grown up in Montana, but no one called him Cowboy, and he was grateful for that, too.

Harry grinned down at him. "The wife's still after me to have you to dinner, Frank. She wants to introduce you to one of her friends."

"I'm not much good at parties. Nice of her, though."

Someone called, "You should go, Parrish. Harry's wife is a wizard in the kitchen."

Someone else said, "He's had to let his belt out three times since he got married." Everyone laughed, and Harry made some jocular response.

Frank breathed a little easier with their attention diverted. He picked up his pencil and slide rule, and with a nod to Harry, bent over the blueprint again. He had lost his train of thought, though, and the corner of the pink message slip distracted him, glaring up from beneath the blueprint. He kept his head down, his chin on his fist, and thought about it.

He wondered if other young women did this now, if this was the new social order. If he accepted Margot Benedict's invitation, what would that mean? In Missoula, a girl's family expected certain things of a young man. He and Elizabeth were hardly allowed to be alone until she was eighteen. When he came home from college at Christmas and Easter, her family and his assumed their inevitable engagement. He didn't have to say anything, or ask anyone. It had all been easy. Everyone knew the rules.

This bold query unsettled him.

He slid the slip out, folded it into a square, and dropped it into his pocket. It was much easier to concentrate on the orderly succession of numbers on his slipstick, to lose himself in comparisons and projections. The implications of a dinner invitation from Margot Benedict were too complex to contemplate.

CHAPTER 6

Blake came in from the garage, pulling off his driving gloves as he scraped his boots on the mat. He had dropped Mr. Dickson and Dick at the office, then driven by the hospital to pick up Dr. Margot and take her to Post Street. It had been a busy morning. Loena was ill again. Leona and Hattie had scurried about, serving the family's breakfast, rushing up the stairs to collect sheets and towels and carry them down to the cellar, where the electric Eden washing machine and mangle stood in their solitary magnificence. The first loads of laundry were already snapping in the spring breeze on the clothesline behind the kitchen.

Hattie labored up the stairs with a basket of wet towels just as Blake was changing his jacket. "Here, here," he said. "Why are you doing that, Hattie? Where's Leona?"

"She's putting sheets through the mangle," Hattie puffed. Her round face glistened with sweat, and she relinquished the heavy basket with a grunt of relief.

Blake shouldered the screen door open, and held it for Hattie to go through. He came after her with the basket, and set it on the grass beneath the clothesline. "We'd better have Dr. Margot take a look at Loena," he said.

Hattie bent to pick up a towel. She spread it on the clothesline, and affixed it with a wooden clothespin. "Dr. Margot has taken a look," she said sourly.

"Well, what's the matter, then?"

Hattie paused, another wet towel in her plump hands, and she fixed Blake with a dark look. "She's gone and gotten herself in trouble."

He raised his eyebrows. "Trouble? What trouble?"

Hattie clucked her tongue. "What do you think? She's nineteen and pretty and has a head full of clouds instead of brains!" At Blake's blank look, she sighed. "She's in the family way. And Mrs. Edith is going to put her right out of the house when she finds out!"

"Drat," Blake said, inadequately, helplessly.

Hattie gave a mirthless laugh, and smoothed her hair with damp fingers so it frizzed even more. "Drat indeed. What's to become of her? Little fool!"

"Who's the—who's responsible, then?" Blake felt like a fish out of water. His knowledge of women was limited to Mrs. Edith and Mrs. Ramona—and Miss Margot. His brief encounters with the whores of Chatham County had taught him nothing about how to deal with women and their problems. When he came to work for Mr. Dickson, he gave up that sort of thing. He'd hardly missed it. Even the memories seemed sordid now, and made him squirm if he thought about them.

"I tried to ask her," Hattie said. "She wouldn't tell me. How long have I known that girl, Blake? Since she was fifteen! But she won't say a thing! Protecting someone, I s'pose. Because she knows—" She shook out a wet towel with a crack, spattering water droplets on Blake's pant legs. "She knows Mr. Dickson would have his hide."

Blake turned toward the house. "I'll go talk to her," he said.

"Good luck with that! I don't know how you'll get anything—"

The screen door opened, and Leona stood staring out at them. Her eyes were round, and she was chewing her lower lip. "Hattie—" she said, then stopped.

Hattie made an impatient noise. "What is it? I thought you were getting Mr. Preston's laundry out of his room."

For answer, Leona held something out, some bundle of white linen, stained dark. Blake scowled at it, not able to understand at first what it was.

Hattie stomped across the grass, and took the thing from Leona's hands. She shook it out. It was a shirt, one of the new ones with an attached collar and mother-of-pearl buttons. And it was stained down the front with great brown splotches.

Hattie said, "Where did you find this?"

"There wasn't nothin' in his laundry basket, Hattie. But I knew there had to be dirty clothes somewhere, so I—I looked under his bed, 'cause I remember my brother always shoved his dirty laundry under his bed, and—it was stuck behind an old box." She gave Hattie a fearful look. "It won't never come clean, Hattie. I run it through the washer twice."

Hattie turned the shirt in her hands, inside out and back again. She tutted, and muttered under her breath. "You bleach it, girl?"

Leona nodded. Blake could smell the bleach from the wet shirt, and he could have told both of them to let it go. The stain was never going to come out.

"What do you think it is?" Leona whispered.

Hattie pressed her full lips together, fixing Leona with a fierce stare. The girl dropped her eyes. "I forgot," she said, her voice fading to nothing.

"Dang right, you forgot, Leona Kinstry," Hattie said with asperity. "We don't ask the family about things like that. Now you just get back in there and tend to the rest of the laundry. I'll deal with Mr. Preston's shirt."

When the girl had disappeared again through the screen door, Hattie folded the shirt over her arm, and turned back to her basket of towels.

"Hattie, shall I take that?" Blake asked. His heart felt heavy in his chest, an old ache he had begun to hope he might not have to feel again. "It's not coming clean. Leona was right."

"You don't know that," Hattie said stoutly. "It's probably chocolate, or somethin' like that. I'll get it clean for Mr. Preston."

Blake didn't answer. There was no point. But his feet dragged as he went indoors to see to the big parlor. No one ever went in there, but it had to be dusted in case it was needed. He opened the windows wide before he started working with his dust rag and furniture polish. It was a lovely spring day outside, full of sunshine and promise. He wished he could enjoy it.

Margot stripped off her rubber surgical gloves, taking her time, dropping them into a steel basket of things Thea would sterilize later. She washed her hands, then smoothed her white coat. When she turned back to her patient, she had composed her face. Pity wouldn't help the girl.

"Miss O'Reilly," she said. "You're about four months pregnant."

Colleen O'Reilly's round cheeks blanched. Her dark skirt was still rucked up around her hips, and her legs, thin as pipe stems, dangled pitifully over the edge of the table, the stockings rolled down to the knees. The white middy blouse and dark vest of her school uniform made her look younger than her sixteen years. "Oh, no." The girl's pupils expanded, and she began to breathe in shallow gasps. "Oh, no. I can't be."

Margot crossed to her, and pulled a blanket from a shelf beneath the table. "Here," she said. "It's all right. Take a good breath." She wrapped the blanket around the girl, tucking it around her bare legs, folding it around her shoulders. "No, no, not like that. Take a slow breath. A deep one."

Tremulously, the girl did. She clung to Margot's hand like a drowning person. "Doctor, please. Couldn't you have made a mistake?"

"I don't think so." Margot spoke gently, but firmly. "It's not the end of the world, you know. It's a baby."

"But I'm not—"

"I know. You're not married. But you're a healthy young woman. You just have to decide what to do."

"My father will throw me out." Colleen O'Reilly's voice flattened. The tears, clear and shining, spilled over her pale cheeks. "He always said he would."

"And your mother?"

The girl had found her way to Margot on her own, slipping away from Holy Names Academy and spending pennies she probably couldn't afford to ride the trolley down Madison.

In a lifeless tone, she said, "Mum has a new baby. And there are already seven of us."

Margot loosened the girl's hand on her arm. "I'll send Thea in with some information. There are places you can go, places you'll be cared for until you come to term."

She had just put her hand on the doorknob when Colleen said, "Dr. Benedict, wait!"

Margot turned. "Yes?"

"Can't you—can't you just—just take care of it? Please?"

Margot sighed, and came back to the examining table. "I understand what you're asking me, Colleen. I'm sure you know I'm forbidden by law."

"No!" the girl cried. Her voice thinned and rose in her desperation. "I thought—if the baby hadn't moved yet—"

"Quickened," Margot said automatically. "It used to be legal if the baby hadn't quickened. That changed about ten years ago." She met Colleen's tearful gaze as steadily as she could. "You must have suspected you were pregnant."

The girl's lip quivered. "I was afraid of it. I tried castor oil to bring on my monthlies."

Margot wrinkled her nose. "That must have been nasty."

"And it didn't work." Colleen looked down at her school shoes, little scuffed Mary Janes waiting beside the examination table. "Please," she whispered. "My pa will be so mad."

"Bring him to see me," Margot suggested. "I'll talk to him."

With a little sob, she said, "He'd never talk to a lady doctor."

"No." Margot gave her head a resigned shake. "No, I suppose not."

"You can give me something, can't you?" the girl pleaded. "My friend Alice said—"

Margot put a hand on the girl's shoulder. "Colleen, listen to me. All girls think they know something that will work, or someone who will do it. It's dangerous. Girls die."

"I know."

"Do you, Colleen? Will you promise me not to do anything foolish?"

The girl's trembling lips firmed a little, stubbornly. "I thought," she said, "that because you're a woman, you would understand."

"I understand better than you think. And I know that these things work out in the end." Margot patted her, as decisively as she could. "Now, Thea will have a list for you, and she'll tell you what you should eat and what you shouldn't. I want to see you again next week. Otherwise, you can go on about your normal activities, at least for a time."

The girl gave a bitter sob. "My pa's gonna kill me."

Margot wanted to believe that wasn't likely, but she had heard the stories. Not in medical school, where family considerations were secondary to medical ones, but in the streets, and in the living rooms where she and other suffragettes had gathered. Abortions killed young women, but so did outraged fathers, even in this modern age.

Margot was about to leave the room, but the misery and fear in the girl's face wrenched her heart. Her attempt at detachment failed her, and she put out her arms. Colleen O'Reilly, old enough to conceive but too young to cope, leaned into her and wept against her shoulder.

Thea knocked on the examining room door, and Margot called, "Come in, Thea."

Her nurse took in the situation at a glance. "Dr. Benedict," she said calmly. "I'll take over here, shall I? The mail came. It's on my desk."

Margot murmured, "Try not to cry, Colleen. Thea has some

help for you." Above the girl's head, she appealed to Thea with a lift of her eyebrows, and Thea nodded. "Tell her about the Good Shepherd Home," Margot said as she gently released herself from Colleen's grasp. "Colleen is Catholic." She wiped the girl's streaming eyes with her own handkerchief. "But first, Colleen, let's talk to your family. You may be wrong about them." She pressed the hankie into the girl's hand, then left her to Thea while she went out into the office, closing the door of the examining room behind her.

She took the mail back to her office. When she heard Colleen's small footsteps in the hall, then the closing of the office door, she came out into the waiting room.

Thea was at her desk. Margot handed her the invoices she had sorted from the other oddments in the mail. "You'll never see a penny from that girl," Thea said.

"If we can get her into the Good Shepherd, I'll count us lucky."

"They usually find the funds somewhere."

"Yes. They do a good job, although I think the nuns are hard on the girls."

"Do you want me to pay the bills?"

"Please. If the clinic account is short, let me know. There's still a bit left in my own."

"I hope this is the way your grandmother would want you to use her legacy," Thea said. She smiled up at Margot.

Margot gave a short laugh. "You should have heard her go on about rising hemlines! I can't think she would have wanted me even to cut my hair, let alone take on a profession."

"That's too bad," Thea said. She pulled the little pile of bills toward her. "I was lucky, I guess. My mother was also a nurse."

"I remember that," Margot said. "You come from a line of working women."

"A mixed blessing," Thea said.

"I expect so." Margot, on her way back to her tiny office, paused. "How's Norman?"

"He's pretty well this morning, I think. He coughed a lot last night."

"Do you need more potassium iodide? I can call Herbert's."

"No. I stopped on my way home yesterday."

"Do you want me to come to see him?"

"Thanks. When you have time."

"Of course. I'll come soon."

Margot went back into her office, and closed the door. There wasn't much she could do for Norman, in truth. He had gone over in the first wave of American soldiers, and succumbed to a chlorine gas attack before he had been in Europe a month. He had been, theoretically, one of the lucky ones. A treacherous wind had blown the worst of the gas into the trenches behind him, then back again, to wash over the Germans who had released it in the first place. But he suffered from chronic bronchial spasms, and nothing—not atropine or even morphine—seemed to quiet them. Margot didn't think much of the potassium iodide solution, but it was all the military doctors had come up with.

Margot sat down at the rolltop desk in her small, spare office. There was just one window, with her medical diploma hanging on the opposite wall. A book lay open, a surgical text with beautiful illustrations of a new procedure for doing skin grafts. She spent most of her free time studying it, though her chances of doing surgery seemed remote. In her internship at Seattle General—which had been hard enough to get—she had had to fight for her turn in the operating theater. Even now she was relegated to assisting at operations, but the intricacy of what lay beneath skin and bone and muscle fascinated her. She turned the pages, losing herself in the wonders of modern medical techniques.

An hour later, Margot heard the outer door of the office open. She listened to Thea's greeting, and to the high piping voice that answered her. She stood up just as Thea put her head around the door. "Please," Margot said. "Tell me that's a patient."

"Oh, it is." Thea was shaking her head, smiling. "She came with her whole family. I don't know where to put them."

It wasn't unusual for patients to arrive with a phalanx of relatives. A trip to the doctor's office was often a communal event. But in Margot's clinic, with its sole examining room and cramped reception room, it was a problem. She hoped, one day, to add another room, but for now, they had to make do.

Four generations of a Chinese family had crowded into the reception area. One was aged and stooped, tottering on tiny bound feet. Another was middle-aged, with a toddler clinging to either hand. Her feet were also bound, folded into silk slippers no more than four inches long. One was a very young woman, surely no more than eighteen or nineteen. Even for a Chinese, she was pale, her skin like ivory. Her feet were straight, though, narrow and small in leather slippers shiny with use. All of them, women and children alike, wore padded cotton jackets over loose trousers. Margot thought this attire eminently practical. She wished she dared wear slacks herself.

The middle-aged woman, who Margot surmised was the young woman's mother, chattered at her daughter in Chinese.

The girl turned her dark eyes to Margot. "I fainted. My mother made me come." Her voice was thin and high, and her hand, as she put it up to brush a strand of straight black hair away from her face, trembled.

"Come into the examining room," Margot said. The girl stepped forward, and her mother started to follow, the children trailing her. The examining room would never hold all of them. "Can your family wait out here?"

The girl turned to chatter at her mother. One of the children whimpered, and she bent to speak to it. When she straightened, she braced herself on her mother's shoulder to keep from falling. The child tried to come to her, but the middle-aged woman held it back, scolding in swift Chinese.

The pieces fell into place for Margot. The children belonged to the girl. The other women were the grandmother and the great-grandmother. When the young mother followed Margot toward the examining room, the toddlers immediately began to wail. The girl turned back, but Thea, smiling and firm, shut the door on the racket.

The girl stood uncertainly beside the examining table.

"Come," Margot said, smiling as reassuringly as she could. She patted the leather surface. "Climb up here, Mrs. . . . ?"

"Mrs. Li." The girl spoke unaccented English, a sign that she had grown up in America. She worked her way onto the table, and Margot helped her to lie back. "How old are your children?"

"The girl is three," Mrs. Li said. When Margot touched her, her flesh jumped. "The boy is two."

It developed, as Margot asked questions and measured pulse and respiration, that this girl had never seen a doctor before. Her two babies had been born at home, which wasn't at all unusual, and often safer than in disease-ridden hospitals. She worked as a hotel maid. When Margot listened to her heart and lungs, the girl stiffened at the touch of the stethoscope, as if expecting it to hurt. Her dark eyes, full of apprehension, followed Margot's every move.

When she was done, Margot helped her to a sitting position and lifted her hands to examine the nails. They were paper-thin, and white. She was cold to the touch, and when Margot released her hands she pulled her padded jacket more tightly around her.

"Mrs. Li, do you know what anemia is?"

The girl shook her head.

"It's called Addison's anemia, for the doctor who discovered it. It can be serious—" A tear escaped one almond eye, and slid down the girl's cheek. "Don't cry." Margot patted the girl's shoulder. It felt like nothing but bone beneath the jacket. "There might be something to help. Just wait here for a moment." She went to the examining room door. "Thea, will you ask Mrs. Li's mother to come in, please? See if the children will stay with their great-grandmother."

This was not accomplished easily, but in the end the mother came, her bound feet pattering across the floor. She stood beside the examining table, hooded dark eyes flickering around the little room, the glass-fronted cabinets with their syringes and needles, glass jars with instruments soaking in alcohol, folded bandages and brown glass bottles. Margot followed her glance. If this family was not used to doctors' offices, it all must seem alien and alarming. She tried to look reassuring and confident.

"Will you explain to your mother what I said, please?" she asked Mrs. Li. The girl spoke to her mother with tears spilling down her face. Soon the mother, too, was weeping into her handkerchief, leaning against her daughter's shoulder.

"Mrs. Li," Margot said. "Listen to me, and translate for your mother. Just last week I read an article by a man named Whipple, showing that eating liver—beef liver, specifically—can help this sort of anemia."

The girl sniffed, and choked out a few words. The mother turned tear-glistened eyes to Margot. A rush of Chinese spilled from her, while she clutched her daughter with one arm.

"Tell her," Margot went on, "that it must be a lot. Half a pound daily."

At this the girl's eyes widened. "A half pound?"

"Yes. Eight ounces, every day. Can you do that?"

"It will be very expensive. I don't think we can—"

Margot put up her hand. "I know a butcher who might help. I'll write you a note."

The girl spoke to her mother again. They looked at each other, tears drying on their faces. "You need rest, too, Mrs. Li," Margot added.

The girl's head drooped. "I have to work," she said. "We have a flower shop in the Market, but it doesn't bring in much money. My husband is away on a ship, and . . ."

"Have you fainted at work?"

The girl bit her lip, and looked away. Her mother asked something, and she muttered a short answer. Margot, suppressing a sigh, said, "Well, Mrs. Li. The liver at least. I'm going to write to my friend the butcher. And I want you to come to me again next week."

The girl didn't speak again until Margot ushered her back into the waiting room. There all three of the Chinese women bowed, and Mrs. Li thanked her formally, the note to the butcher clutched in one hand.

Margot went back to the office, leaving Thea to deal with the bill. She didn't expect anything to come of that. This visit would cost money, not bring it in. The note she had written directed the butcher to send his bill to Benedict Hall.

She closed the door, and leaned against it, wishing there were more she could do.

The economic boom of the war years had evaporated with terrifying swiftness, leaving even those who had worked steadily all their lives worrying about the future. Families like Mrs. Li's had nothing but their labors to save them. Margot argued endlessly—and pointlessly—with her father about social welfare, often losing her temper from sheer frustration. Nevertheless, despite his bluster, she knew him to be a kind man. He would pay the butcher's bill, because she would put a name and a story to it.

Thea knocked on the door. Margot turned to open it, and Thea stretched out a hand. She held a fold of fabric on her palm. "Your payment, Dr. Benedict," she said in a wry tone.

Margot took the folded silk. She shook it out, and gazed down at a cloud of embroidered butterflies, vivid yellow and glowing scarlet, fluttering above a branch of creamy cherry blossoms. It was a scarf, or perhaps a light shawl. The butterflies and the flowers were exquisitely sewn, and so smooth she could barely distinguish the tiny, delicate stitches. "Oh, Thea! Look at this! It's lovely."

"It's not money," Thea pointed out.

"No," Margot said. She smoothed the silk with her hand. Someone—the great-grandmother, perhaps—had labored long and hard over this, doing what she could, offering up what she had to help her family. "No. It's not money." She draped the silk over her outstretched arm, and it fell in shimmering folds nearly to the floor. "This is much better than money."

The spring sun sank slowly behind the gray-green waters of Elliott Bay. Margot had sent Thea home an hour before. There was no point in keeping her in the office when there was no work to be done. She turned off all the lamps and pulled the curtains, then went out into the street, turning back to lock up. She rested her hand on the door for just a moment, reluctant to leave, wishing she could think of some way to encourage more patients to come to her. She knew there were those who needed her. And she needed them.

As she turned away from the office, she realized Frank Parrish had not returned her call.

Blake was waiting for her in the street. The whites of his eyes shone through the dusk, and his familiar silhouette lifted her spirits. He lifted his driving cap, and said, "Dr. Margot."

She gave him a weary smile. "Good evening, Blake. Thank you for coming to fetch me."

"I don't like you on the streets alone at night," he said. His deep voice still retained lingering hints of the South, though he had been with her family since before she was born. She wondered how he had sounded when he first arrived in Seattle—more like Hattie, perhaps. He gestured to indicate where he had parked the Essex, and she pulled on her gloves as she followed him. The streetlights were just coming on, casting spheres of light into the blue dusk. Smaller lights glimmered from the ships in the harbor, like golden fireflies hovering over the dark water.

Blake held the door of the Essex as she climbed into its capacious rear compartment. He got into the driver's seat, and adjusted his mirror. "I trust you had a good day, Dr. Margot?"

"Well," she said. "I had a day, Blake. I think that's the most we can say." She had abandoned her efforts to persuade him not to call her Doctor. She suspected Blake took more pleasure in her accomplishment than her parents did. But then, he was almost a third parent.

This thought made her smile. Her mother would fall over in a dead faint if she ever heard Margot refer to Blake as one of her parents. Her father would roar with laughter.

Blake painstakingly backed the Essex and turned it. When he turned left onto Madison, having to bump over the streetcar tracks and maneuver the big car onto the proper side of the street, he sounded the horn to warn the innocent of this precarious operation.

Margot leaned against the back of the seat, and wondered if she had shocked Major Parrish by inviting him to dinner. That would be too bad. He looked as if he could use a friend.

She could, too, come to that.

Blake pulled up in front of the house, and got out to open her door. She climbed out, and leaned to retrieve her medical bag from the seat. Before she started up the walk she glanced up at him. "You know, Blake, this is very old-fashioned."

He gave her a gentle smile. "I'm an old-fashioned man, Dr. Margot. It helps in life to know the proper way to do things."

She stared up at the welcoming glow of the windows of Benedict Hall. "The thing is," she said thoughtfully, "it only works if everyone knows what's proper. If everyone *agrees*."

He closed the car door, but he stood beside her, gazing at the handsome house with its graceful porch, the old camellia rising almost to the third floor. "You're thinking of Loena."

Margot cast him a glance. "You know about her, then."

"Yes, ma'am."

"She hasn't said who it is, has she?"

Blake didn't speak for a long moment. Margot watched him, knowing that slight pinching of his lips, the downward sweep of his eyelids. She knew him better, perhaps, than she knew anyone else in the family. She prompted, "Blake?"

He shook his head, such a subtle motion she would have missed it had she not been watching him closely.

"Ah," Margot said. He would never say it aloud, of course. It was part of his role as the loyal retainer. "I don't want you to worry about it. You can leave it to me."

In the light spilling from the porch, she could see the furrow in his brow. "You be careful, Dr. Margot."

"Thank you, Blake, but I'm not a child anymore," she said. "I can take care of myself."

He touched his cap, and Margot walked toward the house. Despite her declaration of confidence, she felt a shiver of unease. As she opened the front door, she told herself she was being silly. Everything was different since the war. *He* was different, and they were all grown up, all three of them. They had put childish conflicts behind them.

Loena would lose her job, though. Edith would never tolerate such indiscretion in her household staff. And she would never, under any circumstances, believe that her son could be responsible. Especially not her youngest son.

CHAPTER 7

Preston stared at Margot across the little piecrust table in the small parlor, loathing her mannish features and the blunt cut of her hair. She could never have been called pretty, of course. When she was a girl Mother had done her best with hairstyles and dresses and trips to the beauty parlor. He should have told her then to give it up as a bad job. Margot had the Benedict jaw, the long legs, her father's strong hands. She refused to pluck her eyebrows, and she had made everything worse with her haircut. Bobs were swell on girls with rosebud lips and pointed chins—girls like Ramona. Margot should wear her hair pinned up, away from her face. When he had suggested it, she laughed, and said it was too much trouble. He wouldn't put it past her to start wearing trousers. Really, she was an embarrassment to the whole family.

He set his drink down, hiding his fury behind a woebegone smile. "You seem awfully confident that Loena's—delicate condition—is my fault."

She put up a hand to rub her eyes. Her hand was spotless, with short, perfectly clean nails, but the thought of where those hands had been, what they had touched, made Preston's stomach turn. Sores, infections, blood. Meat. It didn't matter how clean her hand was. It was revolting.

"Preston," she said tiredly. She had turned down his offer of a drink. She kicked off her shoes to stretch out her legs, and gave the little sigh of disdain he had been forced to tolerate since he was four years old. "I saw Loena coming out of your room a few months ago. The right number of months."

"You surprise me. I didn't think you were able to tell Loena and Leona apart."

"I can now," she said. "She's four months along. She's stopped throwing up every morning, but she's starting to show. Hattie and Blake already know. Mother will soon."

Preston had to drop his eyes to hide the rage that must blaze in them. He put his hand to his chest, pressing his palm over the stone hanging beneath his shirt.

"Are you all right?" Margot's tone changed all at once to one of concern or, at least, of interest. She sat up straighter, eyeing him. "You have a habit of touching your chest like that. You don't have pain there, do you? Burning?"

He lifted his head. "You're so sweet, Margot." He liked his voice like this, boyish, vulnerable. "You don't need to worry about me. I'm fine. I just—" He put up his hand to riffle through his hair. "I feel terrible about this. I've been trying to believe it wasn't me. I see now what a stupid mistake I've made."

Her eyebrow lifted, and doubt flickered in her eyes. "Do you?"

"Oh, Margot. It was a silly thing. She surprised me, and I— well, you know how they act around me, both of them. When she slipped into my room, I just didn't—" He gave his most diffident gesture, a little lift of one hand, a rueful drop of the eyelids. "I didn't show any discipline at all. Any self-control. I should have ordered her out, but I didn't, and now . . ."

"Mother will be furious," Margot said uncertainly.

Preston's anger turned to amusement. His sister had girded her unfeminine loins, no doubt, to do battle with her naughty little brother. She hadn't expected him to concede without an argument. He picked up his glass again, sipped at it to hide his smile. "I know," he said. "I wish it hadn't happened." Which, in a way, was true. It was a bloody nuisance, the girl catching like that. Just one moment of weakness, and now he would have to arrange something. Maybe Carter could make himself useful at last.

That was something else he wished hadn't happened. It had never occurred to him that Carter would arrive in Seattle uninvited. When Blake gave him the message that his former "military colleague"—Blake's words—had shown up at Benedict Hall, Blake hadn't even tried to conceal his distaste.

Not that Preston disagreed about Carter's unsavory character, but Blake was a bloody Goddamned servant, and a black one at that. Who was he to look down his nose? At least Preston had been able to stow Carter in one of the flophouses down on Fourth Avenue. He had told him not to show his face at Benedict Hall again, but he knew Carter. He was like a bad penny, always turning up where he wasn't wanted. He wouldn't lie low forever.

Margot interrupted his reverie. "Preston, we'll have to find a place for her. I can help with that."

He made his eyes round and innocent. "Someplace that will take good care of her?"

Margot sighed, and rubbed her eyes again. She was going to get wrinkles if she kept that up, but he wouldn't tell her. Who cared? She was bound to be an old maid anyway.

"We can try the Good Shepherd Home. They do good work with girls in trouble." She let her hands fall to her lap. "It's been my week for unwed pregnant girls."

"Has it?" Preston said. "I'm sorry."

Her eyes, the same dark brown as Father's and Dick's, bored into his. What did she think, that she could read his mind if she stared at him long enough? Finally, she said, in a dry way, "Are you really, Preston?"

He quelled the fresh surge of anger that burned his throat. He didn't touch the sapphire, but he took a breath so that it moved against his skin, cooling his temper, steadying him. It was as if *she* were steadying him, Roxelana, who had faced so much, and triumphed over it all. "I was a spoiled boy, Margot," he said, with what he felt sure was a convincing little catch in his voice. "I know that. But I've been to war. I'm a man now. If you think I need to tell Mother—" He made a helpless gesture. "I will, but it will upset her."

Margot shook her head. "I'll have a word with Blake. Perhaps we won't have to trouble Mother. If Loena will go without a fuss . . ." She gave him another of her penetrating glances. "You'll have to pay her expenses."

"Of course. Oh, of course."

She raised both eyebrows this time. "Well. I'm glad you understand. Shall I talk to her, or do you want to do it?"

Preston paused for a long, long moment. He stared into the cold fireplace as if searching for the answer between the polished brass andirons, then picked up his drink and leaned back, exhaling heavily to show his sorrow. "I'll do it, Margot. I should do it. It's my problem."

They got up to go in to dinner. Preston held the door for Margot. He would take care to seem abashed, to seem suitably chastised. He would maintain a restrained demeanor throughout the meal. That might convince her. He could go in search of Carter afterward.

Carter'd been living down there with the rest of the human trash for three months. He should know how to find anything, procure anything. Damned good thing he hadn't killed the bugger when he first showed up! The thought had crossed his mind.

Preston smiled absently at Hattie as she pressed an extra serving of dried-out halibut on him. Maybe he should just have Carter do Loena, put the wretched slut out of her misery. It would be a simple thing, catch her on the street or even in the backyard, haul her down behind the train station or to one of the cribs and put an end to the whole episode.

He felt Margot's quizzical glance on him, and he gave her a slight, sad shake of the head. No, he would have to be more subtle. Margot was paying attention to this. He would make a good show of speaking to Loena, then go out and set Carter to finding what they would need.

And if everything went well, maybe Margot would stop looking at him as if he were some sort of germ to be Pasteurized.

Frank couldn't bring himself to call Margot Benedict from the Red Barn. He told himself the noise from the workroom was too loud. And if he picked up the telephone on the manager's desk, to ask the operator to connect him, every head in the drafting room would turn to listen. The whole building would know before lunch who he had called and what he had said.

Mrs. Volger was proud of the brass and cherrywood Sultan telephone recently installed on her hall table. She told Frank he was welcome to use it, as long as he left a dime in the little silver dish beside it. Frank picked up the receiver once, but the moment he heard "Number, please?" he put it down again. Every other house on the street knew when someone made a call, because the telephone clicked and buzzed. Curious housewives would pick up their telephones. More than once, a neighbor came across the yard to ask Mrs. Volger about someone she had been speaking to. There was no chance of making a call with no one listening in.

For two days he tried to put Margot's invitation out of his mind, but he found as he bent over blueprints or sat in meetings that his mind kept straying to that slip of paper, now buried in his desk drawer. Why, he asked himself, did he hesitate? He liked her, at least what he knew of her. Her father had been more than kind to him. Preston was only an irritation, with his affectations and odd manner. And it was, after all, only dinner.

But when he tried to see himself escorting Margot Benedict—or any woman, for that matter—he saw again the horrified expression on Elizabeth's face as she stared at what was left of his arm. No, not horrified—worse. Disgusted. Repelled.

As he closed his desk and retrieved his hat and coat at the end of a mostly wasted day, he told himself Margot Benedict was a physician. She must have seen worse than Frank Parrish's botched amputation. On the other hand, he argued with himself, he didn't want to be her patient. He was tired of being a patient. He wanted—what did he want? To be a friend. And that didn't mean taking off his shirt and showing an interesting woman the shameful thing his arm had become.

He swung up into the streetcar. A pert young woman smiled at him, and he touched his hat brim to her. He saw her eyes drop to his empty sleeve. Her smile stiffened, fixed on her face as if it were her duty to hold it there. He nodded to her, trying to pretend he hadn't noticed. He made his way to the back of the car and took a seat, wondering if he would ever get used to that.

When he reached Yesler he got down, and turned his steps toward Post Street.

He walked past the little businesses, the barbershop, the grocery, the shoe repair. The diner's door stood open, and the smell of frying onions issued onto the street. The clinic was just a few steps farther, a small wooden building with a single step separating its front door from the street. Its windows, a large one in front and a much smaller one at the side, glowed with light, assuring him the office was still open. A sign swung over the tiny stoop, proclaiming in brave red letters: M. BENEDICT, M.D. Frank straightened his hat, checked that his sleeve was tucked into the pocket of his coat, and opened the door.

A woman of middle age, with graying hair and a sprinkling of tiny moles on her forehead, sat at a desk in the small reception room. There were two chairs and a low divan, all empty. To one side a glass-fronted cabinet held rows of files. On the other side stood a coatrack with two hats and two coats hanging from it. The woman at the desk looked up, and her gaze swept him with an air of professional assessment. "Good evening, sir. May I help you?"

Frank took off his hat, and crossed the room to stand in front of her desk. "I was hoping to see Dr. Benedict," he said.

The woman stood up. "I'm Dr. Benedict's nurse. Come this way, please. The doctor can see you in a moment."

"Thank you." Frank followed her toward the back of the office, not realizing until she opened the door of a small room that she had misunderstood. He stood awkwardly in the doorway, looking at the examination table, the autoclave on a metal counter, the jars of swabs and cotton and alcohol arranged on a shelf. "Oh," he said. His cheeks flushed, and he pressed his hat to his chest. "I didn't want—that is, I'm a—a friend of Miss Benedict. Doctor, I mean."

The nurse glanced back at him. "Ah. Sorry." Her eyes began to drop to his empty sleeve, but she caught herself. Her smile was tired, but sincere. "I should learn not to make assumptions, shouldn't I? Have a seat in the waiting room. I'll tell Dr. Benedict you're here."

He walked past the desk again. She called after him, "Your name?"

"Frank Parrish." She nodded, and turned to the other side of the office, disappearing down the cramped hallway. Frank took one of the chairs, and belatedly wished he had combed his hair.

"Major Parrish."

Frank jumped up. "Dr. Benedict." She looked at ease here, in her own space, exactly the opposite of the way she had looked in the *Times*. She wore a white cloth coat over a straight skirt. Her stockings were of the new flesh tone that made her ankles look bare, and her shoes had almost no heel. Her straight bobbed hair was perfect with her doctor's clothes, and he found himself smiling with pleasure at the sight of her.

She came toward him, holding out her hand, giving his a strong shake. "I worried you might not have received my message," she said. There was no coquetry in her glance, no shyness in the smile she gave him.

His discomfort fell away. He was aware of her nurse watching them, but that didn't seem to matter. "I did," he said. "I didn't have a private telephone to call you back, so—" He gestured around the tidy office. "I thought I would take a chance on catching you here."

She released his hand. "I'm glad you did." She turned to her nurse, and said, "Thea, as Major Parrish is here on a personal call, I think we're done for the day."

Thea nodded, and went to the coatrack. Frank, awkwardly, one-handedly, helped her into her coat. "Thank you." As she tucked her pocketbook under her arm, she said, "I'll see you tomorrow, Margot."

"Call me if Norman is worse tonight," Margot said. "I should be home by—" She gave Frank a quizzical glance. "What do you think, Major? Dinner, then home by ten or so? That is, if you came here to accept my invitation."

A wave of gratitude for her directness swept over him. He had spent months marveling at the ease with which the other engineers at Boeing seemed to chat with women, flirt with them, tease them. He was, he feared, really and truly a mere cowboy, especially when it came to women. He couldn't put all of that into words, of course. He said only, "Yes. Good."

The nurse went down the hall and out the back, where Frank heard the creak of a door that needed sanding. Margot took up her coat and hat. "Now," she said. "No more Dr. Benedict. I'm Margot. And if I may, I'll call you Frank."

He was surprised to hear himself say, "Just so it's not Cowboy."

She laughed, and he felt a little shiver of pleasure at having amused her. "I hope you'll forgive Preston. He may not realize you don't like it."

Frank held the door for her, and the two of them went out into the twilight. The streetlights had come on. Post Street looked cleaner, more inviting than it did in the full light of day. Frank was about to suggest a restaurant—having thought hard about this choice on the streetcar—when Margot said, "Good evening, Blake."

Frank turned to see the Negro servant from Benedict Hall, the butler. The Essex was parked at the end of the street. Blake lifted his cap, saying, "Major, it's nice to see you again." He had a deep voice, with just the faintest reminiscence of a Southern drawl. He sounded more like a college professor, Frank thought, than a servant.

Frank remembered not to try to shake his hand. Instead, he lifted his hat as Blake had done. "Hello, Blake."

Margot said, "Major Parrish and I are going out, Blake. Perhaps you could drop us, and then tell Mother I won't be home for dinner."

"Of course," the butler said. "The Royal, do you think, Dr. Margot?"

"Perfect."

The Royal Bar and Café was an elegant place, with low lighting, white tablecloths, and candles flickering in pottery holders. Frank held the door for Margot. A man with a spotless napkin folded over his arm hurried forward, smiling. "Miss Benedict! How nice to see you." Without asking, he led the way up a set of narrow stairs and into a semiprivate dining room. Several tables were already occupied, diners talking quietly amid a gentle clink of glasses and flatware. The waiter pulled out a chair beside an empty table, and held out his hand for Margot's coat. When she was seated, he turned to Frank.

Frank shrugged out of his overcoat and let the man take it. As he smoothed his left sleeve into the pocket of his suit coat, the man averted his eyes, saying to Margot, "I hope your father is well? He wasn't in for lunch this week."

"He's fine, Richard, thanks," Margot said. She accepted a menu, and took Frank's for him, laying it at his place. "I believe he and Dick order in when things get busy."

"And you're busy, too?" The man—Richard—unfolded a napkin, and draped it across Margot's lap. To stop this embarrassing service being performed for him, too, Frank shook out his own.

"Busy enough," she was saying. Frank was watching her, and he caught the tension around her mouth, the slight flicker of her eyelashes.

"Good, good. Well. I wish I could offer you a decent drink, Miss Benedict."

Margot lifted her eyebrows. "You can't?"

Richard spoke in an undertone. "The Dry Squad has been here twice. The boss says we have to be careful for a while."

She looked across at Frank. "Do you mind?"

Even as he shook his head, saying, "Of course not. It's fine," his arm began to ache.

When they had ordered, oysters and steak for both of them, Margot sat back, smiling at Frank. Her little hat, a cream-colored affair with a sequined tulip on one side, fit close to her head. It matched her shirtwaist, and made her eyes look very dark in contrast. "I almost forgot I called you," she said. "I'm glad you decided to come and find me."

"Awfully nice of you to think of me."

"Not at all." The oysters came, and while Richard busied himself squeezing lemon juice over them and arranging fish forks beside their plates, Frank felt Margot's gaze searching his face. When the waiter had gone, she said, "You look well, Frank. Much better than when I first met you."

"Good to be out of the hospital," he said.

"No doubt." She scooped an oyster out of its shell with the tiny fork, and put it in her mouth. Frank watched her carefully. He didn't want to tell her he had never eaten oysters. He stuck the fork in the grayish lump of meat as she had, and tried to tug it free while holding the shell down with his little finger. The shell skidded away from him, across the table.

Deftly, Margot stopped it. Without hesitation, she plucked the meat out with her own fork, and held it out to him across the table.

He knew his cheeks were burning, and blessed the dim light in the room. He let her put the oyster in his mouth, feeling her eyes on him as he tried to chew it. It was slippery and salty, escaping his teeth as he tried to bite into it.

Margot chuckled. "You haven't eaten oysters before, I'm afraid."

He swallowed, finding that it slid easily down his throat, and left a wonderful ocean tang in his mouth. When he could speak, he said, "No."

"Do you like it?" she asked.

Frank grinned at her. "I do. Not the kind of oyster we have in Montana."

She raised her eyebrows. "You have oysters in Montana?"

He shook his head, laughing. "When I know you better, I'll explain."

She smiled again, and without asking, extracted another oyster from its shell and fed it to him. As he chewed it, she said, "Tell me how things are going at the Boeing Company. Interesting work?"

It was a welcome topic, and as he explained what he had been doing recently, working with new materials and adapting existing engines, she listened and nodded as if she not only understood but found it interesting. The steaks arrived. Richard set Frank's plate down without comment, and Frank saw that it had been neatly sliced for him, artistically arranged with roasted potatoes and grilled onion slices.

Margot nodded her thanks to the waiter. To Frank she said, "It must be a nuisance for you."

"Sometimes."

"It's wonderful that it doesn't hinder your work."

He tried to keep the bitterness from his voice. "Lucky, I guess," he said. He picked up his fork, took a bite of the excellent steak. "Certainly luckier than some."

"I know. I saw some terrible tragedies."

Frank said, "I admire you for doing what you do."

She lifted one shoulder, and sliced a generous chunk of steak. "It was all I ever wanted. My family hates it, of course. My mother wanted a normal daughter, you know—a debutante in a white dress, pearls around her neck and flowers in her hair. My father would have liked a son-in-law to bring into the business."

Frank laid his fork down. "Surely they don't all feel that way?"

She looked across the table at him. The candle flame shone on the strong planes of her face, and something stirred in his belly. He liked her face. He liked the steadiness of her dark gaze. He liked the length of her fingers as she cupped her chin in her palm and answered his question.

"No," she said thoughtfully. "Not all of them. Dick—my older brother—he's a good sort, and he doesn't mind, though his wife . . .

well, Ramona is much more traditional than I. And Blake . . ." She hesitated. "Maybe you'll consider it odd that I think of Blake as family."

He shook his head. "A fine man."

"He is." She dropped her hand to pick up her fork, and applied herself to her steak again. The smooth curve of her hair brushed her jawline when she bent forward. Frank found himself wishing he could touch it.

He picked up his own fork again. "Is your practice growing?"

Her mouth full of steak, chewing unselfconsciously, she gave him a wry look. When she had swallowed, she said, "My clinic is surviving on the money my grandmother left me. I can make it perhaps six months more, and then—" She gestured with her fork. "Then I don't know. I'll have to go to work for someone, I suppose. Charity work, probably." She laughed. "As if I don't already do an abundance of that!"

Frank suspected the casual way in which she spoke of failure, of losing her clinic, was an affectation. He wanted to ask, but it seemed too personal.

She went on. "But perhaps things will improve. I've had patients this week, actually. Even one or two who could pay." She cut another piece of steak, and changed the subject.

By the time they had finished their meal and drunk their coffee, Frank's arm had begun to burn in earnest. As he put on his coat, he couldn't resist touching the stump, trying to quell the nerves that flamed beneath the scar tissue. He felt her eyes on him, watching, and he hastily put on his hat. They were at the head of the stairs when he suddenly remembered. "Oh! We didn't get the bill!"

She was on his left, and she took what there was of his arm as naturally as if it were whole, tugging him gently toward the stairs. "This was my invitation," she said. "And my treat. We have an account."

Frank felt helpless before her decisiveness, and humiliated by the gesture. His arm throbbed beneath her fingers, so hot he was afraid it would burn her hand. Richard stood nodding, wishing them a pleasant night. When they emerged from the restaurant, Blake was waiting with the Essex. Frank forced himself to speak politely to Blake, though frustration constricted his throat. He couldn't even escort Margot home. Gently, he extricated his arm from her grasp, and held the car door for her.

She climbed in, and looked up at him. "Get in, Frank," she said. "Blake will drop you at your place."

"No, thanks," Frank said. He saw her blink, and he supposed he had spoken harshly. His arm hurt like the very devil, and his wounded pride hurt even more. He tried to soften his tone. "I appreciate it, but I can use the air. It's not a long walk."

Seeming uncertain for the first time all evening, Margot said, "Well. Good night, then."

Frank knew he should say something elegant, something casual. He had no idea what it would be. He blurted, "Thanks for the dinner. It was swell."

She looked at him for a long moment, then nodded, and turned her head away. Blake closed the door, touched his cap to Frank, and got into the driver's seat. Frank watched the curve of Margot's cheek glistening in the light that spilled from the restaurant's open door. He stood where he was, hating himself, as the Essex pulled away. Margot didn't look back.

"Everything all right?" Blake asked as he started the Essex and drove south on First at a ponderous pace.

"Fine, Blake, thanks," Margot said. She smoothed her gloves, and concentrated on keeping her face turned forward, not looking back to see in which direction Frank Parrish turned. What had happened, there at the end of their pleasant evening? Was it the issue of the bill? She had never considered letting him pay for it. She was the one who had asked him to dinner, but—did men feel differently about those things? In this modern era?

Exasperated, she folded her arms, and let her head fall back against the plush of the seat.

"Major Parrish seems a pleasant man," Blake said.

Margot lifted her head, and saw that he was watching her in

the rearview mirror. "Very," she said. There was a pause as Blake negotiated the turn onto Madison.

"Proud sort," Blake said.

Margot pondered this. She had no experience with men outside of medical issues. There was her father, of course, and Dick, but they had always treated her as an equal, argued with her as their equal. She thought about Edith, and Ramona, with their soft voices and fluttering manners. That was probably what men expected. What they wanted. Her mouth twisted, and she saw that Blake was watching her again. "I'm hopeless with men," she said.

In the darkness, he flashed his white teeth at her. "You want to talk about it?"

Margot managed to smile back at him. "I don't even know what to say, Blake. I don't know what went wrong. It was really a lovely evening, and then . . ." She shrugged.

"He'll come around," Blake assured her. "For a woman like you."

Margot shook her head. A woman like her. What did that mean? A blunt, awkward, unconventional woman? Probably Frank Parrish had someone just like Ramona back in Montana, someone soft and pretty and winsome. He was a good-looking man. He was wounded, but he was obviously smart, and surely strong despite the lack of an arm. There could be a dozen girls waiting for him to come home and claim them.

Margot went straight up to her room, bypassing the small parlor where her father and mother were listening to a radio program. She meant to have a long bath, put Frank Parrish out of her thoughts, and retire with a book. Blake had loaned her his copy of *This Side of Paradise*. Margot couldn't remember the last time she had read a novel. It might be nice to read something that wasn't a medical text or a professional journal.

Leona tapped on her door just as she was gathering her robe and nightgown to go down the hall to the bathroom. Margot opened the door. "Did you need something?" she asked.

Leona looked back over her shoulder, though the corridor was empty. Margot hesitated just a moment, then held the door wide. "Come in," she said. "And tell me what's wrong."

Leona slipped inside, and shut the door hastily, guiltily, behind her.

Margot scowled, feeling impatient and irritated. "You're allowed to be in my room, Leona. You're in here every day, aren't you?"

"Oh, yes, miss," Leona said. "In the morning. I do your bed and dust. But now—"

"It's not the usual hour, I understand. But it doesn't matter. No one's going to notice."

"Oh, but *he* will!" Leona said in an urgent whisper. "If he sees me, he'll know—"

"Who?" And when Leona bit her lip and dropped her eyes, she said, "Oh. I see. You're thinking of my brother."

Leona nodded, staring at the pattern in the Oriental carpet.

"Well. We'll be careful." Margot shifted her robe to her other arm, and took her hairbrush from the dresser. "Tell me why you came, and then I'll see you back to your own staircase."

Leona blanched, and gave Margot the wide-eyed look of a frightened doe. "No!" she whispered. "He's up there!"

"Ah." Margot blew out a breath, and leaned her hip against the foot of her bedstead. "Preston *did* talk to Loena, then."

"You knew he was going to?"

"We're going to arrange for her to go to a place where she can come to term, and decide what to do with the baby. Preston and I spoke about this a few days ago."

"But does she have to go tonight?"

Margot's brows drew together. "What do you mean, tonight?"

"Miss Margot—Doctor Margot, I mean—" Leona broke off, in a fluster of confusion.

Margot waved a hand, and snapped, "Tell me what's happened, for God's sake."

Leona's eyes reddened, and Margot could have kicked herself. Edith was right. She terrified these girls. "I'm sorry," she said more gently. "I'm a bit tired. Just tell me."

Leona stammered, in a voice so faint Margot had to lean forward to hear her, "Loena's packing her things. He's taking her somewheres."

"Where?" Margot asked sharply, forgetting her intention.

Leona took a half step backward, and her tears spilled over. "She thinks he's going to take care of her. But I don't know if—" She gazed fearfully up at Margot, lips parted, eyes wide.

"What?" Margot demanded. "What don't you know?"

In a rush, as if she were diving into cold water, the girl said, "Begging your pardon, miss, because he's your brother and all, but I don't know if I trust him!" Leona choked on a sob, and covered her face with both hands.

Margot threw her things on the bed, and brushed past Leona on her way to the door. She didn't bother to put her shoes on, but strode down the hall to the servants' stair in her stocking feet. Leona sniffled as she trotted behind her.

Margot took the stairs two at a time, and threw open the door to the twins' dormer room. It was empty. Two drawers in one of the dressers had been pulled out, and one of the beds was mussed. It looked as if Loena had been in bed when he came to get her.

Leona came in behind her, and stood forlornly in the doorway. "Where did they go, Miss Margot? Will Loena be all right?"

Margot set her teeth together. There was little she could say. He had taken matters into his own hands, and though she wouldn't say it to a servant, Leona was right. Preston's were not hands to be trusted.

Margot slept poorly that night, and rose early for hospital rounds. She was in the kitchen, waiting for the coffee to be ready, when Leona dashed in, still tying on her apron. "She's home, Miss Margot!" she cried. Her eyes shone with relief, and the color had returned to her freckled cheeks.

Margot, holding her empty coffee cup, turned to face her. "Home?" she said. "Loena?"

"Yes!" Leona finished the bow on her apron and gave the ends of the sash a final tug. "About an hour ago. She's in her bed now, resting."

"What did she say?"

"She said he took care of her."

Margot set her cup down carefully beside the electric percolator. "What does that mean?"

Leona went to the cupboard to get a coffee cup for herself. She gave Margot a defiant look. "He took care of her. She's all fixed up." The percolator ceased bubbling, and she lifted it to pour coffee into her cup.

"Fixed up." Margot knew the euphemism. She sank into a chair beside the table, oppressed by a feeling of helplessness.

"It's better this way," Leona said in a determined voice. She blew over the hot coffee, and took a sip. "Now Mrs. Edith doesn't need to know."

Margot picked up her own cup and lifted it to her lips before she realized it was empty. Leona, seeing, unplugged the pot so she could come and pour for her. Margot held the cup in both hands, trying to decide what she should do. "Have you seen Mr. Preston this morning?" she asked in a low tone.

"No, miss. I haven't seen nobody yet today, not even Blake."

Blake. Blake would know. Margot set down her cup again. She left Leona placidly sipping coffee and gathering flatware for the family's breakfast. Margot went out the back door, and hurried down the short walk to the converted carriage house. At the single side door, she knocked.

Blake had his rooms—an apartment, really, though small— above the garage. Margot knew he rose early, and often made coffee in his kitchenette rather than disturb the household. At her knock, he came down the narrow staircase and opened the door. "Dr. Margot?" he said. He was fully dressed, except for his coat.

"Blake, I need—I have to tell you what's happened."

"Come in, then," he said. He stepped back, and she went in, turning up the steep stairs. "Have you had coffee?"

"Not yet." She hurried up the narrow staircase. It gave directly onto a kitchenette, with a rickety table at which she had first learned to read, years ago.

As a child, she had been taught to stay out of servants' rooms. Her mother would have been shocked to learn of the many hours she had spent here with Blake among his books and newspapers, drinking cocoa he made on his hot plate or poring over volumes of an illustrated encyclopedia he kept on a low shelf. Margot had been happy in Blake's rooms. She had been safe.

As he set a cup of coffee in front of her, she said, "We need to get you a better table."

"Sure," he said. He pulled a bottle of cream from his tiny icebox, set it close to her hand. "It's not very cold," he said. "I'll get a new block when the cart comes this morning."

She poured the cream into her coffee, and stirred, swirling white and black together. "Blake, it's Loena. Or maybe I should say, it's Preston. He took her for an abortion."

Blake straightened, one hand on the door of the icebox. "When?" He didn't look surprised. He looked thoughtful.

"Last night."

"Is she all right?"

Margot gave him a guilty look. "I—I haven't seen her yet. I came straight here."

He nodded, and came to sit across from her. As he set his cup down, the table rocked on its uneven legs. He put out his big hand, and covered Margot's where it lay on the bare wood. "It will be all right, Margot," he said quietly.

"Blake, I sent him to her! I told him he had to take responsibility, take care of her—but I meant a home, a place to come to term, not—not this!" She turned her hand over to grip his, clinging to him as she had done so long ago, a terrified little girl.

"It isn't your fault."

"It *feels* like my fault."

"But it's not." He patted her hand with his free one. "Drink your coffee. Then we'll go into the house and you'll have some breakfast. After you've eaten, you can have a look at Loena and see that she's all right."

Margot gave him a grateful look. "Do you ever get tired of saving me?"

His smile brought deep creases to his shaven cheeks. "Never."

"You used to let me sit on your lap for hours when I was upset. It was so kind."

He shook his head, and released her hand. "Nonsense. Come now, Dr. Margot. Drink your coffee. I'm going over to the kitchen and see that Hattie gets started on breakfast."

"Oh—Hattie!" Margot said, stricken.

Blake stood up. His jacket hung neatly from a rack of pegs at the head of the stairs. He picked it up and put it on. "You know Hattie. She'll think whatever Mr. Preston decided to do was best. Now you just sit there for a few minutes, and come in when you're ready."

Margot listened to his slow footsteps on the stairs, and a fresh wave of guilt made her put her head in her hands. Blake was too old to have to deal with these crises. She should find a way to handle this herself.

Of course, Father would be the best one to deal with it, but Edith had convinced him long ago that her youngest was misunderstood. Margot had learned by the time she was eight or nine not to go to her mother with complaints about Preston. Bleeding, weeping with fear and frustration, she had turned to Blake instead. He had never failed her.

CHAPTER 8

The day after his dinner with Margot, Frank went directly from work to one of the high stalls in the Public Market. He put seventy-five cents on the counter, and an elderly Chinese woman in a padded black coat and wide trousers snatched up the money with a wrinkled grin. She sang, *"Ni hao, ni hao,"* as she gestured around her, inviting him to choose something.

The stall was a profusion of flowers and greenery. At the back, a narrow doorway opened on a work space with wooden benches and a foliage-littered floor, where a young girl sat on a stool tying lilies and daisies into bunches. Two little children crouched at her feet, rolling a wheeled wooden toy between them. The girl looked familiar to Frank, but he couldn't place her. The old woman chattered at him, and he shook his head to show that he didn't understand. "A bouquet," he said. He tried to show her, holding his hand a foot above the counter. "A big one."

The girl rose and came forward. She, too, wore the jacket and trousers, with some sort of flat shoes. She said, "Grandmother is asking what the occasion is." Her accent was purely American, but she kept her eyes down, her head slightly bent as if to speak directly to Frank was an imposition.

Frank said awkwardly, "No occasion. I just want to give some flowers."

There was more swift Chinese. The girl translated, "Grandmother wants to give you the right flowers." She hesitated, looking up into his face for just a moment, then down again. "She says flowers have meaning. If you are proposing marriage, for example—"

Startled, Frank laughed. "Oh, no! Not a proposal. More like an apology."

This brought a flood of chatter, while Frank stood blushing at the counter. The girl said in a soft voice, "For a girl, sir?"

"Yes. A lady." He added, a little foolishly, "A doctor."

When the Chinese girl translated this, the old woman fixed her bright black gaze on Frank's face. "Dr. Benedict?" she said. Her lips labored over the foreign words.

Startled again, Frank nodded.

The grandmother gave him a luminous smile, showing surprisingly good teeth. She opened her hand, and dropped all of Frank's money back on the counter. She began pulling colorful stems out of buckets, clipping them with shears, piling them into a cone of butcher's paper. The girl smiled at Frank, too. "There is no charge for these flowers," she said. "Not for Dr. Benedict."

Frank felt a thrill of something like pride shoot through him. Silly, of course. He had no right to be proud of Margot, but still— he was. And now he remembered this girl. "You worked at the Alexis Hotel," he said. "But you look different."

She touched her temples with her small hands, an odd gesture that made her seem much older. "I was very ill. Dr. Benedict made me well." Behind her the children trilled in their musical language, and she turned and said something to them. They quieted, and Frank wondered if the girl was their sister. She was surely not old enough to be their mother.

The grandmother gave a deft twist to the butcher's paper, and held up her creation with a flourish. It was very pretty, blue and pink and white blossoms among spears of green. He reached for it, and she gave it to him, then pushed his coins toward him on the counter. Frank said, "But—I want to pay you."

The old woman said something sharp and short. The girl murmured, "She won't take your money today. She says you will buy flowers from us another time."

He cradled the bouquet in his good arm. "Tell her it's beautiful."

She reached across the counter to point to the flowers. "Hydrangeas, the blue, are for gratitude. Peonies are for peace. Grandmother says she is sorry she has no narcissus, for good luck in business. Dr. Benedict needs luck for her clinic."

Frank scooped up his money with some difficulty, careful not to disturb the bouquet. He dropped the coins in his pocket, and nodded to the old woman. "Well," he said. "Thank you." To the girl he said, "I'll tell Dr. Benedict I saw you looking well."

She smiled again, and he was struck by her transformation. She had gained weight, and her cheeks bloomed like the flowers around her. Whatever Margot had done, it had made a profound difference. As he walked away, he felt another irrational flush of pride.

Frank stepped down from the streetcar at the intersection of Broadway and Aloha, and walked up the hill. It was one of the prettiest parts of Seattle, he thought, with great brick and white-painted mansions rising majestically above the street. Elaborate gardens, like private parks, surrounded each of them. He felt the approach of summer in the warmth of the evening, in the mellow light that glowed on rooftops and tree branches. Rhododendrons were already shedding their blossoms, littering the ground with petals of white and scarlet and pink. The big camellia tree in front of Benedict Hall was in full leaf, and adorned with white flowers. As he started up the walk, the Essex emerged from the garage behind the house, and came to a stop in the street. Frank had just stepped up onto the porch when the front door opened.

A barrage of sudden noise streamed out into the twilight as if a lid had been lifted from a boiling pot. Frank fell back in surprise. Margot appeared, hurrying past him. She was supporting one of the little redheaded maids with her arm. The other maid was at her heels, wailing. From the hallway the cook, whose name Frank couldn't remember, called, "Y'all hurry now! Leona, stay with your sister! Miss Margot—"

Blake had come up from the car to the porch, and he and Margot between them helped the ashen-faced girl down the walk. Her weeping twin followed close behind, nearly tripping over Margot's shoes. Frank stood helplessly to one side, his flowers half crushed beneath his arm. The cook bustled out onto the porch, and she, too, was weeping. Margot, climbing into the Essex, looked back once at Frank. She spread her hands in a gesture of helplessness as Blake closed the door. More raised voices sounded from inside the house, a domestic crisis in full spate.

The Essex pulled away. The cook—Hattie, that was it—sat down on the porch step, threw her apron over her face, and sobbed. Frank heard a man's harsh voice through the open door, answered by the protesting one of a woman. He heard a voice he knew, Preston's, soothing his mother, answering the man, whoever that was, his father or his elder brother, perhaps both. Frank, cursing his bad timing, backed away from the door and went down the steps to the walk, careful not to step on the weeping Hattie. He started back down the street, the flowers forgotten in his hand.

He had gone perhaps half a block when a voice called his name, a new voice, with a different accent. He turned back.

Coming around the side of Benedict Hall was a heavyset man in a flat wool cap and, incongruously, the khaki tunic of a British Army infantryman. The man crossed the lawn, and loped up to Frank, grinning.

"Cowboy!" he cried. "Remember me? Carter. Sergeant Carter, that was Captain Benedict's batman." He sketched a comic bow. "At yer service, Major!"

"Carter," Frank said. "Oh, yes." He started to put out his hand, then remembered the flowers. He gazed helplessly at the bouquet, wondering what to do with it now.

"Big ruckus up there in the house," Carter said with a gurgle of laughter. His voice was high and thin, odd in a big man. "Our Preston's got his arse in a twist."

"What are you doing in Seattle?"

Carter touched his hat brim with a thick finger. "Invite of Mr. Preston Benedict, that's what. We do a little business together, here and there." He winked. "But he's been having it off with one of the maids, and got caught at it."

The front door of Benedict Hall slammed behind them, and Frank heard Hattie yelp. He spun about in time to see Preston hurl himself off the porch, having bumped the sobbing cook with his polished wingtip shoe. She dropped her apron, and called after him, "Mr. Preston! Wait!" He ignored her, stamping out to the street. He caught up with Carter and Frank in three long strides.

"Goddamn it," he snarled to Carter. "Who was that butcher you took her to?"

Carter was a head taller and forty pounds heavier than Preston Benedict, but he took a step backward as if he had been struck. His face and shoulders sagged so he looked like a beaten dog. "You said, find someone fast. I found someone! You can't blame me if he made a bad job of it!"

"I can, and I do," Preston snapped. He started down Aloha toward Broadway, his shoes clicking on the pavement. Carter trotted after him, emitting high-pitched protests.

Frank followed at a slower pace, the now-bedraggled flowers dangling at his side. Preston ignored him, haranguing Carter with every step. "Fucking great idiot!" he shouted. "Now my mother's upset, and the whole house is in an uproar, all because you couldn't do one simple thing for me."

Carter tried to interrupt, but Preston was in full cry. If it hadn't been so obscene, and so serious, it might have been funny. Frank trailed well behind them, but he could hear every word. This was the Preston he had known in the East, with his sneering insults, his curses, his hair-trigger temper. He hadn't known Carter well, because the batmen stayed in the shadow of the officers, but it was telling to see the thickset man cowering before the slighter man's onslaught.

He couldn't laugh, though. The maid, whichever of them it

was, had looked really ill, and the stricken look on Margot's face told him it was serious.

Preston and Carter reached Broadway, and turned left. Only when they had to stop for a gray Packard to make a cautious turn did Preston acknowledge Frank's presence.

"What the hell are you doing, Cowboy, trotting after us like some sort of bloody spaniel?"

Frank said mildly, "Just catching the streetcar."

Preston snapped, "What was your business at my house?" His eyes dropped to the battered bouquet. "Oh, my God," he sniggered. "Flowers?"

Frank stopped in his tracks. He had been on the point of throwing the flowers onto a bench, but now he lifted them, and tried to tidy them against his chest. Mrs. Volger might like them.

The Packard pulled away, but Preston still stared at Frank, his blue eyes dark with anger, a spot of scarlet flaming on each cheekbone. "You look such a fool!" he said. "Please tell me you're not courting my god-awful sister!"

Frank's jaw tightened. Preston's glare reminded him of the mindless fury of a recalcitrant bull. There would be no reasoning with him. He grated, "None of your damned business, Benedict."

"Maybe it is." Preston took a step toward him, his head thrust forward.

Frank stiffened. He answered Preston's step with one of his own. He was taller, but he wasn't sure how much strength he had left in his arm. His only arm.

With a visible effort, Preston took hold of himself. He drew a sharp breath through whitened nostrils, and pulled himself up, thrusting his hands into the pockets of his jacket. "Well," he said. His voice dropped to an intimate whisper, and his eyes glittered with malice—or madness. "I suppose my sister is the best thing for a cripple like you."

Even Carter sucked in a breath at this crudity. Frank took another step forward, bringing himself chest-to-chest with Preston Benedict. He didn't realize he had dropped the flowers until his hand came up to seize Preston's well-cut lapels. "You're a clod," he said between his teeth.

Preston's laugh was light and insulting. "What! You didn't know you were a cripple?"

"I mean the way you speak of your sister!" A rush of fury strengthened Frank's arm. He shook Benedict like a puppy, then shoved him backward so he stumbled into the street, soiling his fancy shoes in the gutter.

Frank became suddenly aware that a little knot of people had paused to watch this altercation. He gave them an apologetic glance, and stepped back, straightening his coat, adjusting the brim of his Stetson.

Preston jumped back onto the sidewalk. He gave their audience a tight smile, and spoke in an undertone so that only Frank could hear. "You're making a mistake, getting sweet on *Doctor* Benedict. I'm not sure she likes men at all. You'd better find yourself a real girl, Cowboy."

"Don't be a jackass, Benedict."

With an unsteady hand, Preston pushed back the lock of blond hair that had fallen across his forehead. He looked down at his wet shoes, and laughed. When he looked up, his eyes were as bright a blue as ever, and he was smiling as if the storm of his temper had passed off all at once. He turned to walk away, with Carter a step or two behind him. Over his shoulder he said lightly, "I don't fight with cripples. But you'll regret this, Cowboy. That's a promise."

Frank, bending to pick up his battered flowers, didn't answer.

Margot spent the whole night in the hospital with Loena. When morning came at last, she left the girl in Nurse Cardwell's care, with Leona on a stool at her bedside. Somehow, she got through her hospital rounds, forcing herself to concentrate. Not until she was done could she allow herself to think of Loena again, lying so pitifully still in the white iron bed.

There was little else to be done for her, Margot reflected, as she stepped out into the sunny morning. She had done her best to clean up the mess the abortionist had made, but the uterine cavity already showed signs of sepsis. She had removed all the clots and necrosed tissue she could see, and disinfected the area with Eusol. She had packed the wound with iodoform gauze. When she came back in the evening, she would try irrigating with Dakin fluid. The bleeding had stopped, but as always, infection was the real danger.

Loena was feverish and confused. Cardwell, who was as knowledgeable as any physician, looked grave. Margot was furious.

She stalked down Fifth, her legs stiff with rage. Her heart pounded so she could feel her pulse against her collar. Her fingers, curled around the handle of her medical bag, throbbed. Her steps were quick and hard against the pavement as she hurried toward the *Times*. She was overdue at the clinic, but she couldn't help that. She meant to have it out with him, and consequences be damned.

She was about to cross the street when the Essex pulled up beside her. Blake climbed out more swiftly than she would have believed possible. He blocked her path as she stepped off the curb.

"Dr. Margot," he said. "Let me take you to your office."

Her voice scraped in her throat. "Thank you, Blake, but no. I have to see Preston."

She tried to pass, but he stopped her, taking her arm with his hand. She stood still, feeling the beat of her blood against the warmth of his palm. She wouldn't shake him off. She cared too much for him. A passerby stopped, staring at the odd sight of a Negro man with his hand on a white woman's arm. Blake dropped his hand, but he still stood in her way.

"Blake—" Margot began. Her voice broke, and a sob of pure frustration rose in her throat.

"Margot," he said. "Not here, sweetheart. Get in the car."

He was right, of course. She was about to shame herself, right here on the street. He held the door, and she slid into the car, dropping her bag beside her. As he came around to settle into the driver's seat, she stripped off her gloves and pressed her fingers against her eyes.

"Oh, God, Blake, I could kill him. I could just kill him," she grated. "You should have seen what that—that *meat cutter*—did to poor Loena! She'll never be the same." She dropped her hands, picked up her gloves, and twisted them into a knot.

Blake put the Essex in gear, and pulled out into the street. He didn't speak, but Margot knew he was listening. "I have to do *something!*" she exclaimed. "I can't let this pass. She could have died! In fact," she said, her voice trembling with the real emotion that underlay her anger, "she may still die. It looks as if someone used a pair of pruning shears on her."

Blake pulled the Essex up to the end of Post Street. He turned off the motor, but instead of getting out, he turned, stiffly, his right arm stretched along the back of the seat. His eyes were reddened and troubled. When he spoke, it was in the old Southern drawl, something she rarely heard.

"You have to be careful," he said. His eyes were intent on hers. "I know you're upset, and rightly so. So are Mrs. Edith and Hattie. But mind you don't humiliate him in public. He's not a little boy anymore. He's a man now. And he was a soldier."

"I know," Margot said miserably. They sat in silence for several minutes, until she drew a long, shaky breath. "I know. Thank you, Blake. Again."

"It's what I'm here for," he said.

"You haven't called me sweetheart in so long. You used to call me that all the time."

"Mrs. Edith didn't like it. She said it wasn't proper."

Margot made an exasperated sound as she put on her gloves again. "Oh, Mother! I suppose she's more worried about the scandal of all this than she is about the danger to Loena."

"It's the way she was raised. It's her culture."

"What about *your* culture?" Margot said peevishly.

That won a chuckle. "Your daddy gave me a new start in life, young lady. I owe him a lot. Everything. And then, when you children came along—" His gloved hand lifted and fell on the back of the seat.

Margot wanted to say more, to find the words to explain how important he had always been to her, but they wouldn't come to her weary brain. She put her hand on the door handle. "I'd better get to the office. You go on home, Blake, and please get some rest. If the hospital telephones, have them call me here."

"I will."

She opened the door, and when Blake made a move to get out of the car, she said swiftly, "No. I've got it." She reached in to retrieve her bag, then closed the door. "I'll see you tonight."

"I'll be right here."

She gave him a small wave as he backed and turned the car. Sleeplessness made her eyes gritty, and though she had drunk some orange juice and coffee in the hospital canteen, she felt parched. She glanced down the street at the diner. Its door stood open, propped by a doorstop in the shape of an iron rooster. She probably should eat something, but she couldn't face it just yet. She kept seeing Loena's wan, shocked face, Leona's terrified one, Nurse Cardwell's stern features. Margot sighed, unlocked her office door, and went in to begin her day. Sleep seemed a very long way off.

Frank wished he had thrown the damned flowers into the gutter after all. He had carried them home, and presented them to Mrs. Volger with a story of an impulse purchase. She had fluttered and preened like a girl, delighted by the bouquet, and had arranged it in a vast pink vase on the hall table. Now, as he walked past it, it reminded him of his clash the evening before with Preston Benedict. Such an ugly scene. He would much rather forget all about it.

His day passed in a blur. Something had gone wrong with one of Bill Boeing's private seaplanes, and that distraction helped. Frank tried to follow his routine, stopping for supper, picking up the *Times*, strolling up to Mrs. Volger's through the long, pale June evening. The flowers in the hallway brought it all back, the look on Margot Benedict's face as she bundled her maid into the

Essex, Carter's amusement, the sneer on Benedict's face. Even more, he remembered the feeling of having Benedict's lapels in his hand, the sense that he could have shaken him until his teeth rattled. Until his neck broke. Frank didn't like that feeling. Any inclination to violence his younger self had possessed he thought he had shed forever.

But there was something about Preston Benedict that made his scalp crawl and his fist yearn to strike something. What was it? Benedict was a selfish man, spoiled no doubt, with his smooth features and bright hair and family money. But there was something more there, something dark and frightening. He reminded Frank of a horse they had when he was twelve, a good-looking bay gelding with a well-cut head and the ironic name of Softy.

Softy had been a strange one. He had a nice gait, and a nice manner when he felt like it. But sometimes, without warning, he would whirl and kick at whoever was trying to saddle him, or bare his teeth and bite at someone walking past. He bucked the hired man off in the road on the way to Missoula, then tried to stomp him with his forefeet. The hired man had hidden beneath a cattle guard until Softy lost interest and went to grazing on a grassy bank. Frank's father refused to sell him, saying it wasn't fair to stick an unsuspecting stranger with an unpredictable horse. He put him down instead, leading him out behind the barn and putting a bullet into his handsome head. There was nothing else they could do.

Frank settled at his small table, and unfolded the newspaper. He skimmed the headlines: more news of unemployment and union complaints. He turned the pages as he sipped his evening whisky, his mind drifting, not really paying attention until he reached Benedict's column. He spun his glass over the title, "Seattle Razz," obscuring the words with wet circles. He wouldn't read it. It would only irritate him further. He picked his glass up again, closed the newspaper, and stood to go to the window. The sky had begun to darken at last, the long summer twilight coming to a close, a bank of clouds building in the west and casting shadows over the waters of the bay.

He tossed back the last of the whisky, and told himself he wouldn't have a second tonight. It worried him that he might come to need more and more. He'd be like one of those dipso-maniacs hanging around the waterfront, wrecked human beings so dependent on alcohol that the search for it consumed their whole lives. He had a job, a good one. He didn't want to lose it.

He took the tooth glass back to the bathroom, washed it, and left it there. He pulled his curtain, undressed, and got into bed, but when he lay back on his pillow, he couldn't sleep. The fabric of Mrs. Volger's cotton sheets, which smelled so sweetly of bleach and sunshine, seemed to grate against the nerves of his amputa-tion. He tried putting his arm outside the blankets, but that didn't help. He twisted this way and that, trying to get comfortable, ar-guing with himself over more whisky.

At last, when he could see by the darkness outside that it must be at least midnight, he got up and retrieved the flask from the inner pocket of his overcoat. He unscrewed its cap, and tipped it up to take three good swallows. At last, with the liquor burning his stomach, he went back to bed, and fell into an uneasy slum-ber. He dreamed of the gelding, and then of Preston Benedict, until the two of them seemed indistinguishable in the turmoil of his brain.

It was raining when he woke. Rainstorms in Montana tended to be the sudden, drenching sort, often with thunder and light-ning to accompany them, and floods of water to turn beige fields green overnight. Here in the Pacific Northwest, the rain was of a more hesitant kind. It was wet enough to create mud puddles in the streets, and to make some commuters carry umbrellas, but not heavy enough to do more than dampen his hair and face. It suited his mood of the morning. He had overslept after being awake too long in the night, and he hurried through his break-fast. He trotted to the streetcar with his briefcase clamped under his arm.

When he reached the Boeing offices, the men in the workroom looked at him strangely. Self-consciously, he ran a hand over his hair in case something was out of place, and refolded his sleeve into his pocket. He tried to catch a glimpse of himself in a window, but he couldn't find anything wrong. He went upstairs, and set his briefcase down under his drafting table. As he turned to hang his coat on the rack, Harry came across to him.

"Good morning," Frank said. Harry, too, had an odd look on his face.

"Have you seen the paper, Frank?" Harry asked. He had a folded copy of the *Times* in his hand, and he held it out.

Frank said warily, "Read it last night. Why?"

"Did you read 'Seattle Razz'?"

"No. It's a gossip column."

Harry shrugged. "Well, sure, gossip. The wife loves it, though, reading about all the rich bitches and what they wear."

Frank waited, his hand in his pocket, for the explanation. Harry held out the paper. "You'd better read it," he said. Curiosity vied with apology on his ruddy face. "You're sure to hear about it sooner or later."

Frank took his hand out of his pocket and accepted the newspaper. He left Harry standing beside the coatrack, and went to lay the paper on his drafting table. It was folded back to Preston Benedict's column. Reluctantly, Frank began to read.

Anyone who hoped the rough-and-tumble Seattle of the unlamented Klondike era was past would have been disappointed last night. The peace of the summer evening was broken on Broadway by a brawl initiated by an employee of the Boeing Airplane Company. This tale is, sadly, a firsthand report. There were no charges filed, out of sympathy for a war amputee. Though no lasting harm was done this time, it was an undignified and ill-bred display of violence more suited to the mountains of Montana than a civilized modern community. This reporter believes the mayor and his chief of police must do more to quell the violence that still erupts all too often on the streets of our fair city. One can't help but wonder if Mr. Boeing is aware of the proclivities of one of his engineers. And one can wish a decorated war hero would display more discipline.

As Frank stared at the paper, his arm flared as if someone had held a match to it. He dared not lift his head. He was sure the rage in his face would convince everyone in the room that Benedict was right about him. The audacity—and the overwhelming unfairness of it—stunned him. It was obvious everyone here knew Benedict was talking about him. What good would it do to try to explain? Harry and the others were collegial with him, but they didn't know him. In his inclination to solitude, he had prevented any opportunity for a relationship to develop. It had not seemed to matter, until now. Now, he lacked a single friend to defend him.

He shoved the paper away. It teetered on the edge of his desk, and fluttered to the floor. From the corner of his eye, he saw Harry cross the room and bend to pick it up. When he straightened, he hesitated, as if he wanted to speak, but couldn't think what to say. Frank couldn't bring himself to meet his gaze, to encourage him. His heart beat furiously, so hard he was afraid Harry could hear it from where he stood.

"Mr. Parrish?" It was the stenographer from the workroom. She was standing in front of his desk, a slip of paper in her hand.

Frank forced himself to look up. "Yes?" He heard how stiff his voice was, hard with anger.

"Mr. Boeing wants to see you. In his office downtown." She held out the paper.

Frank took the note and tucked it into his pocket as he went back to the coatrack. He put on his coat, and carried his Stetson in his hand as he walked toward the stairs.

"Frank," Harry called softly.

Frank stopped, his eyes on the staircase, his jaw aching with tension.

Harry came close enough to speak in an undertone. "Listen," he said. "Everybody loses their temper now and again."

Frank nodded.

"And you—Frank, you're a great engineer. We all like you."

"Kind of you," Frank said through tense lips. He felt every eye on him, and he felt as if he were being stripped naked, his broken body exposed for all to see.

Harry cleared his throat, and rumpled his hair with nervous fingers. "If you—if there's anything I can do—"

Frank stood where he was for a long moment, the note from Bill Boeing a dead weight in the pocket of his trousers. At last he turned to look into Harry's sympathetic face. "Thanks," he said. He glanced up at the rest of the men, and saw their eyes skitter away from him. "It's okay, Harry," he said in a stronger tone. "I'm fine." He settled his hat on his head, nodded to Harry, and started down the stairs to the front door.

Thea came to Margot's office a little before noon. "There's a call from Seattle General," she said. "Your patient—the abortion case—Matron says she's burning up with fever."

Margot pushed aside the surgery text and stood up. "I'll have to go, Thea. She doesn't have another doctor."

Thea stood aside as she passed through to fetch her coat and hat. "Shall I call Blake?"

"I don't think there's time. I'll walk."

Thea didn't ask, but Margot sensed her curiosity. As she pulled on her gloves, she said, "It's one of my mother's maids. She got an abortion from some backstreet quack—she was hemorrhaging. I was worried about septicemia. Unfortunately, it looks like I was right."

"I'll handle the office," Thea said.

"I may not be back today."

"You'll need your umbrella, Dr. Benedict."

"Right." Margot clamped the umbrella under her arm as she hurried down Post Street, then up Madison, weaving through lunchtime crowds. As she turned on Fifth to approach the hospital, she slowed her steps, trying to catch her breath. She wanted to appear calm and professional, not race into the ward like a madwoman.

She found Leona huddled in a corner of the ward, weeping steadily into one of the hospital towels. Cardwell sat beside Loena's bed, sponging her forehead with cool water. A student nurse was just leaving with a bundle of bloody cotton in her hands. The other beds in the ward were blessedly empty. Watery sunlight gleamed on the white iron frames and turned the bleached linens a silvery gray.

Margot washed her hands at the sink, then crossed the ward. She could see at a glance how bad Loena's condition was, and when she lifted the sheet to examine her, she saw that the matron had washed the wound again, and re-packed it with gauze. Margot touched her hot skin with a fingertip. The white mark left behind was like an accusing finger. "She needs fluids," Margot said.

The matron nodded. "I've been giving them to her, but her fever is so high."

"Rectally?"

"I did, although she didn't like it. Shall I do it again?"

Loena moaned, and rolled her head on her pillow. Margot took the compress from the nurse's hands and pressed it gently to the girl's forehead. Leona whimpered from her corner, and Margot pursed her lips. "Could you take Leona out? Send her to the canteen, or even get her to go home."

When Cardwell had shepherded Leona out of the ward, Margot sat down beside the bed. "Loena, can you hear me?"

The girl's eyes opened, and she fixed a glassy gaze on Margot's face. Her lips parted, but nothing intelligible came out.

Margot took one of her hands and held it between both of hers. She said quietly, "Loena, if you're in pain, we can give you something. We don't want to give you too much, because—"

Loena's fingers tightened suddenly, clutching at Margot's hands. "He said—he said—" she whimpered. Her eyelids fluttered closed, and her voice trailed off.

"I know," Margot said, as gently as she could. She waited to see if the girl would speak again. A moment passed, and another.

Margot was about to rise when Loena breathed, her eyes still closed, "He promised. All fixed up. He said I would be all fixed up."

Margot freed one hand, and laid it on Loena's hip. She could feel the fever through the sheet and thin blanket.

Hoarsely, Loena said, "I'm going to die."

"No," Margot said. "We're going to do everything we can for you."

"I can tell," Loena said. Her dry lips worked, and her closed eyelids shivered. "I'm going to die. He killed me."

For long seconds, Margot didn't dare speak for sheer fury, and for the paralyzing fear that Loena was right. She drew a long breath through her nostrils to cool her temper. She could be angry later. Could deal with Preston later. "Loena," she said tightly. "Who was it? Where did he take you?"

The girl didn't answer.

Margot sat with her as Cardwell came and went, and the student nurse refilled the basin and brought her a fresh compress. At last the matron said, "Dr. Benedict, you need to get some rest. Leave her to us."

Margot was about to demur, but she saw the steely expression in the nurse's eyes. Cardwell was right. There was nothing to be done now in any case but keep Loena as comfortable as possible.

As she rose, her back ached sharply, and she looked up at the aluminum-rimmed clock on the wall. It was after four. She had been sitting in that straight, hard chair for four hours.

"Let's give her a half grain of codeine phosphate," she said.

"I have it right here," the matron told her. She held up a medicine tray.

The student nurse sat down beside Loena's bed, reaching out her hand as Margot had done, laying it softly on her body as if she would hold the girl's spirit where it was. Margot's voice caught in her throat as she said, "Thank you. Thank you both."

The matron walked with her to the door of the ward. "I sent her sister home," she said in a matter-of-fact tone. "I told her she could come back after supper."

"All right. I don't want Loena to be alone."

"She won't be. Bailey and I will watch over her." As Cardwell handed Margot her things, she said, "You should prepare yourself. You can't save them all, Doctor."

Margot turned her head to hide the sudden reddening of her eyes. "I know. Thank you, Matron." She tried to achieve a dignified pace as she strode away from the ward.

Leonard Whitely caught her on the stairs as she was going down to the lobby. She nodded to him, and murmured a good evening, meaning to pass by without stopping.

He put his white, soft hand on her arm. "Just a minute, Doctor."

Margot stopped where she was. "Yes, Dr. Whitely," she said. Standing on the same step, she was half a head taller than he. He took a step back, and lifted his chin to look into her face. His face was puffy, the nose and cheeks red with broken capillaries, but there was no smell of alcohol about him today.

"Matron tells me you have an abortion case," he said. He spoke softly, as if it were a secret.

"Yes, I do. Septicemia, I'm afraid."

"Most unfortunate."

"Yes. She's very ill."

His eyes flickered to the side, then back to her face. "I feel obliged to tell you, Dr. Benedict, though it's distasteful to me. There are—" He cleared his throat. "There are rumors about you."

Margot sighed. She was hungry and exhausted and worried. She was in no mood for Whitely's maneuvering. "What do you mean, rumors?"

He shrugged a little, dismissively. "I hate to listen to gossip, of course, but . . ."

Margot set her jaw. "And yet, evidently, you *have* been."

Whitely spoke a little louder. "I was inclined to be understanding, but with this young woman lying near death, I'm afraid steps will have to be taken."

"Understanding?" Margot was so tired. It seemed to require the last shreds of her strength to restrain her irritation. "Dr.

Whitely, I don't know what you're talking about. Take what steps, and why?"

"That little clinic of yours," he said. He tipped his head to one side, and adopted a patronizing expression. "I know you see a lot of poor patients, and some of them are desperate."

Margot snapped, "Do you think you could get to the point, Doctor?"

"I should think the point would be obvious," he said smoothly. "A young woman physician, in a poverty-stricken area. No doubt you feel sympathetic, feel it's all right to take the law into your own hands."

"For God's sake, Dr. Whitely! What is it I'm supposed to have done?"

She couldn't mistake the light of triumph that gleamed in his eyes, quickly quenched by an avuncular look of concern. "Why, abortions, of course, Doctor. Most conveniently located, your little office, isn't it? But we can't have violations of that sort taking place. It reflects badly on the hospital."

"You think *I* performed the abortion?" Margot's voice rose, and two nurses at the bottom of the stair turned to look up at her.

"The girl works for your family. I suppose it's logical—you hoped to avoid a scandal."

"Dr. Whitely—" Margot struggled for words, appalled by the injustice of his accusation. "I did not—I *would* not—"

"Oh, come, Doctor. I heard just today that the word is out among women in the city," he said. "Dr. Benedict will 'put you straight,' I believe is the term?"

"What term?" Margot heard her voice ring in the stairwell, but she no longer cared. "Is that the current euphemism, Doctor? And who told you this story?"

He shrugged again. "It doesn't matter. I've just spoken to the directors. They'll initiate the investigation." He started up the stairs. "You had better hope your patient doesn't die."

He went through the door, letting it slam behind him, and leaving Margot shaking with unspent anger and overwhelming fatigue.

CHAPTER 9

For once, Margot made no protest when Blake dropped her off in front of the house. Her medical bag felt as if it were stuffed with bricks as she dragged herself up the rain-slicked walk and into the house. She had not felt so worn out since her residency. She put her bag on the floor inside the front door, hung her coat and hat on the rack, then stood in the hallway, irresolute. She needed to eat something, and she craved sleep. But she would have to deal with her mother sooner or later. Edith should know the truth about what Preston had done, whether she liked it or not. And surely she would want to visit Loena in the hospital. Margot needed to make her understand how seriously ill the girl was. There might not, indeed, be much time.

Hattie had heard the door open and close, and she came into the hall, wiping her hands on her apron. "Miss Margot, Loena will be all right, won't she? Leona says it's bad."

"Oh, Hattie." Margot crossed to her, and patted her shoulder, a little awkwardly. She could see Hattie had been crying, and she supposed Leona had been, too. She pictured the two of them weeping at the kitchen table over a pot of coffee. She wished she could have done the same. It would be a relief to cry. Instead, she had to control her feelings, keep her voice level. Be in command. "Hattie, Loena has an infection and a high fever. We're doing all we can, and she's in good hands. I'll be going back to her first thing in the morning."

"Oh, sweet Jesus," Hattie said, fresh tears filling her eyes. "She won't die, will she? Just tell me the poor little thing won't die?"

Margot couldn't bring herself to lie. She was trying to dredge up something safe to say when the door to the small parlor opened, and Preston emerged into the corridor. His eyes, when he saw Margot, flashed blue fire, a look of pure triumph. She recognized that look all too well, though she had not seen it for a very long time. A shudder broke through her self-control.

The look on Preston's face melted seamlessly into one of earnest concern. "Hattie," he said, "Mother asks if you could put dinner back half an hour? She wants some time to talk with Father when he gets home."

Hattie sniffled, "Yes, Mr. Preston. Of course." She dabbed at her eyes with her apron as she shuffled back to the kitchen.

Margot started past Preston, but he stopped her. "Is she going to be all right?" There was no hint of hypocrisy in his face or his voice, no violence in the fingers that barely touched her sleeve. He merely looked worried, his eyes darkening, his lips soft with sorrow.

She glared at him. "I don't know, Preston." She didn't try to soften the brittle timbre of her voice, and she moved her arm away from his hand. "She has septicemia."

"Blood poisoning?" His eyes widened. His mouth actually trembled.

"It's a serious infection. I want the name of that butcher you turned her over to."

His eyebrows lifted. The gleam returned to his eyes for one heartbeat before he dropped his gaze, and shook his head as if too overcome to speak.

"Other girls might die," she snapped. "I want his name—or hers—to give to the police."

"The thing is," Preston said, with every indication of real misery in his voice, "I don't know it. I asked Carter—my old batman—to find someone. He did. I took Loena to Carter, and he took care of it."

"You've told Mother, I gather?"

"Of course. Clean breast, and all that." He sighed. "I know it's my responsibility, Margot. I'm just heartbroken."

"Oh, for God's sake, Preston," she said, thrusting past him. "Spare me."

He drew a sharp breath, but she strode on down the hall, anger banishing her fatigue for the moment. Behind her she heard him bang the front door.

She didn't realize Blake was in the hall until she put her hand on the door to the small parlor. She glanced to her right, and realized he had been standing in the back entryway, watching her exchange with Preston. She met his worried gaze, and shrugged.

Edith was seated at the writing desk beneath the side window. When Margot came in, she looked up, but she didn't put down her pen. "Margot, good! You can tell me what to do." She didn't look particularly upset. Her cheeks were tinged with pink, and a few wisps of hair had come loose from her chignon, but otherwise she looked much as usual.

"What do you mean, Mother? Do about what?"

"Why, about Loena! And Leona! Loena will be discharged, naturally, but do I have to send Leona away, too? What if she wants to stay?"

Margot crossed the room and pulled a chair up across from her mother. "Mother, listen."

Edith had been about to write something more, but she stopped with her pen poised above a sheet of monogrammed stationery. "Yes, dear?"

"Loena needs us right now, Mother. And so does Leona. The situation is grave."

Edith laid her pen down, crossing it precisely over the corner of the sheet of paper. "Of course it is, Margot. It's shocking. I have given your brother the scolding of his life!"

Margot sagged back in her chair. Weakly she said, "Scolding?"

Edith's cheeks grew rosier. "Of course! Preston is far too old for such nonsense with one of the hired help, and so I told him. And Loena! I trusted those girls in my home, trained them myself! They know their place. Such a—a transgression—it's unforgivable. Everyone will be talking about it."

"Mother—" Margot began, but Edith interrupted her.

"Now don't you start with any of your women's rights prattle, Margot Benedict! I know what's right and proper, and I expect my servants to do the same." She picked up her pen again. "I'm just trying to decide whether to write a reference for Leona— which is only right, as *she* is not the one who got herself into trouble—and send her packing with her sister."

"Mother, listen to yourself! You're saying Loena got *herself* into trouble? What do you think, that she knocked Preston down and raped him?"

"Margot!" Edith pressed a hand to her throat. "How dare you speak to me that way?"

Margot made an exasperated noise. "Good God, Mother, this isn't the eighteenth century! We don't throw pregnant unwed girls out into the forest, and we don't hold them responsible for their own seductions!" She folded her arms around herself, and pressed her lips together to stem the tide of angry words. It wouldn't help to antagonize her mother.

Edith pursed her lips, and gazed at Margot for a moment. "You know, dear, you may be a doctor, but you're very young. You have no experience of men. You don't know how they are."

"Oh, I think I do, Mother. I know how my brother is, in any case."

Edith lifted her slender eyebrows. "Men have strong urges, Margot. It's the way of the world. And girls—girls like Loena, though I was so fond of her—know how to take advantage of that." Margot started to speak again, but Edith put up a hand. "No, it's true. I've heard a dozen stories just like this, of maids in well-to-do homes seducing the sons of their employers. No doubt they think they will improve their station. I imagine that when Loena discovered it would do her no good, she demanded Preston's help. She brought all of this upon herself."

Margot gazed at her mother in helpless frustration. Edith was wearing a pastel dress of silk voile, which no doubt cost months' worth of Loena's salary. Her hair had been dressed. She wore a delicate face powder that Margot had heard her say was imported from Paris. Her eyes, the same clear blue as Preston's, were untroubled by the slightest self-doubt.

Edith went on, "Preston is properly ashamed of himself, of course. And he will never do such a thing again, not under my roof. I hardly want my first grandchild born to a housemaid! But I won't have such a girl in my employ, and that's all there is to it."

Margot, weary beyond belief, could think of no fresh argument. In a flat tone she said, "Well, Mother. You may not need to discharge Loena in any case. She is very ill. It will be a great surprise if she survives."

Edith folded her hands in her lap. "Well. That's very sad, I'm sure. We will all pray it doesn't come to that."

Margot stood up, and restored her chair to its original position. "You do that. Sit here in your fashionable parlor and pray for Loena while she burns up with fever in a hospital bed. And try to remember, if you can, that Preston put her there." She turned away. Edith uttered a mild protest, but Margot's patience was at an end. She strode out of the parlor and up the stairs to her room, where she stripped off her clothes, drew the blinds, and fell into her bed with the intent of sleeping twelve solid hours. She tossed on her pillow for a time, restless and angry. She couldn't stop the impressions spinning through her mind: Loena's pale misery, Hattie grieving, Blake's worry, her mother's bland cruelty.

And why had Frank Parrish been at the front door yesterday, as she went out with Loena? Had those been flowers in his hand?

When lightning began to flash through the blinds, and thunder to roll over the Cascades to the east, Margot closed her eyes. The storm comforted her, somehow. It symbolized her torment, seemed to lift it out of her, externalize it, expend its energy into the stormy night. She was grateful, and as branches of the camellia whipped her window, and rain spattered the roof above her head, she slept at last.

Frank stood by the window of his room on Cherry Street and watched the storm approach. He imagined it pouring down from the mountains, sweeping across Lake Washington, roiling up over the hill and down into the city. Lightning flashed, and thunder rattled the windows.

He had no whisky tonight. He had come straight from Bill Boeing's office to this room, to stand here—cold sober—and try to think things through.

It had all been done with such deft and artful malice. He would not have guessed Preston Benedict capable of such subtlety.

Boeing had been reluctant, he could see. He had said, "I'm sorry about this, Parrish. Really sorry. But I'm under a lot of pressure from Mayor Caldwell and the city council. I need their cooperation for our seaplanes to use Lake Union. We dropped one in the lake, you know, and a lot of the council are afraid we're going to crash one onto someone's house. I've had to fight to hold on to our privileges."

Frank had been seated across from him in his paneled office. He rose, and stood with his hat in his hand dangling beside his thigh. "Sir, it wasn't like—like the column says."

Boeing stood up, too. "Look, you've done good work for me. I appreciate it. It's just that the Benedicts have a lot of influence in this city. Maybe when this blows over . . ."

Frank's lips had felt stiff, his mouth unbearably dry. "If I could explain, Mr. Boeing."

Boeing looked as unhappy as a man could. He shook his head. "I can imagine how it was. I was young once, too, Frank."

"You don't understand, sir. I—Benedict and I just—" He

couldn't think how to explain it. He had shoved Preston into the gutter, it was true. But if he could somehow make clear what had provoked him, why he had lost his temper—

"It's not fair, Parrish, that's obvious. I'm not happy about it, but I'm in a corner here."

Frank wanted to protest, to beg for another chance. Pride forestalled him. It was, he supposed, the same pride that had given him the urge to shake Preston Benedict the way a terrier shakes a rat.

He swallowed, put his hat on, and extended his hand to Bill Boeing. "Thanks for the opportunity, sir. I'm more sorry than I can say."

Boeing shook his hand. "So am I, son. So am I."

Frank reflected now that though Boeing's regret had appeared genuine, it hadn't helped. He had been let go. Preston Benedict had succeeded in getting him fired.

His hand itched with the need to strike something. It was as well, he thought, that Preston Benedict was not standing in front of him at this moment. He had nothing much left to lose. He would probably throw away what little remained for the satisfaction of battering an apology out of him, for this and for insulting Margot.

Blake finished his evening cup of hot chocolate, rinsed out the cup and the saucepan, and set both in the strainer beside the sink. He was already in his dressing gown, and when he went into his bedroom he didn't bother to turn on the single bulb that hung from the ceiling. He opened the curtains to watch lightning flicker across the sky. Across the yard the windows were all dark, including Margot's. He hoped she would get a good night's sleep. He feared she would need all her strength for what the morning would bring.

He turned toward his bed, but a flash of lightning brought him back to the window. Thunder rumbled in the east, and he waited a moment to see if there would be more.

When another flash came, it illuminated the yard and the house in a burst of light. More thunder cracked and grumbled, closer this time, but Blake paid no attention. He had seen someone in the yard, someone lurking beneath the kitchen window, near the screen door. A tall man, bulky, wearing a workingman's cap.

Blake hurried into the kitchenette, and seized his canvas jacket from its peg. He pulled it on, and took up his marble-topped cane before he hurried down the stairs and out into the storm. He saw the man plainly, standing between the garage and the house, looking up at the second-floor windows. Rain pelted the grass, and the noise of it covered Blake's approach. When he put his hand on the man's shoulder, the stranger yelped, and whirled, hands up to defend himself.

Blake let him back away. He had seen this man before.

"It's you!" Carter shouted over the sounds of the storm. "No need to get the wind up, mate. I need to see Benedict."

Blake glared at him. "Keep your voice down. I don't want the family disturbed."

Carter bristled as before. "You can't talk to me like that. A guest." He was unsteady on his feet, and Blake could smell, even through the rain, the sour tinge of alcohol.

"It's the middle of the night," Blake said with careful dignity, though rain soaked his hair and ran down his face. "I could call the police and report an intruder."

Carter gave a phlegmy laugh, and the smell of drink intensified. "Why doncha, then?"

"I told you. I don't want the family disturbed."

"I'm not leaving till I talk to Benedict. He's expecting me."

Blake glanced up at the darkened windows of the house. "It doesn't look to me like anyone's expecting company. Come on, let's get out of the rain. I can take a message for Mr. Preston." He pointed back toward the garage. Another distant rattle of thunder seemed to decide Carter, and he nodded.

Blake led the way through the door and into the shelter of the stairwell. He flicked on the light, and stood at the bottom of the stair with his arms folded, his stout stick of Carolina pine tucked securely under his arm.

Carter slurred, "Listen, mate, can't you slip into the house? Get him up?"

"Whatever it is can wait until tomorrow," Blake said stiffly. He tried to stifle his antagonism for the man. The scene was bizarre, the storm battering the roof, the fat man filling his little entryway with the smell of his wet army tunic and the reek of bad whisky.

Carter pulled off his cap and brushed it against his sleeve, spattering the floor with raindrops. "I need money," he muttered. "I need it tonight."

"Why do you need money? And what does that have to do with Mr. Preston?"

"I don't see why I have to tell *you*," Carter said sullenly, staring at his heavy boots.

Blake let a long moment pass before he drawled, "Who else are you going to tell, sir?"

Carter raised his head. His doughy features and small eyes gave him a porcine appearance. "I did some work," he said sullenly. "And now I need to be paid. I have a few shillings, but no one will take 'em. I can't pay my rent. I ain't had anything to eat today."

Blake pursed his lips. "I can probably find a few dollars for you," he said. "But I want to know what the work was."

Carter's gaze shifted, and shifted again. "I don't see how it's any of your business."

"Nevertheless."

Carter shuffled his feet, then shrugged. "Preston wanted a word placed here and there, in the right ears. I been living down there, in the city, and I did it for 'im."

"A word about what?" Suspicion kindled in Blake's mind, but he kept his face impassive.

Carter hesitated a long time. Blake leaned against the wall, waiting. At last Carter said, "Look. I'm afraid if I tell you, Preston won't pay me. I meant what I said—I got nothin'. I ain't et all day. And I did the work, just like he wanted."

Blake eyed him, thinking how remarkably unintelligent the man looked. He suspected he had eaten pigs that were smarter than this pale-haired, pink-skinned creature. With a sigh, he straightened, and gestured at the stairs. "Come upstairs, Mr. Carter. I have some eggs and bread, and a hot plate. I'll give you something to eat. You can sober up a bit, and then you can tell me all about it."

Watching the fat man eat made Blake feel a bit nauseous. He had scrambled four eggs with a bit of butter in the cast-iron skillet he had kept in his room since the children were little. He had made them camp toast sometimes, or poached eggs. He sliced some bread, and gave Carter the wire frame for toasting it over the hot plate. He had half a jar of blackberry jam in his single cupboard, and Carter finished that, along with most of the crock of butter the milkman had delivered the day before. He got butter on his fingers and his chin, and dripped jam on his shirtfront. When Blake handed him a napkin, he took it without apology, and mopped his chest.

When he had finished, he sat back with his hands over his big stomach. "Pretty good," he said. Blake said nothing. Carter scrubbed the butter from his fingers with the napkin, and looked around him at the simple furnishings. "Servant's quarters, eh? Bigger than most, I expect."

"Are they?"

Carter gave a generous burp. "Sure. My place in London was like a shoebox."

"I wouldn't have thought you were in service."

"Right-ho, mate. I never was. Me own man, I was, till I went into the army. I was a drayman, had me own cart and everything. There wasn't nobody in the city could lift as much as me." He rubbed his belly, and laughed. "I was a bit younger then, of course."

"So," Blake said slowly. "You don't lift anymore. You . . . what was it you said? Place a word here and there?"

Carter looked a little abashed. "Well, look, mate, it's hard getting work these days. A bloke has to take what he can get."

"I see."

Carter squinted at him briefly, then glanced away again. Rain dripped down the windows, glistening under the raw light of the bare fixture above the table. Blake could feel the man softening, soothed by food, comforted by being out of the rain.

"Everything's different since the war," Carter said. It seemed an irrelevant thing to say. Blake waited. The thunder had moved on. The late hour and the patter of the rain made the room feel isolated, an oasis in time for two unlikely travelers.

Carter went on. "Nobody needs a drayman now." His eyes fixed on the dark window, following the raindrops' meandering path down the glass. "There's vans, even war-surplus trucks to haul things. Nobody knows what they're supposed to do. At home, half the men got killed, and the women take their jobs." He rubbed his stomach with the flat of his hand. "It was better out there. Out East. A man knew what to do every day."

"Follow orders," Blake said.

Carter nodded, and his little eyes glistened in the light. "Right-ho," he said heavily. "That's what a man like me does. Follows orders."

"So Preston gave you orders."

"He gave me orders, and I followed 'em. And now I need my money."

"Tell me what your orders were."

The little eyes flicked from side to side. "Can't tell you. Preston wouldn't like it."

"No. Probably not." Blake cleared his throat, and stood up, straightening his dressing gown. He had hung his jacket on its peg again, but kept the marble-headed cane leaning against his chair. "Well, then, Mr. Carter. If you've finished your meal . . ."

Carter gave him an aggrieved glance. "You said you might have a few dollars!"

"I said I believed I could find some money if you told me what you've done."

"Aw, come on, mate. You know how Preston can be, doncha?"

"How is that, Mr. Carter? How can he be?"

Carter lumbered to his feet, hitching his trousers with both hands. "Well, you know. If he loses his temper."

"What happens if he loses his temper?"

Carter was shaking his head. "It's bad. It's real bad."

Blake indicated the stairwell with his head. "I'll say good night now."

"Aw, come on," Carter pleaded. It was unpleasant, a big man whining. "Come on, mate, just a few bucks."

Blake shook his head. "You chose your company, sir. I can't help you."

Carter's fists curled, and his little eyes narrowed, almost disappearing into the folds of his cheeks. Blake put his hand on the cane. It had been a long time since Chatham County Convict Camp, but Abraham Blake had not forgotten how to defend himself.

When he lifted the cane, its marble lion's head shone faintly in the muted light. The fat man reared back like a frightened horse. His pale eyebrows rose, and the flesh of his neck quivered. "Better watch yerself, mate," he said in his reedy voice. "Preston wouldn't like it if you hurt me."

"You seem to know a lot about what Mr. Preston doesn't like."

Carter nodded, his jowls trembling. "Yeah. Yeah, I do."

"Perhaps you need a friend, Mr. Carter."

The Englishman said mournfully, "Yeah."

"I believe I have four dollars in my wallet. Let's make our exchange, and you can find someplace to sleep tonight."

"Four?" Carter looked hopeful.

"As I recall. I don't carry cash as a rule."

"You won't tell Preston?"

Blake considered, pursing his lips. "Let us say that I will not tell him where I learned—whatever it is."

Carter squinted his pale eyes through the gloom. "Five, maybe?"

Blake took a firmer grip on the cane. "Let me see what I have. Stay here."

It took only a moment to go into his bedroom. He made a show of bringing his wallet out to show Carter he had no more money than he had claimed.

"Nice wallet," Carter said.

"Yes, it is. A gift from Mr. Benedict last Christmas." He opened it, and shook out the bills. There were, as he had expected, only four dollars. He dug inside the change compartment, and found seventy-five cents. "That's all there is, Mr. Carter." He laid it all on the table with one hand. He kept the cane firmly gripped in the other, but Carter, eyes glittering at the sight of the money, had given in. He leaned close to Blake, and whispered his secret as if some midnight listener might overhear him.

Blake nodded, unsurprised, but saddened. He said, "No more spreading rumors, Mr. Carter. Or I will report you."

Carter scooped up the money and stuffed it into his trouser pocket. He grabbed his coat from the back of his chair and lumbered down the stairs, sober now, fed, but a sorry sight nonetheless. At the bottom he threw Blake a strange look. "I can't figure you," he said.

"No," Blake said tiredly. "I don't suppose you can." When Carter had gone out into the wet night, Blake went down the stairs, still carrying the cane. He took care in locking the door. He turned out the light in the stairwell, and stood there for a long time, watching the quiet house across the yard. When he finally trudged up the stairs for the third time that night, the burden of Carter's secret bowed his shoulders and dragged at his steps.

CHAPTER 10

Margot startled awake in the darkness, wondering what was wrong. She lay on her pillow, listening. The house was quiet, and she realized, after several moments, that it was the silence that had wakened her. The thunder had stopped. Even the rain had ceased, though water dripped noisily from the gutters. Faint gray light showed through the opening of the curtains. She rolled over to look at the brass dial clock on her bedside stand, and lay a moment longer, debating whether five o'clock was too early to get up. She thought about what awaited her at the hospital this morning, and her heart began to flutter. Sleep would not return.

She threw back her covers and swung her feet to the floor, expecting the shock of cold on her bare soles. When she felt the relative warmth of the wood, she remembered. It was June, nearly summer. The days were growing long.

Margot was startled to hear, as she crept down the stairs with her shoes in her hand, the percolator bubbling in the kitchen. She smelled eggs and bacon frying. She stopped in the kitchen doorway to put on her shoes. "Blake. What are you doing up at this hour?"

"Dr. Margot," he said with an ironic smile. "What are *you* doing up?"

She sighed, and reached for the mug of coffee he handed her. "I'm going to the hospital."

He moved to the stove to turn the simmering bacon. "You're having breakfast first."

Margot pulled out a chair, and sat down. "I will, thank you. I don't think I ate last night."

"You're worried." He dished up the eggs and bacon, and set them in front of her. He took a fork and knife from a drawer, and set those beside the plate.

Margot set her coffee down to pick up the fork. "There's nothing I can do for her now but be there."

He sat opposite her with his own coffee. "I'm sure you've done all you can."

"That was precious little." She heard the knife edge in her voice, but she couldn't help it. It was a relief not to worry about her tone. Blake would understand how she felt, and why. He understood all of it.

She took a bite of egg, and followed it with half of a strip of bacon. She had been afraid she couldn't eat, but anxious though she was, her body welcomed the food. She finished the eggs in a few bites, and picked up her coffee again. "Whoever did this to Loena," she said, "wasn't a doctor. Not only was the procedure a mess, but there couldn't have been any antiseptic measures. The infection took hold too quickly."

"Dr. Margot," Blake began.

She drained the coffee, and stood up. "Sorry, Blake. I'm thinking out loud."

He stood up, too, slowly, leaning on the table.

"Your back hurts again."

He shook his head. "Let's not worry about that now."

"What then?" He smoothed his white apron. She read indecision in his eyes, and worry. "Is there something else wrong?" she asked.

"I don't know." He picked up the plate and flatware, but stood holding them, staring at the remnants of her breakfast. "Last night, that man—Carter—was here, trying to see Mr. Preston."

"Is that the Carter Preston mentioned?"

"The same. He was Mr. Preston's batman, out in the East. His army servant."

"I can see you don't approve of this person, Blake."

"I certainly don't approve of his coming to Benedict Hall in the middle of the night."

"What did he want?"

"Money." Blake gestured with the dirty plate. "He said he did some work for Mr. Preston, and needed his pay."

Margot felt the familiar wave of unease. "Preston said Carter arranged Loena's abortion."

"More than that. He said Preston wanted a word placed in certain ears. Here and there, he said."

"A word." Margot patted her lips with a napkin and laid it on the table. "You have an idea about this, I gather."

"I don't like to believe it of Mr. Preston. And I hate to speak of it in case this Carter made it all up."

Margot snorted, and turned to fetch her coat. "It's probably something to do with that scandal rag he writes for. Nothing to do with us."

"Do you read his column?"

"Not since he printed that ghastly photo of me. I'm afraid of what I might see."

He came after her into the hall, and helped her into her coat. "Are you sure you don't want me to drive you?"

"No. It's a beautiful morning." She put on her hat and gloves. "There's something else I have to worry about, Blake." He cocked his head, and raised his gray eyebrows. "It's Dr. Whitely, Leonard Whitely. He claims I performed Loena's abortion. And that I've been doing others, at my clinic. He's threatening to revoke my hospital privileges."

Blake hesitated for a long moment, as if he were trying to decide something. Finally, when she bent to pick up her bag, he cleared his throat. "Dr. Margot. You should speak to Mr. Dickson. He can have a word with the directors."

"Father would probably think it served me right. You know how he feels about the clinic."

"Let me speak to him, then."

"No, Blake, but thank you. I have to fight my own battles, don't I?"

"You don't have to fight them alone."

She gave him an affectionate smile before she went out into the cool sunshine and walked quickly down the hill toward the streetcar. The storm had left the lawns green and the air sparkling. The fresh air cleared her head. She tried to enjoy the quiet of the early morning streets, and not to think too much about what she would find when she went into Loena's ward.

But she knew, just as Cardwell had known. It was a death-watch. There was nothing in her power that could change it.

Preston dressed carefully in a vested suit. He smoothed his tie and took his hat from the shelf above his wardrobe. It was surprising, really, how much he enjoyed writing his column, hearing the bit of buzz around the newsroom as people leafed through the paper. The latest one, in particular, had been a swell bit of fun.

The scents of griddle cakes and bacon floated up the stairs, drawing him down to the dining room. Griddle cakes were one thing Hattie did well. Her bacon tended to be limp and greasy, but the crisp edges of her griddle cakes made up for that.

He was seated at the table with his coffee when Hattie carried in the breakfast tray. As she arranged the platters in front of him, he glanced up. "Where's Leona?"

Hattie's eyes were swollen, and her lips trembled. She plucked at the pinafore of her apron as he served himself two griddle cakes and the crispest rashers he could find. She said in a teary voice, "Leona's at the hospital, Mr. Preston. Loena's real bad, she says."

Preston repressed a flare of irritation. He made himself lay down his fork, though the griddle cakes were cooling on his plate. "I thought she was going to be all better, once she got to the hospital. Margot—"

"Miss Margot sat with her almost all day, Leona says. Then she got a nurse to sit with her all night." Hattie stepped back from the table, and flapped a hand at him. "Eat, Mr. Preston. Have all you want. Hardly anybody here for breakfast."

"Mother?"

"I took Mrs. Edith a tray, and Miss Margot left before anyone else was up."

Preston reached for the pitcher of warm maple syrup, but he didn't pour it yet. He held it in his hand, as if his appetite had disappeared. "I should go to the hospital, shouldn't I, Hattie?" he said sadly. "Take Loena some flowers."

Fresh tears welled in her eyes. "Oh, that's sweet, Mr. Preston. That's just so sweet of you. That poor girl!" A sob broke from her throat, and she hurried from the dining room, sniveling as she crossed the hall to the kitchen.

Preston poured syrup over his griddle cakes, and ate two rashers of bacon as it soaked into them. The griddle cakes were delicious. He sat back when they were finished, and sipped the strong black coffee to counteract the sweet taste in his mouth. He put his hand over his breastbone, pursing his lips as he thought about his mother's lecture and Hattie's grief. Then, with a decisive motion, he pushed his plate away, set his cup down, and rose.

His father came into the dining room just as he was on his way out. Dick was walking down the stairs at the same moment. "Leaving already, Preston?" Dickson said.

"Early day," Preston said. "I hope you'll excuse me, Father."

His father nodded. Dick, behind him, said, "Quite the busy bee, aren't you?"

Preston flashed him a grin, then remembered, and pulled his lips into a grave expression. "Well," he said, "work goes on, despite domestic crises."

"That's right," Dickson said heavily. "Nothing we can do but carry on." He nodded, mostly to himself, as he went on into the dining room.

Dick stood where he was, one hand on the knob of the dining room door, as Preston made his way to the coatrack. As he adjusted his fedora, Preston glanced back at his brother. "Something to say, old man?"

Dick's face had the same hard look Margot's so often wore. "Mother and Ramona are both terribly upset, Preston," he said stiffly. "I fully expect there to be no more shenanigans."

Preston opened the front door, letting a rush of rain-washed air into the hallway. "Shenanigans," he mused, just loud enough for Dick to hear him. "Shenanigans. Is *that* what they are?" He gave a silent laugh as he went out into the sparkling morning.

There was a little flurry of activity in the hospital corridors as breakfast trays were being delivered. Preston wrinkled his nose at the smell of medicine and disinfectant mixed with the odors of fried ham and oatmeal. He had to ask directions once or twice before he found his way to Loena's ward. He peered around the doorway.

The girl lay still as death, the spare shape of her body barely visible beneath the stiff white coverlet. A gray-haired nurse in a long apron bent over her, sponging her forehead. On her other side sat Leona, pale and nearly as still as her sister. She had Loena's hand in hers, stroking it over and over. It looked as if she had been making the same gesture for hours.

Preston gave a slight, warning cough, and walked into the ward. The nurse glanced over her shoulder to scowl at him. When Leona looked up, she seemed to go even paler, a phenomenon Preston could have enjoyed under other circumstances. For now, he needed both of them to leave the ward. He put a finger to his lips, and tiptoed across the gray linoleum. He had a slender spray of pink tulips in one hand, bought at the street corner, and he held them out as he came close.

Leona began to reach for them, but the nurse said sternly, "No men allowed in this ward."

Preston stopped where he was, the ridiculous bunch of flowers in his left hand, his right hand pressed to his breast, the perfect gesture of sincerity and concern. "Oh," he said softly. "I'm sorry. I'm—I'm family, really. Preston Benedict."

He kept his right hand where it was, pressing the stone, as he watched the nurse's expression change. "Benedict? Are you Dr. Benedict's brother?"

His belly gave a twinge of fury. "I am," he said. "I came to see how our girl is doing."

"Well," the nurse said. She had a beaky, sharp face, like a crow. "I suppose you can come in for just a moment."

As he drew closer to the white iron bed, Leona reached again for the flowers, but Preston held them out to the nurse. "I know it isn't much," he said sadly. "But do you have a vase somewhere? When she wakes up, a spot of color might cheer her up, don't you think?"

He flattened his free hand against the stone. The nurse's wrinkled lips pinched, making her look even more crowlike, but she took the flowers. "I'll see," she said primly, and bustled away, her long apron fluttering. "I'll be right back."

Leona said, "Dr. Margot just left. She had another patient to see."

Preston ordered, "Go help the nurse, Leona."

At the change in his tone, two little spots of color flared in her cheeks. "Yes, Mr. Preston," she whispered, and fled.

Loena lay unmoving beneath the bleached coverlet, her freckled nose pointing at the ceiling, her white lips a little open. She was more than pale, he thought. She was—waxen, was the word. He liked thinking that. Thinking like a writer, he reflected, not that he would write about this. The girl was a wax image of herself, nearly lifeless. No, bloodless. He wondered for an instant just how much blood she had lost. She looked, in a way, as if she were already dead.

He watched her as he undid one button of his shirtfront with quick fingers. Her breath moved, ever so slightly. And she was so hot! He could feel the heat of her as he leaned close. She moaned, startling him. Still alive. He wondered if, left to her own devices, she might make it. It didn't look like it to him, but then, he wasn't a medical man.

He glanced swiftly over his shoulder, but there was no one about. He pulled the stiff coverlet back to expose Loena's small body in a flimsy nightgown. There was a pungent smell about her, a foul smell, as if something was rotting. His nose twitched, but he bent over her, pulling the silver chain from inside his shirt.

He pressed the sapphire to her chest, between her two small breasts. They had been delightful, those breasts, firm and pink, with nipples like new pennies. Now they seemed flaccid, flat. Not that it mattered. He wouldn't want to see them again.

In truth, he thought, he would be just as happy not to see the girl herself ever again. But his mother—and Hattie—

He closed his eyes, and let the stone sing its ancient song through his fingers, a long-buried song of power. The girl's eyelids trembled, and lifted. Her eyes opened, and a jolt of energy shook her slight frame when she saw him.

"Preston!"

Startled, Preston palmed the sapphire, and thrust it into his shirtfront even as he took a step back, away from the bed, and from the girl looking up at him with glassy, frightened eyes.

"You shouldn't be here!" There was no mistaking the authority in Margot's voice nor the suspicion in her eyes. Her shirtwaist was creased and limp beneath her white coat. Her stethoscope looked like a tired brown snake hanging around her neck.

A moment later the nurse returned with Leona trailing behind her. The nurse carried a plain glass vase, with the tulips' pink heads drooping this way and that. Leona exclaimed, "Loena!" and scurried to her sister's bed.

Margot followed more slowly, her hard gaze fixed on Preston's unbuttoned shirt. It softened as it shifted to Loena. Preston tugged his jacket lapels forward, and stood to one side.

Margot was already pulling on a pair of rubber gloves, and

folding back the coverlet, exposing Loena's abdomen. "Out, Preston," she said. "I'll talk to you in the hall." She bent over the girl, turning her to one side, touching the soiled bandages with her gloved hands. It made Preston feel sick to see it.

"I'll wait for you," he said.

"Five minutes." She didn't even bother to glance at him.

His belly cramped with resentment. Why should she speak to him that way? She always treated him as if he were slow, or stupid. Even when they were little, when he was only three and she five, she had ordered him around, treated him like a baby, a nuisance.

Of course, he mused, smiling to himself as he strolled out of the ward, he had put the fear of God into her then. And now, in a way, he had done it again. A few harsh words didn't matter. A ruined reputation did.

Margot and Cardwell exchanged a look as they pulled Loena's covers up again. The girl had fallen asleep the moment Preston left the room. Perspiration beaded her face.

"She was awake for a moment," Cardwell said.

"Let's push more liquids," Margot said. "She's sweating, and that's a good sign."

Cardwell nodded, and went to a cupboard, coming back with a bowl of vinegar water and the enema apparatus. She moved to the opposite side of Loena's bed, so that Leona had to move out of the way. Cardwell began to uncoil the enema tube.

"Is she better?" Leona asked hopefully.

"Half an hour ago I was sure she was going to die," Margot said bluntly. Leona gave a gasp, and clasped her hands before her. "But she's started to perspire, Leona. That might be a sign her body is beginning to deal with the infection."

"I've been praying so hard!" Leona crossed herself. "To St. Jude."

Cardwell murmured, "Saint of lost causes. Good choice."

"Keep it up, Leona. It's good you're here with her. I'm sure it gives Loena courage." Margot removed her stethoscope from her neck and folded it in her hand. "I have to go speak to my brother," she said. "Matron, are you all right to stay for the time being?"

"Yes, Doctor. I'll take care of the enema, and then see if I can wake her again, get her to swallow some broth."

"Thank you."

Margot half expected Preston to have fled, but he was waiting in the corridor, as promised. His shirt was buttoned now, and he lounged against the wall, his hands in his pockets, one knee bent, the heel braced behind him. "How is she?" he asked. His tone was one of sincere concern, but his eyes were bright, his lips ready to curve into a smile.

"She might have taken a half step back from death's door," Margot said. "That's all I can say at the moment." She scowled at her brother. "What were you doing in there?"

His gaze was one of pure guilelessness. No happy toddler's eyes could have looked less troubled. "Me? I didn't do anything."

"Damn it, Preston," Margot snapped.

"Margot, darling," he said smoothly. He dropped his foot to the floor, and straightened. "You shouldn't curse. Talking like a man won't make you one, you know."

She put her hands on her hips. "I came into the ward, and you were bent over her. Doing something. What was it?"

He smiled at her. "You're imagining things, Margot. Too much ether, I would guess."

"I'm not imagining anything." She glared at him. "What is it you keep under your shirt, Preston? That you keep pressing on?"

His smile faltered, just a bit, but enough to set her intuition tingling. His voice sharpened. "Really, Doctor. Do you try to get everyone's clothes off?"

"I don't want you to take your clothes off. I want you to answer me."

"Well, I'm not going to." He put his hat on, and straightened his lapels. "I just came to visit Loena. As I told you—" His smile returned, wide and angelic. "I feel responsible."

"You *are* responsible."

He spread his hands, his smile broadening. Margot's fingers tingled with a sudden desire to snatch at her brother, to tear the buttons off his carefully pressed linen shirt. She knew in her bones there was something there. She dropped her hands, and linked her fingers in front of her. "How will you feel if she dies?"

"She won't."

"You can't know that, Preston. No one can know that."

"Even the great lady doctor?"

"I can't believe you're making jokes at a time like this. I've been expecting the girl to die any moment."

"And now you're not?"

"Now I'm not so sure."

His lip curled. "Well, isn't that swell! I think I prefer my doctors to be better informed."

She couldn't repress the weary sigh that rose from her throat. "We learn as we go, Preston, and do the best we can. Medicine is an inexact science."

"You're telling *me*," he said, and laughed. He touched his hat brim with two fingers. "See you at dinner, doc, back at the old shack." He sauntered down the gray corridor, sleek and elegant, the picture of insouciance.

She could only stand and watch him go. She didn't realize how tightly she was gripping her hands together until her fingers began to ache.

Before she left, she peeked into the ward one more time. Her eyes widened, and she put a hand to her throat as she saw Cardwell spooning broth from a cup, Loena's pale lips parting to receive it. Leona was at her other side, dabbing at the drops that escaped down her sister's chin.

CHAPTER 11

Frank spent two days in an agony of indecision. He went out each day, not wanting to alert Mrs. Volger to his lack of employment. He walked the pier in the early morning hours, listening to the calls of seagulls and the shouts of the fishermen as they set out into the misty sunshine. He went back to the café at the Public Market, but he drank only coffee. He paced through the high stalls, giving the Chinese family at the flower shop an embarrassed nod when they recognized him. He felt as if everything had gone wrong, and the flowers he had intended to offer Margot, and which had decorated Mrs. Volger's hallway until they were brown and drooping, symbolized the wreck of his life.

On the third day, he woke with the sense of a decision being made. The whole thing was silly. Benedict had responded out of all proportion to the actual offense—if there had been an offense. They had been to war together, Frank thought. They had fought on the same side. While they could not be called friends, they were hardly enemies. They had provoked each other, struck at each other's vulnerabilities. An injustice had been done, but surely, with calmer heads and a little thought, it could be undone.

Frank recalled, as he walked out into the salt-scented wind, how the summer sun had seared the Montana fields, even in June, drying his mother's lawn and flowers, parching the wheat and hayfields. Here the sun was soft, filtered through rain-laden clouds that puffed over the mountains before spreading themselves thin above the waters of Puget Sound. Roses and daisies bloomed in pots and beds. Rhododendrons grew wild in every open space, struggling toward the light from thickets of evergreen shrubs. There was a restrained beauty about all of it, a gentleness that mocked his black mood.

He rehearsed what he would say as he swung up, one-handed, into the streetcar. He meant to be courteous, but firm. Perhaps an apology was more than Benedict would countenance, but a retraction was necessary. Frank wanted his job back, and he thought Bill Boeing would keep it for him, at least for a time. The plans for the GAX triplane were in full swing, and he needed every engineer on his staff. Frank had been the point man for the project. No one understood the requirements of mounting cannon and machine guns better than he did.

Surely Benedict could be reminded they were war comrades. They had been over there longer than other Americans. They had known what it was to be outsiders in the King's army, as well as to be under fire.

All these thoughts tumbled through his brain as he walked up Aloha and turned left on Fourteenth. He hesitated only a moment on the sidewalk outside Benedict Hall. Margot should have left early for her hospital rounds. Dickson and his elder son were no doubt already at their office. Preston probably set his own hours at the *Times*. He might catch him at home.

Frank straightened his jacket and hat before going up the path and taking the porch steps two at a time. He lifted the knocker and let it fall twice. The confident sound of brass on brass strengthened his determination.

Blake and Hattie looked at each other in surprise at the sound of the door. Blake set down the tray of cups he had been about to carry back to the dining room sideboard. "Everyone's gone, aren't they?" he asked.

"Everybody," Hattie said. "Mrs. Edith and Mrs. Ramona went shopping. Leona went to the hospital with Miss Margot, to sit with Loena." She pulled the stopper in the sink, and paddled the water with her hand to disperse the soapsuds. "Loena'll be home in a week, Miss Margot says. Praise the Lord."

"Yes, indeed." Blake reached for his jacket, and shrugged into it. "Well. I'll see who it is." He moved down the corridor with a dignified step, allowing this unexpected visitor to wait a bit as a sign of the family's importance.

A wave of compunction swept him when he saw that it was Frank Parrish waiting on the porch, his hat in his hand, sunlight glinting on the faint gray streaks in his black hair. "Major Parrish," Blake said, trying to hide his surprise. "Good morning."

Blake had read Mr. Preston's column, but it seemed no one else had. Miss Margot would have been furious, so he had refrained from pointing it out to her. She had enough to worry about at the moment. Mr. Dickson would have remonstrated with his son for exposing a private conflict to public scrutiny, but he couldn't have undone the damage. It had seemed best to let it go unremarked.

Frank Parrish looked strained, but he spoke with his usual reserved courtesy. "Good morning, Blake. I'm sorry I didn't telephone ahead. I wonder if Preston is available?"

Blake stepped back, opening the door wide. "Please, come in, Major. Mr. Preston left early today—in fact, all the family is out—but let Hattie give you a cup of coffee. Have you breakfasted?"

Parrish hesitated on the doorstep, pressing his hat against his thigh.

"Please do come in," Blake said. "Dr. Margot would want us to make you feel at home."

Parrish gave a nod, and stepped past him into the hall. Blake shut the door, and held out his hand to indicate Parrish should go into the dining room.

"Nice of you, Blake," Parrish said. "But if everyone's gone—"

Blake considered for a moment. "Do you mind the kitchen, then?" he said. "I could use a cup of coffee myself."

He saw the relief on Parrish's face, and when they had made their way into the kitchen, he seemed more at ease. As Blake busied himself with the percolator, Parrish offered, "We always ate in the kitchen at home."

Blake glanced over his shoulder. "Home is Montana, I recall?"

Parrish nodded. "Missoula."

The coffee began to perk, filling the sunny kitchen with its cheerful bubble. Blake pulled out a chair for Parrish, and sat in one himself. "You don't plan on going back?"

Parrish sat down. He was silent for a moment, and Blake wondered if perhaps he didn't want to converse with a servant. It was a little out of the ordinary, having a guest in the kitchen, especially with the family away. But he guessed Parrish had come to tackle Mr. Preston about the column. The major's mouth was set in a hard line, and he looked as if he had not slept well.

At length, he answered. "It's a ranch," he said. "Cattle and horses. Wheat." He lifted the remnant of his arm in explanation, and raised his eyes to meet Blake's.

Blake pursed his lips. "Surely," he said gently, "there are things you could do. Help you could give your family."

"I wish I could. The thing is—" His mouth twisted. "The damned arm is worse than useless, Blake. I can't bear anything to touch it. Even the shirt sleeve hurts."

"Is that a problem in your work, then?"

Parrish gave a short, bitter laugh. "Not anymore."

Blake got up to pour the coffee, and brought two cups back to the table. He set one in front of Parrish. "What's happened?"

Parrish drew a breath, and released it in a rush. "Lost my job." He said it swiftly, as if to get it over with, as if the words themselves caused pain.

Blake's heart ached with shame. This was why Preston had written the column. The war had not changed the youngest Benedict at all, except perhaps to make him more wily, more subtle. More dangerous than before. He said heavily, "I'm so sorry, Major. That's bad luck."

Parrish, with his cup halfway to his lips, said, "Bad luck. Yes."

Blake sat back in his chair, holding his cup, watching the swirl of steam rise from it. What could he say? It was not for him, a servant, to offer counsel.

Frank watched the old Negro's face. It was odd to be sitting here, in this gleaming kitchen, with someone like Blake. He experienced an irrational urge to tell him everything. He wouldn't, of course. He had been raised to keep his feelings to himself. Even at dinner with Margot he had been constrained by his sense that to reveal anything of his feelings was to show weakness. And he had no idea how people normally dealt with servants.

The hired men at home were like family—they slept in the bunkhouse, or at least Danny Jones had, before he died in France—but they ate with the family, attended church with the family, went along with them to weddings and dances and picnics.

Blake was different from the hired men Frank had known. There was something elegant about him. Something refined and appealing.

When Blake looked up from his coffee cup, the expression on his face was one of sympathy and some other, more complicated emotion. Frank had the fleeting thought that Blake looked ashamed. But that was foolish, of course. What would he have to feel shame over?

"Major Parrish." Blake's deep voice resonated in the high-ceilinged kitchen. "I'm very sorry about your post at Boeing. I was under the impression things were going well there."

Frank shrugged. "Not well enough, it seems." Again he felt that absurd urge to tell this kindly old man everything—about his dinner with Margot, his confusion, the damned flowers, the insult Preston Benedict had thrown at his sister. Of course he couldn't do that. Blake was no doubt as loyal to Preston as he was to Margot and the rest of the Benedicts.

And Frank didn't want Preston's words to reach Margot's ears. It could only hurt her to hear what her brother had said.

He looked away, fearing his weakness would show in his eyes. He fixed his gaze on the large aluminum clock hanging on the kitchen wall. "I'll find another position."

"Of course you will. I'm sure Mr. Dickson would be happy to help."

Frank wasn't at all sure that was true. Unless he could set things straight with Preston Benedict, he feared his friendship with the family would be at an end.

He drained the coffee cup, and set it on the table. He stood up, automatically smoothing his left sleeve into the pocket of his jacket. "Thank you for the coffee, Blake. I'll let you get on with your day."

Blake stood, too. "Before you go—could I ask you something, Major?"

"Of course." Frank stood, his hand on the back of the chair, as Blake took both their cups to the counter.

Blake turned to face him. "There was a man here. A man who was with Mr. Preston in the war. I wondered if you might know him."

"You mean Carter."

"So you do know him."

"Not well. He was Preston's batman. And I saw him when I— that is, I saw him the other day. With Preston."

Blake nodded. "He was here the other night, very late. He said he needed money."

Frank raised his eyebrows. "He asked *you* for money?"

"He wanted me to wake Mr. Preston. Naturally, I refused—it was after midnight, and the family was asleep."

"Why should Preston give him money?"

"This Carter said he had done some work, and needed to be paid. I gave him a meal, and I offered him what money I had if he would tell me what the work was." Distress pulled at his mouth and creased his forehead. "He said Mr. Preston paid him to put a word in certain ears. A rumor."

"Did he tell you what it was?"

"He did." Blake looked grave. "It was about Dr. Margot. I didn't tell her, because I knew how it would hurt. I don't like to repeat it, and I don't think it will come to anything, but—I've been wondering if this Carter is a dangerous man. We have ladies in the house. I have to think of their safety."

Frank considered this. He didn't want to add to his troubles with Preston, but Blake was right. There were other people in Benedict Hall to consider. He said carefully, "If the Benedict ladies were part of my family, I wouldn't want Carter around them. He—"

The telephone rang in the hall, interrupting him. Blake excused himself, and went to answer it. Frank followed, turning away from the hall table where Blake was speaking into the receiver. He heard his name as he walked to the coatrack and plucked his Stetson from its hook. He was just settling the hat on his head when Blake said, "That was Dr. Benedict. I'm going to fetch her from the hospital for a house call. She wants me to offer you a ride, since I'll have the car out."

An automatic refusal rose to Frank's lips, but he didn't speak it. He couldn't help thinking how nice it would be to see her again. She wouldn't have time, he supposed, for a meal, but he could ask. Try one more time. "Thanks," he finally said to Blake. "Awfully nice of you. Of both of you."

Margot sat beside Frank in the back of the Essex, first tossing in her medical bag. She said, "It's good to see you, Frank. I'm sorry about the other day. You could see—"

"It's all right," he said. "Good to see you, too."

And it was. He had forgotten how dark her eyes were, how much he liked the firm line of her jaw and the way her short hair brushed her cheeks. Her long calves looked elegant beneath her short skirt.

She said, "I need to go to Thea's. Her husband's taken a turn for the worse, and she got a neighbor to call me at the hospital. Their house is in West Seattle, and the trolley doesn't reach. Blake, we can drop Frank at Boeing on our way."

Frank's eyes met Blake's in the mirror. "Well," Frank said. "Drop me anywhere convenient. Not Boeing."

Margot turned to him in surprise. "You're not working today?"

He made himself meet her gaze. "I lost my job."

"No! But I thought—" She stopped, and put out her hand to him. Her fingers were firm and strong through her gloves, and before he could think better of it, he took her hand and held it. It felt good to touch her, and to be touched, even through the thin leather of her gloves.

"Afraid so," he said. "Two days ago."

"I'm so sorry, Frank. You must be terribly disappointed."

"I liked the work," he said.

She was shaking her head and frowning. "I don't understand. I know Father spoke to Bill Boeing just last week. He said everything was going well. He was grateful to have you."

Frank was searching for a way to explain when Blake said, over his shoulder, "Mr. Preston printed something unpleasant about Major Parrish in his column."

Margot's hand tightened on Frank's. "What was it? Why would he do that?"

Frank had to look away from her intense gaze, out to the glistening waters of Elliott Bay beyond the pier. "We had a disagreement." He saw they had reached Cherry. "Here will be fine, Blake. Thank you."

Blake pulled the car to the curb, and Frank released Margot to put his hand on the door.

"Wait," she commanded. "Blake, what's this about? What's Preston done?"

The edge in her voice, the quick fury, made Frank look at her again. She was leaning forward, tension in every line of her body.

"Margot, I don't—" Frank began.

She cast him a swift look, and he saw in an instant that she knew what her brother was. She understood, perhaps better than he did. There was no need to explain.

He opened the car door. "You have a patient waiting," he said. "Let's talk soon." Before she could object, he stepped out of the car, only bending to say briefly, "Thanks for the lift, Blake."

Margot said, "Come to the house tonight, Frank."

"I don't think that's best." And then, fearing she would misunderstand, he said, "Perhaps another time." But as he closed the door and the car pulled away, he doubted there would be another time. He stood watching, lifting his hand, as the Essex pulled away.

"Blake," Margot said. "What did Preston write about Frank?"

"It wasn't good," Blake said heavily. He drove with his usual deliberate speed. "He accused him of brawling in the street. He didn't use Major Parrish's name, but I have a good idea there's no other amputee engineer working at the Boeing Airplane Company."

"Why didn't you tell me?"

"All of this happened in the middle of Loena's illness, Dr. Margot. It was my judgment that you had more pressing concerns."

"But why would Boeing fire Frank over one of Preston's silly columns?"

"Mr. Dickson would know more, but I suspect there's pressure from the city government. I've heard your father say that the mayor and the council have their doubts about Boeing using Lake Union to land the seaplanes. There was that crash, you remember. In the lake."

"So Preston did this on purpose. But why?"

Blake only shook his head, and Margot leaned back in weary frustration. "I like him, Blake. Frank, I mean."

"I like him, too, Dr. Margot."

"Do you think Preston did it just to hurt me?"

Blake hesitated before he said, slowly, and in a voice rough with sorrow, "I'm not sure Mr. Preston needs a reason."

*   *   *

Thea's house was small and dingy, with a flat roof and a neglected patch of lawn in front. The next-door neighbor was pushing a mower around his own yard, and he looked up curiously when the Essex pulled up and parked. When Margot went in, calling out to Thea that she had arrived, she was struck by how spare everything was. A brown divan rested beneath the curtained front window, with a matching armchair drawn up before an empty fireplace. The kitchen opened to the right, a narrow, dark room with a wooden table and two chairs. There seemed to be only one bedroom at the end of a short hallway. Margot felt a twinge, thinking of the beauty and space of Benedict Hall compared with the meanness of the Reynolds home, to say nothing of the Essex waiting in the street outside. It occurred to her for the first time that she had no idea how Thea got to work.

Thea emerged from the bedroom, her face haggard, her graying hair straggling from its pins. "Margot, thank you for coming. I'm so sorry about the office—"

"Nonsense. Where's Norman?" Margot said.

"He couldn't get out of bed this morning. His breathing is so bad."

"Let's have a look at him." Margot took off her gloves as she followed Thea down the short hall and into the bedroom.

Here a small window had been opened to the fresh air, and dimity curtains billowed slightly in the breeze. A lamp beside the bed burned weakly, shedding just enough light so Margot could see. An emesis basin and a small stack of towels rested beside the lamp, along with a pitcher and a glass.

Norman Reynolds lay propped on pillows, but his head was pulled back as he struggled for breath. His lips were blue, and when she picked up his hands, the nails were gray. Despite the open window, the odor of necrotic flesh overpowered the scents of salt air and newly mown grass.

She said quietly, "Good morning, Norman."

Thea said, "It's Dr. Benedict, Norman." Her husband's closed eyelids flickered.

Margot opened the clasps of her bag, and took out her stethoscope and a pair of rubber gloves. She pulled on the gloves, then affixed the earpieces. Thea opened Norman's flannel nightshirt, and Margot bent to press the chestpiece to his skin. She was interrupted by a spasm of his coughing, while Thea pressed a towel to his lips. When she tried again, she found that it was, as Thea had already surmised, very bad. Norman's lungs bubbled as if he were trying to breathe thick liquid through a straw. She imagined the seared tissue struggling to flex, to open and close. There was little she could do beyond another dose of potassium iodide.

When she had done what she could, she drew Thea back into the front room. "There's one other thing we can try, Thea. A physician named Haldane has been administering oxygen with an anesthetic mask. It may help. I'll have to find a source for oxygen bottles."

"Thank you."

"And don't worry about the office. Stay here with Norman."

Thea nodded wearily, and Margot asked, "Do you have anyone to come and help you?"

"A neighbor. The one who telephoned."

"Good. I'll come back tonight."

"What will you do about the clinic, though? You'll need someone."

"I'll manage."

"And what about Dr. Whitely? Are you going to have to go before the board?"

"I am. But I can manage that, too." Margot touched Thea's shoulder. Thea looked up, her eyes full of the grief that was drawing nearer by the moment. "I'm so sorry, Thea. I wish I could do more for him."

"I know. Thank you."

As Margot walked across the neglected lawn to the Essex, she drew a deep, rib-expanding breath. Such a simple act, breathing, filling her lungs right to the brim with sweet, fresh summer air. It was a sensation Norman Reynolds would never again experience. As Blake drove her away, she glanced back at the little house that looked so tired and worn. As worn as poor Thea. "Good God, Blake," Margot said softly. "What human beings do to each other!"

"I know, Dr. Margot. I know."

Suddenly, she didn't think she could bear to be alone, to think about this all by herself. She wanted the company of someone who understood. Who liked her. She blurted, "Blake. Do you have a telephone number for Major Parrish? At his rooming house?"

She heard the smile in Blake's voice. "I believe I can find it, Dr. Margot. Would you like me to call him?"

"No. No, just get me the number, if you please. I'll call him myself."

CHAPTER 12

Preston cursed, and kicked at a skinny mutt nosing around a trash bin near the *Times* building. He had succeeded in getting Parrish fired, but his other plan had gone awry. He had no one he could blame, in this case. He had ruined it himself. He must be getting soft, living the way he did, with his mother and Hattie fussing over him, and all the old biddies crowding around in hopes of a mention in his column. He should have let the stupid girl die.

It had been a moment of weakness. Of believing his own press. Of wanting to remain the hero in his mother's eyes, and not wanting his father to give him that measuring look, or Dick to eye him as if he had just popped out of a sewer.

And now everyone thought Margot had saved Loena's life! As if all of her witch doctoring could have done it—enemas, for Christ's sake, or vinegar soaks. It was a great shame he couldn't have just shown her the sapphire, told her its story, made clear to her that it was *he* who had allowed the little slut to live. Instead, Dr. Margot Benedict was now the great healer, the miracle worker! Resentment at the irony made his teeth ache.

This morning, over breakfast, Father had fixed him with his gimlet eye. "Preston," he said, "how are things at the *Times*? Going well?"

Preston had looked up over his plate of eggs and ham, and grinned. "Just dandy, Pater."

His mother beamed from the other end of the table. She had a copy of the paper folded beside her plate. "Lovely column today, Preston," she said. "You should read it, Dickson dear. Listen to this:

> Will Seattle's Pine Street be the Western version of New York's Fifth Avenue? If Frederick & Nelson's devoted clientele is any measure, it could well happen, and happen soon. Ladies of fashion know that Frederick's is the place to find the latest hat or frock, the finest gloves or stockings, in designs to rival anything New York can offer. Frederick & Nelson offers a ladies' luncheon every Tuesday in their tearoom. When this reporter dropped by, he was treated to an elegant display of the latest *modes* worn by the leading ladies of Seattle fashion. The Misses Sorensen, of the West Seattle Sorensens, both sported long Parisian scarves of painted silk—"

Dickson put up a hand, and Edith's voice trailed off. She said, with a tentative smile, "But Preston writes very well, don't you think? Everyone says so."

"Do they." Dickson raised one thick gray eyebrow. He put one fist on the table as he turned his dark gaze back to his son. "I saw Bill Boeing yesterday. There was evidently some unpleasantness with one of his engineers. He tells me you saw fit to write about it in the paper."

Edith's smile faded, and she turned a confused look on Preston. "What unpleasantness? What happened, dear?"

Dick, across the table from Preston, laid down his fork.

Ramona said, "Oh, it was nothing, really."

Dick said, "You read it, Ramona? You didn't tell me."

"Or me," Edith said. She frowned. "When was this?"

Ramona said, "Mother Benedict, I didn't think you would—that is—well, I liked it, because it was interesting to read something that wasn't just parties and dresses and things. I didn't think you'd care for it, though."

"I would hardly call it nothing," Dickson said. "Bill Boeing certainly thinks it's something. It caused him a lot of difficulty with the city council. It should have been kept private, in any case."

"Why private?" Preston said. He strove to keep his tone light. "I'm a journalist. I write the news as I see it."

"Journalist." Dickson waved his hand, brushing the term aside.

Preston had to breathe to release the pressure building in his gut. When he dared trust his voice, he said, "I don't see how this concerns you, Father."

"Everything to do with my family concerns me."

Dick said, "I told you to watch your step, Preston."

"Mind your own fucking business, Dick," Preston snapped.

Edith gasped, and Ramona said, "Preston! Please!"

His father glared, and Preston said hastily, "I'm sorry, Mother. Ramona. Too much time with soldiers." He contrived an innocent, round-eyed look of chagrin.

Edith said faintly, "I suppose so, dear. But that word. My goodness."

"You're absolutely right, Mater. I hope you'll forgive me." He pushed back his chair, hoping to escape the whole absurd scene.

His father, however, like the bulldog he resembled more every day, persisted. "Preston, our family business stays out of the paper in the future."

Preston stared at his half-finished breakfast. Tension grew in his belly, an explosion waiting to happen. His breastbone throbbed with it. "Father. I think you're overreacting."

"I still don't know what happened," Edith said in a plaintive tone.

Dickson said, "Preston was in a street fight with Major Parrish. A one-armed man! Then he wrote about it in the paper where anyone could see."

"He attacked *me*," Preston protested, and then wished he hadn't. He sounded like a wounded child.

"You cost him his job," Dickson said. "Bill Boeing is none too happy about it. And neither am I."

Ramona glanced sideways at her mother-in-law. "Does Margot know?"

No one answered her.

Now, remembering that scene, Preston yearned to break something, to bash someone, but he didn't dare. Not after his pose of innocence in the whole Parrish altercation. He had his column to write, and a deadline looming, but he couldn't go to the *Times* in this mood.

He turned away, striding back the way he had come. He would go down into the Tenderloin, to that flophouse where Carter was living. He would pay up, maybe take the silly sod for a drink. It was probably best to let everything blow over, calm down for a while. He had time.

He pressed the sapphire against his chest, and let its weight ease the tension in his belly. Yes, he had time. Of course. He had plenty of time. It could wait.

Margot swept the floors of the examining room and reception, and stowed the broom and dustpan in the back storage closet. She had run the autoclave, and disinfected the examining table. She washed her hands, and went around turning out the lights. It had been a quiet afternoon, but she had seen three patients. She felt a modest sense of satisfaction.

She was putting on her hat when Frank stepped in through the front door. His eyes were a vivid blue beneath the brim of his Stetson, and he looked very tall in the cramped clinic.

"I hope I'm not late."

She smiled at him, and pulled her gloves from her pocket. "Your timing is perfect. I've just finished."

He held the door for her to pass through, and took her medical bag from her as they turned down Post Street. She stepped to his left side. He flinched, but she let her fingers rest, with the lightest of touches, just under his upper arm. His gaze came down to hers, and she leaned a little closer. "Just enough to hold on to," she said. He blinked, and then laughed.

She liked walking next to him down the street. She liked him being taller, and she liked the tilt of his hat brim and the length of his steps. He smelled like soap and fresh air and, just faintly, of whisky. Once or twice someone turned a head to watch them pass, and Margot didn't mind that at all.

He led her toward Pioneer Square, to the Merchant's Café. "I booked a table," he said. "Hope it's all right."

"Of course," she said. She wondered if he knew the upper floor of the building was a brothel, and decided he couldn't. He would never have brought her here if he did. She hoped he wouldn't find out. She said, "You've seen what the food is like at home! We all love Hattie, but the Benedicts eat out a great deal."

Holding her bag in his right hand, he struggled a bit with the door handle. Margot stood back, resolutely leaving him to it. In a second he had the door open, and he propped it with his shoulder as she went through. As the waiter held her chair, she noticed how deft Frank had become, setting her bag down quickly beneath the table so his hand was free to help her with her coat. He shrugged out of his own overcoat, and smoothed his empty sleeve into the pocket of his jacket before he sat down.

"You're getting used to it," she said.

He glanced at her in surprise. "Used to what?"

"Doing everything one-handed. It's hardly noticeable."

"About time, I guess."

"I would imagine, in the hospital, the nurses did everything for you."

"They did a lot."

The waiter bent to ask if they cared for a drink. Margot said,

"Are you serving?" He nodded, pencil poised over his pad. "Not Vine-Glo, I hope?"

The waiter laughed. "Not here, ma'am. I promise."

Frank said, "If you have scotch, I'll have one."

"I'll have the same," Margot said. She hoped Frank had enough money, but she didn't dare ask. She would not repeat her previous mistake.

He murmured, "So much for Prohibition."

"The farmers in the valley are making more money on moonshine than on their crops."

"So I've heard."

"A milk bottle full of gin for three dollars. It's a lot worse than letting people buy legitimate alcohol at a decent price. And a lot more dangerous."

He looked away, as if there was something interesting on the wall behind her. There was silence until she ventured, "How's the job search?"

He leaned back in his chair. "Frustrating." She waited, eyebrows raised. He seemed to fumble for words. "No one will talk to me. It's as if—"

"As if what?"

He looked around the room at the other diners, then to the window, where the lights of Pioneer Square flickered in the long summer twilight. "Never mind," he said. "No point in talking about it. Tell me about your day instead."

She said ruefully, "I didn't think anyone wanted to hear about a doctor's work. My family certainly doesn't. Ramona thinks it's disgusting. My mother always changes the subject."

Frank shifted his left shoulder, as if trying to ease it, and smiled a little. "I wouldn't ask if I weren't interested."

"Father thinks I should turn the large parlor at Benedict Hall into my office. He offered to put in a separate entrance, and he says I would have a better class of patients on Fourteenth Avenue than on Post Street."

"And would you?"

She grinned. "Probably. But can you imagine Mother tolerating a lot of sick people marching through her house?"

Their drinks came, neatly disguised in teacups and perched on saucers. Margot lifted her cup, and the gesture seemed to mirror the lifting of her heart. It was lovely to be sitting here with a handsome man. It made her feel girlish and young. Happy. "Here we go, then, Frank. I'll tell you about my day, and when you've had enough, stop me."

He drank from his own cup, then set it down, slightly too far from his hand. "Tell me."

"Without Thea, it's a bit difficult," she began. He watched her with an intentness that was both flattering and a little unnerving. "I didn't realize how much I depend on her."

His fingers twitched, reaching toward his cup, then resisting. Margot noted the movement, and filed it away to think about later. "I did have patients today, though."

"You don't always?"

"Not private ones. Plenty of them at the hospital." She sighed. "Mostly poverty cases! They give me the leftovers, I'm afraid."

"Because you're young." His restrained smile gave her that burst of giddiness again.

She took another sip. "And female."

He gave a measured nod. "I didn't see a single female doctor in the army."

Margot raised her eyebrows. "Really? There are a few, but . . . Actually, there were more women physicians in America twenty years ago than there are now."

"Didn't know that."

The waiter put a menu in her hands. She held it without opening it, frowning. "You know, Frank, they've made it harder for women to get into medical school, deliberately harder. Rules and restrictions, reduced hospital privileges, all sorts of things. They want women to be nurses, not physicians."

He seemed to consider this for a time. He picked up his cup and took a shallow sip. As he set it down, he said, "All the more credit to you, then, for making a success of it."

"I'm not there yet!"

"You will be," he said. "You had patients today, after all."

"None with any money. That's what Father would point out."

Margot watched as he took another careful sip of scotch. Rationing it. She wondered if it was because he couldn't afford another.

The waiter came and Margot hastily opened the menu and scanned it. They ordered, baked salmon for both of them, with fried potatoes and fresh greens from the valley. When the menus had been whisked away, Margot put her elbows on the table and cupped her chin with one hand. "Tell me more about Montana," she said. "And don't say there's nothing to tell."

Frank dropped his eyes, and his fingertip traced the edge of his cup. "Dad runs around five hundred head of cattle, mostly Angus with a few Herefords. He keeps about two hundred acres for seed stock, too, kind of a specialty of our ranch." He pushed the cup in a circle, then released it, tapping his fingers on the tablecloth. "His ranch."

Margot resisted an urge to take his hand, to still those restless fingers. "And your mother?" she asked.

"She works just as hard as Dad. Always has. They want me to come home, but . . ." He lifted his left arm, as if that explained everything.

"Frank," Margot said. "Amputees do all sorts of jobs. You're getting better at handling things with one hand every day."

He turned his face away from her, and the lights from the square glistened on his profile. His jaw flexed, and his fingers stretched toward the teacup again.

"What is it?" she asked.

He was silent for a moment. She watched his profile, saw the twist of his mouth. When he began to speak, his voice was so low she had to lean forward to hear him. "I had a pony when I was small," he said. "An Icelandic pony, about twelve hands, black as coal. My dad bought him cheap at an auction somewhere, probably because he was so small no one wanted him. He wasn't big enough to do much work. But I rode that pony everywhere, every day." He chuckled, but it was a mournful sound. "I would have slept in his stall if my mother had allowed it.

"We were riding in the snow one day, and the pony stepped in a gopher hole. Broke his leg." His mouth twisted again, a look Margot was coming to recognize as the only reaction to pain he allowed himself. "I ran back to the house, screaming all the way. Dad made me go back with him, and watch as he put my pony down. Shot him in the head with his rifle. I had hysterics."

Margot hardly dared breathe for fear he would stop talking.

"He waited till I stopped crying enough to hear him, and he told me, 'Real life, son.' That was all he ever said about it." Frank sighed, and opened his hand, as if to let the story go. "A ranch is no place for soft hearts, Margot. It's a place for men with two arms, two hands. It's no place for a cripple."

She could barely find her voice. "That's a terrible story, Frank. But you're not a cripple. You have so much—"

"Don't." The expression on his face was like iron, his vivid eyes gleaming in the candlelight. She would have bet his father looked just like that when he made a little boy watch him shoot a beloved pony.

Their food arrived, and Margot let the matter drop. She finished her drink, and Frank, finally, emptied his as well. The salmon was drenched in good dairy butter, and sprinkled with chopped parsley and chives. The potatoes were crunchy with fried onions. Frank seemed to throw off his moodiness, and they both ate with good appetite.

Over coffee, she told him that Loena would be going home from the hospital soon, and that her mother, under pressure, had agreed to have her back at Benedict Hall. She didn't tell him about having to face the board of directors in the morning. She wanted to speak of cheerful things, casual things.

The bill came, and Frank took money from his pocket and paid it. As they left the restaurant, Margot took his arm again. She meant to be careful, but she stumbled slightly on the sill, and gripped it harder than she intended.

Frank sucked in a noisy breath, and she looked up at him in surprise. "Did I hurt you?"

He shook his head, but his lips had gone white. She felt heat blaze through his sleeve.

She dropped her hand, alarmed. "Frank! Is it painful?"

He blew out the breath. "Sorry," he said. And then, through gritted teeth, "Goddamn it."

"Why Goddamn it?"

"Can't even walk my girl down the street," he said. He took a few steps. She stayed close beside him, but didn't touch him.

"Frank, it's been too long for you to still have that much pain! You should be healed by now. Is something wrong?"

He didn't answer. In the dim light, she saw the muscles of his jaw ripple.

Margot bit her lip as they walked, searching for a way to talk to him. When they reached the ironwork pergola with its carved benches, she said, "Let's sit a moment."

He stopped. There were a few people on the street, but the benches were empty. The lights of the square twinkled cheerfully through the dark. A couple passed, their heads bent together. Margot sat down, and scooted over to make room on her left. Frank sat, too, but he put her bag between them. With a decisive movement, she picked it up and set it on her other side. "Tell me about the arm," she said. "And about the surgery."

He was silent for a full minute, staring off into the summer night. She waited, pleating her gloves in her lap. She had learned that patients would often tell her what she needed to know, given enough time. It was important not to rush them.

Finally, he blew out a long breath, and let his stiff spine sag against the slats of the bench. "Sorry about swearing."

"Don't be silly."

He shook his head, and she felt that heat from him again, as if something burned inside his body, some banked fire that blazed up at odd moments. She resisted the impulse to take his wrist, feel his pulse.

"I understand the new prostheses are quite good," she ventured.

"The arm hurts all the time," he blurted, as if he were admitting some sin. She noted that he said "the arm," not "my arm." "They botched it out there in the East, in the field hospital. Tried to repair it in Virginia, but no dice. Turned out I couldn't tolerate the prosthesis. And—" Another pause. "It looks like hell, Margot."

"Let me see it."

"No."

She didn't argue with him, but she did battle inside herself. The surgery manual she had been studying had an extensive section on nerves of the arm, and amputation techniques. The physician in her wanted to examine him, to see what she might be able to bring to the problem. The other side of her clung to the sentence he had let slip in his moment of pain. "Can't even walk my girl down the street." His girl.

She gave him a sidelong glance. His lips were not so white now, and the heat radiating from him seemed to have lessened. His eyes were closed, his jaw set against whatever emotion troubled him.

"Frank," she said softly.

He opened his eyes, and looked into her face. "Have I ruined another evening?" he said.

"Of course not. It's been a lovely evening. But I'm worried about you."

"Don't. It's okay."

"But chronic pain—"

"I can deal with it." He stood up, and put out his hand to help her up. "It's getting late. I'll see you home on the streetcar."

"I could telephone for Blake."

He shook his head. "Let's not bother him. By the time he could get here, I'll have you at your front door."

In the streetcar, Margot took care to sit on Frank's right side, and when they stepped down and walked up Aloha, she put her hand under his right arm, though he was carrying her bag in his hand. The air was warm, sweet with the smell of pine and fir and the occasional fragrance of roses. It was beguiling, Margot thought, to walk this way, a man and a girl strolling together through a summer evening as if there were no tomorrow to worry about, no board of cynical physicians to face. It made her feel wistful. Vulnerable.

She knew better, by now, than to let herself be vulnerable.

Still, standing in the shadows of the front porch, looking up into the masculine face of Frank Parrish, she felt as soft as any naive girl. Her lips felt tender, and her belly trembled with a sensation that had no medical definition.

She felt him hesitate, and she wished she understood the protocol for such moments. It seemed to be one of those secrets people like Ramona knew, or her mother. She gave a small shrug. "Frank. I know I'm not like other women. I can't help it."

His chuckle was quiet. Intimate. He bent to set her bag down on the mat beside the door, and when he straightened, he put his arm around her waist and pulled her to him. Her eyes closed before his mouth found hers. His lips were firm, and his hand against her back was strong. She noticed, briefly, how clean his skin smelled, and then she stopped noticing anything but the feel of his mouth, the warmth of his chest against hers, and that tremulous feeling in her stomach. She kissed him back, leaning into him, tilting her head to the perfect angle.

It seemed she knew the protocol after all.

When he said good night, she stood where she was, watching him walk to the street. Her knees felt like water, and she leaned against the doorjamb until they steadied, smiling into the darkness. She waited a few more minutes, to allow the flush in her cheeks to subside, before she opened the door.

Preston twitched the parlor curtain back into place and turned to watch Margot pass the doorway. "Hey, doc," he called.

She stopped, and turned to face him. The room was dim, lit

only by the light of the fire. She squinted through the gloom. "Hello, Preston."

He crossed the parlor, raising his glass to her as he did so. Ice tinkled in the cut crystal, and light from the fire gleamed in the dusky liquid. "Not very dignified, was it?"

"Was what?"

"Necking on the front porch. You're not a schoolgirl!"

"You were watching me?" Her eyes narrowed. "That's rude."

"Anyone could have watched you!" he exclaimed, laughing. "You were out there giving it away in full view, like some twit of a housemaid."

"Stop it, Preston." She stepped into the parlor and shut the door behind her. "We're not children anymore." She pulled off her hat in a careless motion, and stuffed her gloves into it. "This has to end."

"What has to end, sister dear?" He cocked his head to one side to give her his most winning smile.

"You know damn well."

He spread his hands, nearly spilling his drink. "Tell me. *Doctor*."

She took another step, until she was no more than an arm's length away from him. "I've never understood, Preston," she said. "All these years, I've never understood why you hate me."

He turned away and walked to the sideboard at a deliberate pace to pour more scotch into his glass. "You're an embarrassment, Margot. To the whole family."

"That's not true."

He faced her, his glass in his hand. "Oh, but it is. That revolting little clinic, those filthy people you see—you touch—"

"What do you care? It doesn't hurt you."

He gave a sour laugh. "It's loathsome."

"It's not, but never mind that." She crossed the room, and leaned one hip on the back of the sofa. It was utterly unfeminine, a man's posture. She folded her arms, and jutted her Benedict chin at him. "It started long before that, in any case. Years before

I went to medical school. I thought when you went to war, you would change. Grow up. Get over it."

"Get over it!" he spat. A fountain of rage began to build inside him. His face grew hot, and he tossed back the scotch in his glass. "What, like a bad cold?" His voice rose. "I was *stuck* with you, Margot! The big sister, the smart sister!"

She raised her eyebrows. In an infuriatingly mild tone, she said, "Why me, Preston? Dick's also older than you. And probably a whole lot smarter."

He thought he might choke on his anger. She gazed at him with those dark eyes as if she knew something. Anything. He wanted to take her by the neck, strangle her until she admitted her ignorance. "You don't fool me!" he shouted. "Father might not see through you, but I do!"

"See what?"

How he hated her, standing there, growing calmer by the moment as he grew so agitated he could hardly draw a breath. "Conniving! Pretending to be better than everyone else! All to make yourself Father's special, smart little girl! That's why—" He bit back the words, and turned his head away to stare into the fire crackling in the grate.

"That's why you did those things, Preston?" she asked. "That's why you bit me, and burned me, and shoved me out of trees or down stairs? Because you thought I was pretending?" He kept his gaze on the flames. "Answer me," she insisted, in that maddening, controlled voice. "You started torturing me when I was six years old. No one would believe me, no one would stop you. If it weren't for Blake—"

His head snapped up. "Blake! He's the worst of all!"

"Worst of what, Preston? What did anyone *ever* do to make you behave that way?"

He stared at her for long seconds, while fury simmered in his chest, vibrated in his fingers. She had no idea, at this moment, how close she was to death. At last.

"Maybe if you tell me," she said with that infuriating calm, "if you try to explain—maybe you'll be able to let go of it, to—"

"Goddamn it!" he shouted, so loudly the windows vibrated. She fell back, and he thought he had frightened her at last. "Don't play doctor with me, you phony bitch!" He heard the parlor door open, but he didn't look to see who it was. He was past caring.

He threw his heavy glass at Margot. Ice spattered over the floor as the thick cut crystal spun past her head. It struck the far wall with a heavy *thunk*.

"Preston!" It was Blake's deep voice, and Blake's heavy step. "Take control of yourself!"

Preston whirled to glare at him. He found he was panting, his throat burning as if he had swallowed fire. He hated the way his voice sounded, rising, thinning, the shriek of a child. "Leave me alone! You've been telling me to take control of myself all my life, and I—I—" He had to take a breath, his head spinning, his lungs aching for air. "I *hate* it!" He wished he had a knife in his hand, a gun, a sword. Something to make Blake back away, to bring fear to his face. He wanted to take control, all right, but not of himself. He wanted to control *them*. He *needed* to control them, and everything they stood for, the unfairness, the favoritism, the—

"Preston," Margot began.

He spun back toward her, one fist raised. "Goddamn you, Margot," he shouted. "Always the favorite, Daddy's precious girl! *Blake's* favorite! I wish you'd just—just—*die!*"

He lunged forward, but Blake's heavy hand, dark and strong, seized his wrist, held him back. There were more people in the room then, voices, cries of concern, lights coming on. Preston's free hand moved toward the sapphire. Margot watched him with that sharp gaze of hers, but he couldn't help that. It had all gotten away from him. He had to smooth this over.

He drew a shuddering breath, and pulled free of Blake's grasp.

From the doorway his father's voice rumbled, "What's going on down here?"

And his mother's quavering voice crying, "Preston! Darling, whatever's the matter?"

He let his shoulders slump, and pressed both hands to his face. "Oh, my God," he moaned. "What just happened? It's like—it's like Jerusalem all over again!"

In moments Edith was soothing him on the couch, ordering Blake to bring her a cold compress for his hot forehead. His father retrieved the glass, and poured him two fingers of brandy. Dick and Ramona hovered near the fire. Ramona, in her dressing gown, clutched Dick's arm and whimpered questions.

Margot stood against the far wall, her hands on her hips, her lips pressed into a line. Her eyes looked nearly black in the lamplight, and she watched him as if he were the devil himself.

He closed his eyes against her angry gaze. He would have to deal with her. He had let it go on far too long.

Roxelana had known what to do in a situation like this. She had persuaded the sultan to have his firstborn put to death, making way for her own son to rise to the throne. It had not been pleasant, but she had courage. She had not shrunk from what was necessary.

He would use her as an example. A model. It was past time to get Margot out of his way for good.

CHAPTER 13

As Frank relaxed onto the bench seat of the streetcar, he found himself smiling despite the fierce ache in his arm. The taste of Margot's mouth clung to his lips. His good arm could still feel the lean, vibrant warmth of her. She had kissed him back. She had leaned into him, her body pressed to his, her arms around his neck. He had no idea what he would do about all of it—he was a man with one arm, no job, and no prospects—but it felt good just the same. Elizabeth had never—she always kept a distance between them, and her kisses had been chaste and restrained. He could still sense the pressure of Margot's breasts against his chest, the bite of one hip bone as she moved closer to him, closer than he had been to any woman in a very long time. He let his eyes close, recalling that moment.

" 'Scuse me, mate?"

Frank opened his eyes, and flinched. "Sergeant Carter!"

Carter's light hair was limp and greasy beneath his dilapidated flat cap, and his jacket looked like he had plucked it out of a rubbish heap. His cheeks sagged, and his pale lashes clumped together. "Yeah," he said, with an aggrieved air. "It's me, right enough."

"What are you doing here?"

Carter tugged at his collar. His head hung at a sad angle, making him look like a beaten dog. "I was trying to see Benedict," he said. He had a worn duffel bag, and he pushed it between his feet. "But there was some sort of ruckus after you left."

Frank straightened. "A ruckus? What do you mean?"

"I was about to knock on the front door, and I heard shouting inside."

"Shouting? At Benedict Hall? I only left there ten minutes ago."

"I know, mate. I saw you."

Frank said tightly, "Explain yourself, Sergeant. What the hell happened?"

"I waited till you was gone, and then I went up on the porch. I heard Preston yelling at someone, and then there was a bang, and a whole bunch of people started talking."

Frank tensed, and a chill ran through him. "Preston was shouting?"

Carter blew out his lips. "Something fierce! That bloke has a terrible temper."

"What kind of bang was it?" Frank reached for the cord to ring for the streetcar to stop.

"Sounded like someone threw something." He sagged forward, and put his elbows on his knees. "It calmed down pretty fast after that. But I didn't dare knock."

Frank dropped his hand, and eyed Carter doubtfully. "That's the third time you've been up to Benedict Hall."

Carter's glance was mournful. "Yeah. How'd you know that?"

"Blake told me."

Carter made a face. "That nigger butler?" He shook his head. "Thinks he runs that family. Wouldn't let me see Preston."

"He fed you, I believe," Frank said.

"Oh, yeah. He did give me some eggs, now you mention it."

"And money."

"Not much."

"He didn't telephone for the police."

Carter heaved a wheezy sigh. "That's true."

"What were you doing there tonight?"

"I still need money. I want to go home."

"You think Benedict will give it to you?"

"Yeah. He owes me."

"Go back tomorrow, then. Or go to the *Times*."

"Oh, he wouldn't half like it if I showed up at his work!"

Frank shifted his weight on the bench seat, not liking to be close to the man. "Why do you care what he likes, if he's in your debt?"

Carter mumbled at his boots, "Don't dare cross Benedict. He'll do things to you."

"You're twice his size."

"Don't matter. He has ways."

Frank thought for a moment, as the streetcar rattled beneath the lights of Broadway. When it turned down Madison, he said, "My stop is coming up, Carter."

Carter's eyes flicked up to his, then away, then back again. "I thought I might tell you something, if you got some of the ready."

Frank hesitated. "You're not afraid Benedict will find out?"

Carter lifted his cap and scratched beneath his dirty hair. "Look, Major, I'm just trying to get enough scratch for a ticket home. I thought—if you had it—I'd get a train tonight. Get away before Benedict comes looking."

Frank put his hand in his pocket, and fingered the bills he had there. He thought hard for a moment. It would be good to know what Preston had been up to, and it would be good to get Carter away once and for all—that would give Blake some peace. It would be tough, though, if he couldn't pay Mrs. Volger his rent. He had spent half his cash on dinner. What remained was the last of his final paycheck. And he needed whisky.

The streetcar slowed. Carter said, "It was him blackballed you. Benedict."

"I guessed."

"There's more."

The streetcar clanked to a stop. Frank stood up, his hand still in his pocket. He gave Carter a hard glance. "You'll really go, if I give you the money?"

Carter stood up, too, a gleam of hope in his pale eyes. "Too bloody right," he said. "I want to get back to England and find a proper job."

Frank led the way down the steps. He stood beneath a street-light, not wanting Carter to follow him to Mrs. Volger's. He counted the money in his hand. "It won't get you to England," he said. "Maybe as far as New York."

Carter looked at the money, and his thick lips parted. Frank shoved the money back into his pocket, and Carter whined, "You ain't going to give it to me?"

"You have something to tell me first." Frank nodded in the direction of King Street Station. "I'll see you to the train, Sergeant. You can bare your soul on the way."

"Bare my—?"

"Tell me what's on your conscience."

They left Madison, and cut across on Fourth, heading toward the clock tower glowing above the city rooftops. Carter, with the air of one relieved to be divesting himself of a burden, told his story as they walked. He recited it with an impressive lack of compunction, nearly boasting as he spoke of planting rumors about Margot's practice. "Easy, it was," he said. "Just told all the whores if they needed fixing, Dr. Benedict would do it. Preston's sister. Word spreads fast through the cribs, and the blokes carry it home to their wives and girlfriends."

Frank gave him a look of pure loathing, but Carter wasn't watching him. "Wasn't hard puttin' the word out about you, either, Major, beggin' yer pardon." Voluble now, he chattered on as if none of his actions signified in the least, as if the ruining of careers was hardly worth mentioning. "Just chatted up a few blokes here and there, the docks, the factories, out in the alleys where the men stand around and smoke."

"But Preston's column—"

"Oh, yeah," Carter said, with another phlegmy laugh. "That

took care of Boeing. But Benedict wants you right out of Seattle. Whatcha do to him, Major? He don't like you one bit."

Frank said, "Seems he doesn't like you much, either, Sergeant."

"He used to do. Now I know too much."

"Why would you do those things for him? Why not just get an honest job?"

They walked in through the glass doors to the brightly lit lobby of King Street Station. It bustled with activity despite the late hour, dozens of voices echoing under its great dome. Frank walked with Carter to a booth, and he himself paid for the ticket, then handed it over. "You're going to get all the way to Grand Central in New York. Maybe you can get working passage on a steamer. Or go to the British Embassy."

Carter murmured something evasive. Frank gave it up. The man would probably steal what he needed, but there was nothing he could think of to forestall that. They sat on long wooden benches, waiting together in an uncomfortable silence, watching the people pass to and fro, wrangling their luggage and calling instructions to one another. Frank's arm had begun to burn in earnest, making him shift again and again in his seat. The sleeve of his coat chafed maddeningly. He wanted a drink, but having decided to get Carter out of the way, he meant to see it through.

When Carter's train was announced, Frank stood. Carter rose, shouldered his duffel bag, and looked down at the ticket in his hand. "Look, Major," he said. "You're a decent chap. I'm sorry I—well, I been pretty rotten to you."

Frank made no answer. He had no doubt Carter would go somewhere else and be just as rotten to other people.

Carter lifted his head as the conductor called the train a second time. "I just—look," he said again, evidently struggling with something. "You should know something. Something else about Benedict."

"What?"

Carter started shuffling toward the gate. Frank stayed beside him to see that the man boarded the train, and stayed aboard. "What else do I need to know, Carter?"

Carter held out his ticket, and the conductor checked it, then pointed to a car down the tracks. Carter went through the turnstile, then turned to face Frank across the iron rail that separated passengers from the terminal. "There's this jewel," Carter said. "A big old sapphire. Benedict got it out in Jerusalem."

Frank frowned. "He bought it?"

Carter barked an ugly laugh. "Hardly. Killed the bloke what owned it."

"You mean . . . murder."

"Bloody murder, yeah. Nasty scene, but that's not the point. There's something about that thing, Major. I can't explain it, but you want to watch out. He wears it around his neck. And that thing means Benedict can pretty much do whatever he wants."

"Sounds like superstition to me, Sergeant."

"Maybe." Carter's small eyes flicked from right to left, and Frank supposed he was choosing fresh marks for his time on the train. He shifted his duffel, and half turned, ready to walk away. "Leastways I've warned you, Major. You oughtta get that stone off him. It means trouble."

Frank shook his head. "Fairy tales. Forget it." He touched his hat brim with his fingers, and Carter took a last look at his face. Frank said quietly, firmly, "Have a good trip, Sergeant."

Breakfast at Benedict Hall was a chilly affair, despite the warmth of the July sun that brought out the gloss on the camellia leaves. Margot was still angry, and couldn't bring herself to speak to Preston when he came into the dining room. Her mother was having a tray in her room, and her father was as silent as she, glowering over his paper. Ramona drank coffee in silence, and nibbled at a piece of toast. She avoided Margot's eyes, but Dick grimaced at her across the table. "Rotten day for you, isn't it," he said.

Dickson looked up. "Why? What's rotten?"

Margot said, "I have to go before the hospital board this morning."

Dickson shook his paper with an angry rattle of pages. "Bunch of damned lady aunts, all exercised about nothing. You should let me put a flea in Peretti's ear, Margot!"

"Thanks," she said. "It's tempting, Father. But I think I'll have to manage this myself."

At the opposite end of the table, Preston worked his way through a plate of bacon and eggs without looking up. Margot made herself eat an egg and a piece of toast. Blake came in to refill the coffee cups. He gave her a speaking glance, and she managed to smile at him.

"They can't convict you with gossip," Dick said stoutly. "Just stand up to them, Margot."

Margot gave him an affectionate glance. "I'll do my best, Dick. Unfortunately, it's not about a conviction so much as an impression."

"What can they really do to you? They can't close your clinic."

"No. But they can deny me hospital privileges."

Silence fell again, broken only by the clink of flatware and the sounds of Blake and Hattie talking in the kitchen. Leona came in to collect empty plates. As she reached for Preston's, he looked up. "Loena comes home today, doesn't she?" he said. Leona nodded. "Good. That's good news."

Margot looked down the table at her younger brother. He looked so well it was almost unnatural. His skin was ruddy, his eyes clear, his fair hair springing vigorously over his forehead. He met her gaze, and gave her a limpid smile. "Good luck today, doc. I mean it."

Margot felt everyone looking at her, waiting for her to accept Preston's peace offering. She was aware of Blake standing guard in the doorway, and her father's worried glance. Ramona touched her finger-waved hair with one hand as she raised her painted eyebrows.

Margot couldn't do it. Better to say nothing than to reignite the fiery exchanges of the night before. Only Dick—and Blake—

could understand. Her father had made it clear long ago that he wanted no part of sibling struggles. And her mother, or Ramona—

Blake saved her from answering. "Are you ready to go, Dr. Margot?"

"Yes. I'll put in an hour at the clinic before I go to the hospital." She rose, pushing her chair back from the table. Just as she laid her napkin beside her plate, she saw the look of naked hatred that crossed Preston's face. It was gone in a heartbeat, but there was no mistaking it. She had been seeing that look all her life. Blake's expression, the swift lowering of his eyelids and the tightening of his lips, told her he had also seen it. It wasn't imagined, that look. They both knew what it meant.

Margot took a straight chair opposite the long table where the directors of Seattle General Hospital sat. There were four of them, gray-haired men who had been at the hospital for years before she entered medical school. Their long white coats, their grave expressions, and the coldness of the gray walls oppressed her. She wondered, as she took off her gloves and hat and laid them on a second chair, if this was the way patients felt when they came to the hospital, as if every element was arrayed against them.

She folded her hands in her lap, crossed her legs at the ankle, and waited.

"Dr. Whitely has leveled a serious charge, Dr. Benedict," said Dr. Peretti. He was the oldest of the physicians on the board, and he came from an old Seattle family. He laid his hand on the slender file in front of him. For a single faltering moment, looking into his cold gray eyes, Margot wished she had let her father put a flea in his ear after all.

She straightened her already stiff spine. "I'm aware of it, Dr. Peretti," she said. Her voice sounded thin in the spare conference room. "He told me—at a moment when I was dealing with a patient who was seriously ill—that he had heard a rumor I was performing abortions at my private clinic. There is no foundation

whatsoever for such a charge. There is no truth in it." She met
the eyes of each of the men, ending with Whitely.

Whitely gave her a tight smile. "This is not the only complaint
against you, Doctor." He had no folder, or papers of any kind. He
had a fountain pen in his fingers, and he toyed with it, tapping it
on the table. He glanced at the other doctors, then back at Margot. "You have displayed a pattern of disrespect."

"To whom?" Margot snapped. She knew she was glaring at
him, but she couldn't help it. Even now, the ruddiness of his nose
and cheeks bore ample witness to his addiction.

"To me, for one," he snapped back. He leaned back, tucking
the pen into the pocket of his coat, and giving her that cramped
smile again. "Your job, as a younger and less-experienced physician, is to follow my lead and learn from me in the operating theater. It is not—" His voice rose. "It is not to tell me how to do
my job!"

"You're speaking of Sister Therese?"

He made a gesture with one hand. "I don't remember the
name. Appendectomy."

One of the other men said, addressing Margot, "Can you explain yourself, Doctor?"

Margot found she was gripping her fingers so tightly her hands
had begun to ache. Deliberately, she released them, and let her
hands lie palm up in her lap. "Sister Therese presented with ab-
dominal pain characteristic of appendicitis. It was quite late in
the evening. As I am not yet allowed surgical privileges, the hospital called Dr. Whitely."

Whitely's eyes were like shards of ice, and his reddened cheeks
grew redder. She could tell he was gritting his teeth by the dis-
tortion of his fleshy jawline.

Margot had thought this through before she arrived this morning. She had discussed it with Blake, and thought over what
Alice Cardwell had said. There would be no better moment than
this. And no worse one.

"Dr. Whitely was intoxicated," she said bluntly. There was a
little indrawn breath, but she couldn't tell whose it was.

Peretti said, "I have to advise you to take care what you say, Dr. Benedict."

"Yes, Doctor," Margot said. Her voice still sounded fragile to her, but it was steady. Without inflection, she said, "The attending nurse was very concerned, as was I. I watched carefully, but I did not intervene until Dr. Whitely nearly punctured the appendix. I recalled his attention to the patient, and the surgery went forward without further incident."

"Ridiculous," Whitely grated. "If you thought that, you should have filed a complaint."

"I should have indeed," said Margot. "That was my error." She looked at Peretti as she added, "I was afraid of just such a situation as this one. My position at the hospital is tenuous."

Peretti said, "Why do you feel that, Doctor?"

Margot considered carefully before she answered him. "The hospital has been slow to grant me surgical privileges."

One of the other doctors said, "Perhaps that's just a question of caution."

Margot raised her eyebrows. "Caution? I had a successful residency, and my evaluations were all satisfactory. Male colleagues with similar resumes are already operating."

"Are you accusing us of prejudice?" Whitely demanded.

Margot's shoulders began to ache with the effort of controlling herself, and she knew she was hunching them. She tried to relax them as she addressed Peretti. "It wasn't easy for me to get into medical school. Since the Flexner Report, as I'm sure you know, requirements for women are considerably more stringent than those for men."

"If it were up to me," Whitely put in, "you wouldn't have hospital privileges here at all. Only your father's influence got you in to begin with."

Margot was shocked, for a moment, into wordlessness. When she could speak again, her voice shook. "That's neither true nor fair, Dr. Whitely. I earned my position at Seattle General."

He bristled. "Incompetence is—"

"*You* accuse *me* of incompetence, Doctor?" Her voice rose, echoing in the spare room.

Whitely folded his arms, and nodded down the table to his colleagues. "You see? It's a pattern. Insubordination, rudeness—and we still haven't dealt with this issue of performing illegal abortions in that little clinic of hers."

"I'm not performing abortions in my clinic, or anywhere else," Margot said.

"You've never performed one?" Peretti asked.

"In my residency, I did two therapeutic abortions, under supervision."

"So," Whitely said nastily, "you admit you know how."

"I can read a surgical manual as well as anyone, Dr. Whitely. That's why I knew you were about to kill Sister Therese."

Whitely leaped to his feet. His reddened cheeks darkened to an alarming purple, and he shrilled, "How *dare* you?"

Margot fixed him with a steady gaze. It was over in any case, that was clear. She might as well get it off her chest. When she spoke this time, she thought she sounded like herself again, her voice deep and steady. "Come, gentlemen. We all know it's true. You're protected, Doctor, because of your status, and because you've been here a long time. Sister Therese is not the first patient you've endangered, and everyone in the hospital knows it."

She turned her head to Peretti. "Should I assume, Doctor, that this entire meeting is for show? Since you've asked no substantive questions, I gather the decision about my future with Seattle General was taken before I arrived."

Peretti regarded her for a moment, his chin on his hand, his mouth pulled down. Finally, he said, "We know you performed your maid's abortion, Dr. Benedict."

"What do you mean, you know? How could you, since it's not true?"

"Evidently, it is true." Peretti straightened, and leaned back in his chair with a weary air. "Dr. Benedict, your brother came here this morning. He told us what you did, and why. He thought, for the honor of your family, that we should know."

Margot's lips parted, but she couldn't catch enough breath to speak. Whitely gave her a triumphant glare as he sank back into his chair.

"Your younger brother," one of the other doctors said. He was a friend of the family, someone who had known her—and Dick and Preston—since they were children. "It was Preston."

Margot's breath returned, but her composure was lost for good. She said shakily, "Of course. It would be." On trembling legs, she stood up. She tried to put on her gloves, but she fumbled with them, unable to match them to her fingers. She gave up, and kept them in her hand as she put on her hat.

"We can't have physicians who perform illegal surgeries practicing at Seattle General," Peretti said. "Your privileges here are terminated, Dr. Benedict. I'm sorry."

Margot said, through trembling lips, "I want you to know, Dr. Peretti, that it isn't true. My brother Preston was responsible for Loena's pregnancy, and he arranged for her to have an abortion down in the Tenderloin."

"Now, why should we believe that?" Whitely said. "And why would your brother lie about his own sister?"

Margot met his gaze with hers. "Why should you believe him?" she asked.

None of the men answered.

Margot walked slowly, carefully, fearful her knees would give way beneath her. Blake was waiting, and he held the car door for her without speaking. Not until she was inside did he turn in his seat to give her a look full of sympathy.

"Yes," she said in a whisper. "It was awful. As bad as I feared."

"Did they rule?"

"They revoked my hospital privileges."

He clicked his tongue and said heavily, "What can you do?"

"Not much. I can try another hospital—maybe that little children's hospital on Queen Anne, but that won't keep the clinic going. I need those emergency calls to pay my mortgage."

Blake turned forward to press the ignition. He adjusted his gloves and his hat, and put the car in gear.

Margot said hollowly, "Preston went to see them this morning, Blake. He told them I performed Loena's abortion. And they believed him."

Blake put out his arm to signal before he nosed the car into the street. "I saw him leave the house after I left you at your clinic," he growled. "He told Mr. Dickson he was going to work. He never mentioned the hospital."

They rode in silence for a few moments. Margot watched the buildings pass, then turned her eyes toward the bay, where the Pacific waters shifted and churned beneath a lowering sky. Dully, wearily, she reflected that it would rain soon. It always did.

Blake pulled up at the end of Post Street. He turned off the motor, but made no move to get out. "Dr. Margot, I have a little money put by."

"Absolutely not, Blake. I would never accept it. But I thank you, with all my heart."

"I should have done something before this."

"What do you mean?"

His gloved hands gripped the wide steering wheel, and his gaze was fixed on something beyond the windscreen. "I tried once," he said, his accent softening and broadening into the old Southern drawl. "I spoke to Mr. Dickson, because I knew Mrs. Edith wouldn't believe me."

"When was that?"

"It was getting bad," he said. "You were ten, I think, and Mr. Preston was eight."

"Oh. The stairs."

"Yes." He drew a slow breath. "No one could believe that a little boy like that . . ." His voice trailed off.

It was true. Despite the bite marks, the bruises, the cuts, once a burned hand, no one had believed Preston capable of deliberate violence. It had become a conspiracy of silence, and Blake had been Margot's only protector. Preston was the shadow that had darkened all of her childhood and adolescence.

Now, he had found an even more damaging way to hurt her.

She put her hand on the door. Blake made a move as if to get out and help her, but she said, "No. Don't get out, Blake, please."

She climbed out of the car and stood looking down at him. "It's worse since he came back from the war," she said. "He shouldn't have had any power in this. Any power over me."

Blake said, in a voice she barely recognized, "Never you mind, Dr. Margot." *Nevah.* "You let me handle it."

Her indrawn breath ached in her chest. "Be careful, Blake. He's strong now."

"Yes." Blake put his hand on the gearshift. "Don't you worry. Go to your clinic, see your patients."

"But what are you going to do? What *can* you do?"

He smiled up at her, a bleak smile that made her eyes sting. He started to say something, then evidently thought better of it, and turned his face forward.

As he put the car in gear, she stepped back. She stood very still, watching him turn the car and proceed up the street at his usual deliberate pace. She had a terrible feeling she should do something, call him back, stop him. She was tempted, despite the indignity of it, to run after the car, shouting his name.

She didn't, of course. He would have hated that. But she would wish, later, that she had done it anyway.

Blake had never been to Dickson Benedict's office. In the normal way of things, he would pull the Essex up in front of the Smith Tower and wait for his employer to emerge. Now, for the first time, he parked the automobile on the street. He brushed his coat with his gloved hands before he walked up the steps and into the paneled lobby.

The elevator operator, a Negro like himself, wearing a neat red-and-black uniform, gave him a strange look. "Floor?"

"Eighteen." He stood at the back, stiffly, as the bars of the elevator swept past floor after floor.

When the doors of the elevator opened, the operator said, "Eighteen. Uh, sir." Blake nodded to him as he stepped out.

He scanned the doors until he found the Benedict name. He lifted his hand to knock, then judged it was better to simply open the door. A receptionist seated behind a large black typewriter glanced up. "Good morning," she said in a frosty tone.

He crossed the room, taking off his cap as he went. "Good morning, ma'am. I'd like to see Mr. Benedict, please."

"Senior?" The young woman was pretty, rosy-cheeked and smoothly coiffed, but there was ice in her gaze. Briefly, Blake wondered if that ice melted when she was away from her wide, official-looking desk.

"Yes, ma'am," he said. "I'm Mr. Benedict's driver."

"Oh, yes. Blake, isn't it." This was not a question. She rose immediately. "Let me see if Mr. Benedict is free."

She went through a heavy oak door, closing it behind her, but she was back in only seconds. "Mr. Benedict will see you, Blake," she said. She stood to one side, holding the door, and shut it after he had walked through.

Dickson sat at a massive mahogany desk. Papers and ledgers were scattered across it, with an assortment of pens and ink bottles of different colors. He looked up as Blake came in, lifting his bushy eyebrows high. "I hope nothing's wrong, Blake?"

"I can't reassure you on that count, Mr. Dickson." Blake stood opposite the desk, his hat in his two hands, looking down at the man who had made the renaissance of his life possible.

Dickson's brows fell, drew together. "Everyone all right at home?" Blake nodded, and Dickson waved at a chair. "Sit down."

Blake would have preferred to stand, but he thought if he sat this conversation might seem less like a confrontation. He pulled the chair forward, so that when he sat down, he was facing Dickson directly. He held his cap on his lap. "Sir," he began. *Suh.* A pronunciation he had schooled out of himself years ago.

Dickson said, "Something to drink, Blake?"

Blake shook his head. "No, thank you, sir."

Dickson leaned back in his heavy wooden chair. It had armrests six inches wide, and he propped his elbows on these, steepling his fingers before him. "You sound very Southern today, Blake. What's happened?"

"It's the hospital, Mr. Dickson."

There was no mistaking the look of sorrow that pulled at Dickson Benedict's features. He gave a slight groan. "They didn't," he said, half under his breath.

"Yes, sir. They revoked Dr. Margot's privileges."

"Goddamn it. Those chickenhearted bastards." Dickson made a fist of one hand, and punched it into his other palm. "I wish Margot had let me—"

"Mr. Preston was there this morning, Mr. Dickson. At the hospital."

Dickson's brows rose again. "Preston? Why on earth? Was he visiting Loena?"

"I don't believe so."

"What was he doing there, then?"

Blake drew a deep breath. "I have something to say, Mr. Dickson. It's not easy. I would appreciate it if you would hear me out."

"Of course, Blake. You've earned the right to tell me whatever you think I should hear."

Blake nodded. It was the best thing Dickson could have said, and it was no surprise. He had always been fair. Hard sometimes, but fair. As he thought for a moment how best to begin, his employer waited, watching his face.

Blake let his gaze rise to the wide window. Beyond the glass, the clouds had dropped to hide the Olympics from view. A freighter chugged across the bay, its gray hull nearly the same color as the water. He said, "I blame myself for not trying harder to make you understand, years ago." Dickson shifted in his chair, but he didn't speak. "It's not seemly, a full-grown man complaining about a little boy. Especially a Negro telling tales about a white child."

Blake heard the short, small hiss of Dickson's breath. He kept his eyes on the somber view, watching the plume of smoke from the freighter's chimneys rise to blend with the rain-laden clouds. He began a slow nod, a rhythmic, repetitive movement to accompany the painful words he spoke. "It started when he was very young, no more than four. He bit Miss Margot, and he hit Mr. Dick with his toys. They complained, but everyone put it down to childish fights. As Mr. Dick got bigger, Preston left him alone. But Miss Margot—"

Blake dragged his gaze back to Dickson. Dickson was watching him from beneath his brows, his lips pulled into a hard line. He didn't speak.

Blake said, "He burned her, and got scolded for playing with matches. He drowned a kitten she was fond of, but no one believed he did it. I hoped he would grow out of it. I tried to believe it was just sibling jealousy, as you and Mrs. Edith did. Until the day he pushed Miss Margot down the stairs. She could have been terribly injured then, even killed." He hesitated. "I started watching, trying to be there as much as I could. He wouldn't hurt her if Mrs. Edith was around, or Mr. Dick. You may remember, sir, I spoke to you about it once."

Dickson nodded, gazing at Blake through heavy-lidded eyes.

One way or the other, Blake thought, this was the end of his position at Benedict Hall. He had understood that the moment he heard the news. It made him immensely sad, but he saw no other choice. He said, "We thought it might be better after he came back from the war."

Dickson growled, "Who thought?"

"Dr. Margot and I, sir." He hesitated. "It's worse, though. Worse than ever." *Evuh.*

"How?"

Blake explained the night visit of the man Carter. "I gave him what money I had, Mr. Benedict, and he confessed to me that Mr. Preston had paid him to spread rumors. And then today—sir, Mr. Preston went to the board and told them Dr. Margot performed Loena's abortion."

Dickson closed his eyes, and pressed his forefingers against the lids. He said in a voice like gravel, "Blake. Are you sure she didn't?"

Blake stared at Dickson in disbelief. "I am," he finally said. *Ah am.* "Aren't you?"

Dickson opened his eyes, dropping his hands to the arms of his chair. "I can't see why Preston would lie."

Blake paused as he searched for the words he needed. He decided, in the end, there were none good enough, none that could explain. He could only be blunt. "I'm so sorry, Mr. Dickson." He spoke ponderously, painfully. "There's something wrong with Mr. Preston. There's something wrong in his soul."

Dickson gripped the armrests of his chair as he spoke. "Blake. I don't know the man you're describing. That's not my son. It couldn't be." He didn't sound angry, which was odd, Blake thought. He sounded sad.

"No one wants to hear such things, Mr. Dickson. I understand that."

"He can be foolish. He's a bit frivolous—young men are."

Something sharp and hurtful twisted in Blake's chest. He said, "Yes, sir," very quietly.

Dickson said, a little defensively, "I offered to help Margot with the board."

"Yes, sir. She wanted to handle it on her own. Perhaps now—"

"I don't see why Preston would speak against her. But I'll ask him."

It was the same old argument. Justification. Rationalization. Blake turned his cap in his lap, one revolution, then lifted his hands from it. He had no further argument to make.

Dickson said, with some gentleness, "What is it you would have me do, Blake?"

Blake could only shake his head. He had run out of words. There was nothing left for him to do but take action. He would have to confront Preston himself.

He wished he had done it when he was a younger man.

CHAPTER 14

The rain cleared away in the middle of the afternoon, and the roads and lawns and sidewalks dried quickly in the mild sunshine. The populace adopted a sort of giddy mood, celebrating the fragile summer weather. They walked the streets in shirtsleeves, hatless, tipping up their faces to feel the sun on their cheeks. It still felt cool to Blake, despite thirty years in this northern city. He should have gotten used to the pallid Seattle summers by now, but somehow, when August came, he yearned for the melting heat of the Carolinas. Old bones, he thought now. Old bones are always cold.

He drove home from the Smith Tower to Benedict Hall, and left the Essex in the drive. He saw no point in going into the house. There was no one he could confide in.

He felt every one of his years as he climbed the stairs to his apartment over the carriage house. How had it come to be that he was so lonely? He was hardly ever alone, yet there was no one to share this burden with him. The only person who would understand would also adamantly try to dissuade him, and he couldn't allow that. He would do this for her sake.

He spent the afternoon alone, gathering his few defenses. He wished he had said just one more word to Dr. Margot, something she would understand later, but it was too late for that now. He took comfort in knowing she would understand. Someone had to protect her, or one of these days Preston would do more than just ruin her reputation and destroy everything she had worked so hard to achieve. One of these days, Preston Benedict would succeed in killing his sister.

Blake carried his teacup to the sink, rinsed it, and set it in the strainer. He stared through his window at the elegant house on the other side of the lawn. It looked peaceful and well organized. The lawn was clipped and green. The walls glowed clean and white in the sunshine. The camellia stood proud and tall, its glossy leaves shading the north-facing windows. It was the most beautiful place Blake had ever lived, and it was hard to leave it.

But it was time. He took off his driving coat and hung it over the back of a chair. He took his old canvas jacket from its peg and put it on. He left his cap on the table. On his way out, he picked up his marble-topped cane. He opened the front passenger door of the Essex and laid the cane on the seat, where he could quickly put his hand on it. He saw Hattie looking at him from the kitchen window, where she had begun dinner preparations. He nodded to her as if there was nothing unusual about the afternoon. He got into the driver's seat, pressed the ignition, and rolled the big car out of the drive, turning left on Fourteenth Avenue, then right down Aloha.

Preston was just emerging from the *Times* building, chatting with an older man, when Blake pulled up to the curb. Blake didn't get out of the car, but waited while Preston, looking pleased to have the car come for him, said good-bye to his companion and opened the door to let himself into the backseat.

As he settled himself, he said, "Blake? Where's your cap?"

"I left it home." Blake heard the soft slur of his Carolina accent, but Preston didn't seem to notice. He pulled the car out into the road, and drove south on Fifth, then east on Madison.

"So, what's the occasion? You made me look important to my

editor, back there." Preston leaned back in the seat, and chuckled. "Thanks for that, Blake."

Blake said nothing.

A moment later, Preston said, "Blake—you missed the turn."

"Yes, sir." *Suh*.

Preston leaned forward to peer out through the windscreen. "What are you doing? Where are you taking me?"

For answer, Blake depressed the accelerator, and shifted into a higher gear. Preston fell back against the seat with a little intake of breath. A moment later he laughed. "A surprise, eh? You must have something up your sleeve!"

Blake still didn't speak, but he glanced into the rearview mirror. He saw Preston smooth his tie, then slip his hand beneath it and hold it there. He didn't notice Blake watching him. He had turned his head to gaze out the window in an unconcerned fashion.

Blake turned south again, toward the Rainier Valley, where the Italian farmers grew peas and corn and summer squash. He turned into an unpaved road that ran up a gentle hill and wound through groves of pine and fir and cedar. Every detail of the landscape, the blue sky, the scudding clouds, seemed preternaturally sharp. The air through his open window smelled sweeter than he could ever remember. Below the rise stretched the Jefferson Park golf links, green and rolling, with flashes of blue water here and there. The road dwindled to a track, ending in a cleared space, where broken wagons and outdated farm equipment had been abandoned. Blake pulled the car up between a rusted axle and half an iron plough, turned off the motor, and set the brake.

Preston said lightly, "What is it you want, Blake? Why have you brought me here?"

Blake secured the keys in the breast pocket of his jacket before he unlatched his door and climbed out. He reached back inside the front seat for his cane, then opened the passenger door and held it wide. "Get out of the car, Mr. Preston."

Preston gave his most cherubic smile. "Are we having a picnic?" His eyes flicked over the cane, but he had seen it many times before, propped innocently against the wall of Blake's apartment. He didn't move.

"Get out."

Preston appeared to consider for a moment, then, with a negligent shrug, slid across the seat. He stepped out of the car without glancing again at the cane. He stood for a moment, looking down at the golf links. "Funny," he said. "The golf course looks different from here."

"I wouldn't know." Blake took a firmer grip on the cane as Preston turned to face him.

"What are you doing with that?" Preston asked. His smile was as cheery and untroubled as a child's. "You always told us never to touch it."

Blake turned the cane so he held it in both hands. "I have used this twice as a weapon, Mr. Preston," he said slowly, pedantically, the way he used to teach the children the alphabet or instruct them in the use of a hammer. "I spent six years of my life in Chatham County Convict Camp for murdering one Mr. Franklin Blake. That murder, as it happens, I didn't do. I did, however, commit two others. I went into the camp an innocent boy. I was not the same when I came out." The marble lion's head glittered in the lowering sun as he reversed the cane to point its rubber tip at Preston.

Preston's brows lifted, and his mouth quirked in amusement. "And why should you need to worry about that now? Faithful retainer of Benedict Hall, longtime butler of Mr. Dickson—"

His words broke off. He flinched as Blake pressed the tip of the cane against his chest.

Blake said, "When I was a good deal younger than you, I felt the bite of this wood more times than I can count."

Preston's smile faded.

Blake's resolve hardened his mind. It was a tool in itself, like iron molded in the fire, then chilled in a barrel of water. He had reached his destination. There was no going back. "I'm nearly fifty-five years old now, Preston. An old man."

Preston tilted his head to one side, and regarded him, unsmiling now. "You *are* old, aren't you, Blake? You probably feel you can waste away an evening, lazing in the sunshine. But I'm a young man, and I have things to do. Could we get on with—whatever this is?"

Blake pressed harder with the cane. Something moved beneath the tip, something hard that rolled beneath Preston's shirt. "I want you to set things right for Dr. Margot. Tell the hospital board the truth."

Preston laughed in his face. "*You* want? Who are you to tell me what *you* want, Blake?" He didn't look at the cane, and he didn't flinch again.

Blake had not expected anything different. "I've served your family well and long, Preston. I cared for you when you were in short pants. I drove you around when you were in school. I've picked up after you and fed you and cleaned up your messes."

"So?" Preston's eyes narrowed. "Your job, old man. And a damned good one, if I may say so. Especially for an ex-convict."

"Yes." Blake pushed a little harder, and Preston was forced to take a step back, trapped between the cane and the rear door of the Essex. "A very good job. I've earned the right to have a say in what happens to the Benedict family."

"That's debatable. You're not, after all, a Benedict."

"And you don't deserve to be a Benedict." Blake gave the cane a shove. The object under Preston's shirt slid aside, and the tip of the cane found skin and bone beneath it. "I've had to protect Miss Margot from you since she was a tiny girl."

"You'd best watch yourself, old man. You don't know who you're dealing with."

"I think I do." Blake lessened the pressure on the cane, but kept it poised close to Preston's shirtfront. "There's something not right about you, Preston. No one else sees it. No one wants to."

Preston's lips thinned and pulled back from his teeth. He no longer looked angelic. He looked feral. He hissed, "How dare you? Who do you think—"

"You've been trying to destroy your sister for a long time, and this time you've nearly done it. I'm not going to let that happen."

Preston's hand whipped up to seize the cane. He twisted it, but Blake was ready. He was a big man. His hands and arms were still strong, and he was prepared. He gripped the cane with both hands, bracing his elbows against his belly. Preston snarled, "What do you think you're going to do, Blake? Thrash me like a wayward boy?"

"Yes, sir." Blake tore the cane free, lifted it high, and brought it down.

He could see Preston hadn't thought he would do it, couldn't believe Blake would strike a Benedict. Only at the last moment did Preston duck, so the cane caught him on the point of his shoulder. He stumbled to one side with a grunt, more of surprise than pain.

Blake had learned in the camp that once you made up your mind to something, hesitation could be fatal. There was no time for compassion, no more room for discussion. He struck again. Preston threw up his arm, and the cane cracked against the hard bone of his forearm. He tried to scramble out of the way, falling to his knees near the front wheel of the car. He was reaching for his shirtfront when Blake lifted the cane again to slash at his back.

He missed. In a flash Preston was on his feet, dancing out of Blake's reach. His grin returned, but there were white lines around his mouth. "You think I'm going to stand here and let you thwack me with that thing?" He backed away, one hand to his forearm. Blake knew how it must sting. He remembered how that Carolina pine could bite into flesh.

Blake felt a bit out of breath, and he didn't want to waste it talking. He thought of Margot's stricken face as she walked out through the hospital doors, and the memory strengthened him. He slammed the rear passenger door of the car with his left hand. Preston said, "You don't intend to leave me here—" but Blake set his belly muscles and swung the cane again before he could finish the sentence.

The polished wood whistled through the air, a sound that brought back the smell of the indigo vats and hot Carolina nights, the sensation of bare feet on wood chips, and the face of Franklin Blake, contorted with rage. The cane struck the side of Preston's head. Blood sprang from his scalp to darken his hair and drip down his stiff white collar.

Preston roared something wordless. He staggered, and his fingers scrabbled at his shirtfront. Blake struck again, his blow not so swift this time, but wielded with both hands and all his strength. It caught Preston's forehead with enough force to break the skin above one eyebrow. Blood poured into his eye, and down his cheek. He reeled, and fell. He lay panting on the ground, peering up at Blake with his one clear eye.

Blake meant to finish it. He had made his decision hours before, on his way home from Dickson's office. It would be the end of his life at Benedict Hall, but Margot would be safe.

Preston, half blinded by blood, peered up at him. "You wouldn't kill me," he rasped. "You haven't got it in you."

"You have no idea what I have in me." Blake's accent was pure, broad South Carolina.

"Do it, then, old man! What are you waiting for?" Preston's right hand clung to his chest, and his unbloodied eye glared.

Blake took a deep breath and lifted the cane high over his right shoulder. Preston pulled something from his shirtfront and held it up, something that dangled on a silver chain and flashed blue in the twilight. "Too late, old man," he panted. "Too slow."

Blake swung the cane, slashing down and to the left, intending to put an end to the whole ugly business.

The pain that seized his chest, before he could complete the blow, was worse than any he had known, either at Mr. Franklin's hands or under the overseers' whips. It was huge, a giant fist seizing his heart, squeezing his lungs, pinching the air from his throat. He groaned, an involuntary sound that rose from his groin and bubbled up from his belly to his throat. The blow he had meant to strike never happened. Instead, the cane slipped from his nerveless fingers to rattle uselessly against the gravel. His knees buckled, and his left arm went numb. The sunny evening turned black around him as he crumpled to the ground.

Preston laughed as he got to his feet. Blake couldn't see him. He couldn't see anything. He could only hear that cold laughter, like a rush of icy water. He felt fingers probe his breast pocket for the car keys, then felt hands tugging at him, lifting him, bundling him into the passenger seat of the Essex. It may have been moments, or it may have been an hour, but the motor sputtered to life, and the tires crunched and spun as the car backed and turned. There was nothing Blake could do. The grip of pain was irresistible, and he longed only for it to end.

As the car rolled back down the hill toward the main road, Blake struggled to breathe past the boulder crushing his chest. He felt the upholstery of the seat beneath him, the roughness of the unpaved road beneath the tires. He had just time to wonder why Preston hadn't left him in the woods when a sudden great jolt threw him to the floor. There was a crash as the bonnet of the car struck something hard. Glass burst, and the horn sounded, over and over. The boulder on Blake's chest grew heavier, until no air at all could get past it.

He gave up trying to breathe. The pain vanished seconds later, and he felt suddenly light. Free. His chest didn't hurt. His back didn't hurt. The blackness receded, and around him the twilight glowed faintly golden.

Then, in the middle distance, as if someone had opened a window, he heard her. He heard a voice he hadn't heard in nearly fifty years, and she was calling his name.

"Abraham! Oh, Abraham!"

The sweet, husky, familiar sound filled him with joy.

CHAPTER 15

The telephone on Thea's desk rang just as Margot was gathering her things, ready to go out to wait for Blake. Thea spoke into it, then looked up at Margot with wide eyes. "Margot. There's been an accident."

Margot had just pulled on her gloves. She strode to the desk, dropping her hat on the pile of invoices. She took the receiver from Thea's hand and spoke into it. "What's happened?"

"Margot." Her father's voice rumbled in her ear. "Blake crashed the car. Hit a tree, apparently, down near Jefferson Park. I don't know if—I can't imagine what they were doing there—but they're both hurt. They're at Seattle General."

"Who's the emergency physician?"

"What?"

By the strain in her father's voice, Margot knew it must be bad. She was afraid to ask which of them was in real danger. "Who's the attending physician, Father?"

"I—I don't know. Can you just—"

"Where are you?"

"The hospital."

"All right, I'm on my way. I want you to sit down, Father. Loosen your collar, and take deep breaths. I'll be there as soon as I can."

She gave Thea a swift explanation, and a moment later was striding down Post Street, pulling on her hat as she went. The evening traffic was heavy, and she doubted she could find a taxicab without calling for it first. It would be faster just to walk up the hill on her own.

She hurried, and in fewer than fifteen minutes she was walking into the hospital, stripping off her gloves and hat. The receptionist led her to where her father sat on a straight wooden chair outside the accident room, head in hands, elbows on knees. When he saw her, he grasped her hand in both of his and squeezed it. "Thank God, Margot. They made me wait out here. I was going to call Peretti, but then I thought—I thought you could find out what's happening. Can you get them to tell you something?"

"I will," she said. She circled his wrist with her fingers, and eyed his pale face. "Do you feel all right, Father? Dizzy? Short of breath?"

He gave her a wan smile. "Stop it, Doctor. I'm fine. Please go see how Blake is."

A rush of cold ran through Margot, though she was so warm from her hurried walk. "Blake? I thought it was Preston."

"Both of them." Dickson ran his hands over his face. "Blake wasn't moving. Or talking. He looked—" His voice broke, and he drew a rasping breath.

"And Preston?"

"He's pretty banged up, but he was conscious. He drove Blake back to the city."

"Preston can drive?"

"I don't know if he can, but he did. They made it here. The car's a mess." He shuddered suddenly, a spasm that shook him from head to foot. "Oh, God. I don't know why I said that. I don't give a damn about the car."

Margot pressed his hand. "You're in shock, Father. It's hard to say the right thing."

Her father pressed his shaking hands over hers. "Go and see them, will you?"

"I'm going in now."

"I should telephone Edith."

"Yes. That would be good." Margot helped him up, and he turned down the corridor toward the reception desk. She turned the other way, and pushed through the door into the accident room. It was a forbidding place, with its big sinks and glass and enamel cabinets. Steel surgical instruments ranged on countertops, with basins and jars and, in one corner, a bulky autoclave. Margot hurried past all of this to the four beds in the back. Preston, with a nurse bandaging his head, lay on one.

The nurse, a young, rather stern-looking woman with her hair pinned into a tight chignon beneath her white cap, glanced up at her as she approached. "Are you family?" she demanded. Margot saw the corner of Preston's mouth twitch.

She said evenly, "This is my brother."

"Well," the nurse said crisply. "Dr. Miles has seen him. You don't need to worry. He's going to be fine, in time."

One of Preston's eyes was covered with cotton, and strips of linen bound his head. He had a sling over one arm. Gingerly, he turned his head to look at Margot. "It's Blake," he said in a sorrowful voice. "I'm so afraid—"

"Where is he?" Margot demanded.

The nurse said, "You mean the chauffeur? He's in the colored ward."

"Is there a doctor there?"

She raised her eyebrows, and Margot was sure that if she hadn't been a head shorter, she would also have looked down her nose. "I wouldn't know, of course. I don't work on that side of the hospital."

Margot bit back an irritated remark. She eyed Preston, and saw that his color was good, and the pupil she could see looked normal. She didn't touch him, but nodded to the nurse. "I'm going to find Mr. Blake," she said, emphasizing the *Mr.* She strode out the back of the ward, and started down the long corridor to the far side of the hospital.

She had been in the Negro wards of the hospital several times, when none of the Negro physicians were available. Most of her colleagues wouldn't treat Negro patients, but the hospital staff had learned that Dr. Benedict had no objection.

This section of the hospital was understaffed. The corridors were deserted, and Margot only found the right ward by trying doors. When she opened the right one, she found the room eerily quiet.

Blake was the only patient, and he lay terribly still. Too still. Margot struggled to sustain a flicker of hope as she hurried across the ward.

Blake lay beneath a brown wool blanket. His face looked faintly gray, as if someone had dusted him with ashes. His eyes were closed, and his hands lay outside the blanket, one palm up, the other down. She touched the hand nearest her. The fingers curled blankly upward, and it was ice-cold. Freshly alarmed, she reached for her stethoscope, then realized it wasn't in its usual place around her neck. She had left it behind at the clinic. She put her fingers on his wrist, and found his pulse thready and fast.

Her heart sank like a stone in a pond. She held Blake's wrist in her fingers, no longer as a physician, but merely as a friend. A daughter. Someone who couldn't bear to lose him.

A nurse appeared in the doorway and crossed to the foot of the bed. She was a dusky-skinned girl with enormous brown eyes and kinky hair pinned back beneath her nurse's cap. She was small, nearly dwarfed by her voluminous white apron, and her voice was high and girlish. "Excuse me, ma'am—you do know this is the colored ward?"

Margot answered sharply, her voice edgy with fear. "I do. Is there no doctor?"

"Not right now," the nurse said. "There's only me. They carried this man here from the street, and I—I didn't know what to do for him. I don't even know his name."

"No one told you his name?"

"No. They just brought him in and laid him here, and I was so afraid he would—"

"I need a stethoscope," Margot said abruptly, to stop her speaking the thing they both feared. "And he's cold. We need more blankets. Two, at least."

"I'll get them," the nurse said. And then, with a hopeful expression, she asked, "Are you a doctor?"

"I'm Dr. Benedict."

"Oh! I know your name."

"Our patient is Abraham Blake. He works for my family."

"Oh! Very good, Doctor. Good! I'll be right back." The nurse hurried to a cabinet, and came back with two more of the brown blankets and a stethoscope. As she spread the blankets over Blake, Margot put the earpieces of the stethoscope into her ears and pressed the bell to Blake's chest.

Now she could hear the struggle of his lungs, rales and rhonchi all over the chest, and the irregular heartbeat she had already detected with her fingers. She took the earpieces out, and hung the stethoscope around her neck. "Does he have visible injuries?"

The nurse said, "I checked under his shirt, and I took his shoes off. All I can find is that bruise." The mark on Blake's forehead was nearly black against his dark skin, contrasting with the silvery gray of his hair. "They said he was in a crash."

"Yes." Margot gazed down at Blake's gentle face, the full lips and prominent jaw, the high forehead. His cheeks sagged now, and she saw the wrinkles in them, pale threads like delicate cobwebs stretched across his dark skin. She had not noticed he was getting old, except for the grizzle in his hair. Feeling helpless, she pressed her palm to his cool forehead.

"Why is he unconscious, Dr. Benedict?"

"It's his heart." The worst possible news. Despite everything they knew about cardiac events and their symptoms, there was a paucity of steps they could take to address them.

"Is there anything else we can do?"

Margot glanced up at the nurse. She looked terribly young, hardly older than Loena and Leona. She didn't look afraid, though her patient was very likely dying. She looked—curious, Margot thought. It was the way she had been herself, when she first began treating patients. Curious about what was wrong, what she could do to help, how she could ease their discomfort or repair their wounds. Margot said, "What's your name, Nurse?"

"Church. Sarah Church."

"Well, Nurse Church, we'll want to hydrate him. We'll see if we can get him warm, and we need to get the rest of his clothes off, make sure there are no injuries we've missed. Then . . ." Her voice broke suddenly, in a most unprofessional way, and she clutched at the stethoscope around her neck as if it were a lifeline. Then . . . what? She had to do something. She couldn't give up. Blake needed her. He had no one else.

Nurse Church used scissors to cut away his trousers. Margot scanned his legs and ankles, probing them gently with her fingers. She found no trauma. The little nurse watched with interest as Margot palpated his abdomen, not finding anything unusual nor getting any response.

"He hasn't moaned, Nurse, tried to move his legs, to speak?"

"No, Doctor. It didn't seem right—that is, I didn't think—" The girl's voice broke off.

"What? What did you think?" Margot fixed her gaze on the nurse. She knew she was being abrupt, but Sarah Church seemed to understand. She was a courageous little thing, Margot thought. Any number of more experienced nurses could learn from her example.

Nurse Church drew a determined breath through her wide, delicate nostrils. She met Margot's look with a level one of her own. "It didn't seem right to me that he should be unconscious. The bruise on his head isn't that big."

"I see that." Margot bent to gently lift Blake's eyelids with her fingers. The pupillary response was normal, neither fixed nor dilated. She let his eyes close again, and smoothed the blankets over him. "His symptoms are contradictory, it's true. Prolonged unconsciousness is not good, but no doubt you know that."

"Yes," Nurse Church said sadly. "It seems you were fond of him, Dr. Benedict. I'm sorry."

"Thank you." Margot understood the implication of the past tense, but she thrust the thought away. "Dr. Henderson is the cardiologist. Place a telephone call to him, will you? Ask him to come and see Mr. Blake as soon as possible."

For the first time, the nurse hesitated to follow her orders. When she didn't move immediately, Margot scowled at her. "What's the matter?"

"Dr. Benedict—I don't know if he'll come."

"Why wouldn't he?"

With an air of patience, as if speaking to a child, little Sarah Church said, "Dr. Henderson is white. He might refuse to see a Negro patient."

Margot stared at her, thunderstruck. She was right, of course. Margot might think of Blake as a third parent, her protector, her precious friend, but to another doctor—a white doctor—he was just a Negro man. He was only a patient in the colored ward of the hospital. Dr. Henderson might consider that such a patient was neither his responsibility nor his duty.

A wave of anger replaced her fear. She looked down at Blake again, lying so deathly still beneath his pile of brown blankets, and she said firmly, "Nurse Church, stay with Blake, will you, please? I'll place the call to Dr. Henderson myself."

"Don't worry, Dr. Benedict. I'll be right here."

Margot glanced back once as she hurried away, and saw Sarah Church chafing Blake's wrists with her small hands. It was a simple gesture, even an old-fashioned one, but Margot approved. It might be all they could do just now.

At least, if Blake were to die in this moment, he wouldn't be alone.

*　　*　　*

Margot found Preston sitting up in his bed in the accident room. His head was braced against the iron bed frame, his unbandaged eye closed. His bloodstained shirt was open to the waist, and there were bruises purpling on his chest. The stern-looking nurse hovered near him with a glass and a carafe of water. She gave Margot an indignant glance when she appeared, as if her territory had been invaded.

Margot approached the bed, ignoring the nurse's challenging gaze. She eyed the pattern of marks on Preston's chest and the angle of the wounds on his head. "What happened, Preston?"

He didn't open the eye she could see. The nurse murmured, "Mr. Benedict was so heroic. Bleeding, injured—somehow he managed to get to the front door of the hospital, to get someone to come to the car."

Margot ignored her. "Preston?"

Preston said thinly, the eye still closed, "I don't know. Blake was driving, and . . ."

"Where were you going?"

"Jefferson Park."

"Why? You don't play golf."

"I wanted to see someone at the links."

"Really. But I'm told you weren't at the golf course."

Preston's lips trembled, and he lifted one hand as if to steady them. "Blake must have taken a wrong turn."

The nurse said, "Come now, Mr. Benedict, lie down. Dr. Miles said you mustn't talk. You need to save your strength." She sent Margot a warning frown from the opposite side of the bed.

Margot said impatiently, "What's your name, Nurse?"

"Morris."

"Well, Nurse Morris. I'm Dr. Benedict." The nurse's eyebrows rose, and Margot could see she wasn't sure whether to believe her. "I want you to go out and find my father. He's waiting to see Preston."

For a moment, Margot thought the woman might refuse. There was a rebellious set to her lips, but in the end she gave in. She said stiffly, "Very well." She touched Preston's arm once, possessively, before she bustled away, her apron rustling against her uniform.

When she was gone, Margot said, "I want the truth, Preston."

His eye opened, and fixed on her. "Is Blake dead?" he asked, in a voice as matter-of-fact as if he were asking the time.

"No."

The eye blinked, slowly.

"I want to know what happened out there."

"Don't be an idiot, Margot. There's nothing I can tell you."

"Yes, there is." She pointed at the round bruises on his chest. "How did you get those?"

"That sweet Nurse Morris told you all about it," he said. "Blake crashed the car."

"Don't *you* be an idiot, Preston. You're a mess of odd bruises, and Blake is nearly untouched."

Preston managed a one-shouldered shrug. "I guess the steering wheel protected him." He shifted against the pillows, and something showed beneath his unbuttoned shirt, something blue and heavy on a silver chain. He pushed it out of sight with his good hand.

"What is that?"

He blinked, slowly, deliberately. "None of your business, doc."

"You're wearing a necklace?"

He turned his head away from her.

Margot folded her arms. "Tell me what happened, Preston. Did you hit the gearshift? Roll over it several times? What made that bruise pattern on your chest?"

Preston turned his head away from her. "While I appreciate your sympathy over my wounds, Margot, I don't really want to talk about this now. I've just been in a car smash. I would think you'd be more sensitive."

An angry retort was on her lips, but her father's arrival forestalled her. He crossed to Preston, and patted his shoulder, murmuring something about being glad he was going to be all right. Preston, tremulous now, nodded, murmured something. When

Dickson was reassured about his son, he turned to Margot and asked to see Blake.

She held her father's arm as they took the long walk back to the colored ward. "I've just spoken to Dr. Henderson on the telephone," she said as they moved down the empty corridors. "I used your name, Father, or I don't think he would have agreed to come."

"Blake's alive?" Dickson's step faltered, and Margot gripped his arm. "He looked dead."

"He's not dead," Margot said in a low voice. "But he hasn't regained consciousness."

"What's wrong with him, Margot?"

"I can't be certain yet, Father. Let's wait for Dr. Henderson."

She opened the door of the ward, and held it for Dickson to pass through. Dr. Henderson was there ahead of them. He was a gray-haired man in his sixties, still wearing his street clothes, a suit coat and flannel trousers. His fedora and a rolled umbrella lay on a chair nearby. He was bent over Blake, stethoscope pressed to his chest. Sarah Church, true to her word, was at Blake's side, one hand on his arm. Blake still lay as if lifeless, but Dr. Henderson was frowning, listening with care, moving the bell of the stethoscope here and there.

Margot held her father back from crossing the ward. He trembled under her hand, and she squeezed his arm as reassuringly as she could. They stood just inside the door, waiting for the cardiologist to finish his exam. Henderson did what Margot had done, palpating Blake's abdomen, lifting his eyelids. Sarah met Margot's gaze, nodding slightly. When Dr. Henderson straightened, removing the earpieces of the stethoscope, Sarah murmured something to him.

He looked up at Dickson and Margot, and came across the room, his hand out. "Dickson. It's been a good while. Sorry we have to meet under these circumstances."

Dickson shook his hand, saying, "Thanks for coming, Thomas. How is he?"

Henderson included Margot in his glance as he said, "It's hard to tell. This is your daughter, isn't it? You're the one who called?" He put out his hand to Margot as well.

She shook it. "Margot Benedict, Dr. Henderson. I'm grateful to you for coming."

"Well, you were right, Miss Benedict."

Dickson said, half under his breath, "Doctor."

Henderson arched an eyebrow. "What's that, Dickson?"

"Margot is a doctor. Dr. Benedict."

"Ah. Yes, I've heard the name, but I didn't realize—" Henderson's mouth pursed and he eyed Margot more closely. She had no doubt he had heard about the board and their decision. She hoped he hadn't already formed his own opinion. His mouth relaxed, and he said, "Well, Dr. Benedict, you were right to call me. Your patient has suffered auricular fibrillation, and as you probably have surmised, a likely cerebral thrombosis."

Dickson gave Margot a helpless look. She said, "Blake had a heart attack, Father, and probably a stroke, which would explain why he's still unconscious."

Her father's ruddy face paled. She saw that he understood the implications all too well. He said in a low voice, "Thomas. Can you do anything for him?"

"We can try."

"He was in a car crash," Margot said.

"He was driving?"

"We believe so."

"Did he lose consciousness before or after the impact?"

"I've been trying to find that out," Margot said. "There is . . . some confusion."

"Why?"

Both men were looking hard at her, her father's gaze uneasy, Henderson's sharp.

"My brother was in the car," Margot said. "His injuries and Blake's are inconsistent."

"Well," Henderson said. He pulled at his lower lip with his fingers as he thought. "It might help to know—but there's no history of heart problems? Nausea, breathlessness . . . ?"

"None that he ever complained of."

Dickson said, "Can I see him?"

"Yes, of course." Henderson led the way back to Blake's bed.

Margot stood with Dr. Henderson at the foot of Blake's bed. Dickson went to his side, and leaned over him. He said, in a tender voice that made Margot's throat constrict, "Blake. Blake, it's Mr. Dickson. I don't know if you can hear me. You've been in an accident, but Dr. Margot is here to watch over you. We just want you to rest. You're not to worry about a thing."

Margot watched for any indication that Blake heard. There was nothing. Not even when her father added, "Preston is going to be all right. You'll want to know that," did Blake show, by a flicker of his eyelids, that he heard.

Margot prepared to spend the night at the hospital. Sarah Church brought her a bit of casserole from the canteen before her shift was over. Margot bid the young nurse a grateful good night just as another nurse, a heavy woman with graying hair and worn features, came on shift. She had two patients in other wards to look after, and Margot assured her she would stay with Blake until Sarah could return. She still hadn't seen any other physician, and she began to wonder if any of the Negro doctors made regular rounds.

She turned off the ceiling light, leaving a small lamp illuminated at one side of the room, and returned to the chair Sarah had set up for her, one with wide wooden armrests, cushioned now by pillows taken from empty hospital beds. For a long time she simply sat, gazing into the darkness, her ears straining for the whisper of Blake's shallow breathing.

It was ironic that although she had lost her hospital privileges, no one on that board of white male physicians would care—or even be aware—that she was spending the night in the colored wards, watching over a single patient.

She rose after a while to place her hand on Blake's wrist, on his chest. She could perceive no change in him. His stillness was eerie.

It seemed to her, indeed, that this entire side of the hospital was eerie. She was often in the hospital at night, and was accustomed to the clanking of bedpans and the click of heels on the tiled floors, of patients calling out in their sleep, of the hushed voices of consulting physicians or gossiping nurses. This part of the hospital was as silent as a tomb.

The thought made her shiver.

She stood beside Blake in the darkness, her hand on the nest of blankets in which she and Sarah Church had cocooned him. She felt more alone than she ever had in her life. The impending death of this kind, courageous man was more than she could take in. Where would she find the strength to bear it? Who could comfort her in such a loss, or even begin to understand what it really meant to her? She thought of Frank Parrish and wished, no doubt inappropriately, that he were here beside her.

After a time, she propped herself in the chair as best she could with a pillow beneath her head and another behind her back. She rested there through the night, dozing fretfully, waking often. Even when she managed to nod off, dreams of death and dying and smashed automobiles made her twist in the chair, and wake unrefreshed.

When the early summer dawn brightened the single window of the ward, she gave up trying to sleep, and went to wash her face and hands. She smoothed her rumpled hair with her fingers, but her pleated dress was beyond help. She borrowed a white coat from a closet and pulled it on, striving for a semblance of professional decorum.

Dr. Henderson came back before his morning rounds. "No change?"

"None," Margot said. "He hasn't moved at all, the whole night."

Henderson gave her a narrow-eyed glance. "You stayed here? Why?"

"This side of the hospital is short on staff, Doctor."

He glanced around, as if surprised at the empty ward. "Dr.

Peretti told me you've lost your privileges at Seattle General," he said. "For performing abortions."

"I haven't performed abortions," Margot responded tiredly. "But it's true that my privileges were revoked. I shouldn't be here."

"Well. I appreciate your devotion to your—to your family retainer." He gazed at her quizzically for a moment. "He is fortunate to have you."

Margot couldn't think how to answer that.

"Well," Henderson said. "At the moment, all we can do for him is hydration."

"Yes. I did that during the night," Margot said, pointing to the intravenous equipment coiled on a metal tray nearby. "I administered a liter of Ringer's formula."

"Very good."

"When Nurse Church comes back, I'll instruct her to give him another."

They stood together, watching the infinitesimal movement of Blake's chest. His color, Margot thought, was a bit less ashen this morning, but that could be her imagination. She wasn't thinking clearly. Her eyes burned with fatigue, and she pressed the tips of her fingers to them.

"You're exhausted, Doctor," Henderson said. "That won't help Mr. Blake."

Margot dropped her hands. "I know. I wish I knew what would help him."

"Sometimes," Henderson said, "time and patience are all the medicines we have."

She nodded. If only there were some way to look inside Blake, to know for certain what had happened, to know what was wrong and be able to fix it—but there was nothing more they could do. Electrocardiography was still experimental, and even if it were available in Seattle, she doubted anyone would be willing to use it on a Negro patient.

Henderson said, not unkindly, "Do you need me to remind you,

Dr. Benedict, that our patient may very well never regain consciousness?"

"No, Dr. Henderson." Margot drew a steady breath. She had tried not to think of that, all night long. She had kept the thought at bay during the hours of darkness, but now, in the full light of day, she could no longer pretend. Sorrow choked her, and she had to swallow before she finished. "I'm aware he may die. I'm going to Benedict Hall now, to warn my family."

As Margot stepped out of the hospital, she blinked. It hardly seemed possible the sky was blue and clear above the city, that sunshine glittered on the waters of the bay, and flowers and grass and trees all glowed with color. She would not have been surprised to find that winter had come overnight, to turn the sky and the Sound as leaden and dark as she felt. Her feet were heavy as she turned toward Madison to catch the trolley. When a taxicab pulled up to discharge a passenger, she hailed it on an impulse.

She regretted it at once. When she slid onto the backseat, her skirt caught on something sticky. The windows of the taxicab were cloudy with fingerprints and soot. The driver barely looked at her as he asked, in bored fashion, "Where to?" She gave him the address on Fourteenth Avenue, which made him turn to look at her more closely. "Benedict Hall?" he said.

"Yes."

He sniffed. "Why dincha just say that?"

Margot thought of Blake's dignified courtesy, of the sparkling windows and spotless upholstery of the Essex, and she felt an irrational urge to slap the back of the cabbie's head. She settled for a curt, "Do you want the fare or not?"

"Sure I do. No need to get—"

"Drive, please," she commanded.

"On my way," he said, shoving the gearshift into position. The gears ground unpleasantly before they engaged, and he pulled out into the sparse traffic. Margot folded her arms around herself, and stared blindly through the dirty windows.

At least when he reached the house, the man got out of the car and opened her door for her. She found a dollar tucked into the top of her medical bag and gave it to him, waving off the change. He smiled at this, showing missing and broken teeth, and tipped his greasy cap as she went up the walk.

The door opened at her approach. Hattie waited, her hands twisted in her apron, until Margot had stepped inside, and dropped her medical bag beneath the coatrack. "Miss Margot," she said, as Margot took off her hat and began peeling off her gloves. "Is Blake—Blake didn't—" Her voice broke on a sob, and Margot could see she had been crying for some time already.

"Blake's still alive," Margot said wearily.

"Oh, thank the good Lord!"

"He's very ill, though, Hattie. I don't want you to misunderstand."

"Oh, no, Miss Margot. I understand." Hattie began to weep again, tears running freely down her full cheeks and dripping from her chin.

"Where's Mother?" Margot asked. "And Father? The rest?"

"They're all in the dining room," Hattie said, swiping at her face with the hem of her apron. "They're having breakfast. I made ham steak and fried eggs, but it doesn't seem nobody's eating much. Poor Mr. Preston, he's looking so poorly, it's just like to break my heart. Now, you go on in—" Her voice broke as she sobbed again. "Go on in, Miss Margot, and I'll send Leona with your coffee."

"Thank you, Hattie," Margot said tiredly. "Now, try not to cry. You'll wear yourself out."

"Yes, Miss Margot," Hattie said, but she sniffled freely as she padded down the hall toward the kitchen.

Margot did her best to smooth the crumpled pleats of her dress as she walked to the dining room, but she was sure she looked a fright. She wished she could slip upstairs for a shower before speaking to anyone, but it didn't seem fair. She knew her father, like Hattie, would be terribly worried.

She opened the door to find a quiet group around the table. Hattie was right. No one was eating much except Preston, who, despite the plaster of Paris cast on his arm, was working his way through a thick slice of ham. The bandage on his head was fresh and unstained, and both eyes were now uncovered. He said brightly, "Margot! So good of you to stay with our Blake all night! I don't think Mater would have slept a wink otherwise!"

Margot moved to her chair, and Leona was there with the coffee before she had sat down. The girl stood back, the pot in her hands, and Margot nodded to her. "Thank you, Leona," she said. "You can stay and hear about Blake. Then please explain everything to Loena."

Leona bobbed a curtsy before she stepped forward to pour the coffee. Margot was too tired to feel even a flicker of annoyance at the curtsy. She picked up her cup, and took a grateful sip before she looked around at her family's faces.

Dickson looked as worn as she felt. Dick wore a worried frown, and his eyes flicked between Margot and Preston. Margot met his gaze, and gave a brief shake of her head. She thought she would speak privately to him later.

Edith and Ramona, other than looking a bit pale, seemed as always. Edith leaned forward and said in her breathy voice, "Margot, dear. Is Blake all right? We're just shocked to see how badly Preston was injured—he might have been killed!"

Preston took a mouthful of ham steak, and chewed it. She watched him as she set her coffee cup down. She said quietly, "I'm sorry, Mother, to bring bad news, but I'm afraid Blake is not all right."

"Oh, dear," Edith said.

Preston lifted his head, his blue eyes as innocent as a child's. "He's going to get better though, isn't he, doc?"

"I wish I could say that with any confidence. He's very ill."

Leona gave a small hiccup of a sob. Edith breathed again, "Oh, dear. Poor Blake."

Dick leaned forward, pushing his half-eaten breakfast out of the way. "Father said he hit his head and then had a heart attack. Does that make sense?"

Preston put down his fork, saying irritably, "Come on, Dick.

Use your brain. He must have had the heart attack first, and that caused him to crash the car."

Everyone turned to Margot for confirmation of this. She sighed. "We just don't know. Preston was there, and if he can't tell us what happened, we may never have an answer."

"I told you what happened!" Preston said indignantly. "Why don't you believe me?"

"Now, Preston, dear, you mustn't excite yourself," Edith said.

Dickson spoke over her. "You haven't explained, Preston. Why not tell us now?"

"Tell you what?" Preston demanded. "I told you Blake crashed the car! What else do you need to know?"

Margot dropped her hands to her lap and wound them together. Perhaps she could hold on to her temper with her two hands, stop herself from throwing her coffee cup at Preston the way he had thrown his cut-glass tumbler at her. She spoke past a knot of anger in her chest. "Did Blake complain of chest pain while he was driving? Was he rubbing his arm, or doing anything to indicate he wasn't feeling well?"

Preston glared at her. Margot noted that his color rose, and she could see the pulse speed in his throat. She liked it. Offense felt ever so much better than defense. She held Preston's gaze with her own, and relaxed her hands beneath the table.

"Preston?" Dick prompted.

"How do I know how Blake was feeling?" Preston snarled. "He was the chauffeur—"

"*Is*," Margot said icily.

"Oh, damn it, Margot. Slip of the tongue. *Is* the chauffeur! Am I supposed to notice everything about him? He was driving, I was thinking of something else. Bang!" He slammed his good hand on the table, making the china and both Edith and Ramona jump. "The car smashed into a tree."

Margot's own heart beat faster, as if she were running a race. Or doing battle. Preston's gaze bored into hers, and she had no doubt he knew exactly what she was doing. He knew she didn't believe a word he said.

She didn't, in fact, believe him. It was not just that his injuries and Blake's were so utterly different. She felt it in her belly, in her bones, that her brother had been lying from the beginning. She might never know the truth, but she would not give him the satisfaction of thinking he had deceived her. She pressed him. "How did you break your arm, Preston? How did you get that cut on your head?"

He suddenly sagged back in his chair, putting his hand to his face and causing his mother to lean close to him with concern. "I don't know," he said in a piteous voice. "I can't remember. It's all—it's all black." He dropped his hand. "Is that normal, do you think, Margot? Will it ever come back to me? I mean, a trauma like that—"

Margot said, "Blake is lying unconscious in the hospital, Preston, and you're the only one who was there when he was injured."

Ramona snapped, "For heaven's sake, Margot. It seems you're more concerned about a chauffeur than your very own brother!"

Margot turned swiftly to face her sister-in-law with cutting words rising to her lips. Dick forestalled her, saying, "Ramona, Blake is much more than a chauffeur to this family. He's been with us since before I was born. You know that."

Ramona cast an irritated glance at her husband, but she subsided. Hattie came in with a plate of freshly scrambled eggs and set it before Margot. She guided Leona out with her when she left the dining room. Margot picked up her fork and began to eat.

When she had finished the eggs, and declined a piece of ham steak, she lifted her coffee cup again. Edith said, "I'll ring for fresh coffee, dear," but Margot shook her head.

"This is fine, Mother." She looked around the table at her solemn family. "I wish I had better news for you. I thought I should warn you, though—" Awareness of what might happen rolled over her again, all at once, and her hands suddenly trembled. Her eyes stung, and she thought, for a terrible moment, she might cry. She couldn't do that. She didn't dare. Not with Preston watching her across the table, searching for signs of weakness.

She made herself drain the coffee cup before she put it down. "I thought I should make you aware of how serious it is."

"Edith, we'll go to visit Blake in the hospital," Dickson said.

His wife turned a wide-eyed look on him. "In the colored wards, dear?"

Dickson, with a sudden movement, shoved his cup away from him so that coffee slopped over the white tablecloth. He growled, "Why the hell not, Edith *dear?* You didn't mind if he took care of your children all of their lives! If he served your meals, managed your house, drove you to your endless luncheons, or waited in the car while you shopped for face powder or had your hair dressed. Why wouldn't you walk into the hospital ward to see him?"

He pushed back his chair and stood. His jaw clenched as if to forestall more angry words. Everyone stared, shocked into silence, as he stalked out of the dining room.

Margot waited until he was gone before she, too, excused herself. She placed a call to Thea to explain why she wouldn't be able to keep her clinic hours, then went up to her room, showered, and fell into bed to sleep for six solid hours.

When Margot woke, she dressed in a fresh skirt and shirtwaist before she went downstairs and out through the kitchen to go up to Blake's apartment. She wanted to fetch him a proper set of nightclothes, perhaps a dressing gown. She stepped out the back door and looked up at his little window, the one that faced the lawn, the one where he often stood gazing at Benedict Hall. It was unthinkable that Blake might never again cast his protective eye over the house before he went to bed.

She was halfway down the short walk when the Essex rolled into the drive. It made a terrible scraping noise as the wheels turned. Her father was in the front passenger seat, and Frank Parrish was driving.

Margot stopped to watch Frank negotiate the turn toward the garage. He seemed to manage the gearshift without trouble, moving his hand quickly back to the steering wheel when he had shifted down. He nodded grimly when he saw her, and turned off the motor.

Both men climbed out of the car and stood in front of it. The hood was crumpled, its hinged top flying open on one side. The windscreen was cracked, with great chunks of it gone. The fender on the driver's side was scraping against the tire. Frank glanced up as Margot approached. "I'm so sorry to hear about Blake," he said.

"How did you—" Margot looked at her father.

Dickson said, "I knew Major Parrish wasn't working, so I called his rooming house. I was the one who bought this automobile, but I have no idea how to drive it. I didn't know Preston did, either."

"We all drove bits of machinery out in the East," Frank said. He stepped away from the smashed car, and came to Margot. He took her hand, and said again, "So sorry, Margot . . ."

She clung to his hand, grateful for its warmth and strength. "Is it bad inside?"

"No. Just what you see, the fender and the hood and the windscreen."

Startled, she turned toward the car. "There's no damage inside at all? Blood, jagged bits of metal, maybe broken glass?"

"None that I saw."

"Did you look in the backseat?"

He shook his head. Together they walked to the car, and Frank opened the rear door. He bent to look inside, and when he straightened, he said, "Don't see anything."

"But Preston—Preston was bleeding, and he has wounds on his head and face."

"Maybe he was in the front."

"He could have been, but there would be some sign, surely, if he hit the windscreen or the dashboard. . . ." Her voice trailed off as her father came around the car.

"I'd better go in. I'll have to apologize to your mother," Dickson said.

"She's in the small parlor, I think."

He nodded. "Thank you again, Major," he said. "I don't know what I would have done."

"Happy I could help, sir." Frank's hand found Margot's again as Dickson disappeared through the back door. As it closed behind him, Frank squeezed her fingers. "Are you all right?"

"He did something, Frank. Preston did something to Blake."

"Your father said Blake had a heart attack."

"He did." She edged closer, yearning toward Frank's strength and steadiness. "And a subsequent stroke. But there's something strange about the whole thing, and Preston—he won't talk about it. Now he claims he doesn't remember, but I don't believe him."

"How is Blake doing now?"

She took an unsteady breath. "I've just spoken to the hospital. He's still unconscious. I want to get back there as soon as I can."

"It's not good, is it?" he asked.

"No." She shook her head. "There's not much hope, I'm afraid. We're doing all we can."

He looked down into her face, and said softly, "Awfully hard on you, Margot."

"Frank, I can hardly bear to look at him, lying there, so . . . so vulnerable."

"I know." His arm slipped around her, steadying her. It seemed impossible that only the night before they had laughed over dinner, that he had kissed her on the doorstep as if they were courting. As if they were innocent young lovers.

"I learned something last night," Frank said. "After I left you. It's something I think you should know."

It didn't take long to tell her about Carter, and about what he had done. Frank didn't mention his money problems, because he was afraid she would try to give him money, and he couldn't have borne that. He would have to find a way to explain his imminent departure from Seattle without sounding pitiful.

He followed Margot up the garage stairs to the small apartment where Blake had lived. It was painfully neat, just a few small belongings tucked into a cupboard. The door stood open to a narrow bedroom with a single bulb hanging from its ceiling. The little kitchen had a hot plate and a woodstove. A teacup rested in a strainer beside the tiny sink. A winter coat of brown wool hung on a peg rack, and over the back of a chair, Blake's driving jacket. His cap lay on the table.

Margot sat down, and drew the cap toward her. She gazed at it as Frank explained that he had seen Carter out of town, that he had thought it best under the circumstances. "I hoped, if the rumors stopped—"

She nodded. "I appreciate that, Frank. It's too late, unfortunately."

"Is it?"

"It hardly seems to matter now, when Blake is all I can think of." She turned her dark eyes up to him, and they were so sad his heart twisted with sympathy. "I went before the board this morning. They revoked my hospital privileges, because Preston told them I performed Loena's abortion. As if I would have botched such a simple procedure!"

He sat opposite her, shaking his head, stunned by the unfairness of it. His arm ached, but that was no surprise. The whole world was full of pain.

"Blake found that out, and he was furious," Margot said. "He was going to talk to Father, he said. I can't think why he was driving Preston, or where they were going. He never did that." She looked around the cramped kitchen. "Blake used to fix us cocoa up here," she said in a small, flat voice. "Sometimes when it rained. And cinnamon toast. He let me use the toasting rack. Mother was never around, you know, and Blake was—he was—" She made an awful sound in her throat, more a groan than a sob. She buried her face in her hands and hunched forward, as if she could hold in her grief that way.

"Margot!" Frank got up, kicking his chair out of the way, and went to kneel beside her. He was on the wrong side, and it was awkward to try to reach his right arm around her, but somehow he managed. "Margot, for God's sake. Cry if you need to."

"He's a *servant!*" Her voice was muffled by her hands. "Everyone will say he's a *servant*, only Father's Negro butler—but he's so much more!" Her shoulders shook, and he held her tighter, as tightly as his one arm and strained position would allow. "No one will understand." She shook with emotion within the circle of his arm. "Without Blake, I wouldn't have survived my childhood. No one believes me, not even Dick, but Frank—Preston would have killed me! He tried, over and over again, and only Blake—"

Frank wanted to pry her hands away from her face, to draw her head to his shoulder, but he had no way to do that. Frustrated, feeling useless, he could only whisper, as she sobbed into her hands, "It's all right, Margot. It's going to be all right. Sweetheart, I'm right here."

Margot, when the storm of her tears subsided, was afraid to show her face. She knew it must be red and swollen, and her nose as runny as an urchin's. She drew a shuddering breath as she sat up, and tried to turn to one side.

She found Frank's handkerchief, neatly ironed and folded, in front of her. With a little hiccup of thanks, she took it. When she had dried her eyes and blown her nose, she kept it. "I'll see it's cleaned," she said lamely.

"Throw it away." He helped her up, but she kept her eyes averted.

In a voice raw with weeping, she said, "I'm so sorry."

"For being human?" She felt his arm come around her again, and she pulled away for fear the flood would return. He stepped back, a little stiffly.

"I don't—I just don't want to cry anymore, Frank. It won't help Blake, and it never does any good that I can see."

He said with a touch of irony, "I wouldn't know."

She managed a shaky laugh. "Most women cry often, I guess. I learned a long time ago that tears are a waste of time."

"Not if they make you feel better."

"Well." She made a futile attempt to smooth her hair, then

gave it up. "I suppose I feel a little bit better." She looked at him then, and tried to smile. Her lips felt thick and unsteady. "Maybe you should try it."

He gave her a rueful smile. "No, thanks," he said.

"No. I didn't suppose you would." She wiped her eyes again. "I'd better get back to the hospital. Blake's nurse will need time off, and I don't know if there's anyone else to stay with him."

"I'll take you there."

She gave him a grateful look. "Thank you," she said. "That would be good, Frank." She turned to Blake's bedroom. "I want to take some things to him," she said. "Nightclothes. A dressing gown. Maybe his toothbrush—what else does a man need?"

"Razor. Shaving soap and brush. Comb."

"Oh, yes, of course."

Together, they went in search of these things. They were easily found among Blake's simple, orderly possessions. There was a suitcase on the top shelf of the wardrobe, as well, an ancient cardboard one with a cracked handle. Frank pulled it down, and Margot looked at it doubtfully. "It's awfully old," she said. "I've never seen it before."

"Doesn't smell too good," Frank said.

"I'll get one of mine. I have an overnight case we can use." They turned toward the stairwell, Margot's arms full of clothes, and Frank carrying the shaving things.

Just at the top of the stairs, Margot stopped beside the peg rack. A sweater hung there, one he sometimes wore on cool nights. There was nothing else. "Why wasn't he wearing his driving coat? And—where's his cane?"

"He carried a cane?"

"No, he never carried it, but he had one. It had a marble head on it in the shape of a lion—we always loved looking at it when we were children, though we weren't allowed to touch it. I think it belonged to someone he knew, out in South Carolina. His parents were slaves, you know. That cane always stayed right there, leaning against the rack. Always."

"Was it worth stealing?"

"I don't think so. The head was marble, but it wasn't very big. The wood was cracked. It looked old."

"Maybe he took it with him."

Margot touched the spot on the wall where the carved lion's head had always rested. The violets on the wallpaper were darker there. "You can see," she said softly. "It was just like Blake—always where it was supposed to be. I can't imagine what happened to it."

They went downstairs and took another look inside the car, behind the seats, in the back. There was nothing there. Margot touched the steering wheel with her hand, remembering Blake driving away from her, supposedly on his way to speak with Dickson.

"I wonder if he changed his mind," she murmured. She straightened, and stepped back. Frank closed the dented car door with some difficulty. Side by side, they went into the house.

CHAPTER 16

Preston watched from the window at the back of the hall as Margot and Frank Parrish emerged from the door at the side of the garage. They had been, obviously, in Blake's apartment. Parrish carried what looked like a shaving mug in one hand. Margot had clothes folded over her arm. Her face was awful, red and swollen. Probably sniveling on Parrish's shoulder, running on and on about Blake's fine qualities.

Preston withdrew from the window and dropped the curtain back over it. He turned toward his own bedroom, thinking a bit of a lie-down was in order. His broken arm hurt like the devil, and the dose of morphine prescribed for him by that twit Miles barely touched the pain. If he propped himself on pillows, though, and laid the sapphire on top of his cast, that seemed to help. He would do that, and keep a quilt over him in case someone came in. He would double the dose, too. His supply was getting low, but if he ran out, Leona could go on the streetcar to Bartell's.

It was too bad to be laid up this way. He would have to dictate his column to a stenographer instead of writing it out. Of course, he would contrive to look wan and noble as he did it, and that wouldn't be bad at all. He would see her admiring him—the uncomplaining victim of a terrible accident, the humble savior of an elderly servant—that would be fine. The role of hero suited him.

He drew his bedroom curtains against the lowering sun, and folded himself beneath the embroidered quilt, the stone with its silver chain draped over the plaster of Paris immobilizing his arm. He lay back against the pile of pillows, and stared at the crown molding above his head.

It was too bad about old Blake, really. But he had gone too far. Pushed Preston to the edge one time too many, and paid the price for it. Pity he hadn't turned up his toes right away. Would have been easier on everyone if he had. But that was Blake for you. You had to give it to the cagey bugger—he was tough, especially for an old man. From what Margot said, though, it shouldn't be long now.

The double dose of morphine began to do its work. Preston smiled drowsily up at the ceiling. It had all worked out rather well, actually. They all believed Blake's heart had given out, and even though Margot had her doubts, in a matter of hours Blake should be out of the way for good, and the matter settled. Parrish, with no job and his name on every blacklist in Seattle—nice bit of work, that—would surely have to go to some other city in search of work. There would be only Margot to settle.

He closed his eyes. Of course it had all gone just as he planned. There had never really been any doubt. Once he made up his mind, set his course, he would always have what he wanted, what was rightfully his. Nothing could stop him, just as *she* had let nothing stop *her.*

He folded his right hand around the sapphire and fell into an easy, satisfied sleep.

When Preston woke again, the light had begun to fade in his room. He lay for a moment, feeling a little fuzzy from the morphine, wondering why no one had called him for dinner. He pushed the quilt away, and retrieved the sapphire from where it had slipped beneath him. He looped the chain around his neck, and got up to push back the curtains.

It was true, the sun had set beyond the Olympics. He could see a ferry with lighted windows sailing across the inky waters of Elliott Bay, and the mountains were only gray silhouettes against the dim sky. Preston dug a fresh shirt out of his chest of drawers and worked his way into it. It was damnably difficult with just one hand, and he felt a rush of irritation at his mother. She should have known he needed help. And she had let him miss dinner, which was strange. Hattie, he felt sure, would have insisted someone wake him.

He found a way to put his shirt on with relative ease, but the buttons were a struggle, and the tie was impossible. How did Parrish manage this every day? It must take a lot of practice. Parrish was getting that, of course. He himself didn't intend to be one-handed long enough to become adept.

When he opened his bedroom door, the aroma of frying chicken met him, and he heard the clatter of Hattie cranking the potato ricer in the kitchen. It was damned odd that dinner had not yet been served. He started down the stairs, and met Leona coming up.

She stopped when she saw him, and bobbed a nervous curtsy. "Mr. Preston," she said, keeping her eyes on her shoes. "Mrs. Edith sent me to fetch you. It's dinner soon."

"It's almost nine o'clock!" Preston said irritably.

"Yes, sir," she said. She stood aside so he could pass her on the stairs, then followed him down the hall. She ducked into the kitchen, and Preston went on into the small parlor, where he found his brother and sister-in-law and both his parents gathered. Preston stiffened when he saw that Frank Parrish was there, as well, with a tumbler of Father's good scotch in his hand.

Edith jumped up from her chair when she saw Preston. "Oh, Preston, dear," she said, hurrying across the room. "Your tie! Let me help you!"

He wanted to slap her hands away, but he did need the help.

He stood still as she worked the knot, looking down at her fair head, and made himself say sweetly, "No dinner yet, Mater?"

"Your father asked Major Parrish to go to the hospital to fetch Margot, so I put dinner back. They've just arrived. Margot ran up to change her frock." She patted the finished tie. He looked down, and saw she had done a creditable job of a four-in-hand knot. In fact, she had bought him this tie, one of the new bias-cut ones. He experienced a little rush of affection for her, and as she stepped back, he bent to kiss her cheek. "You're a peach, Mater," he said.

She smiled up at him. "Come now, you must be ravenous," she said, taking his arm. She guided him toward the door, saying over her shoulder, "Major Parrish, please do come to the dining room."

Parrish, silent as usual, followed at a little distance. Preston debated how to behave toward him. It was a nuisance to have him here, of course, but obviously he and Margot had formed an attachment, and to object to it now would only make him look petty. Who else was ever going to be attracted to a woman like Margot? He could afford to be generous, surely. After all, Parrish should soon be out of the picture.

Preston patted his mother's hand as they reached the door. "Go on without me, Mother," he murmured. "I'll be there in just a moment." He waited in the doorway, letting Ramona pass, Dick, then his father. When there was only Parrish left, he put out his hand, keeping his face solemn. "Cowboy. Thanks for helping the pater out with the car. It's all such a bloody mess."

He could see Parrish hesitate. He, too, must wonder how they should go on after their little skirmish. Of course, he couldn't know Preston had blackballed him, but . . .

Parrish looked down at his outstretched hand, but he made no move to touch it. He brought his gaze to Preston's face, and his eyes were like blue ice edged in charcoal, cold and hard and unforgiving. Preston's neck began to burn. He pulled his hand back, and shoved it into his pocket.

Parrish said, "Delighted to help Mr. Benedict in any way I

can," and then, infuriatingly, stepped right past Preston and on down the hallway.

A scathing insult rose in Preston's brain. It almost reached his lips, but before he could speak it, Margot came dashing down the stairs to catch up with Parrish at the door to the dining room. She smiled at him as she took his arm, and the two of them went inside without giving Preston so much as a courteous glance.

There was nothing he could do but follow. Every atom of his body seethed with sudden fury, but he had to paste a smile on his face and pretend that nothing had happened. There was a bit of fuss and bustle as everyone took their chairs. Preston sat next to his mother, as usual. When he looked up, he saw that Margot was still smiling, looking less tired and worn than earlier. He leaned forward, hoping to take control of this damnable situation.

"Doc?" he said, his voice throbbing with what he thought was appropriate gravitas, preparing for terrible news. "Tell us about Blake. Is there any improvement?"

Margot turned to face him. Her voice sounded sharp and deliberate, as if she understood very well how deeply her words would cut. "He's awake, Preston. Blake is awake, and resting comfortably."

Frank watched Preston as Margot gave him the news. His smooth features hardened, changing the shape of his face. His full lips thinned, and Frank thought they might actually pull back from his teeth like an angry dog's.

The moment was gone in an instant. Preston recovered himself, cooing, "Wonderful! Mater, isn't that the best news?" in a way that made Frank's skin crawl.

"It's marvelous," Edith said. She put one hand on her delicately powdered cheek. "We're all so relieved. Do tell us about it, Margot."

Hattie and Leona came in with the platter of fried chicken and a bowl of mashed potatoes. Margot waited until everyone was served before she said, "We decided to try a Nativelle's granule of digitalin, and watch him closely. The side effects can be—"

She broke off, and her glance slid sideways to her mother. "They can be unpleasant," she said.

She had explained the specific risks to Frank: nausea and diarrhea. Vomiting, she had told him, was dangerous in an unconscious patient, so she and the nurse—Nurse Church—had watched Blake closely as they gave the first dose. She had described all this to him, whispering in his ear as they rode in the streetcar, then speaking in a normal voice as they climbed the hill to Fourteenth Avenue. She had conferred with Henderson, then administered the digitalin with the greatest care.

Her eyes glowed now as she said to her family, "Blake responded almost at once, moving his hands, trying to lift his head. We waited two hours, as Dr. Henderson suggested, and gave him another granule. He opened his eyes, and when I touched his hand, he squeezed my fingers."

Preston said, "Doesn't sound like much, doc."

Margot responded calmly. "No, I suppose it doesn't. But now that we know he tolerates it well, he'll receive more digitalin in the morning. I expect soon he'll be able to speak, to tell us how he feels. We should know more then."

"And his heart, Margot?" Dickson asked.

"The heartbeat is significantly stronger, and much more regular already," she said. "I'm so grateful to Dr. Henderson for his advice. It would have been hard to make this treatment decision on my own."

Frank heard a sniffle, and looked up to see Hattie standing inside the doorway, listening. She was dabbing at her eyes with the hem of her apron. Margot turned in her chair. "Hattie, it will take some time, but I think Blake will recover."

"Oh, thank the good Lord, Miss Margot!" Hattie dropped her apron and smoothed it. "Thank the good Lord! You tell him we're all just so glad!"

"I will," Margot said. "You can tell him soon yourself."

Hattie, with a tearful smile, nodded, and turned. "Oh, I'm sorry! I forgot the gravy boat." They heard her heavy step down the hall, and the swish of the kitchen door.

Dick said, "Gosh, Margot, that was good work. I'm so glad."

Edith said, "Yes, indeed, dear. We're all proud of you." Dickson nodded, and Frank thought his chest puffed just a bit as he regarded his daughter across the table.

Even Ramona said, "It's wonderful, Margot. First you saved Loena, and now Blake!"

"I don't know that I saved either of them, but I'm flattered you see it that way." Margot smiled again. Frank thought she looked transformed. Her cheeks glowed with a bit of color, and even her dark hair seemed to shine. She looked as if she'd had a week of rest, though he knew she had slept no more than a few hours in the last two days. Blake, he reflected, was a very special man to have won such devotion.

Only Preston was silent. They all began on Hattie's fried chicken, and general conversation sprang up around the table. The riced potatoes and cream gravy were delicious, and if the chicken was a little dry, Frank thought Hattie could be forgiven because of the delay of dinner. Loena, he knew, was resting upstairs. Dickson had persuaded his wife, with some difficulty, to allow her to return to her post when she was recovered, though she was forbidden to ever mention her "little difficulty."

Peace, it seemed, reigned in Benedict Hall.

Margot, despite her relief at Blake's improvement and her own weariness, found it difficult to sleep that night. The house was breathlessly hot, and though she opened her window, there was hardly enough breeze to stir the drooping leaves of the thirsty camellia. She folded back her quilt, and lay down under just the sheet, wearing her thinnest nightdress.

It wasn't the heat, though, that kept her wakeful. She found herself listening for the furtive creak of a floorboard, the muffled click of a door opening in the bedroom across the hall from her own. She wanted to call the hospital and leave strict orders that Abraham Blake was to have no visitors, but since she was not officially on his case—and in fact was violating the board's edict even by treating him in the hospital—she didn't dare.

After dinner, she had walked with Frank as far as Aloha. The fading light outlined his clear profile, the set of his chin, and she had felt a swell of admiration for this taciturn man. She kept her hand under his right arm as they walked, and she confessed her fear that Preston would try to get to Blake, to stop him reporting on whatever had happened above Jefferson Park.

Frank said, "I could stay and watch the house."

"You can't just sit in the park all night."

He nodded back toward the great brick water tower. "Could lounge on the stairs there, in the dark, and see that no one leaves Benedict Hall."

She shook her head. "The police patrol the park every night. If they saw you watching the house, they'd probably put you in jail."

"They don't have to see me."

"Frank. Can you imagine if they did? After what you've already been through?"

They reached Aloha, and paused at the corner. Frank put his arm around her shoulders, and pulled her close enough to kiss her cheek. "Go back now, Margot. Go to bed. You need to rest."

"Promise me you're not going to do anything foolish. Anything risky."

This time he kissed her mouth. The feel of his lips, so warm and smooth, sparked a hunger in her body that surprised her. As tired as she was, she still wanted more of him, wanted to throw her arms around him and kiss him until neither of them could breathe, and never mind the neighbors who might be watching from their shadowed porches.

Instead, they parted decorously, and smiled at each other. "Promise," Margot whispered.

"I promise. Nothing foolish."

"Go to your own bed, Frank."

He didn't answer that, but pushed the curve of her hair back from her cheek. "Good work today, Dr. Benedict," he murmured.

Even in the darkness, she saw the twinkle of his eyes, the

slight curve of his lips. She wanted so much to keep kissing him that she could hardly catch her breath, but she resisted. She only said, knowing her own eyes must be glowing in the dusk, "Thank you, Major. Sleep well."

"See you tomorrow."

He was gone a moment later, striding down the steep curve of Aloha Street, a tall, lean, one-armed figure disappearing into the gloom.

Now, wakeful and anxious, Margot rose to open her bedroom door. She left it ajar about six inches, and went back to bed. She dozed restlessly, rousing often at the small sounds the house made through the hot night. Not until the sky began to turn gray beyond her curtained window did she sink into a hard, heavy sleep. She didn't wake until Leona tapped on her door, and by then the sun was already well up over the hills. "Miss Margot? Breakfast."

Margot said hoarsely, "Yes, yes, I'm coming in a moment. Thank you." She waited until the maid's steps retreated down the hall, then crept to her door to open it, and look across to Preston's room.

With a jolt of alarm, she saw that his door stood open. His bed was already made, the coverlet smooth, the pillows plumped and rearranged against the headboard. Fully awake now, she hurried to wash her face and drag a comb through her hair. She thought, under the circumstances, her mother would forgive her coming to breakfast in her dressing gown and slippers.

When she reached the dining room, the only person left at the table was Ramona. She raised her eyebrows at Margot's appearance, but said only, "Good morning, Margot. I thought you were going to miss breakfast altogether."

"I didn't sleep well," Margot said. She glanced down the table at Preston's place, and saw a clean plate and an unused coffee cup.

Leona appeared with the coffeepot, and poured for her. "The toast is cold, I'm afraid, Miss Margot," she said. "Shall I get Hattie to make more?"

"No. It doesn't matter," Margot said. "But leave the coffeepot, will you?"

When Leona had gone, Margot said, "Do you know where Preston is, Ramona?"

Ramona was wiping her fingers on a linen napkin, preparing to leave the table. "He was already gone when Dick and I came down. Probably off to do an interview or something. I just don't know how he'll manage with that cast on his arm." She stood up, and pushed her chair back into its place. "I hope Blake is better today," she said.

Margot, her mouth dry with anxiety, managed to say, "Thank you. I'll tell him you said so." She drank her coffee, and waited until she heard her sister-in-law's step on the stair before she pushed away from the table and hurried toward the kitchen.

She found Hattie at the sink, her arms elbow-deep in soapy water. Leona was just starting out with a bucket and several cleaning rags in her hands. She stopped, and bobbed one of her maddening curtsies. "Miss Margot! Did you want that toast after—"

Margot said, interrupting her, "Never mind the toast. I want to know if either of you saw Mr. Preston this morning."

Leona shook her head, and Hattie, twisting to see over her shoulder, said, "No, Miss Margot. I guess he'll be having his breakfast downtown, though I wish he'd told me. I fried up those sausages special because I know he likes them, and I thought he might want somethin' extra good with that broken arm and all."

Margot turned swiftly and left the kitchen. She heard Hattie say, "Miss Margot? Don't you want breakfast, neither?" but she didn't take time to answer. She hurried up the stairs to dress, and in fifteen minutes was on her way to the hospital.

She could see from the street that the reception area of Seattle General was already busy with the change of nursing shifts and the arrival of physicians for their rounds. She hesitated on the steps, but seeing Dr. Peretti just climbing out of his automobile decided her. She spun quickly, hoping he hadn't spotted her, and strode down the block and around to the back entrance.

There were visitors now in the cramped corridor of the colored section of the hospital, a woman in what looked like a maid's uniform whispering with an elderly woman leaning on a cane. They cast wide-eyed looks of surprise when the tall white woman appeared. She nodded as she paced past them to Blake's ward, and paused outside. She heard a man speaking inside. It wasn't Blake's deep voice, nor was it her father's hoarse growl. It sounded familiar, though it was hard to hear, and fresh anxiety made her hand tremble as she opened the door.

Sarah Church, in her long nurse's apron, looked up from the sink where she was coiling a length of intravenous tube into a basin. She flashed Margot a white smile and went on with her task. The man whose voice she had heard still lounged in the chair near Blake's bed, the same chair Margot had tried to sleep in, his long legs stretched out, his head resting on a pillow. It was Frank, smiling sleepily up at her. "Good morning, Margot," he said.

She exclaimed softly, "Frank! Have you been here all night?"

He pushed himself upright, letting the pillow fall to one side. "Seemed like the thing to do," he said.

Nurse Church pushed the basin to the back of the counter, and turned, wiping her hands on her apron. "I told him he didn't have to stay, but he insisted. It was good, because we were busy last night, and I didn't like to leave Mr. Blake alone."

"Thank you," Margot said with sincerity. She crossed to the bed to take Blake's wrist in her fingers. As she did so, his eyes opened. The wrist she held didn't move, but his opposite hand did, lifting unsteadily to reach across his body and touch her arm.

"Good morning, Blake," she said, trying to summon a cheerful smile. She bent to look directly into his face. "How are you feeling?"

His eyelids flickered, and his fingers grazed the back of hers with a faint pressure before his hand fell limply away.

The nurse, coming up beside Margot, said, "He hasn't spoken, Dr. Benedict. He did take some broth, though, and his color is much better. At least, I think so," she added hastily.

Margot held Blake's hand in both of hers. "You're absolutely right, Nurse Church," she said. "His color is better, and his pulse is steadier. We'll continue with the digitalin, and perhaps we could get him to take a bit of breakfast, if he can swallow it."

"Yes, Doctor," the nurse said, her tone touched with pride.

"You've done very well with our patient," Margot said.

The nurse looked up at her, a quick flash of brilliant dark eyes and thick lashes. She showed a single dimple in one smooth cheek before she turned toward the door. "I'll go to the canteen myself," she said, and swished out into the corridor, the long hem of her apron flicking behind her.

Frank stood, stretching his shoulders. Margot released Blake's hand, and his eyes closed once again. She watched him for a moment, then crooked a finger at Frank to invite him out of the room. When the door of the ward was closed behind them, she said, "Did anything happen?"

He leaned against the wall, gazing down at her with a grave expression. "Preston showed up about four this morning."

"Oh, my God."

"Wasn't a bit pleased to find me here, either."

Margot released a long, slow breath. "What did he do?"

Frank's mouth tightened, and he gazed past Margot at the blank wall. She could see he was choosing his words deliberately, as if he was still trying to make sense of it all. "There's something else Carter told me," he said. He glanced up and down the hall, as if he didn't want anyone to hear him. It was empty now, though Margot heard voices coming from other wards.

"What was it?" she asked.

Frank looked into Margot's face, and even now, in the brittle electric light of the hospital corridor, the intense blue of his eyes in their frame of black lashes made her breath catch in her throat. The few silver threads in his black hair gleamed, a reminder of the toll the war and its aftermath had taken. "I thought Carter was being silly. Superstitious. Not a smart man at the best of times." He gave a slight shrug. "But Preston has it, just as Carter said."

"Has what?"

"A stone. Heavy, old-fashioned. Carter said it was a sapphire, but I wouldn't know."

Margot frowned. "He wears it around his neck."

"You've seen it?" Frank's jaw rippled, and Margot saw that it wasn't fatigue drawing deep lines in his cheeks. It was anger.

"A glimpse. I thought it was just—an affectation. What happened, Frank?"

He described Preston's visit to Blake in the tersest terms, with a minimum of drama, but Margot could see it clearly, feel the tension, understand the threat. Preston had crept into the darkened room at a moment when Sarah had just gone out. He had opened the door only wide enough for him to slip through, and closed it soundlessly behind him. When Frank, drowsing in his chair on the far side of Blake's bed, startled awake, Preston was standing at the head of Blake's bed. He was holding the stone in his hand, poised above Blake's heart.

Frank leaped to his feet with an exclamation, and Preston swore, jumped back, and was gone from the room almost before Frank understood what had happened. When he leaned over Blake to be certain he was all right, he saw that Blake's eyes were open, showing the whites as they followed Preston's movements.

Frank said now, "Carter said the stone makes Preston stronger."

"Foolish, isn't it?" she said. "But I could see him convincing himself it's true."

"That would make Preston no smarter than Sergeant Carter."

"Well. This isn't my field of expertise, but there are a number of studies on how war experiences affect the mind. Not just battle fatigue, but delusions and paranoia. Preston has always been difficult, but since the war . . ." She put up a hand to rub the tight muscles of her neck. "I don't know. I'm not sure anyone understands him, including Preston himself." She gave him a helpless look. "He has always hated me, since we were little children."

"Why?"

"He says I'm in his way. I don't see how, but he told me just the other night that I've always been in his way."

Frank's voice was low and hard. "It's jealousy."

"What does he have to be jealous of?"

"Your father is so proud of you, Margot."

She gave a surprised laugh. "Proud of me? We argue all the time!"

"Your father loves that. Anyone can see it." She shook her head doubtfully, but Frank pressed on. "Preston came here to hurt Blake last night, Margot."

Margot's answer was so soft Frank had to lean closer to hear her. "I think he already hurt him, Frank. I think they fought, out there near Jefferson Park. Preston had these round bruises on his chest, and . . . I keep thinking of Blake's cane. Could he have tried to deal with Preston himself? If my father wouldn't do it?"

"Blake's not young," Frank said grimly. "A fight with a younger, stronger man—"

"Yes. That could have caused his heart attack, and the resulting stroke." She shivered suddenly with fatigue and tension. "Blake did it for me, Frank. That makes it my fault."

"No," he said, and gripped her arm tightly with his hand. "No, it's Preston's fault. He caused all of this."

"And he's not done, it seems."

Frank straightened, gazing past her. She turned and saw Sarah returning with a tray carrying a small, steaming bowl. She smiled up at them, and said, "Porridge." Margot nodded approval of this choice as she and Frank stepped aside to let the nurse go into the ward.

When Margot started to follow her, Frank held her back. "I have no doubt that Preston came to finish what he started. Came to shut Blake up forever."

"It's a nightmare."

"Blake won't be safe at Benedict Hall."

She answered sadly, "I know."

Margot arrived home after her day at the clinic just as the family was gathering in the small parlor for drinks. Preston already sat next to his mother, leaning close to whisper something in her ear. She laughed, and touched his shoulder with her manicured hand. Ramona sat across from them, and Dick was at the sideboard, pouring sherry into two tiny glasses. Margot met her father in the doorway. He stood back to let her pass through, and she assessed him with a swift glance. He was looking worn and worried, thick eyebrows drawn together, the pouches beneath his eyes heavier and darker than usual.

They would have to talk later, she thought, when they could be alone.

"Doc!" Preston cried when he saw her. "How's our patient tonight?" He leaned back in his chair, crossing his neatly flanneled legs. His suit jacket draped over one shoulder, where the cast was too thick to allow him to put his arm into the sleeve. He contrived somehow to make it look chic that way. His tie was perfect, and she supposed Edith had helped him with it. His eyes were as bright and clear as if he had just arisen from a refreshing sleep. If she had been creeping around the hospital at four in the morning, she was sure she would have looked like hell.

But she would make no accusations. They would only be energetically denied. She said, "I assume you mean Blake, Preston. He's doing remarkably well, all things considered."

"Henderson concurs?" Dickson rumbled.

Margot nodded to her father. "He does. With good care and a lot of rest, we expect Blake to improve significantly. He may even, one day, make a full recovery."

There were murmurs of relief around the room. Margot fixed Preston once again with a hard gaze, and he met her look with a challenging one of his own. Any pretense of fraternal affection between them was at an end. The battle between them was joined, even if they were the only two who knew it.

Preston said, with a nonchalant air, "Is he talking?"

Margot let a beat pass, watching her brother's face, before she said, "Why do you ask that particular question, Preston?"

His lips curled in a cherubic smile, and his eyes didn't flicker. "Well, of course, I'm not a medical man—like you—" The subtle insult didn't escape Margot. She felt her father tense beside her on the sofa, but she let it pass. "But you know—a fellow hears the word *stroke* and he thinks speech problems. What's that word? A—a—"

"Aphasia?"

"That's the one."

Margot turned slightly on the sofa so she was facing her father. "Blake hasn't been able to speak," she told him. "But he's moving his hands and his feet, and he's been able to eat and drink. It's hard to predict how much movement he'll recover."

Dickson said, "We'll bring him here. We can hire a nurse, and—"

"I don't think that's best, Father. He needs more care than one person can provide."

"What will we do, then?"

Margot let her eyes flick over Preston, as if by chance. "I've moved him to a convalescent home," she said. "He was transported there by ambulance this afternoon."

"Where?" Preston asked, and Margot thought his tone was a bit sharper than he intended.

She said mildly, and untruthfully, "Oh, it's a private home out of the city. There was no place in Seattle for a colored man to go."

Preston was about to press her, she could see, but Dickson said, "They'll send me the bills, of course."

Margot nodded. "Of course, Father. I knew I didn't have to ask you."

"Can he have visitors?" Dickson asked.

"For now, it's better he has complete rest. I've left orders to that effect, and arranged a special nurse. He'll have the best of care, Father."

Edith said, "That's very good news, Margot. Isn't it, dear?"

Dickson nodded, and in a rare display, turned his hand over to grip Margot's. "Thank you, daughter. I know you're doing all you can for him."

She squeezed his hand just as Leona appeared in the doorway to announce dinner.

When dinner was over, Dickson went out onto the wide front porch to smoke his cigar. Margot followed, taking a seat next to him on one of the white wicker chairs. The summer twilight glowed over the city, and in the distance the waters of Puget Sound glistened with faint starlight. The heat of high summer had given way to a cooling evening breeze, scented by the roses Blake had nurtured all around Benedict Hall. Margot shivered a little in her short-sleeved frock, but she didn't want to go in for a wrap. It wasn't easy to find a moment alone with her father.

He leaned back in his chair, cigar clamped between his teeth. He stared across at the park, where the brick water tower rose into the darkness. "What was it between you and Preston tonight?" he asked in a low tone.

She said, just as quietly, "I think perhaps you already know."

He heaved a smoke-filled sigh. "Blake came to see me," he said.

"He told me he was going to do that."

"He said Preston told the hospital you had performed Loena's abortion."

"Yes. I haven't had a chance to tell you about my meeting with the board."

Her father turned his head to her, and his heavily lidded eyes were sharp and sad. "You didn't do it, did you, daughter?"

"I did not."

He looked away again, out into the gathering darkness. A mosquito whined past, but didn't alight. "I couldn't believe," Dickson said slowly, "that Preston would do something like that. I knew Blake would never lie about a member of the family, but—I thought he was confused somehow. That he had misunderstood."

Margot waited in silence. Her father, she thought, had to come to understand about Preston in his own way, and in his own time. Dickson was a canny and insightful man. It was one of the reasons he had been successful in his business and financial affairs. He knew and understood people—except for his youngest son.

"It seems very strange," Dickson said, his voice dropping even lower, "that this terrible thing happened on the same day. Blake looked fine when he was in my office. Troubled, of course. Sad, I believe. But not ill."

"No."

The cigar had gone out, but Dickson still chewed on it, rolling it across his teeth as he ruminated. "I suppose a heart attack can happen like that, out of the blue?"

"Usually there are some warning signs. Not always."

"I guess I have to accept that Preston tried to hurt you." A pause. "Do you think he caused the accident?"

"I don't know any more about that than you do, I'm afraid," Margot said. She went on gently, knowing her words would wound him. "What I do know is that Preston went to Blake's room at the hospital at four o'clock this morning. That's what was between us this evening. Frank was there. He spent the night watching over Blake because he knew I was worried. Frank woke up just in time, and Preston bolted."

Dickson took the cigar from his mouth and turned it this way and that in his fingers, gazing at it as if its dark wrapper might be hiding an answer. He blew out a breath, and shook his head. "No one visits a hospital at four in the morning. Not in any reasonable way."

"No."

"That's why you're not telling the family where Blake is."

"I feel that's best, Father."

He turned his face to her, and even in the darkness she could see how his features sagged, dragged down by sadness and shame. "Be sure the bill comes to my office, Margot. Not here. Not Benedict Hall."

She nodded.

"Can we avoid telling your mother about this?"

It was Margot's turn to look out into the darkness. Gooseflesh prickled at her bare arms, and she hugged herself against the cold. "I know Preston is special to Mother," she said. "But there's bound to be more trouble with him. I'm afraid you can't protect her forever."

"I'll have a word with him, of course."

"I hope it helps, Father. I really do hope so."

CHAPTER 17

The brief season of high summer faded quickly in the Pacific Northwest, and Frank's hopes of a new position disappeared with it. Carter and Preston had made a thorough job of ruining his reputation in Seattle. He made the rounds, asked questions, presented his credentials, but without any luck. His months at the Boeing Airplane Company opened doors to him at first, but when he gave his name, interviews were canceled without explanation, telephone messages not returned. He had sold his British Army greatcoat, but even that money was gone now. It was time to move on.

He had to find a way to explain this to Margot, and that was bad. Even worse, it meant that Preston Benedict had won, and Frank hated that even more than the coming separation. He could hardly ask Margot to leave her clinic and come with him. He had no home to offer her, no income, and for the moment, no future.

On a rainy September afternoon, he retrieved his valise from the wardrobe where he had stowed it when he first moved into Mrs. Volger's and, with a heavy heart, began to pack his things.

He indulged himself, this once, in a good shot of whisky in the afternoon, something to soothe the unrelenting pain of his arm and to cushion the despair that made his eyes burn and his feet drag.

He gave a guilty start at the knock on his door, and he quickly capped his flask and thrust it into his trouser pocket. He crossed to the door, and opened it to find Mrs. Volger in the corridor. "It's the mail, Major," she said brightly. She pulled an envelope from the pocket of her housedress and showed it to him, a thick beige square bearing his name and address in an elegant copperplate hand he didn't recognize. "It looked important, so I brought it right up."

He hadn't opened the door very wide, and she leaned to one side in a not-very-subtle attempt to see what he was doing. He was tempted to take the letter and close the door, to postpone the inevitable and uncomfortable conversation they would soon have. Instead, he stepped back, and pulled the door as far open as it would go.

She stared at the pile of clothes lying on the bed beside the half-packed valise. "Taking a trip, Major Parrish?"

He said, "No. I wish I were. Please come in, Mrs. Volger."

She took a tentative step inside, something she never did when he was home. She was careful to clean and change linens when her tenants were properly away at their work. "What's all this, then?"

The letter was still in her hand, and he wanted to see what it was, but he knew he owed her an explanation. "Mrs. Volger, I'm—I'm sorry to say I've lost my job." It was hard to speak the words, embarrassing. Shaming. He thrust his hand into his pocket, and it encountered the hard, slim silhouette of the flask. He pulled it back out again and stood awkwardly, looking down into his landlady's wrinkled face.

She said, with sincerity, "Oh, no! That's terrible news. You can find another, though, I'm just sure, a nice young man like you."

"I've been trying," he said. "I think I've tried every place there is. The employment picture in Seattle is . . . well, I don't need to tell you how hard times are."

"But you—an engineer. An officer. A—" She waved his letter in the air as she searched for other ways to describe his good qualities.

"I sure wish things were different. I was going to give you my notice today."

She stood shaking her head, gazing at the modest pile of his possessions heaped on the coverlet. "You're my very best tenant, Major Parrish," she said sadly.

He didn't know why that should be, but he let it go. Perhaps it was the flowers that made her say that. Perhaps being a landlady could be as lonely as being a one-armed, unemployed engineer. He said only, "Kind of you, Mrs. Volger. I'm sorry to leave."

She looked up at him suddenly, her faded eyes brightening. "I can give you a month," she said. She tapped her chin with the corner of the beige envelope. "While you try to find work. You can make it up to me later."

Again, he said, "Kind of you, but I think I'm going to have to try a different city. Maybe San Francisco."

Her face fell. "Oh. Too bad. That's so far away."

"I know."

"Well, a young man has to have work, I suppose."

"Yes. I'll be on my way by the end of the month, if you want to rent the room."

She sighed, and turned toward the door. Over her shoulder, she said, "You remember. I can give you a month on account, if you change your mind."

"Thanks." She stepped through into the hall, and it seemed she had forgotten her original errand. "Er—Mrs. Volger?"

She turned back to him, eyebrows raised, then remembered the letter in her hand. "Oh! Oh! Yes, your letter. I do hope it's good news, Major Parrish. I expect you could use some."

He took the letter from her. She watched him for a moment, as if hoping he might read it while she was there, share its contents.

That was too much for him. He nodded to her, thanked her again for coming up the stairs, and closed the door.

He sat down by the window, first pulling the flask out of his pocket. He uncapped it, something he had become deft at doing with one hand, and took a healthy swig before he set it on the round table beside the letter. There was no return address, but it was clearly his name, in full, written above the address of the boardinghouse. He turned it over and worked his thumb under the flap of the envelope. It was only lightly glued. It popped free easily, and he shook out the card inside.

It was one of those engraved things, an invitation, the typeface all curlicues and sweeping capital letters, deep burgundy ink on heavy beige card stock.

Mrs. Dickson Benedict
requests your presence at a garden party in honor of
Miss Allison Benedict
Saturday, September 18, 1920
Benedict Hall
at four in the afternoon
Cocktail attire
Respondez, s'il vous plait

Frank stared helplessly at this incomprehensible missive. Why on earth would Edith Benedict invite *him*, of all people, to an event honoring someone he had never heard of, much less met? He was about to reach for his flask, to soothe this new irritation, when he heard the telephone shrill in the downstairs hall. Moments later, Mrs. Volger's heavy step sounded again on the stair, followed by a knock on his door.

With an exasperated laugh, Frank tucked the flask underneath the day's newspaper, and went to answer.

"Major Parrish, you have a telephone call," Mrs. Volger panted. "She says it's—Doctor something. Dr. Benedict? Does that sound right?"

With a rush of relief, Frank said, "Yes, Mrs. Volger. It sure does!" He hurried out, pulling the door to his room closed behind him. "Thanks!" he said over his shoulder as he pattered down the stairs to the hall table. It was a bit tricky for him, holding the earpiece of the telephone in his hand, leaning down so he could speak into the receiver. "Hello? Margot, I hope that's you!"

Her deep chuckle reassured him. "Hello, Frank. I tried to catch you before it came, but I suppose you already have it."

"If you mean this invitation, yes. What have you got me into?"

She laughed. It was good to hear, after the stress of the past weeks, and it made him smile even as he bent nearly double over the little table. "I've got you into some silly party, Frank. I hope you won't mind too much. It's my cousin—my mother's niece. Allison. It's her debutante year, and they wanted to have her first public party at Benedict Hall."

"But, Margot—why me?"

"Oh! Mother insisted I have an escort. She says it's improper for me to attend on my own, and she insists I be there." There was a brief moment of silence, filled only by the faint clicking of the telephone line. Or someone listening in. Margot said, "You can say no if you want to."

In fact, Frank's first thought had been to refuse. Of course he would feel out of place and awkward, but it was the perfect excuse to postpone his departure a few days. Perhaps he could find the right moment to explain to Margot why he had to leave Seattle. He said, hastily now, "I'll come, if you want me to. Can't have Dr. Benedict going to a party unescorted."

"It's so silly, isn't it? All the things I do in the clinic, in the hospital—but I can't go to a garden party without a man holding my elbow!"

"You'd better explain what Mrs. Benedict means by cocktail attire," he said. "I've never heard of it."

"No one has," she answered in a wry tone. "That was Preston's idea. He says they're holding 'cocktail parties' in New York, and if Mother wants to be a fashion leader in Seattle, she should, too."

"Does she want that?"

"What she wants—as always—is to make Preston happy. He's going to write up the party in 'Seattle Razz,' so everyone has to look modish and up-to-date."

"I don't have a dinner jacket, Margot. All I have is my dress uniform."

"Oh, Frank," Margot said, and she laughed again, a deep sound that filled him with pleasure. "Please do wear that. Mother will *love* it!"

Margot, wary of another disaster like the photograph of her in the *Times* at the hospital benefit, turned to her sister-in-law for assistance in the matter of her dress for the garden party. Ramona looked wise when she approached her. "We must go shopping, Margot."

"Do we have to? We couldn't just order something . . . ?"

Ramona's laugh dismissed that idea without even a discussion. They were at breakfast, and Ramona rose from the table with a determined look.

"Absolutely not, Margot," she said, with an air of authority. "There's no time for you to be properly fitted, of course. We'll have to get something *prêt-à-porter* down at Frederick's, and there's really no time to lose. Why not go this morning?"

Meekly, Margot put down her coffee cup and stood up, pushing back her chair. The men were already gone. Edith had disappeared with the debutante and her mother to choose flowers and ribbons for the event. Loena and Leona stood together just inside the door, waiting for the last of the family to finish their breakfast. As Margot and Ramona approached the door, both maids curtsied. Margot rolled her eyes, and Loena giggled, making Ramona cast her a sharp glance.

"That girl is getting above herself," Ramona said when they were in the hall gathering their things.

"She's not, really, Ramona," Margot said. She made an effort to keep her tone mild. "I saw her yesterday at the clinic for a follow-up exam. She's just a bit giddy, happy with life in general. She knows how close she came to dying."

Ramona sniffed, but said nothing more. She made a brief telephone call to order a taxi, and it was soon waiting for them at the foot of the walk. They went out, side by side, and the taxi driver jumped out of his automobile to hold the door for them.

Ramona, it seemed, knew the proper taxi company to call. This driver was neatly dressed, and his vehicle was spotless. Margot found herself, in a very short while, stepping out on Pine Street. The Frederick's doorman, a well-spoken Negro in a billed cap and black leather gloves, opened the door of the taxi, then scurried ahead to hold the door of the store for the ladies. Ramona, without giving him so much as a glance, swept past. Margot followed, smiling at the man as she passed him. He bowed, and she thought, with a pang, of Blake.

She had gone to see Blake the night before, after her clinic hours. It required a streetcar ride and a walk of a half dozen blocks, but she had been rewarded by seeing him sitting up, listening to Sarah Church read from the *Times*. His eyes had brightened when he saw Margot. He managed to mumble a hello, and to take her hand in both of his and squeeze it.

The East Madison Convalescent Home was modest, even shabby, but it was clean and the staff was friendly. Sarah saw to it that Blake had everything he needed, but still Margot went to check on him every evening she could. His whereabouts were still a secret, even to Dr. Henderson.

"Margot?"

Margot blinked, startling out of her reverie. She had followed Ramona automatically, up in the elevator to the third floor, and now a saleswoman in a tidy coatdress, with a tape measure draped around her neck, was looking her up and down as if she were a mannequin to be adorned. The saleswoman said, in a cool voice, "Madame has a lovely figure."

Margot bit her lip to keep from laughing at this, but her sister-in-law clearly didn't find it amusing. She nodded sagely, one finger to her lips, and said, "Yes, she does. She won't need a corset, that's certain. Her legs are terribly long, though."

"Your message said cocktail attire?"

"Yes."

"So very chic," the woman murmured.

"It's to be a garden party at Benedict Hall. My cousin's debutante year, you know."

"How lovely," the saleswoman said smoothly. "Well. Most frocks are above the ankle this season, so I'm certain we can fit Madame. If Madame will permit?" She whipped off the tape measure with a practiced gesture, and began to measure Margot's shoulders, her hips, her waist. She conferred with Ramona over colors and fabrics before she disappeared into a back room. Margot stood, bemused, while Ramona toured the racks around them, fingering dresses, eyeing displays.

"This will be excellent for Madame, I think," the saleswoman said. She had returned with a gown draped over one arm, a silk slip and a long gauzy scarf over the other.

"Oh, good," Ramona said. Margot found herself a moment later in a dressing room. The two other women helped her out of her simple day frock and into the slip and the proposed evening gown. The saleswoman led her back out into the showroom, and pirouetted her before a long mirror while Ramona watched with a professional air. Margot had never seen her sister-in-law so confident. Ramona, clearly, was in her element.

She had to admit that Ramona and the Frederick's saleswoman knew what they were doing. The gown was long and narrow, a silk georgette crepe in a warm peach color. It sparkled with crystal beads, flowing easily over Margot's narrow hips. Its scalloped hem fell just to her ankles. The saleswoman stood to one side, her hands clasped to her cheeks in admiration. "Oh, Madame! So elegant. It's perfect."

Margot gazed at herself in the mirror. "I—I must say—" she said, then stopped.

Ramona, forgetting her dignity, giggled like a girl. "Oh, say it, Margot! You look swell!"

They caught each other's eyes in the mirror, and suddenly both were laughing. "Ramona, you're amazing! How did you know what would look good on me?"

Ramona shrugged a little, and pursed her lips smugly. "I've had practice," she said.

The saleswoman tweaked a seam here, a sleeve there, then stood back. "We'll just take in the waist a bit, shall we? And perhaps a bit in the shoulders. I have other gowns, naturally," she said. "But this sets off your coloring so nicely. And elbow-length gloves, I think?"

"Yes, definitely. Hair?" Ramona asked. She addressed the saleswoman directly, as if asking Margot would be a waste of time.

It would have been. Margot kept her hair short so she wouldn't have to fuss with it. She listened with bemusement as the two other women discussed what might be done to dress it up. In the end, she accepted Ramona's recommendation of a beaded bandeau to encircle her forehead. She only drew the line at a sweeping white silk feather. "I'd feel like a parrot," she protested.

Ramona held the feather this way and that near her face, then, surprisingly, nodded agreement. "You're right, Margot. It's too much. But promise you'll wear the bandeau!"

"As long as you don't think it makes me look like a Red Indian."

"Oh, no, Madame!" the saleswoman exclaimed. "All the ladies in New York and Paris are wearing them this year. They're very smart. Very *avant-garde.*"

Ramona had recovered her air of importance. "Have it all wrapped and sent to Benedict Hall, will you?"

"Of course, Madame. It's been my pleasure to assist you."

Margot couldn't help but notice that there was no mention of the bill. It would appear on Father's desk, she supposed, and be dealt with accordingly. Not until she and Ramona were shown to a table in the tearoom did she realize she hadn't the faintest idea how much money they had just spent. Ramona ordered their tea without looking at the menu, and Margot accepted that as well.

"Ramona, thank you for your help today," she said, when the

tea and a plate of finger sandwiches were set in front of them. "I never know what to wear."

"You're going to look beautiful," Ramona said with pride.

Impulsively, Margot said, "You're so good at this! You could be a designer, or a buyer for this very store."

At this, Ramona's eyebrows rose. "Why would I do that? Take a *job?*"

"I just meant—" Margot began, and then let her voice trail off. Women in aproned uniforms and frilled white caps moved among the tables, serving ladies in modish hats and summer wraps. She thought, observing the scene in the Frederick & Nelson tearoom, that she identified more with the waitresses than she did with the ladies at the tables. Than she did with her sister-in-law, or even with her mother.

She smiled across the china tea service at Ramona, and let it pass. For once, her sister-in-law had found something she could do for Margot, some way to showcase her own special abilities, and Margot felt real gratitude for it. For this one day, in this one instance, she supposed she didn't need to point out the irony of the situation. She had just bought a very pretty frock, and she could hardly wait to see Frank's face when he saw it. It was enough.

"After tea," Ramona said decisively, "we must find you some shoes. *Peau de soie*, I think, and not too high a heel! You don't want to tower over your escort."

Frank approached Benedict Hall past a line of cars crowding Fourteenth Avenue. Saloon and touring cars, Model Ts, even an imported Stanhope were parked in the street. Drivers in caps and gloves leaned on their automobiles, smoking, waiting for their passengers. Music floated from the garden, a small ensemble playing light classics and popular tunes. Frank was a little late, as Mrs. Volger had labored over his uniform with her cleaning cloths and irons longer than he had expected. She had also insisted on laundering his shirt and polishing his shoes, fussing over him in a maternal fashion that made him smile even as he squirmed under the attention.

He had decided not to bring flowers, and as he came up the walk, he was glad of it. Benedict Hall was awash in flowers. They massed in white wicker baskets, draped over decorative arches leading into the garden, bloomed in nosegays in small crystal vases on every surface he could see. The sounds of conversation and clinking glasses spilled out through the neighborhood. A man he had never seen, wearing a butler's coat and gloves, met him at the door, accepted his overcoat, and guided him around the wide porch to the garden. He announced him to the gathering, though no one seemed to pay the slightest attention.

Frank stood awkwardly at the edge of the porch, looking down on the colorful scene of women in silky long dresses and men in dinner jackets and bow ties. He didn't know anyone except the Benedicts, and they were scattered among the guests. Edith stood near a woman who looked very much like her, and with them was a nice-looking young girl in a white dress and long white gloves who Frank guessed to be the honoree.

"Oh, you're here. What a relief."

Frank turned just as Margot came up the porch steps and walked toward him, her hand outstretched. He thought, if he had not known her voice, and recognized her purposeful stride, he might not have recognized her. He knew nothing of clothes, but the narrow, flowing dress she wore suited her perfectly, and the tiny crystal beads in it glittered subtly in the slanting sunshine. She had a narrow shawl of embroidered Chinese silk, sprinkled with butterflies and cherry blossoms, draped around her shoulders, and she wore a strip of beaded fabric around her forehead. It rather neatly contained her shining dark hair, and somehow fitted her strong features. He couldn't find the words to tell her, but he saw by her smile, and the confident way she reached up to kiss his cheek, that she knew. He said, finally, inadequately, "You look so beautiful, Margot."

She laughed. "Ramona's doing. She has a real talent." She came around to his right side so she could take his arm with her gloved hand. She led him down the steps and through the chattering crowd to a linen-covered table where cups and glasses were laid out. "We don't really have cocktails, I'm afraid. Not out here in the open. Lemonade, some root beer, and tea, if you prefer it."

"Nothing, thanks. I'd just have to put the thing down if anyone wants to shake hands."

"Maybe later, then, Frank. Thanks so much for coming to stand by me."

He smiled at her, resisting an urge to kiss her in front of everyone, settling for pressing her hand close under his arm. She took him to meet the debutante, who was shaking hands with a line of well-wishers.

Allison Benedict still had a girlish plumpness, and had fair, fine hair that curled around her face. Her eyebrows were painted in thin arches, and her features were as delicate as those of a porcelain doll. Her expression was one of pure boredom. Frank wondered, as he waited his turn to be presented, if that was a fashion among young people, or if she really found the party enervating.

Edith was standing beside her niece. When they approached, she said, "Oh, Major Parrish! You're in your dress uniform! How handsome you look. Allison, this is Margot's friend, Major Frank Parrish. Major, Miss Benedict."

The debutante took in Frank's uniform, his major's insignia, his flattened sleeve folded into his pocket, and her blue eyes brightened, banishing the impatience in her expression. "How *do* you do, Major?" she said. As she shook his hand she leaned forward to add in an undertone, "I'll bet *you* have something more fascinating to talk about than the weather!"

Margot said, "Allison, behave yourself."

The girl pressed her cheek to Margot's. "Oh, Margot," she whispered, just loud enough for Frank to hear, "you're the only interesting one in the family. Trust you to bring the best-looking man!"

Margot laughed, and with a gentle tug, urged Frank away.

"That girl will cause everyone trouble one of these days, I can promise you."

Frank thought that was a reasonable prediction, but he grinned over his shoulder at the youngest Benedict before he followed Margot to a spot where they could stand out of the swirl of people. He saw Preston wandering here and there, a glass in his hand, a notebook and pencil prominently displayed in his jacket pocket. He looked stylish and self-possessed in his white linen dinner jacket, but he avoided the spot where Frank and Margot stood.

Dickson Benedict found them, though, and shook Frank's hand with a firm grip. "Thanks again for your help with the car, Major."

"A pleasure, sir. Anything I can do."

"Good man. Glad you could come tonight. Damned foolishness, this coming-out nonsense!" Frank thought his best recourse was to let this remark go unanswered.

Dickson disappeared into the crowd, but Frank found himself shaking hands with several other people, men in dinner jackets and women in dresses festooned with long necklaces and chiffon scarves. He would never remember who they were, but he did his best to appear polite.

As the sun set, the music grew louder. The hired butler came out to light the Chinese lanterns that had been hung from tree branches and from the latticework above the porch. A dance floor of polished boards was set up to one side. The strains of "Where the Lanterns Glow" filled the garden, and in the fragrant dusk, couples began to dance.

Frank leaned close to Margot and murmured in her ear, "I don't dance, I'm afraid."

"Oh, thank God, Frank! I always feel like an idiot when I try to dance. Let's just go up on the porch and sit down."

Together they forded the crowd, and went up the steps, where Margot leaned against a pillar, and Frank braced one hip against the porch railing. "How's Blake?" he asked.

"He's getting better," she said. "It's slow, but that's to be expected. You remember Sarah Church?" He nodded. "Father hired her to care for Blake in the convalescent home. He's walking a bit, with her help."

"Good." They were quiet for a moment. It was probably, Frank thought, a good time to tell her he had to leave Seattle, but she seemed to be enjoying the evening, and he didn't want to spoil it. Instead, he said, "What's your father going to do about the car?"

"It's still in the garage. I don't think he can bear to look at it."

"I could drive it to a mechanic for him. Get it repaired. Then he can sell it, or do whatever he wants. Has anyone started the engine recently?"

"No." She put out her hand to him, and when he took it, she pulled him up. "Let's go try it. We've made enough of an appearance, I think."

He followed her off the porch and across the close-cut grass toward the garage. The circle of light cast by the Chinese lanterns didn't reach past the middle of the lawn. Warm darkness enveloped them, and Frank liked the feeling that they were suddenly alone, though the music still rang behind them, and chatter and laughter filled the garden. Margot fumbled in the dimness for the door latch. When she found it, she pulled the door back, and they walked into an even deeper darkness smelling of gasoline and rubber. Frank could just make out the gleam of the Essex's headlamps and the shape of its crumpled fender. He said, "Is there an electric light?"

Margot, from the side wall, said, "I'm trying to find the switch."

She was several steps away from him, feeling along the wall with her hand, when they heard Preston's drawl. "What do you two think you're doing?"

Frank spun to face the open garage door. Preston lounged there, his white jacket making a languid silhouette against the yellow lantern light. He said, lightly but coldly, "Hardly the moment, do you think, old man?"

"I beg your pardon?" Frank said. Margot started toward her brother. With each stride, the beads of her dress cast tiny prisms of light in the gloom. Frank said, "What are you talking about, Benedict? The moment for what?"

"Shall we say—an assignation? Or is it something nastier?"

Margot said, "Don't be ridiculous, Preston."

"Ridiculous? Come on, doc. It's pretty clear you're no better than you should be."

Frank's jaw tightened, and his arm began to burn. He made his voice as even and expressionless as possible. "Watch what you say to your sister, Benedict." He walked toward the door. The best thing, he thought, was to take Margot's arm, lead her back to the party, and deal with the car another time.

Preston took one step to the side, right into Frank's path. "You know, Cowboy," he said. "You should really go home to Montana. You don't fit in here, do you? Why not go back to your cows?"

Frank stopped, an arm's length from Preston. "Whatever your trouble is, Benedict, this isn't the time or the place for us to have it out."

Preston's chuckle held no humor. "We're not having it out, old man. I'm merely making a suggestion."

"You'll forgive me if I don't take it." Frank took a step to his right, to go around Preston, but his adversary matched his movement.

Preston raised his head and sniffed. "Is that cow manure I smell?"

Margot said, "Preston, for God's sake."

Frank gritted, "Look, Benedict. I'm ready anytime if you're itching for a fight. Right now I'm going to take your sister back to the party. I'm only here to support her."

"Support her? With what?" Preston lifted his two hands, palms out. "This is what a man has, Cowboy. Two strong ones."

"I don't see that," Frank snapped. "You have two hands, don't you? They don't stop you from acting like a spoiled boy." Preston's angry breath hissed in his throat. Frank took a long step forward, shoving him to one side with his left shoulder. He put out his hand to Margot and she reached to take it.

At that moment Preston seized his arm—his left arm, the stump—and yanked at it.

Pain blazed from the damaged nerves. Frank's vision blurred under its onslaught, and a gasp of agony escaped him. He stumbled, and had to fight to keep his balance. Through a haze of pain, he heard Margot's voice.

"Back off, Preston," she snapped. Frank felt her hand on his arm and another on his back, steadying him, supporting him as he had meant to support her.

"Better keep your voice down, doc," Preston said. "You'll upset the mater."

Frank blinked to clear his vision. Fury burned in him, hotter even than the fire in his arm. "What the hell do you want, Benedict?" he demanded. He sensed the eyes turned to them, and he realized the music had stopped some moments before, but the agony in his arm and the humiliation of having to lean on Margot inflamed his temper. "You've cost me my job, cost Margot her hospital privileges. Isn't that enough? What's left?"

Preston grinned, his teeth shining white in the reflected lamplight. He said, almost gaily, "Just trying to preserve the dignity of the Benedict name, old man."

"By causing a scene at a party?"

"I don't like seeing my sister keep company with a cripple," Preston answered. He made a negligent gesture with one hand, a flick of the fingers as if he were brushing away cobwebs, as if the cruelty of his words was hardly worth noticing. "It's bad enough she puts her hands all over whores and drunks and God-knows-who-else, but you . . ."

Frank said, "You're a head case, Benedict."

The insult struck home. Preston made a guttural sound, as if he were a dog that had been kicked. He raised his hand, hissing, "I want you to stay away from my family!"

A flood of light suddenly glared on them, light from a single unshaded bulb hanging from the garage ceiling. Dickson Benedict was there, his hand on the light switch, his thick eyebrows raised in question. The light caught Frank with his fist cocked, ready to defend himself.

Preston cast a sidelong glance at his father, and he pressed the flat of his palm against his shirtfront, beneath his dinner jacket and his striped silk tie.

Dickson said, "Preston, what—"

Frank exclaimed, "I'll be damned! You're still wearing that stone—the one you murdered for."

Preston balanced on the balls of his feet, like a boxer. Two spots of color flamed high on his cheekbones, and he hissed, "Back away from me, Parrish, or you'll regret it."

Frank's belly tightened, and his nostrils flared at the scent of rage surrounding Preston. It was sour and strong, like the scorch of a flatiron on wet linen. Frank grated, "Let's have it out now, then, Benedict. Get it out in the open. I know about you. I know you're a murderer and you're a liar."

"You don't know anything," Preston said.

Dickson demanded, "What's going on?"

Margot said something to him in an urgent tone. Frank was barely aware of them, or of the faces turned toward them from the garden. Everything in him focused on Preston, on his fingers spread wide on his shirtfront, on the glitter in his eyes, the cruelty in his handsome face. "I know enough, Benedict. I know what you are."

Dickson said, "Just a moment, Major—Preston—"

Preston leaned toward Frank, whispering, "What? What am I, Cowboy?"

"You're not right. Not normal. There's something rotten inside you."

Dickson tried to take his son's arm, to step in between the two men. Preston shook him off, never loosening his grasp on what he held.

Frank said, "You think it's a magic amulet, Benedict? *Arabian Nights?* That's insane!"

Preston's eyelids flickered, a brief look of doubt that vanished a heartbeat later. He began to pant, for all the world like a maddened dog. His eyes glittered with the sort of craziness Frank had seen all too often in the East, when bloodlust seized a man and drove all reason away.

Frank straightened his shoulders, wresting control of his own temper. He stepped back, out of Preston's reach. "Look, Benedict. You and I can talk this out at a better time—"

But Preston lunged at him. He caught Frank's amputated arm with both his hands, and with a vicious, deliberate movement, he twisted it. He seemed to know precisely where his fingers would hurt the most. His manicured nails dug into the sensitive nerves until Frank felt, sickeningly, as if his arm had been severed a second time.

His world tilted. North became south. East and west reversed. A cloud of blackness swallowed him. From a distance, he heard Margot say, "Preston, stop it!" and Dickson cry some wordless protest. Frank tried to grapple with Preston, to free his arm from that relentless grip, but he groped into darkness. Something struck his shoulder and the side of his head. He wanted to call out to Margot, to apologize, but he had no breath. He rolled onto his back, away from the pain, but it rolled with him, a searing agony that turned his muscles to water. He lay uselessly on the grass, the harsh light of the exposed bulb shining full on his face, illuminating his weakness.

His humiliation was complete.

Margot took a long step forward and snatched at Preston's hand, pulling it away from Frank. She thrust him backward with all her strength. "Bastard!" He stumbled slightly, but he was grinning now as if it were all a great joke, holding both palms up in mock surrender.

"Don't get excited, doc!" he said. "It was just a little pinch!"

Dickson growled, "Preston, for shame! Get control of yourself!"

"Keep him away, Father!" Margot fell to her knees in the grass beside Frank. She reached across him for his right hand, and chafed the wrist in both of her palms. His eyes were closed, his lips pulled back from gritted teeth. His breathing was shallow, and beads of perspiration dotted his forehead. "Hold on, Frank," she said. "It should be better in a moment. I'll try to find you some—"

She broke off. A hand extended in front of her face, holding a silver hip flask with a cork stopper. Margot, startled, looked up to find her father bending over her.

He pulled the cork out of the neck of the flask. "Give him a jolt of this," he said in a matter-of-fact tone. "That must hurt like the devil."

"Help me lift him first, Father," she said. "Careful—careful of that side."

Cautiously, Dickson Benedict got an arm under Frank's shoulders and lifted him out of the dirt. Margot cupped his jaw with her left hand, and held the flask to his lips. "Can you swallow, Frank? This will help."

His eyelids fluttered open, but his eyes were unfocused, and she doubted he could see her. She touched the cool metal to his mouth, and tipped up the flask.

Frank swallowed one mouthful, then another. He took a shaky breath, and swallowed again. His cheeks pinked up almost immediately, and his breathing slowed and deepened. He blinked, hard, and his eyes focused on her face. "Goddamn it," he muttered.

"Just take a moment," she said.

Dickson steadied Frank with his arm. Frank struggled to sit up, to take control of himself. He said, "Sir, I'm—sorry about the scene. Christ, I'm—sorry."

Margot's eyes were on her father at that moment, and she saw steel in his gaze, and anger in the flush on his neck. He rumbled, "Not your fault, Major."

Dickson released Frank, who had steadied enough to sit on his own. Grunting, Dickson came to his feet, and glowered over his shoulder at Preston, who had faded back into the crowd of people. "I apologize for my son. I don't know what your disagreement was, but that was a damn lousy thing to do."

Margot said, "Frank, surely now you'll let me have a look at your arm. It doesn't need to be like—"

The desperate plea in his eyes made her stop speaking.

Frank refused more whisky, though his arm still blazed with pain. Margot, her face pale and her jaw set, helped him to his feet, then slipped the hip flask into his left pocket, beneath his folded sleeve.

"Come into the house," she said quietly. "We can have our supper in the kitchen with Hattie."

"I couldn't eat anything, Margot. The whole evening is— Lord, what a mess."

"It was hardly your fault."

"I shouldn't have come."

Her hand suddenly trembled beneath his arm. Her shoulders slumped, hunching so that the pretty silk scarf slipped down to her elbows. She said bleakly, "Are we going to let Preston rule our lives, then?"

"He'll write another column about me," Frank said.

"He wouldn't dare. Father won't allow it."

"Well." Frank tried to laugh, but succeeded only in a gulp of misery. "It's not as if I have anything left to lose."

Margot dropped her hand from his arm. She didn't know, of course, that he had no choice but to leave Seattle. That he was about to lose her in any case. He cast about for some way to explain to her, to say that he hadn't meant—

She said abruptly, as they walked side by side toward the porch, "I'm going to move out of Benedict Hall."

"What? But—where will you go?"

"I have the clinic. I'll fix up the storeroom as a bedroom."

"No," Frank said, without thinking.

"That sounds like an order."

He shook his head, powerless to explain his feelings about the idea. "Not an order, Margot, of course. Not—just—just not there."

"It's the best place for me."

"It's not! It's not safe for you, Margot! A woman living alone . . ."

"Frank." She fixed him with her dark, unwavering gaze. Her voice roughened, and she sounded very much like her father. "Without Blake, I'm not safe here, in Benedict Hall. Tonight was a warning."

They reached the porch, ignoring the curious gazes of the partygoers. Supper was laid out on long covered tables, and the hired butler and the two redheaded maids were slicing a roast, dishing out salad, offering baskets of rolls and butter, pouring coffee into tiny china cups. Conversation and laughter filled the garden, and the ladies' dresses spread over chairs and benches like pressed flowers over the pages of a book. Frank's temper subsided under a wave of sadness. Preston was right, he supposed. He didn't belong here. He didn't fit into Margot's life.

She started toward the front door, but he stopped. "I'd better go," he said.

"Come in, Frank. Let's talk."

"I don't think I should."

"Because of Preston?"

"Because of everything. Your family—"

"The family doesn't matter."

"It does. It always will." Frank gazed into her face, her clear dark eyes, her determined mouth. Dickson's flask felt like lead in his pocket, a reminder of his weakness, but a promise of relief. He wanted another drink, badly. He wanted, even more, to explain to Margot, but the words wouldn't come.

She watched him for a long moment, her eyes full of hurt, her shoulders hunched in that defensive way, ruining the drape of her frock. She said bitterly, "So Preston wins."

Helplessly, uselessly, he stared at her. He wanted to blurt it all out to her, tell her how bad it really was, but he had so little pride left. None, really. He couldn't do it. He couldn't find the way to bridge the gap between them.

And she wasn't going to do it, either, he could see. Not this time. A spark flared in her eyes, and her shoulders straightened, stiffened. "So, you don't think I should live alone, but you won't come in and discuss it with me. What do you suggest I do?"

Mute with misery, he could only shake his head once more.

Her eyes were bright now with anger, and her chin thrust out. "I don't know what you want, Frank."

The words were in his mouth, on his lips. In his heart. But how could he speak them? It wouldn't be right. He had nothing to offer her. "If things were different—" he began.

"They are what they are, Frank. I have to deal with it, and so do you." She turned in a glittering whirl of beaded silk, and stalked in through the front door.

They weren't speaking of the same thing at all, but Frank, silent and stunned, couldn't think how to set it right. He stood alone, watching her disappear inside the fortress that was Benedict Hall.

Preston's hand shook with rage, making the curtain rings rattle against the rod. He stood just out of sight in the window of his bedroom as Parrish, healthy and more or less intact, strode away down the hill. Starlight gleamed on his dark hair, making it look polished. His lean shoulders were back, his head high, his steps quick and determined. He should have been dead. At the very least, he should still have been writhing in pain.

Preston dropped the curtain, and spun to gaze at the sapphire, gleaming dully from the coverlet of his bed. He had flung it there in exasperation, and now he glared at it, as if he could vent his anger on it, as if he could wrest an explanation from its depths. He had stood there with the stone in his hand, in front of everyone, risking exposure. He had concentrated, had poured his desire into it, with Parrish no more than an arm's length away. It was just what he had done with Blake, and that had been a triumph. But now, tonight—his heart pounded with fresh fury as he thought of it—there had been *nothing!*

The bloody stone had rested in his hand as if it were no more than a piece of jewelry, some effeminate gem meant for a vain old woman. It wasn't a deep, rich blue anymore. It had faded, its glow dimming to a pinkish hue he didn't recognize. It was as if its fire had gone out. It didn't even call to him now, lying on his bed in the little pool of its silver chain. It was useless.

Humiliation built in his belly, threatened to explode in his chest. Parrish had called him insane. The looks his father—and his insufferable *sister*—had bent on him made him feel like a spider they would as soon crush beneath a shoe as tolerate in the same house with them. His mother and his sister-in-law—oh, God, was he reduced to counting on brainless Ramona?—had fussed over him, tried to defend him to Dickson. But what did they count? Women! God, he hated women! It was too bad the world couldn't sustain itself without them.

He paced his bedroom, around the bed, past the bureau, back to the window. He thought his heart might burst from his chest from the sheer pressure of rage and frustration and injustice. Frank Parrish! Father chose an *outsider* over him, preferred a one-armed cripple to his own son. He expected it of Margot, of course. She had always been hateful. But even Dick had said something nasty as he passed him in the garden, something about disciplining himself.

Preston pounded his chest with one fist, hardly able to contain the tumult building inside him. What had gone wrong? What had changed?

He stopped beside the bed, breathing hard, and gazed down at the stone. For the first time, he allowed himself to think that it might, after all, have been his imagination.

But that couldn't be. "Seattle Razz" wasn't his imagination. His newfound reputation, the admiration of Seattle society, that wasn't his imagination. It had to be something else.

Margot, of course. It had always been Margot, and tonight was the same. She had simply gotten in his way before he could finish what he started.

He would settle her for good. He would do it as soon as possible. Then there would be nothing in the world to hold him back.

CHAPTER 18

Margot went to the telephone in the hall, and asked the operator for the Alexis Hotel. As she waited to be connected, she leaned against the wall, closing her eyes, trying not to remember Frank's stricken face, her own harsh words. She was tempted to put the receiver down, to dash down the street after him. But what would she say? She couldn't beg.

When the hotel desk answered, she booked a room for a week. She estimated her funds would just about cover that while she applied to other hospitals, and saw to a bed and a bureau for the storeroom. She would take Blake's hot plate so she could do a little of her own cooking. Toast and tea she could manage, perhaps a scrambled egg once in a while.

She broke the connection with the hotel clerk and started up to her room to pack a bag. Hattie, wearing her best long white apron, passed through the hall with a carafe of lemonade for the party. She didn't look up, and Margot went on up the stairs.

She gazed at herself in the mirror over her washstand for an uncomfortable moment. She had really thought, before the party started, that she looked well in this dress, fashionably slender, well turned out. Now, her eyes looked bruised, and her hair was disordered beneath the bandeau. She had just enough ego left to wish Frank had not seen her like this.

She took off the gown and threw it over a chair. Ramona could find some use for it. She couldn't imagine she would ever want to put it on again. She pulled on a dressing gown, then took her valise from its shelf, and began to fold skirts and shirt-waists into it.

She was just closing the lid when someone knocked on her door. Her father's voice said, "Margot? May I speak with you?"

She snapped the lock shut, and straightened. "Of course, Father."

He came in, and closed the door behind him. His eyebrows rose at the sight of the valise on her bed. "What's this?"

"I'm leaving." She folded her arms, and stood gazing down at the bed with its virginal white bedspread and embroidered pillowcases. It had been hers since girlhood. A wave of regret at the necessity of what she was doing tightened her throat. "I know you don't want to believe it, Father. And Mother never will. But I'm not safe here."

"Not safe? In your own home?"

"Not with Blake gone. I'm sorry, Father, but that's the truth."

Her father seemed to sag, suddenly, to diminish in size, and in presence. "I was going to tell you—" he began. White spots suddenly appeared around his mouth and nose. "I wanted to explain that when—when Blake came to see me—" His voice faltered.

"Take your time," Margot said, as gently as she could.

"I didn't listen. I should have—" His voice broke completely, and he passed his hand over his eyes.

"Father!" Margot was beside him in a stride, helping him to sit on the lacy stool in front of her dressing table.

He sank onto it, and gently pushed away her hands. "I'm all right, Margot."

Margot knelt beside his stool, her hands on her bent knees. She said warily, "What did Blake try to tell you?"

"He tried to warn me about Preston."

"You mean, the day of the accident?"

"Yes. But before that, long ago, when you were all still young. He tried to tell me—but I thought it was just, you know, hijinks. Childish pranks. You were Blake's favorite, and I thought that made him protective. Stricter with the boys."

Margot pushed herself to her feet and walked to the window. The lights from the Chinese lanterns shone on the front lawn, and the music had resumed from the garden.

Behind her, Dickson said, "I just couldn't believe that my son—my own son—"

Margot remembered Frank's ashen face, his eyes blurred with pain, and her heart hardened. "There are no excuses for him. Not anymore."

"I keep thinking there must be an explanation, a reason. The accident—"

"Preston would do anything that served his purpose."

Her father winced at the harshness in her voice. "But what purpose could he have? Why would he want to harm Major Parrish? Or Blake?"

"As you just said, Father. Blake knew what Preston was. He knew Preston hated me." Her voice sounded like breaking glass.

"But, Margot—*why?*"

Margot sighed. The years of struggle made her feel ancient and worn. It was hard to remember sometimes that she was only twenty-eight.

She crossed to her bed, and sat down beside the valise. "I suppose it's because I came first," she said sadly. "And because you and I—I know we argue all the time, but we—we have an understanding, don't we? And Preston couldn't be part of it."

"But he could have!"

"I don't think he could, Father. He doesn't *think* the way we do."

Her father let his head drop into one hand, and she feared he might actually weep. He said in a muffled voice, "What do we do now?"

She tried to speak bracingly, to steady him and herself. "I don't know yet. But it will help if I'm out of the house."

He lifted his head, and to her relief there were no tears in his eyes, only the same dragging weariness she herself felt. "I don't want you to go, daughter."

"And I don't want to make you choose."

"But where will you live?"

"At my office, eventually. But for now, I'll spend a few days at the Alexis."

Dickson came heavily to his feet, bracing his weight on the dressing table. "Have them send the bill to me."

"No, I—"

For a moment, he looked like his old self, his mouth firm, his chin jutting. "Don't argue with me, Margot. You're going to let me do this one thing. We're not going to discuss it."

Further protest died on her lips. She knew she often looked very much like her father did at this moment, leading with her chin. She understood it. She rose, too, and crossed to her father to press her cheek to his. "Thank you, Father," she said. "That will be a big help."

"And what about Major Parrish?"

She pulled back, and said warily, "What about him?"

"I like him, Margot. I think you do, too."

"I suppose that's obvious."

"It is to me. But I know you, daughter. It may not be so obvious to him." The corners of her father's mouth relaxed, just a little, and his voice was easier. "He's a fine man."

She looked away, back to the starry night beyond her bedroom window. "Yes, he is."

"Does his—his wound—does that hold you back?"

Startled, she whirled to face him. "No! Of course not. What do I care about that?"

"It holds *him* back, though."

She stared at her father, frowning. "What do you mean, it holds him back? From what?"

"Think, Margot. His arm is gone; his job is gone. Probably his money is gone. He feels like half a man."

"Why should he feel that way?" she demanded. "What does any of that matter?"

Dickson shook his head. "Margot. Put yourself in his shoes. What if you were about to lose your clinic?"

"I—" She put a hand to her lips, thinking of it. "Yes. I see what you mean."

"I think you're a match for each other."

Margot dropped her hand, and folded her arms around herself. "I don't know, Father. I'm not sure he thinks so." She gave a small, pained sigh. "He doesn't talk much."

"I noticed that." Dickson picked up her valise. "Come. I'll call you a taxicab."

She led the way out of the bedroom. As they descended the staircase together, Preston emerged from the small parlor and looked up at the two of them. "What's this?" he asked brightly, as if nothing at all had happened. "Going on a trip?"

Margot brushed past him without answering. Dickson said, "Preston, go tell your mother that Margot's leaving. She'll want to say good-bye."

Margot glanced over her shoulder at Preston's suddenly frozen face. "Never mind," Margot said, meeting her brother's gaze with her own hard one. "I'll speak to her myself."

Dickson went to the telephone on the hall table. Margot turned toward the small parlor. Preston came close to murmur, "Watch yourself, Margot. I'm warning you."

She paused, an arm's length away. "Warning me of what?"

"You keep sneaking around behind my back, talking about me to Father, to Mother. Like you did to Blake."

"Preston. You're—" For a moment she couldn't think of the word. She stared at his cold, handsome features, and her belly crawled with revulsion. "You're irredeemable," she finished at last, in an undertone.

His laugh was short and hard. "I don't need redemption."

"What do you need? I've never known."

His eyes were like blue ice, fixed on hers with the baleful attitude of a snake. "I need you out of my life," he whispered.

She shrugged. "You should be happy I'm leaving, then."

As she turned away, she thought she heard him say something like "That won't be enough," but she wasn't certain, and she didn't stop to ask. She had had all she could take of her younger brother.

Frank lay awake most of that night. The morning after the party he got on the streetcar and rode up Broadway, meaning to go to Benedict Hall and try to explain to Margot, but in the end he simply rode it back again, and paced his room trying to think what to do.

He couldn't leave without seeing her. But what could he say to her? That if he were whole, if he had work, if he had a future—he would ask her to share it? Even the idea of broaching the subject stirred the memory of Elizabeth's shocked face as she stared at the devastation of his arm, and made him shudder with shame and revulsion. He would just tell Margot he needed to look for work. He wouldn't tell her what was in his heart. He thought if he ever were to see that same revolted look on Margot's face, he would never get over it.

Half a dozen times that day he passed the telephone on its stand in Mrs. Volger's hallway. Each time he yearned toward it, wishing he had a reason to call her, some excuse that didn't mean further humiliation. Had she kept her vow to leave Benedict Hall? If he called, would Preston answer? Her mother? It was all hopeless. A mess.

He decided, as the afternoon wore on, that the thing to do was to present himself at the clinic when she was ready to close. Blake had usually been there to drive her home, and seeing the street empty when she came out must be painful.

Clouds had rolled in over the city, and the cooler air smelled of autumn. Here and there maple trees had begun to turn, spots of red and gold flaring against the ubiquitous evergreens. Frank walked down Cherry, and crossed Madison, turning onto Post Street at about five thirty. He paused a moment to look up at the familiar sign—M. BENEDICT, M.D. in those strong red letters—

and to gather his courage. Then, after adjusting his hat and smoothing his sleeve into his pocket, he pushed the door open.

She wore her white cotton coat over a shirtwaist and a pleated wool skirt. She was seated at her nurse's desk with an open ledger in front of her. At the sound of the door, she lifted her head. Frank's heart gave a twinge at her drawn look, the darkness beneath her eyes. Her hair was tumbled, as if she had been pushing her fingers through it. He wanted to cross to her, go around the desk, pull her up into his embrace. Instead, he found himself blurting, "Where's Thea?"

Something about the wryness of her sudden smile told him she understood, and the alacrity with which she rose from her chair and came around the desk to meet him told him he had done the right thing, even if the right words had eluded him. His feet carried him forward without his volition. They met in the middle of the little reception room.

It felt so natural he couldn't think why it had taken him a whole day to come. Her long arms went around him, and his good right arm pulled her close. Her lean body melted into his, and she buried her face against his neck. He said into her hair, "I'm so sorry, Margot."

She said in a muffled voice, "Sorry for what?"

He laughed a little, and held her tighter. "Everything. For being—a cowboy."

At this, she laughed, too, and he felt the movement of her small breasts against his chest. For long moments they didn't speak. He let his cheek rest against her hair. He breathed in the scent of her shampoo, mixed with the faint tang of medicine that clung to her coat. Only when she stirred did he release her, and then only to kiss her, firmly and at length.

When he was done, she said mistily, "Oh, Frank! I'm so glad you're here."

He released her, but caught her hand in his, reluctant to let her go. "Last night was just—"

She made a vague gesture, then pulled her hand free, gently, to begin unbuttoning her white coat. "It was ghastly," she said. "And embarrassing. I should have understood that."

"You're not angry with me."

"Of course not." She tossed her coat over the back of Thea's chair. "Thea couldn't make it in today. Her husband is ill again." As she moved toward the rack where her street coat and hat hung, the telephone rang. She went back to the desk and picked it up. "Dr. Benedict speaking."

Frank took her things from the coatrack as he waited for her to finish the call. Her end of the conversation was terse. When she put down the receiver, she said, "That's Thea's neighbor. Norman is much worse, evidently. They're on their way here." She picked up her white coat again, and pulled it on. "Can you help me, Frank? I ordered some bottles of oxygen from the surgical supply house, and they came today. They're in the storeroom, but I don't have an anaesthetic mask. If you could go down to Bartell's, they might have one."

"Happy to help. Where is it?"

She cast him a grateful look as she started on the buttons. "First and Pike. Thank you."

Frank hadn't been to Bartell's before, but he found it easily. It was a modern drugstore, its shelves packed with bottled medicines, boxes of tooth powder, sacks of bluing, cans of pipe tobacco. The clerk quickly found the mask and tubing he needed behind a rack of peanut brittle and chocolate-dipped cherries, but he insisted on wrapping the supplies in brown paper, tying them neatly with string, though Frank told him he was in a hurry. He strode swiftly back to the clinic with the package under his arm.

The taxicab that had carried Thea and Norman from their home was just pulling away when Frank reached Post Street again. At Margot's direction, Frank fetched an oxygen bottle from a row of three in the storeroom. He carried the bottle into the examining room. Thea's husband lay on the high table, a pillow tucked beneath his head, a woolen blanket across his legs. Frank could hear his wheeze while he was still in the short hallway.

Norman was so thin it seemed his bones might break through his skin. His hair was limp and colorless against the white pillow-case, and his lips and nostrils were as blue as the waters of Elliott Bay in the summer. Frank had seen men who looked just that way in the hospital in Virginia. They had all died.

Thea and Margot worked together in efficient silence. Margot fastened the anaesthesia mask to a rubber bag, then connected the apparatus to the oxygen. Thea held the mask over Norman's face as Margot monitored his pulse, and operated the valve on the oxygen bottle with her other hand. After each inspiration, Thea lifted the mask for her husband to exhale, then replaced it. The little room filled with the sounds of Norman's struggles to breathe and his occasional, desperate moans.

Frank went back to the waiting room. He left the door open, so he could hear Margot if she called to him. He didn't bother turning on the light, but leaned against the wall near the door, his hand in his pocket, staring blindly out into the darkening street.

It was all achingly familiar. Sounds like this had been com-monplace in the hospital in Virginia. He had become so accus-tomed to the smells of disinfectant and ether and damaged flesh that he hardly noticed them. Since leaving the hospital he had tried to put them out of his mind, but now, here, he remembered. Norman *smelled* of death. It was only a matter of time, no matter how hard Margot worked over him.

An unexpected yearning swept through Frank. He longed, suddenly, to be home, under the wide, clear Montana sky, breath-ing the invigorating scents of grazing cattle and freshly cut hay. He thought of his mother, kneading biscuits on the ancient board in the kitchen. He thought of his father, climbing down from the hay rig, loosening the harness so the big draft horses, smelling of healthy horseflesh and summer sunshine, could munch grass in the shade. It was all lost to him, all the vibrant strength and sweetness. Norman would die, as so many others had, and leave his grieving widow behind. Frank would have to go in search of some way to support himself, and he would have to leave Margot to do it.

There was no escaping the aftermath of the war. His arm burned, as if chafed by the very memories he had tried to put away. He groped in his pocket, but his flask wasn't there.

Thea said, "His lips are pinker."

"Oxygen relieves the anoxaemia," Margot said. "It's temporary, I'm afraid."

Thea gazed down at her husband. "He's suffered so much." Her brow contracted, and she said in a choked voice, "Perhaps I should just let him go."

Norman's pulse was thready beneath Margot's fingers. "He could go to the hospital."

"If he goes to the hospital, they'll put him in one of the public wards—no one will pay him any attention, and he'll die there, all alone!"

Margot released Norman's wrist. "You and I can't keep this up all night."

"I know," Thea said. She lifted her eyes to Margot's. They were red-rimmed, but steady. "I'm not sure we should in any case. He's not going to get well, is he?"

Margot glanced at Norman. His eyes were closed, all his energy focused on breathing, in, out, in, out. Briefly, she wondered which was harder, the inhalation or the exhalation. It was no wonder he was so thin. It must take constant effort simply to force air through those scarred lungs. She said gravely, "No, Thea. Norman's not going to get well."

"He said, just the other night, that it would have been better if he'd died in France. Died with his buddies, he said. He hates lying in bed all the time. Being helpless."

Margot could sense Frank waiting in the outer office. There was a great deal she didn't know about him, but she was certain he, too, would have hated being an invalid. Bad as he felt things were, as badly as his arm hurt him, he still had a life. He had only to find it.

She wanted to say something hopeful to Thea, but she couldn't bring herself to speak false comfort. It wasn't her way, and her nurse knew that. They looked at each other in the silence of the night, and understanding flashed between them.

It was Thea who reached for the mask. With gentle fingers, she lifted it from her husband's mouth and nose, then caressed his forehead with the back of her hand. Margot coiled the tubing, and took the mask when Thea handed it to her.

"I'll prepare an injection of scopolamine. There's no point in Norman being in pain."

"Thank you." Thea's voice shook only a little. She bent over her husband to press her lips to his cheek, then pulled a chair close and sat down. She held his hand, but she didn't put her fingers over his pulse. Sorrow filled the room. The air was thick with it, its presence as discrete as the smell of alcohol. Though Thea did not weep, nor did Norman make any sound beyond his labored breathing, it was a relief to Margot to step out, to have respite from the atmosphere of grief, even for a moment.

When she came back with the syringe, she found Thea with her eyes closed, Norman's hand cradled at her breast. Norman's lips had gone blue again. His breath scraped through his throat in ribbons so thin his chest barely moved.

She gave him the injection, and his face relaxed a bit. She murmured, "Call me if you need me, Thea. I'll be in the reception room," and slipped out. On her way she turned off the light, leaving Thea and Norman in a comfortable darkness. In the little hallway, moonlight filtered through the small window of her office, just enough for her to see where she was going.

She left the lights off in the waiting room, as well. She removed her white coat and hung it up. She and Frank sat down together on the little divan. She sat on his right side, and he gathered her close to him with his arm. It was comforting to rest her head on his shoulder, to feel his masculine solidity. The weight of his head against her hair felt proprietary, and her burden of responsibility lessened, as if by his very proximity he could share it. She murmured, "Thea doesn't want Norman to die in the hospital."

"Right."

"I can't leave her here alone with him."

"We'll stay."

"You don't need—"

"Hush, Margot. We'll stay together."

She was so tired. Frank wriggled into a more comfortable position, his head back against the frame of the divan. Margot kicked off her shoes and tucked her feet beneath her. She rested her cheek against the rough fabric of Frank's coat, and listened to the rasp of Norman's struggles to breathe. Darkness enfolded the little building, so that there was nothing in the world but the final breaths of the dying man, the faint sounds of occasional foot traffic in Post Street, the steady beat of Frank's heart so near to her own. For a time she dozed.

She startled awake at the creak of the back door of the clinic. She sat up straight, and listened. Frank stirred beside her. "What?"

She put a finger to her lips. She heard nothing from the examining room.

Margot got to her feet. Frank stood up, too, just as a step sounded in the little hallway, and the door to the storeroom opened and closed. Margot said, "There's someone back there."

"Thea?"

"Perhaps she decided to give more oxygen after all." Margot crossed the waiting room in her stocking feet, and peeked into the examining room. Thea still sat beside the bed, her forehead resting against the edge. Norman made no sound at all.

Margot went to him, and put her hand on his wrist.

Thea said in a thin voice, "He stopped breathing a few minutes ago."

Margot found her stethoscope on the counter, and fitted the earpieces to her ears. She put the bell to Norman's chest and listened for a moment. There was only silence. Norman was released at last from his suffering. She straightened, and pulled off the stethoscope. "He's gone, Thea. I'm sorry." Thea only nodded.

From the doorway, Frank murmured, "Margot—there's someone in your storeroom."

She had forgotten the sounds. She turned sharply about, and started toward the door. "It could be someone looking for alcohol," she said. "It's happened before."

Frank put up his hand. "I'll go. Stay with Thea."

He hadn't taken more than two steps before they heard an odd whoosh, just audible in the quiet. Margot couldn't identify the sound, and before she could think about it there was a clatter, as of something being dropped or thrown. Frank broke into a run.

Margot reached the hall just in time to see Frank hauling Preston out of the storeroom by his arm. Preston wore a long coat and a hat pulled down over his forehead, and he tried to yank his arm free of Frank's grasp.

Frank spun Preston around, and shouted something. A sudden rush of fire billowing from the storeroom drowned his words. Glass popped, and burning wood made great cracking sounds. Thea cried out, "What's happened?"

Margot stared in shock as angry red fire roared up behind Frank and Preston. The two men struggled, their silhouettes dark against the flames. It looked as if Frank was trying to pull Preston down the hall, away from the fire. Of course, he would know, the engineer. Everything in that storeroom was flammable: alcohol, ether, cotton, wooden shelves . . . oxygen bottles!

Margot recovered herself enough to cry, "It's a fire! Thea, call the fire trucks!" before she started toward the two men. Halfway there, she saw her brother twist free of Frank's grasp. He flattened himself against the wall, opposite the now-blazing storeroom.

Frank lunged for him.

Preston pulled back his fist and launched it at Frank's face.

Margot found she was screaming. "Frank! Frank, no! Let him go!"

Frank took the punch on his bad shoulder, and Margot heard him choke, "Benedict! You have to get out of here!"

Preston's lips pulled back in a rictus of a grin, an expression made demonic by the lurid light of the fire. The ceiling had caught the flames, and the fire flared across the top of the little building with a rush of sound and heat. Preston pulled back his arm again, readying another blow.

Margot reached Frank and seized his arm. It was the bad one, but it was closest, and there was no time to be gentle. She pulled him back, away from Preston, away from the fire, past the examining room and toward the front door. She gave her office a despairing glance, lamenting her books, her diploma, but there was no time to save anything. The fire was racing across the roof. She could hear it, and she could feel it. Thea, weeping, begged someone on the telephone to hurry. There was nothing to be done about Norman's body, either, and Thea would know that.

Frank resisted her hand. She could tell by the heat of his body that his arm must pain him furiously. She said, "Thea! Outside! Frank, we have to get out!"

Frank shouted, "But he doesn't know about—"

Two concussions shook the building, dull, deep thuds in such quick succession they were nearly indistinguishable. The storeroom, Margot's office, the little hallway, erupted in a wall of flame that sped toward the waiting room with breathtaking speed.

Frank cursed, and dashed toward the front door. "I'll go around back," he shouted. Margot cried, "No! Frank, wait!" but he had already disappeared.

With a thudding heart, Margot guided Thea through the front door into the cool darkness of the street. A handful of men were running toward them, shouting with excitement as they dashed up from the speakeasies on Western Avenue. In the distance a fire bell clanged, but the roar of the fire nearly drowned out its hollow voice.

A single high, thin shriek pierced the din of shouts and splintering wood and the roar of the motor of the fire truck. Thea gave a horrified scream, and turned to stare at the billows of smoke, the spears of orange flames. Her hands to her face, she beseeched Margot, "He was dead, wasn't he? Norman was already dead? Oh, my God, Margot, he's not *burning?*"

Margot gripped Thea's arm, hard. Over the racket, she cried, "No, Thea, no! He was already gone. You know that!"

"Then who—?" Thea began to sob. Margot didn't try to answer. Aghast, she stared at the inferno. Her brother was in there. Despite everything, it turned her stomach to think of her blond, handsome brother suffocating with smoke, crushed beneath blazing timbers. And where was Frank? Was he in there, too? It would be just like Preston to escape, and to allow Frank to perish in his place.

In the midst of the heat and noise and glare, Margot felt frozen. She just managed to move her arm, to put it around Thea, to allow her to weep on her shoulder. They clung together as leather-helmeted firemen streamed past. Thea sobbed, and Margot trembled. There was nothing they could do but watch Margot's dream burn to the ground, taking Norman's body with it.

CHAPTER 19

The heat from the fire reached to Margot and Thea where they stood. An ambulance arrived, and one of the drivers, a man Margot recognized from the hospital, threw her a surprised glance as he ran toward the burning building, a stretcher under his arm. The police arrived a few seconds later. One of them came to Margot and began asking questions. She struggled to answer through lips gone numb with shock and fear.

Where were they? Why didn't he come back, around the corner of the building, away from the danger? She tried to picture them, Frank helping Preston, even dragging Preston. She tried to believe they would emerge from the inferno in just another moment. . . . It was unthinkable that they shouldn't. But everything about this situation, the fire, Norman's body incinerating, was unthinkable. None of it should be happening.

The building was fully engulfed now, flames spearing the dark sky, windows popping as they burst from the heat. The firemen gave up on her clinic. They played their hoses on the surrounding buildings, trying to stop the fire from spreading. Faces glowed sickly orange in the light from the flames, and Margot shook so that even Thea, distraught as she was, looked up at her with concern.

The ambulance driver reappeared from the blur of fire and smoke, a nightmare figure against a scarlet haze. He had the front poles of the stretcher in his hands, and one of the firemen had the back. There was a blanket on the stretcher.

With an exclamation, Margot tore free of Thea and ran forward. She stopped a pace away from the stretcher, terrified at what she might see.

It wasn't that she didn't know how a body could be ruined by fire. She had seen it in her residency, bodies contorted, twisted into grotesque shapes that were no longer human. The heat of her burning clinic was powerful enough to destroy muscle and tendon and bone, to make a body unrecognizable.

Margot the physician stepped forward, put out her hand to lift the blanket. Margot the woman had to stifle the panicked moan rising from her throat as she bent forward. If her brother had caused Frank's death, he might as well have killed her.

She pulled up the edge of the blanket. The stretcher was empty. There was nobody there, dead or alive. The fireman stumbled, and the ambulance driver shouted something. The stretcher fell to the ground, the blanket sliding off onto the pavement.

"What happened?" Margot cried.

The two men stared at the empty stretcher, then looked up at her, mouths open in astonishment and fear. "Where'd he go?" the ambulance driver cried.

The fireman swore, whirled, and headed back into the murk and smoke. The ambulance driver stood with Margot, staring down at the empty canvas stretcher. A silver chain was tangled in the gray folds of the blanket. Margot twitched the blanket's edge with her fingers, and the jewel tumbled out onto the dark pavement. The ambulance driver said something, but Margot didn't hear him. She was gazing at the sapphire, lying in the road, glowing with the reflected light of the flames.

She had seen the stone only once, but she knew what it was. It was the jewel Preston wore around his neck. The one he had pressed against Loena's fevered body in the hospital, the one he had tried to hide after the accident.

As she stared at it, the turmoil around her seemed to recede. Sounds faded from her hearing. The smells of burning wood and chemicals diminished. Hardly knowing she did it, she bent, and stretched out her hand.

When she picked it up, it was still hot from the fire. It stung her palm, and she had to release it, to drop it hastily into her pocket.

A man shouted, and Margot looked up to see a fireman stagger into the street with someone leaning on his shoulder, someone who could barely stand, whose soot-smeared face was twisted in agony. The ambulance driver dashed back across the street to meet them, shouting over his shoulder, "Dr. Benedict! We found him!"

It was Frank, thank God, Frank stumbling beside the fireman, Frank showing his teeth as he gritted them against the pain of his burns.

The relief that washed through Margot left her dry mouthed and weak kneed. She stared for a long moment, wanting to be convinced, longing to be certain. Then, as if waking her from a transfixing dream, her training broke her shocked trance and propelled her forward. She ushered Frank into the waiting ambulance, and climbed in beside him, automatically giving orders all the way. As the ambulance started down Post Street, she was already cutting away his still-smoking shirt. He writhed in pain as she pulled the fabric away from his good arm.

She said, "Sorry," but she kept going. If the hot fabric clung to his skin, he would lose even more. The burns on his hand were already blistering. His good hand, his *only* hand. There was no time to do anything about his pain. The skin was charred in places, a bad sign. She sluiced the burns with cool water, grateful for the well-supplied ambulance. The vehicle careened around the corner, rocking on its wheels as it sped toward the hospital, and she braced Frank's legs to keep him from abrading his burned skin any more. He cursed, "Goddamn it. Oh, goddamn it!"

"Good," she said to him, "you keep that up as long as you can. We'll be there soon."

She forgot about her lost privileges until they were already at the hospital. Fresh fear clutched at her throat. If they turned her away, if she had to hand Frank over to someone else—

But it was Nurse Cardwell on duty, and her cool gaze assessed the situation in seconds. Margot said, "Matron, is the operating theater available? It's the only place clean enough."

Cardwell said, "Of course, Doctor. I'll fetch a gurney."

Margot spoke to a nurse to order an injection of morphine. Frank sighed with relief as it was administered, and Margot said, "Rest now, Frank. We're going to take care of you."

It wasn't until she went to scrub, snatching a surgical coat out of a locker, that she realized the sapphire was in the pocket of her pleated skirt. It felt oddly heavy there. She reached down to touch its smooth surface. Had she actually picked it up, dropped it into her pocket? Why had she done that? She could hardly remember.

"Ready, Doctor?" Cardwell stood in the doorway, already masked and gowned.

Margot lifted her hand from her pocket and turned to the sink. "Two minutes."

In the operating theater, Cardwell and a younger nurse were waiting on either side of the surgical bed. Under the brilliant lights, Margot could see that the burns to Frank's right arm and hand were mostly of the first degree, with the blisters of the second degree limited to the forearm and wrist. The cool water rinse had prevented further damage. She could treat the burned skin as soon as the chloroform took effect. She wasn't going to think about her privileges at the moment. As Cardwell had recognized instantly, only in the operating theater did Frank have a decent chance of avoiding infection. That was the worst risk with such burns. If they became septic, there would be little she could do.

When his eyes were closed and she was certain he was not conscious, Margot began the careful process of thoroughly, gently cleaning his arm and hand with peroxide of hydrogen, followed by a lavage of sterilized saline solution. She opened the blisters and removed the epithelium, repeating the cleansing each time. When she was done, taking great care so as not to miss anything, Cardwell applied clean bandages. Margot watched her carefully for any possible contamination, but Alice Cardwell was as thorough as she had been herself. Margot said, "He should be treated with picric acid as soon the granulation begins."

"Yes, Doctor," Cardwell said.

"And if there's any difficulty, a bath of boracic lotion."

"I'll make a note on his chart." Cardwell finished the bandages on Frank's right arm. As she lifted the sheet to cover him, she paused, looking down at his left arm. She clicked her tongue in sympathy. "Poor fellow!" she said. "This looks like it was done with a saw."

Margot had steadfastly avoided looking at Frank's left arm up until now. She stepped around the surgical table, moving the light with her elbow so she could get a good view. "Oh, Frank," she said. He lay quietly beneath the chloroform mask. His breathing, though light, was steady and clear. "My God. No wonder it hurts so much."

"You know him?" Cardwell raised her eyebrows.

"I do." Margot bent for a closer look. "And I know they tried to repair this in the military hospital in Virginia, but—" She pointed her gloved finger. "You see this swelling? I was looking at an illustration just the other day." It had been in the surgical manual, the same text that was now nothing but ashes, but that didn't matter. A book could be replaced, and the images were as clear in her mind as if she had the book in front of her. "It's an amputational neuroma. The nerves weren't cut short enough, and when they try to regenerate, these swellings adhere to the scar tissue."

Cardwell said, "The pain must be ghastly."

"No doubt." Margot straightened. "The nerves should be resected." She gazed at Frank's face, so still now, so relaxed. She was used to seeing tension in his mouth, and finely drawn lines around his eyes. Who could imagine the courage it took to live with such pain?

"I suppose," the matron began, "you could ask Dr. Peretti—"

"No." Margot pictured the illustrations in the Manual of Surgery, the photographs, the drawings. She remembered the instructions with perfect clarity, as if she had known, when she studied them, that she would need them one day.

"I can do it myself," she said in a low voice. It was true, and she knew it. She felt filled with confidence, brimming with it, as she turned to the matron. Her voice throbbed slightly with determination. "I can do it right now."

Cardwell opened her mouth, then closed it, then opened it again. In a voice as low as Margot's, she said, "Are you sure, Doctor?"

Margot wondered, for the briefest moment, if she should doubt herself. She had never done this surgery, nor had she seen it done. She wasn't even supposed to be here. And Frank—what if she botched it, made it worse? He had said he didn't want her doctoring him. If she did this, he might never want to see her again.

She felt the sapphire shift in her pocket, heavy and warm against her thigh. She took a breath. Was Preston dead? She didn't know. But Frank was here, in the operating theater. He was already sedated, and he had been in pain for far too long. She knew what to do and how to do it. This was no time for faintness of heart, nor did she feel such a thing. She felt only certainty.

With a steady voice she said, "Yes, I'm sure, Matron. I'll need an assistant."

"There's an intern on the second floor." Cardwell turned to the younger nurse. "Robertson, go fetch Dr. Clay. Tell him to hurry. Scrub again when you get back."

Robertson, her eyes wide, scurried away. The matron went off to get a surgical tray, and wheeled it back.

Margot said, "I don't know which of my problems is worse, Matron, my personal relationship with the patient—or the fact that I'm not supposed to be in this hospital at all."

Cardwell scowled, and the web of wrinkles in her forehead clustered beneath her cap. "You have a patient who needs help. Feelings don't matter. Neither do politics."

Margot gave a halfhearted chuckle. "I know. I doubt Peretti will agree."

The intern came in, pulling on his gloves as he backed through the door. When he turned and saw Margot, he stopped.

Margot, her mind already on the task ahead, snapped, "Is there a problem, Doctor?"

He was young, with an uncertain manner. His eyes flicked over Frank, lying quietly beneath the chloroform mask, then up to Margot. "I didn't know it was you," he blurted. He stood where he was for several seconds, reluctance in every line of his body.

She had no time to wonder whether it was because she was in trouble with the board or because she was a woman doctor. "Well," she said testily, "it *is* me. Are you ready?"

He stood with the door half open, his gloved hands held out in front of him to avoid contamination. "I—I don't know. That is—"

Cardwell said, in the voice of authority Margot recognized all too well, "This is an emergency, Dr. Clay. Are you going to assist Dr. Benedict, or am I going to have to do it?"

If the moment had not been so charged with tension, Margot might have laughed at the complexity of the intern's expression. Alice Cardwell had not lost her touch. Every intern and resident in the hospital learned early and well to do what she suggested, and do it quickly.

The young physician cleared his throat, stepped away from the door so it swung shut, and came to stand opposite Margot. She said evenly, "Thank you. This will be a resection to correct an amputational neuroma. We need to dissect out the scar, and the nerve ends. I may need a hand to free these adhesions."

In a voice faint with apprehension, the intern said, "Yes, Miss—Dr. Benedict. Whenever you're ready."

Margot picked up her scalpel, ready to get to work.

Frank woke slowly to brilliant sunshine on his face. He blinked, and tried to swallow. His mouth was dry as dust. He rolled his head on his pillow, and searched for the pain that greeted him every morning. All he found was a dull ache, held at a distance as if someone had put padding between the ruin of his left arm and his nervous system. Surprise brought him fully awake.

He found himself in a hospital room. The painted iron bed, the stiff sheets, the drab walls all made him wonder for a moment if he was back in Virginia.

Cautiously, he lifted his head. No, not Virginia. This room had a window opposite the bed, and the bedside table held a bud vase with a rose and a spray of baby's breath. In all the time he'd spent in the hospital in Virginia, he had never once had flowers beside his bed. There was a carafe of water, too, and a glass, but when he lifted his right hand to reach for it, he found his arm was heavily bandaged, the fingers immobilized. He lifted his left arm, and saw that it was bandaged even more heavily than the right, the stump swathed in layers of gauze. The movement didn't exacerbate the nerves as it usually did. Pain had been his constant companion for so long that its absence shocked him.

He let his head fall back against the pillow, wondering how much medication he had been given. Enough, evidently, to soothe his arm. He wondered how to call for someone, but before he could decide, a plump nurse with sandy curls escaping from her cap put her head around the door. "We're awake!" she said brightly. "How are we feeling?"

Frank considered this. "All right," he said, after a moment of assessing himself. "My head aches, and I'm thirsty. But I feel—" He paused, and then said, wondering at it, "I feel all right." It was more than he could have said any morning, upon any awakening, for more months than he cared to count.

"Well!" the nurse chirped. "Dr. Benedict will be so pleased to hear that." She trotted to the bed with a rustle of her long skirts, and poured a glass of water. "Now, Major Parrish," she said. "Your headache is because of the chloroform. Dr. Benedict left an order for pain medication when you need it." She held the glass to Frank's lips, and he drank it all. "And I'll bring you some breakfast if you're hungry."

"What happened to me?" he blurted.

She smiled at him as she set the glass down. "I only know what I heard from Matron Cardwell when I came on duty this morning. Your hand and arm were burned when you tried to pull someone out of the fire at Dr. Benedict's clinic. They brought you here. Dr. Benedict treated your burns, and while you were in the operating theater, she also repaired your—" She paused, and colored. "Your amputation," she finished.

"She—she repaired it?" Frank said. He closed his eyes, but he couldn't shut out the image of Margot looking at his stump, handling it, all its ugliness exposed to her. *Margot* had operated on his arm?

"Matron Cardwell is so proud of her! She has a special interest in Dr. Benedict, I think. She's telling everyone what a brilliant surgery it was. I'm sure you'll hear all about it. I'm told you're a very lucky man." She touched the flowers, straightened the sheet, plumped Frank's pillow. "Now, Major, how do we feel about that breakfast?"

Frank woke again to find a nurse with iron-gray hair beneath her starched cap standing next to his bed. She held a chart in one hand, a pen in the other. The pockets of her long apron bristled with lengths of cotton gauze, a stethoscope, a large thermometer in a glass case. "Good morning, Major."

"What—what happened? How long have I been here?"

"Two days now. You're a little sleepy from the medication, but you're going to be fine." There was a little bustle on the opposite side of the ward, other nurses attending other patients. The nurse glanced behind her with a stern expression, as if admonishing someone, then turned back to him. "I'm Nurse Cardwell. I was on duty when you came in, and attended your surgery." She turned a straight chair so it faced him, and sat down, her back very straight, her ankles primly crossed. She opened the chart, and said in businesslike fashion, "Can you tell me what you remember, Major?"

Frank frowned, trying to think. The relief from his constant pain made him feel oddly giddy. Nothing seemed quite real, as if he had dreamed the events of the last days. "I remember the fire," he said. "Preston was in the storeroom. He didn't know there was oxygen there. I knew it would flare up, so I ran around the back."

"You burned your hand and arm rather badly."

Frank lifted his bandaged right hand. He looked up at her, suddenly uncertain. "Did he—did he make it?"

"I'm sorry, Major. It seems Mr. Benedict did not survive."

"He—Benedict's dead?" It didn't seem right to him. It seemed unreal, like part of the dream. "I can't believe it," he said hoarsely.

"It's a shock, I know. The building burned right to the ground. There's nothing left."

"They think his body burned, too?"

"I understand they found bone fragments in the rubble."

Frank closed his eyes, trying to take it in. Preston dead?

The nurse put a hand on his arm. "I'm sorry to be so blunt, Major. It's not a pleasant subject, but—"

"No, it's all right. I'm not upset. I'm just—" Frank shook his head, trying to put the pieces together. "A lot to take in. Someone told me Margot—that is, Dr. Benedict—"

The nurse's thin cheeks wrinkled with a restrained smile. "Oh, yes," she said complacently. "Dr. Benedict did beautiful work on your burns and also on your arm. Your burns could have been serious, but they're going to be fine. Your arm—the amputation—was in quite bad condition. I'm sure you're going to be much more comfortable from now on."

"But she—" Frank shook his head against the pillow, wondering if he was just too slow to take it in. "I thought—her hospital privileges—"

"It was a problem, naturally, but there was no time to call anyone. It was the middle of the night, and your burns needed immediate attention. Dr. Benedict was still operating when several other doctors arrived for their morning rounds."

Her smile grew. With a satisfied air, she said, "They could hardly interfere then, so they watched from the gallery." She stood up, tucking the chart into the crook of her elbow, dropping the pen into an already-crowded pocket. "No one could have made a better job of your surgery than Dr. Benedict, Major. It was most fortunate." Then, briskly, "But she can't attend you, because of the other problem. Her colleague Dr. Clay will be in. He assisted Dr. Benedict with your operation. And I promised to keep an eye on you as well."

She bent, and lightly touched the bandages on his hand, and then on his stump. "We'll change these when the doctor comes. No need to trouble you now. Are you comfortable?"

"Yes."

"Good. Mostly you need to rest."

She restored the chair to its original position, and walked out of the room with a purposeful step, nodding to the other nurses as she passed them. Frank stared after her, blinking in the clear sunlight. He couldn't shake a feeling that it was all an illusion, that when he roused from whatever state he was in, his pain would return in full force. And Margot—after seeing the horror of what was left of his arm—she could have accepted her banishment from the hospital as a way to avoid him.

He tipped his head back, and pondered the blank ceiling.

The morning after Frank's surgery, Margot went back to the Alexis. She called Benedict Hall, but no one answered the telephone. She called Thea's neighbor, who reported that Thea was holding up all right, before she fell into bed to sleep for ten solid hours. She woke at six o'clock in the evening to a ravenous hunger. She showered, and put on a linen dress. The skirt and shirtwaist she had worn lay in a pile on the floor where she had dropped them. When she picked them up, she wrinkled her nose at the smell of smoke and chloroform. She dropped them on top of her valise. She had no hat. It had been hanging on the rack in her office, along with her coat and her gloves. All of it was gone, nothing but cinders, along with her precious books, her diplomas—and two bodies, utterly consumed by the oxygen-fed fire.

Hatless, gloveless, she went out to the Royal, where she ate an enormous meal of steak and potatoes. She had no pocketbook, either, but she ordered the bill to be sent to Benedict Hall, then walked out into the twilit street and turned up the hill toward the hospital.

She was just inside the entrance when she saw Dr. Whitely emerging from a stairwell. He started to turn away, as if to avoid her, then seemed to think better of it. With short, quick steps that made him look a bit like a gray-haired robin, he crossed the lobby toward her. Margot stopped where she was. She felt exposed, with neither hat, gloves, nor her medical bag. The absence of her bag, in particular, made her feel she was not fully dressed.

Whitely was wearing an overcoat, despite the heat. He carried his medical bag in one hand, his hat in the other. By the time he reached her, his cheeks were pink with outrage. "Doctor," he said. "You are forbidden to be in this hospital."

Margot strove for a mild tone. "I have a surgical patient to check on, Dr. Whitely."

"Oh, I know," he said sharply. "We all know that. You went against the board's directive! You deliberately took advantage of an emergency situation to—"

"As you say," she interrupted. "It was an emergency."

"Repairing a stump neuroma wasn't an emergency!" His voice rose, and the receptionist and two nurses at the desk turned to look. Visitors were straggling out through the lobby, and they also cast curious glances at him.

Margot thrust out her chin. There was no point trying to placate Whitely. The deed was done now, in any case. "Is it your professional opinion, then, Dr. Whitely, that it would have been better to sedate a patient twice? One who has already been through multiple traumas?"

"It's my opinion," he snapped, "that you should not be allowed in this hospital ever again."

"I believe Dr. Peretti may disagree with you. He observed my surgery last night—that is, this morning—and he can judge for himself."

"Peretti! He's not a surgeon." Whitely's plump cheeks grew

pinker, and he bounced on his tiptoes, looking more than ever like an angry bird.

"I don't think he would appreciate that assessment." Margot drew herself up, so she could look down at Whitely, make him tip up his chin to meet her eyes. "Excuse me, Doctor. I see Matron Cardwell, and I'd like a report on my patient's progress."

"You're not to go up to the ward," Whitely said sourly. He looked over his shoulder at Cardwell. "I'll make sure Matron knows that."

"No need to trouble yourself," Margot said. She brushed past him, and started across the lobby to where Alice Cardwell was just shrugging out of her cape and pinning on her cap. "I'll tell her myself."

Having learned that Frank was resting well, with no fever or restlessness, Margot secured Cardwell's promise to watch his postoperative pain. Reassured, she walked back toward the Alexis through a fragrant autumn evening. It was nearly nine o'clock, and the last sunlight still glowed from the western sea. She hesitated at the corner of First Avenue, and then, instead of turning, she walked on down the gentle slope toward the docks. She wanted to stroll along the waterfront, to breathe the salt air. She wasn't ready yet to go to Post Street and view the ruin that had been her clinic, but she didn't think she could sleep again so soon.

The waterfront was quiet, most workers gone home, only a few other walkers about. The surface of the bay was glossy in the evening light. Gentle silver waves rippled away from the hull of a ferry at the dock. Margot paused to watch the ferry chug out of its berth and set out across the water. She found a weather-beaten bench, and settled onto it to watch the light fade. It had been a long time since she'd simply sat, watching sky and water, her hands empty in her lap. Tonight, there was nothing else for her to do. It was strange to sit idle, to feel no pressing need to go to the clinic, hurry to the hospital, answer a telephone. The stillness helped to clarify her mind, to let her consider all that had happened in the last twenty-four hours.

It was hard to take in the knowledge that her tormentor was truly gone. It was even harder to know how to feel about it. Preston, her brother, her mother's son, had done his best to take everything from her that mattered. He had been willing to do anything to destroy her. She supposed she would never understand that, especially now. She would never comprehend why he had wanted her to fail so much that he had, apparently, destroyed himself.

Night settled over the city as she sat on, staring at the darkening bay. She struggled to absorb the idea that she was free. She still hadn't been able to reach her parents, but she knew they would be devastated by Preston's death. She would have to face that. Help them through it. Her clinic was ruined, but that was something she could consider tomorrow. Frank might never see her in the same light again, and that would hurt more than she dared contemplate.

But Preston—Preston was gone. It would be interesting to learn how to live without looking over her shoulder at every moment.

When the moon rose, and strains of ragtime began to float down First Avenue, she roused herself, and walked back to the hotel. One or two men leered at her, but she took long, strong steps, her back straight and her head up, and they didn't trouble her. She went up to her room, thinking she would have a bath, but when she reached it, she was suddenly exhausted again. She settled for washing her face and brushing her teeth, and fell into bed.

She slept until seven the next morning, when brilliant sunlight pierced the curtains of her hotel room. Groggy with sleep, she climbed out of bed and went to the window to look down on the street. It was going to be one of those surprising autumn days when, even in Seattle, lawns would be parched and flowers and shrubs would droop in the heat.

Hatless, gloveless, she set out to walk to Post Street. She felt strong enough now to face the wreckage of her clinic. She hoped that later she would be ready to face the wreckage that was the Benedict family.

As she passed the rustic café with its GOOD EATS shingle, the proprietor, in his stained apron, came out to follow her. When she reached her destroyed clinic, he stepped up beside her as she surveyed the mass of burned timbers glistening like coal in the sunshine. "Terrible thing, Dr. Benedict," he said, wiping his hands on his apron. "They say it was arson."

He had never spoken to her before. She suspected he disapproved of women doctors, but he was a fellow businessman. Perhaps this disaster made them comrades. She said, "Yes."

"They catch the guy?"

Margot gave him a wary glance. "He died in the fire," she said. The words felt strange in her mouth, but what could she say? Words couldn't describe the import of it, the weight of the fact that Preston was gone.

He raised shaggy eyebrows. "That so? I didn't hear that. Huh. Died in his own fire." And then, easily, "Well. Guess he had it coming."

Margot remembered the long, thin shriek stabbing through the tumultuous night. It had not been Frank. Norman had already been dead. It could only have been Preston, and he had not died easily. Her feelings about his death were complex, but she wished he had not died in pain.

"You see the photos in the *Times?*" her neighbor asked.

She shook her head.

"I saved the paper. Yesterday's edition."

"What did it say?"

"Mostly pictures after the fire was out. A total loss, it says."

She stared into the blackened rubble of her clinic as other businesspeople from Post Street gathered beside her. The barber, the Italian grocer, and the shoe repairman came to murmur over the mess, and offer their sympathies. They spoke kindly, and if their assurances were a little paternal, under the circumstances, it was understandable. And forgivable. She did her best to thank each of them for their concern.

When they disbanded, to go back to their own intact businesses, she approached the mass of burned wood and shattered glass, tiptoeing gingerly around it. It still smelled of chemicals. She peered into the interior, but it didn't look as if anything could be saved. The blackened autoclave lay on its side among other ruined bits of equipment. Somewhere in there was her medical bag, and everything it had contained, all turned to ashes. Everything would have to be shoveled up into wagons or wheelbarrows and carted off. What would be left?

She finished her circuit of the site. Just as she reached the street again, a spot of red caught her eye in the detritus at the front. She crouched down, and pushed away a chunk of something that looked like charcoal, but which had probably once been part of the front door. Beneath it, charred but intact, was the sign she had so proudly ordered and hung the year before—a lifetime before. M. BENEDICT, M.D., painted in red letters and varnished against the weather. The varnish was cracked now, the cheerful red paint darkened.

She pulled the sign free, and stood, brushing ash and dirt from the surface. Her eyes stung at seeing it there in her dirty hands. It was ruined. She had lost her hospital privileges, and she had lost her clinic. She might even have lost her family.

She didn't know about Frank. Would he be glad about what she had done? Or furious?

When Margot reached Benedict Hall and opened the front door, an eerie silence greeted her. She glanced inside the kitchen, but found no one. She peeked inside the small parlor, but it was similarly empty. She stood in the hallway for a moment. The house was unnaturally quiet, no sounds of water running or wardrobes being opened or doors clicking shut. She took a tentative step toward her father's study, and spotted Loena creeping down the staircase on tiptoe.

The maid put a finger to her lips. "Mrs. Edith is sleeping," she whispered. "The doctor gave her something."

Margot kept her voice low. "What about Ramona? And Hattie?"

"Mrs. Ramona went with Mr. Dick and Mr. Dickson to arrange the service for Mr. Preston. Hattie's in her room. She's been crying all morning."

"I'll go see her," Margot said. Automatically, she bent to pick up her bag, then remembered. Gone. She could talk to Hattie, but she had no medicine, nothing to give her. "Fetch the brandy bottle, Loena."

"Yes, Dr. Margot." Loena's eyes were bright and untroubled. No grief here, Margot could see, and probably not for Leona, either. Their illusions about Preston had already been shattered.

She found Hattie huddled on her bed in her little room behind the kitchen, sobbing into her apron. She looked up as Margot came in. Her round cheeks dripped tears, and her eyelids were swollen. "Oh, Dr. Margot," she choked. "I keep thinkin' it ain't true. That he ain't . . . that Mr. Preston ain't . . ." She put both hands over her mouth, shaking her head, swallowing tears. "I can't help cryin', but I been stayin' in my room so I don't start Mrs. Edith off again."

Loena came in with the brandy bottle and, in an unusual display of initiative, a kitchen glass. Margot poured two fingers of brandy, and held it out to Hattie. "Drink, Hattie," she said.

Hattie didn't argue. She took the glass and drank it down. When it was empty, she tried to set it on the bedside table, but missed. The glass rolled across the carpet, and Loena retrieved it. Hattie's eyes pleaded with Margot. "Mr. Preston—was he trying to put it out? The fire? Is that what happened to him?"

Margot could find no answer for this. She said, "Hattie, please lie down. Kick your shoes off. I'm going to cover you with your quilt, and pull the curtains. Try not to cry anymore."

Hattie hiccuped, and sniffled, but she did as she was told. Margot sat on the single chair in her room, and waited beside the bed for Hattie's breathing to even out and her tears to stop. She waved Loena out, and leaned her head back, closing her own eyes, listening to the quiet of the house. Time suspended for a few moments, and in the transient peace, her thoughts stilled.

A slight snore from Hattie told her the brandy had done its work. Margot stirred, and opened her eyes. The dim little room smelled of brandy and soap and that indefinable scent that was Hattie. Suddenly, intensely, Margot longed for Blake, and the comfort of his rooms above the garage. She got to her feet, and slipped out of Hattie's room as quietly as she could. She went through the kitchen, out the back door, and across the patch of lawn. She let herself in through the side door of the garage, and went up the narrow staircase.

Everything was just as she had seen it last, even to the teacup in the dish strainer. Through the open bedroom door, she could see that his bed had not yet been stripped. On his nightstand a carafe of water had dried, leaving a faint haze. A clean glass rested next to it. She opened the little icebox where he had always kept milk and butter and bread. It was unnaturally empty, the ice compartment dry and warm to the touch. The air in the apartment was hot and still.

Margot sat down beside the old table where she had so often sat with Blake, playing checkers or reading one of his books. She knew in her heart it was likely he would never return to these rooms, never stand beside the sink looking across the lawn at Benedict Hall, keeping his watchful eye on them all. She knew the chances of his full recovery were small—perhaps even nonexistent—but her heart yearned to see him here once again. To see everything, and everyone, in their rightful place.

She started at the sound of the door opening at the bottom of the staircase. "Margot?"

"I'm here," she called.

It was Dick, his footsteps sounding heavy on the treads, nearly as heavy as their father's. "Loena saw you come over, although I thought she must have been mistaken. Are you all right?"

"Yes." He appeared, huffing a little from the climb. "You look exhausted, Dick. I suppose you've been trying to hold everyone together."

He waved one hand. "Nothing much I could do. It's a nightmare."

"Sorry I wasn't here. I was up all night after the fire, and I had to sleep."

"You couldn't have helped, anyway."

"Where's Father?"

"He's picking out a coffin."

"But, Dick—we don't have Preston's body. What is the coffin for?"

"We're going to bury the bones they found in the ashes of your clinic."

She stared at him. "The bones?"

"Well, what's left of them. God, Margot, it's all so macabre. Mother's falling apart, I'm afraid. She really needs this funeral, even though it seems a bit—what's the word? Gothic?"

"It makes sense, I guess. She'll cope better if she can have a ceremony, and a place to visit at the cemetery. But oh, Lord, poor Father. What an awful task."

"He's holding up all right. Terribly sad, of course, but—it's almost as if he's not surprised. As if he was expecting some disaster." Dick broke off, and stared around him at the tidy apartment. "I haven't been up here in years. What made you think of coming here?"

"It's silly, I suppose. I've just always felt safe here."

Dick heaved an enormous sigh. "Margot—no one's telling us what really happened. At your office, I mean."

She folded her arms, and regarded her elder brother. "Mother and Hattie will never believe it, but you might as well know. Preston started the fire. He didn't know there was oxygen in the storeroom. The fire accelerated, and caught him. The firemen thought they had him on a stretcher, but it seems in the confusion he fell off."

"What were you doing there at that time of night?"

"Thea—my nurse—brought her husband in. He was dying, and she didn't want him in the hospital. We were all in the dark, just waiting. Preston probably thought the clinic was empty—although I don't know if he would have cared."

"Parrish was there."

"Yes, sitting with me in the reception room. He ran around the back to try to pull Preston out, but it was too late. Frank burned his hand and his arm, and I went in the ambulance with him to the hospital."

"And your nurse's husband?"

"He died shortly before the fire started."

"So those bones could be . . ." Dick raised his eyebrows. "Talk about Gothic!"

"I know. It's better not to think about it too much."

"Is Parrish still in the hospital?"

"Yes."

"His hand okay?"

"It will be."

"My God, Margot. If he had lost his other hand!"

"Unthinkable." Margot lifted her gaze to the window, where a brilliant shaft of sunlight poured into the quiet apartment. She thought of Frank's amputated arm, of the repaired nerves, the clean new surgery. A little swell of satisfaction lightened her grim mood. "But he's going to be fine," she said.

"He's a good man, Margot."

"Yes, he is."

"You two—do you have an understanding?"

Margot pictured Frank's Black Irish eyes, his lean face, and heard again the steel in his voice as he refused to let her examine his arm. She looked into her brother's face, and shook her head. "I don't know, Dick. After everything that's happened . . . I just don't know."

CHAPTER 20

The nurse smiled down at Frank. "There, I've opened the window for you, Major," she chirped. "It's a beautiful day."

He could see that from where he lay, propped on a pile of pillows. Sunshine poured across the linoleum floor, and birds sang exuberantly in the trees outside the hospital. The pain in his arm was different, a healing ache rather than the familiar fire. He woke every morning with a little spurt of surprise at the difference. There had been other men in the ward, but their beds were empty now, with fresh sheets piled on the bare mattresses. "Didn't think warm weather was ever coming," he said.

"Oh, we often get our summer in August and September." The sandy-haired nurse laughed. "Though there are some years it never does show up!"

She fluffed his pillows, and Frank wriggled back against the bed frame so he could sit more or less upright. "When can I get out of here?"

She giggled. "Feeling better, are we? It's only been three days, Major."

"Is Dr. Clay coming today?"

"Someone will come." She gave him a twinkling smile as she produced a washbasin, a cake of soap, a razor, and a comb. She set all of it in his lap, and took a folded towel from a cupboard. "I'm going to shave you," she said brightly.

"Thanks," he said. "Don't think I can manage that on my own just yet."

"No," she said comfortably. "Not with all those bandages. And why not let me do something about your hair? It's getting a bit long on the neck."

Frank submitted to her deft hands. She soaped his chin with a brush, and wielded the razor with efficiency. She used scissors on his hair, then brushed hair off his pillow, and emptied the basin into the sink. When she came back to the bed she stood looking down at him, hands on hips. "Very handsome, Major. I think we're ready."

"Ready?" He blinked. "For what?"

"You'll see." She gathered her things and piled them into the basin. "Breakfast first. Then you'll see."

When his breakfast arrived, the nurse helped him out of bed and into a cane-backed wheelchair. She settled the tray on the bedside stand and pulled a chair close for herself to sit while she helped him to eat eggs and bacon and fresh biscuits. "Well," she said. "We're hungry today. That's an excellent sign."

He swallowed the last of his breakfast, finishing everything, and savored the cup of coffee. "Thanks," he said again, as she dabbed at his chin with a napkin, then picked up the tray. "I'd sure like to get out of these bandages."

"Not just yet, Major. We don't want to risk infection, now, do we?"

Frank felt restless and out of sorts from inaction. He had been taking less and less medication. He had had no whisky at all since coming to the hospital. What he needed now, he thought, was a good brisk walk. So far, he had not been allowed out of bed except to use the latrine, and that was a miserable experience. A man should be able to use the latrine on his own.

The *Times* had been folded on his breakfast tray, and the nurse spread it on the bed for him before she left. He bent over it, smoothing out the creases as best he could with his elbow. The front-page headline screamed that the Poles had "routed the Reds." So much for the war to end all wars. With difficulty, Frank used his bandaged fingers to scrape the front page over. On the second page he found an article about the imminent ratification of the Nineteenth Amendment. He lingered over this, thinking how pleased his mother would be. And Margot.

Because he was thinking of her, it seemed to him he was imagining the sound of her voice. It had appealed to him from their very first meeting, when he heard it from the hallway at Benedict Hall, deep, assured, crisp. Now he turned his head to listen. Who else sounded like that?

The voice came closer, speaking to someone in the corridor, then ceasing. He sat back in the wheelchair and turned it with his feet so he was facing the doorway when she appeared in it.

"Good morning, Frank," she said. She wore her white coat, with her stethoscope draped around her neck. Her hair swung against her jaw as she crossed the ward to him with her characteristic strong steps.

"Good morning." He hardly knew how to address her. She looked dauntingly professional, and somehow polished, hair and skin and eyes clear and glowing. Her gaze assessed him, and he remembered that he was her patient. She had seen—handled, operated on—the horror that was his left arm. The thought made his breakfast churn in his stomach.

"How do you feel?" She stood, tall and slim, beside the wheelchair.

He felt ridiculous and vulnerable, looking up at her. "People keep asking me that."

Her lips curved. "And what do you answer?"

He moved his head impatiently. "I feel fine. Like getting out of here."

Her lips curved a bit more. "I'm glad to hear it." She touched his wrist, held it for a moment, nodded. She touched the bandages on his left arm, but to his great relief, she didn't offer to peel them back. "Dr. Clay says you're healing well."

"Good." He wanted to say more, but the words wouldn't come. He wanted to tell her how beautiful she looked, her dark hair shining in the sun. He wanted to touch her, but at the moment he had no hand to do it with. "You operated on me."

She tugged on the ends of her stethoscope, looking suddenly less confident. "Yes. I know you said—you didn't want me to treat you, but—" She dropped her hands, and thrust them into the pockets of her white coat. "The thing is—it looked so—"

"Hideous," he said, and dropped his gaze. "I told you that."

"No!" She crouched beside him, so he had to look into her eyes. "No, Frank. Not hideous. Painful. You had an amputational neuroma, and it must have been a nightmare to live with. I don't know how you've managed."

To his horror, his eyes suddenly stung with tears. He cleared his throat, and said roughly, "Didn't have a choice." He felt her hand on his shoulder, but he set his jaw, and stared at the blurred blue sky beyond the window.

She took her hand from his shoulder. "You're angry with me."

He didn't dare speak, for fear he would sob. That would be more than he could bear.

"Very well," she said. Her voice changed, a little rough like his own. There was a rustle of fabric as she stood up, and the whisper of her shoes on the linoleum as she took a step back. "I knew you might be, but I—I had to do what I thought was right."

Frank swallowed hard, and took a shaky breath. He turned his head, able to face her again. "Margot," he began.

She shook her head. "You don't have to explain. I took a chance." The pitch of her voice rose, as if her throat, too, was constricted.

"Margot—"

She scowled, and thrust out her chin. "Just so you know, the surgery went very well. You should have no more pain, once the incisions have healed."

"Margot, stop! Listen to me!" Frank made a helpless gesture

with his bandaged hand. He knew he was making a mess of it. "Please."

Her chin dropped, just the tiniest bit. "Yes?"

"I'm lousy with words. You know that."

Her chin relaxed a bit more. "Yes?"

"I want to explain to you why—I thought if you saw my arm—"

She said with asperity, "You underestimate me."

"I'm sorry. But I could hardly bear looking at it myself, and—I didn't want *you* to have to look at it. To—to think of me that way."

Her face softened. "That would never make a difference to me. It's just flesh. Broken flesh. And you're going to find it looks much better now."

He looked up into the face of Margot Benedict, her clear dark eyes, the firm set of her mouth. Suddenly, it was hard to remember Elizabeth's face. Hers belonged to the past, and this one—strong and fine and dear—belonged to the present.

She said, "You're not angry, are you, Frank?"

"It's more than I can take in."

"Take your time."

"I seem to have plenty of that."

"I'm afraid so. We can't release you just yet." She stood up, smoothing her coat, smiling. "I'd better go now. I have patients to see."

She was already out the door before it struck him that she must have had her privileges restored. He hadn't even asked her about that. And he hadn't thanked her.

"Goddamn it, Parrish," he muttered, kicking his wheelchair toward the window. "You really are a cowboy."

Margot was not Frank's only surprise of the day. In the middle of the afternoon, a new nurse bustled in, with another visitor in tow. She opened the door for him, nodded to Frank, and said, "Here he is, sir. Not too long, now. Dr. Clay wants Major Parrish to rest."

Frank was in bed again, and he struggled upright against the pillows, awkwardly, using his elbow. "Mr. Boeing! Sir, I didn't expect—I—" He started to hold out his hand, then dropped it as he remembered. "Sorry."

"Not at all, Frank, not at all." Bill Boeing reversed the chair beside the bed, and straddled it. He held his hat in one hand, and in the other he held out a little bunch of flowers wrapped in a cone of paper. "I saw these at the Public Market. I thought they might brighten this place."

"Thanks," Frank said. "I sure didn't expect to see you."

Boeing laid the flowers on the nightstand. "I'm so damned sorry, Parrish, about—well, everything. Now you're a hero—again—and I don't even get credit as your boss!"

"Hero?"

"Sure, hero. Didn't you see the paper? The *Times?*"

"Only today."

"Preston Benedict was *their* employee, and the report says you tried to save him from the fire. At risk to your—your hand," he added, a little shamefacedly.

"My only hand, you mean." Frank gave him a lopsided grin. "Not news to me, sir."

"No, of course not. But still, now you're a hero in Seattle. Young Benedict didn't make it, they say. Not that they could find his remains, but—well, you probably know that."

"A shame," Frank said cautiously.

"Yes." Boeing turned his hat in his hands, and cleared his throat. "Look, Frank. I need your skills. Douglas has this new airplane—"

Frank sat up straighter. "The Cloudster. I read about that. It's going to carry a load that exceeds the airplane's weight. That should be interesting—if it works."

A light kindled in Boeing's eyes. He leaned forward, as if they were back in his office in the Hoge Building. His fingers curled, and Frank had the impression they yearned for a pencil, and paper to sketch on. "That's the one," he said eagerly. "I want to get ahead of Douglas. We're in a tough spot since the army cut its order in half. We need to look ahead, innovate."

"What about the BB-1s?"

"The market isn't big enough." Boeing spread both his hands in an expansive gesture. "It's going to be the military that keeps us going. And for that I need men like you, men who have seen service, who know how the military does things."

"Are you offering me my job back?"

Boeing grinned, managing to look boyish despite his owlish spectacles and graying temples. "More or less begging you to come back. When you've recuperated, of course." He pointed to Frank's bandaged hand. "You'll need that."

Frank held up his heavily wrapped stump. "I've had surgery on this, too, sir. I'm going to need a bit of time."

"As much as you need, son. As much as you need."

Later, Frank couldn't remember for certain if he had actually agreed to go back to work for Boeing. He stared at the flowers the nurse had put in a pottery vase, and went over the conversation a dozen times. He had a job again! He hoped he had said yes, in so many words. He hoped if he hadn't that Bill Boeing would understand. And would ask him again!

He lay back against his pillows, and waited impatiently for Margot to return.

It felt strange to Margot to go home again, to step out of the hot afternoon light and into the coolness of the foyer of Benedict Hall. She had only been away a few days, but the world had changed in that time. Changed, and changed again.

Leona met her at the door, and took her valise to carry it upstairs. Loena went to draw her a bath. No one else seemed to be around, and Margot supposed her mother and Hattie were still in seclusion with their grief.

While she was waiting for the bath to fill, Margot drew the curtains against the afternoon heat, and opened the valise on her bed to sort soiled clothes from clean ones. A smell of smoke rose from the pile, and she picked the pleated skirt and shirtwaist from the other things, thinking they should probably be washed separately. As she shook them out, the sapphire fell from the skirt pocket and tumbled toward the floor. Its chain caught on the clasp of the valise, and the sapphire in its nest of blackened silver chain hung over the edge of the bed, glowing.

She had forgotten all about it. She found herself, now, reluctant to touch it. She remembered Preston holding it in his hand as he bent over Loena in the hospital, and pressing his palm over it as he convinced everyone he hadn't meant to lose his temper, that awful night in the parlor. He had had it with him when he set fire to her clinic, and she had picked it up from the ground, despite the chaos around her and her fears for Frank.

It had been in her pocket as she operated.

Loena knocked on her door, and put her head around. Her freckled face was solemn, but her eyes were bright, her cheeks rosy. "Your bath's ready, Miss Margot."

"Coming. Thank you."

"Is this your laundry?" Loena reached for the skirt and shirtwaist flung over the chair.

"Yes."

Loena turned toward the valise on the bed. "Is there more?"

"There is, but I haven't unpacked it yet."

Loena made a maternal shooing motion with one hand. "You go and have your bath while it's hot. I'll sort through your things."

"Thanks." Margot took her dressing gown from the wardrobe. As Loena crossed to the bed and the open valise, Margot thought she should make it clear she had finally learned how to tell the twins apart. "Thank you, Loena," she said.

"You're wel—wait. Where did this come from?" Loena lifted the sapphire on its chain. Bits of ash drifted from it to the rug beside the bed. Loena's eyes went wide, and she gazed at the stone, openmouthed.

"It was—in the fire." Margot saw again the empty stretcher where her brother should have been, and a wave of sadness surprised her. "You've seen that before?"

"Mr. Preston never took it off. Not even when . . ."

"Yes," Margot said. She meant merely to imply that she understood, but Loena's cheeks blazed with two sudden spots of red.

She dropped the sapphire onto the bed as if it were still hot from the fire, and put her fingertips into her mouth.

"Loena, it's just a stone. It's a sapphire."

The color staining Loena's cheeks drained away abruptly, and her pupils expanded. "No! It ain't just a jewel, miss. It has— when he was wearing it, he—"

Margot dropped her hand from the doorknob. "He what?" she snapped.

Loena took a step back, and Margot regretted her peremptory tone. She remembered her mother's admonishment. "I'm sorry, Loena," she said more gently. "It's all been a shock."

"I know, miss," Loena faltered. "We're awful sorry about your clinic."

Margot took a breath. "Thank you. I am, too. Now, could you explain what you mean about the stone?"

Loena twisted her freckled hands in her apron, and stared at her shoes. "It's just that—well, I knew better, but he—"

"I know my brother seduced you, Loena. That happens with girls and men."

Loena's eyes flashed up at her, then down again. "Everything he said—when I was with him, it seemed real, with that necklace shining at me. But when I was alone, I knew it couldn't be. The likes of me don't end up with men like Mr. Preston."

"No. I'm afraid that's true. But my brother often got his way."

"Not before he had that necklace," Loena said. This time she brought her gaze to Margot's, and held it. Her voice firmed. "He tried his tricks on me and Leona before he went off to the war, miss, and we wasn't having none of it. We knew Mrs. Edith would turn us out if we did! But when he came back—with that—" She gestured to it, but she didn't touch it again.

Margot didn't want to touch it, either. She put her hand on the door again. "Just leave it there, Loena. I'll think what to do with it later."

"Yes, miss." Loena began to sort through the clothes in the valise, laying the clean ones aside, piling the soiled ones with the others. Margot watched her for a moment, thinking how practical the girl was. She wouldn't have thought her the sort to suffer fancies.

But as she went to have her bath, she reflected that the sapphire seemed to have that effect on people. It was big, and it was obviously old. Maybe that made it mysterious.

Margot lay in the bath for a long time, letting the hot water soak the tension from her muscles. She washed her hair. When the bath water began to cool, she climbed out, and wrapped herself in a thick cotton dressing gown. As she left the bathroom, she tousled her hair with her fingers to dry it.

Her fingers still tangled in her wet hair, she pushed open the door to her bedroom with one bare foot, then stopped.

Her mother was standing by the bed, holding the sapphire in her fingers. The chain dangled past her wrists, glistening in the afternoon light. Edith was staring at the stone, white-faced and very still.

"Mother?"

Edith lifted her head, slowly, as if in a trance. Her gaze seemed to rest on Margot, or to go right through her. It was hard to tell. Her eyes were glazed, their lids red and swollen.

Alarmed, Margot took a careful step toward her. "Mother? Are you all right?"

Edith's lips parted, but for a moment it seemed she wouldn't speak. When she did, Margot could barely hear her. "What is this?"

"It was Preston's."

Edith caressed the stone with her hand. "I saw it once," she said. "Preston showed it to me."

Margot moved closer, frowning as she assessed her mother's waxy complexion and contracted pupils. "Mother, how much laudanum are you taking? You seem a bit—"

"Preston died," Edith breathed. Her eyes filled. "In a fire."

"I know," Margot said carefully. "I was there. You remember."

Edith blinked, and her eyes seemed to sharpen behind their blue sheen of tears. "You were there," she said, a little louder.

"Yes, I—"

"He tried to save your office," Edith said. An edge came into her voice. "Your clinic was on fire, and Preston tried to stop it!"

Margot put out her hand. "Mother, no. That wasn't—"

"I *told* you not to do that, Margot!" Edith's voice rose, and she shrank from Margot's hand. "Put Grandmother's money into that awful place! You just wouldn't listen. You *never* listen! And now—now Preston is *dead!*"

Margot, hand still outstretched, wet hair dripping on her neck, gaped at her mother. "You can't possibly—" she began, but her protest died unspoken. Her mother could, and no doubt did.

Blake should have spoken to Edith. She was the one he should have tried to warn. He would never have thought of it, of course. He naturally turned to Dickson, to the head of the household, the *pater familias*. That was only proper, and Blake had always been proper.

But it was Edith who had been the expert at creating excuses. Preston was sensitive, she had said. Highly strung. He hadn't meant to spill a cup of steaming cocoa on Margot's leg—something had startled him. He hadn't intended to stab Margot with the scissors—he was trying to help her with her scrapbook. He would never have pushed her downstairs—or off the swing, or into the water—she was confused, or jealous, or selfish. Preston had been Edith's beautiful, charming, affectionate boy. Her baby.

Margot gazed helplessly at her mother, standing there with the sapphire glowing in her hand. What could she say now that would make any difference? Preston was gone. Dead. If her mother took comfort in placing the blame on her, perhaps she shouldn't care.

She said, bleakly, "Take the thing, Mother, if you want it."

Edith stared at her as if trying to remember who she was. She opened her hand, letting the sapphire tumble to the floor. "I don't like it," she whispered, in a voice as thin as thread. Her eyelids fluttered, and she began to crumple. As her knees buckled and her head fell back, Margot took one long step, and caught her in her arms.

Her mother seemed to weigh nothing, as if grief had drained

her substance. Margot lifted her without effort. Edith's arms were nerveless, her lips slack. "Loena!" Margot called. She backed to the door, and turned toward her mother's bedroom with the unconscious woman in her arms. "Loena! Tell Hattie to find the smelling salts. Mother's fainted."

"Don't move out again, Margot. Not now." Dickson's mouth drooped, and though he puffed curls of gray smoke from his post-dinner cigar, the action lacked its usual relish. His eyelids were heavy, and his movements—one hand on his chest, the other flicking cigar ash in the vicinity of the cut-glass tray—were sluggish.

"She holds me responsible, Father. I see it in her face every time I pass her in the hall."

"She'll come to her senses. She'll get back to normal."

Margot turned the snifter in her hand, watching light glimmer in the amber depths of brandy. "Actually, Father," she said, "I wonder if you blame me, too."

"No. Of course not." His voice was flat, heavy with grief, and with something else she couldn't place.

"Have you changed your mind, then? About Preston?" Even now, speaking her brother's name recalled that chilling shriek, spiraling out of the horror of the fire. Sometimes she heard it in her sleep. It startled her awake, and she would lie tense beneath her blankets, wondering if she could ever banish the memory.

Dickson sat still for a long moment, staring at the floor between his shoes, the cigar seemingly forgotten in his hand. Then, with a great sigh, he pushed the cigar into the ashtray and got to his feet. "I have to show you something, Margot." She started to get up, but he waved her back. "Wait just a moment."

He moved behind his chair, and she noted with concern how his heavy shoulders stooped, how his feet dragged. Her father had worked hard to keep up appearances, for her mother's sake, no doubt. But he had aged a decade since Preston's death. He had always seemed unchanging, eternal, like granite beneath a mountain. It unnerved her to think that her father could fail.

He bent to pick up something hidden behind his leather arm-chair. When he straightened, and she saw what he had in his hand, she forgot everything. She caught a breath, and pressed her hand to her mouth.

It had been propped against the wall of Blake's apartment, half hidden by coats, for as long as she could remember. She and her brothers had asked Blake what it was for, but it was one thing he wouldn't discuss. He never touched it, either, but left it in place, year after year.

"Father, where did you find it?"

Dickson lifted it in his hands like an offering. There were stains on it that hadn't been there before, rust-colored stains.

"I wanted to—I should say, I *needed* to see where the accident happened." He ran his hand over the cane, as if the old wood and the new stains could tell him something.

"Was Blake's cane there?"

Dickson shook his head. "The car hit a tree at the bottom of a hill. Not much of a hill, really. Just a little slope overlooking the golf course." He propped the cane against the arm of his chair, and stood looking down at it. "I left the taxicab and walked up to the top. I thought if I could see where the car went over, maybe I would know why. Maybe I could understand. . . ."

"You found the cane at the top?"

"Yes. Lying in some gravel." He looked up at her, a level glance. "I'm afraid you were right. Something happened between Preston and Blake." He pointed to the rusty stains. "I wish I knew what it was."

"When did you find it?" Margot asked. She realized the snifter was still in her hand, tilting dangerously, and she set it down.

"It was the afternoon before the fire. I think I knew what it meant, but I—" He looked away from her face, staring blindly at the darkness beyond the window. "I argued with myself. I wasted time looking for another explanation. If I had just accepted what was obvious, perhaps it wouldn't have—he wouldn't have—"

"No." Margot rose, and crossed to her father. She put her arm around his shoulders, as if she were the parent, and he were the child. "No, it wasn't obvious. And there could be another explanation." He shook his head, but she said, "In any case, it doesn't matter now. It's all done, and we can't change it."

She felt the uneven breath he drew, and heard the shame in his voice. "It's your mother," he said. "Perhaps if I tell her—if I explain. She would know then that you're not to blame."

"I think it would only hurt her further." Margot released her father, and went back to pick up her glass. She had not expected to finish it, but now she swallowed what was left in one draught. "All she has left of Preston are her illusions. That's some comfort to her. In truth, I don't think she and I will ever have a close relationship, no matter what you tell her or don't tell her."

The armchair creaked as Dickson sat down again. He picked up the cigar and turned it in his fingers. It had gone out. "You know, Margot, when you were small—you were so smart, even then. You argued with me all the time, about anything you could think of. Whether horses were better than cars. Whether gaslight was better than electric lights. Even—" He chuckled. "Even whether corsets should be against the law."

Margot had to laugh. "Corsets? I don't remember that."

"Oh, yes. You decided it was bad for women to have their spines held up by whalebone, and their stomachs squeezed in so they couldn't breathe."

"I was right, as it turns out."

"I know." He reached for a match, but he didn't strike it. "What I'm getting at, daughter, is that your mother felt left out by all of that. She's not that sort of woman."

"I wasn't the sort of daughter she hoped for."

"And Preston, you know, was different. He was a little blond angel who looked just like her. He wasn't stupid, but he wasn't like you and Dick. He liked clothes, and he liked trailing around after Edith when she went shopping. He liked to sit on her lap. You never did that."

Margot watched in silence as her father struck the match to relight his cigar. He blew a gout of gray smoke, and squinted through it. "Having children is never what you think it will be," he said.

"I suppose not."

"And losing one—even one so troubled—is the worst thing a parent can experience."

"I know. I'm so sorry, Father. I would never have wished it for you."

He gestured with the cigar, and harrumphed, but she saw his eyes redden. She wanted to go to him, to embrace him, but she knew if his tears spilled over, he would hate it, so she stayed where she was.

"I just want to say, Margot," he began, then stopped to clear his throat. "I just want to say that you are—you are more than—more than I ever expected in a child. In a daughter. I'm so damn—" His voice caught, and he looked away. "Proud," he finished, in an undertone, then loudly cleared his throat again. "I'm proud of you."

Helplessly, as loath to lose control as her father was, Margot murmured, "Thank you."

"And I'm sorry I didn't believe you, about Preston."

Margot made herself say, "It's all right. It's forgotten now," a lie told out of affection.

With obvious effort, he smiled at her, and waved her back to her chair. "Come now, tell me what Peretti said when you met with him. And Whitely."

Margot settled back into her chair and linked her hands in her lap. "Dr. Peretti didn't exactly apologize," she said. "But he did mention observing Frank's surgery. He said the board had reconsidered, and now feels that the evidence against me was flimsy. His word, *flimsy*." She gave a wry smile. "Is that synonymous with nonexistent?"

This won a wheezy laugh from her father.

"In short, I have my privileges restored. And some surgical privileges, under supervision."

"Good for you, Margot."

"Thanks."

"Have you seen Whitely?"

"No." She lifted one shoulder. "He's never going to forgive me. I embarrassed him."

"Does it matter?"

"Maybe not."

"I don't think so. Peretti's the one who counts at that silly place." Dickson ground his cigar into the ashtray, and got to his feet again. "I'd better go up to your mother, I think. See if she wants anything."

Margot rose, too, and walked with him to the door. He held it for her to pass through, and as she walked by him, he said, "I want to help you rebuild your clinic, Margot. The people down there need a doctor."

She paused, the automatic refusal poised on her lips, but she didn't speak it. She saw that her father was sincere in his wish to help. And, she thought, he *needed* to help. He needed to help her, and she needed his assistance. She could put aside her pride this once.

She leaned forward to kiss his whiskered cheek. "Thank you, Father," she said. "I appreciate it. And you've helped me make up my mind."

CHAPTER 21

"Hattie, don't climb the stairs," Margot protested. "Just set everything there at the foot. I'll get it."

"No, ma'am, Miss Margot," Hattie said stoutly. "You got nobody else to help you, and I'm right here to do it." She shifted the linens and towels to her other arm, and grasped the banister as she huffed up the narrow staircase into Blake's apartment.

Margot followed, her own arms full of clothes from her wardrobe. The air was stuffy and stale in the apartment. Margot saw that the marble-topped cane had been replaced beneath the peg rack, stains and all. Her father must have been here. It seemed right that the cane was back in its proper place, though it would never look the same.

She went into the bedroom and threw the clothes on the bed, then hurried to open the window. She went back into the kitchen to find Hattie straining to open the little window over the sink. Perspiration dripped from her neck and cheeks.

Gently, Margot moved her aside. "I'll get this," she said. "You can put those towels in the bathroom."

"I don't like this much," Hattie said. She picked up the towels and stepped into the little bathroom just off the kitchen. "It don't seem right, you living in this little place, and nobody to look after you."

"You'll be looking after me, Hattie," Margot said. "I'll still be having all my meals in the house—most of them, anyway. And Leona and Loena will do my laundry and dust once in a while." She unlatched the window, and pushed it open. Air began to stir through the apartment, and she turned and surveyed with satisfaction the three little rooms that were now hers. "I should have thought of this before."

Hattie came out of the bathroom, and picked up a set of sheets. "What if Mr. Dickson finds a new butler?"

"I believe he's decided against that. We're all hoping for Blake's return one day."

"How is Blake, Miss Margot? I mean, truly?"

Margot turned to look into Hattie's sweet, plump face. "I'll take you to see him, Hattie. Would you like that?"

"Oh, yes, ma'am, I would!"

"You'll find he doesn't speak very well. Not yet, in any case. But there are some good signs, and I think a visit from you would lift his spirits."

"Thank you, Miss Margot. Oh, thank you!"

Margot preceded Hattie into the bedroom to move her clothes out of the way. Hattie snapped out a sheet, and Margot went to the other side of the bed to help. "Father's going to learn to drive the car himself, he says." Margot began arranging her clothes on the peg rack behind the bedroom door. She had never noticed before that Blake had no wardrobe. The whole apartment, in fact, was only sparsely furnished. But then, Blake's personal possessions were sparse.

Hattie shook her head as she smoothed the linen over the ticking. "I just wish they'd get rid of that motorcar," she said. "Mrs. Edith won't never ride in it again."

"No. I don't suppose she will." Thinking of her mother made Margot pause, a lawn shirtwaist in her hands. "Hattie—does she talk to you?"

Hattie straightened with a little grunt, and reached for a pillow-case. She didn't meet Margot's gaze. "A little, Miss Margot. Just a little."

"About Preston?"

"No. She don't talk about him at all."

"I know she blames me."

"Now, you just stop that." Hattie plumped the pillow and set-tled it at the head of the bed. "She gonna come to her senses one of these days. It was an accident, that's all. Can't go back and undo it." Hattie bent for another pillowcase, and as she straight-ened, Margot saw that her eyes had reddened, and they glistened with tears. "He was such a sweet little boy," Hattie said, half under her breath. "Such a pretty smile, he had."

Margot turned back to the kitchen without responding. Surely it was better to let them remember Preston the way they wanted to. What good would it do now to dredge up old hurts? She went to the sink to run a glass of water, and as she drank it, she gazed out across the yard just as Blake always did, one last look to be certain everything was in order before he went to bed.

She paused, and lowered her glass. Her mother was at the win-dow of her upstairs bedroom, lifting the lace curtain to peer at the garage. She looked like a ghost of herself, pale, thin, ephem-eral. Why was she looking out here? She avoided Margot when-ever she could, closing doors or stepping into other rooms when Margot was near. It had seemed the best thing to simply remove herself from her mother's presence. Edith had not roused herself to make any comment or any objection.

"There," said Hattie behind her. "Your bed's all ready. What else do you need?"

Margot set her glass in the sink, and turned. "Nothing. I'm fine."

"You come over for lunch now, you hear?"

"Just a sandwich, thanks, Hattie. I'm due at the hospital this afternoon."

"Best come soon, then."

"I will."

There wasn't much left to do. Margot put her lingerie in the little chest of drawers. Hattie had sent one of the twins to clear out Blake's things and store them in the attic. She had hung towels and washcloths in the tiny bathroom. Margot put her hairbrush and other toiletries in the cabinet over the sink, and checked to see that there was soap in the little wire basket hanging from the edge of the claw-foot tub. Margot touched the soap, wondering if Blake had used it, but it was a new cake of Ivory, the letters still prominent on its surface. Hattie must have set it there.

In fact, there seemed to be nothing of Blake left in the apartment except the cane. There had been books, but they had disappeared. She hoped the twins had decided to take them to their own room, but she wouldn't ask. She intended not to frighten Loena and Leona anymore, and quizzing them about some old books might do just that.

She took one last look around before she started down the stairs and walked across the yard. She let herself in through the screened porch, and came in the back door to the kitchen. Hattie had left her a sandwich on a plate, wrapped in a cloth napkin. Margot pulled out a chair, and was ready to sit down, but Edith startled her, stepping inside the door, leaning against the wall.

"Mother?" Margot said.

Her mother was so pale and colorless that she looked oddly transparent, like a creature made of glass. She wore no powder, no lipstick. Margot wondered if she had had her hair done since Preston's death. It looked ragged, even dirty. Her eyes had an unfocused look, and Margot thought she had better speak to someone about the laudanum.

"Mother?" she said again. "Do you need something?"

Edith crossed to the table, and sat down next to Margot. It was the closest they had been to each other in weeks. Margot was shocked to find that her mother smelled bad, as if she wasn't bathing regularly, or cleaning her teeth. "I keep hearing him," Edith said in a hoarse whisper. "You have to take it away so I won't hear him."

"What do you hear, Mother?"

"It's—it's Preston—" Edith's eyes swam with tears, and her lips trembled. "Screaming! He keeps screaming, and he won't stop!"

Horror made Margot's belly crawl. She felt the blood rush from her face until she feared she had gone as pale as her mother.

"Please," Edith said again. "Take it away! If you take it away, it will stop!"

"Mother—take what away? I don't know what—"

"That sapphire! The jewel—I can't stand it in the house!"

Margot stood up abruptly, scraping the legs of her chair on the linoleum. She put a hand under her mother's arm. It felt as thin and brittle as a twig. "Mother, you need food, and a bath. You need to stop taking so much laudanum. I'll make you a cup of coffee, and then—"

Her mother tried to twist away. "No, no, Margot! I don't want coffee. I want you to take that—that *thing*—" Her voice rose to a wail. "Take that *thing* away!" She clamped both hands over her ears, and burst into hysterical sobs.

Margot stared at her, open mouthed. In seconds Hattie was there, bundling Edith into her arms like a weeping child, urging her out of the kitchen and up the stairs. Loena and Leona came in, shoulder to shoulder, looking at Margot with wide eyes. "What is it? What happened?"

Margot said, inadequately, "Mother's upset. Hattie's taking care of her." She wrapped her sandwich up again in its napkin, and left Leona and Loena staring after her as she went out of the kitchen and up the stairs to her bedroom.

Her room looked bereft without her toiletries and books and the little oddments of daily life. The dressing table was bare, its lace-draped stool tucked beneath it. Nothing was left but a few winter clothes in the wardrobe, and some bits of lingerie and jewelry she rarely wore abandoned in her bureau. She crouched, and opened the bottom drawer.

She had wrapped it in a chemise and left it there, hoping—

hoping what? That she would forget about it? That someone would take it?

She unfolded the chemise, a lacy thing her mother had given her for Christmas, and which she had never worn. The sapphire lay innocently in its folds of silk, a stone as long as the first joint of her thumb. She knew nothing of jewelry, but it looked like a museum piece, with its heavy silver chain and filigree setting. Why hadn't Preston had it reset?

She picked up the stone and cradled it in her palm. It reminded her of a time when she was small, when she and the family had picnicked on Alki Beach, on the shores of Puget Sound. Blake had laid a starfish in her hand, and though the creature didn't move, she felt the potency of its life through her fingers. She had held it gently before laying it reverently back in the tide pool.

Margot clicked her tongue at her own fanciful thinking. It was nothing but superstition. If she allowed this silly thing to continue to haunt her, it would be as if Preston were still here, badgering her, lying in wait to trip her up. She twisted the chain around the sapphire, and thrust the thing into her pocket. She carried the chemise over her arm as she went out of her room. Perhaps she would find a time to wear it when Frank returned.

As she went down the stairs, she heard Hattie in her mother's bedroom, speaking soothing words. Margot paused on the landing, listening, wondering. Edith couldn't know that Preston had screamed as he was dying the night of the fire. She had told no one. Edith had never met Thea. Frank would never have mentioned it, and certainly not to her mother. So where did Edith get an idea that she heard Preston screaming? And why did she turn to Margot to make it stop?

Margot walked slowly down the stairs. Her brother's story was a tragedy, but it had come to an end. She could not allow him to go on tormenting her—or anyone else—from his grave.

She went out through the back door and across to the garage apartment, where she found an empty coffee can under the sink. She stowed the sapphire in it, and shoved it into the back of the cupboard.

* * *

She spent a quiet afternoon at the hospital. She saw a child with a high fever, and settled him in the children's ward with plenty of hydration and a nurse to give him sponge baths. The little boy's color was good, and he was talkative, so she wasn't worried about him. His mother stayed in the ward with him, and Margot promised to see them again in the morning. She saw a case of alcohol poisoning, which meant she had to pump the man's stomach. It wasn't pleasant, but it was routine. Afterward, she sent him up to a public ward with orders to restrain him if he became violent, and to give him as much water as he could drink. She stopped by to visit two other patients, both of whom were resting comfortably.

At the very end of the day, she was called down to the reception area, where she found a slender, freckled girl in a school uniform waiting on one of the straight wooden chairs. The girl jumped up when she saw her. "Dr. Benedict," she said. "Do you remember me? Colleen O'Reilly?"

"Yes," Margot said, hesitant at first, then smiling. "Of course I do. You've had your baby."

Colleen's eyes were bright and clear, her freckled cheeks rosy. "Oh, yes, that was weeks ago. I went to your clinic to see you, but—it's all burned up."

"We had a fire." Margot tipped her head, assessing the girl's appearance. "You look very well, Colleen. And you're back in school."

Colleen smoothed her dark vest and pleated skirt. "Well, yes. I'm a year behind my class, though."

"I'm glad to see you," Margot said. "Are you here to see your doctor?"

The blue eyes, still fresh and innocent despite everything, lifted to hers. "I want you to be my doctor again," she said. "I didn't like the Good Shepherd doctor very much. But now your clinic is burned up."

"We're going to rebuild it. There will be a new one in the

same place," Margot told her. "Do you need to see me now? Is there anything troubling you?"

"No. I'm fine. I just don't want to see that doctor anymore. I don't think he liked us much—us girls at the Good Shepherd."

"Well. If you need care before my new clinic is ready, you can come to me here."

The girl smiled, and put out her hand in a grown-up fashion. "Thank you, Dr. Benedict."

As she turned to leave, Margot said, "Colleen." The girl turned. "You must be back with your family."

"I am."

"What did you do about your baby?"

Colleen's gaze was frank now, and a wise expression came into her eyes. It reminded Margot of the look in Mrs. Li's eyes, with her toddlers at her side. Mrs. Li was only four years older than this girl.

"You were right about my family," Colleen said. "They didn't throw me out after all. Mama and Pa are raising Peter as their own. Pa said no grandson of his is going to be given away to people he doesn't know."

Margot smiled behind her hand as she watched the dark skirt and shiny Mary Janes swish away from her.

As she left the hospital for the evening, she encountered Alice Cardwell just coming on for the evening shift. "Good evening, Matron."

"Dr. Benedict," Nurse Cardwell said. "Are you going to rebuild your clinic?"

"Yes. The builders are going to clear the site next week, and start on the foundation."

"But you lost your office nurse."

Margot nodded. "She went back to her people in Chicago."

"Well," Cardwell said. She carried a charge book in one hand, her cap in the other. "I have several student nurses who show promise. Let me know if you would like a referral."

"I would indeed," Margot said. "Once the building is under way, I'll ask you."

"Good. Good evening, then, Doctor." Cardwell walked off, her long apron rustling. As Margot went out through the front doors, she saw Dr. Whitely walking across the lobby with another physician. He looked away, avoiding her eyes.

She smiled to herself as she stepped out into the Indian summer sunshine. It was a relief not to have to worry about him, or to pretend a respect she didn't feel. And it was a damned good thing his wasn't the only voice on the hospital board.

She arrived back at Benedict Hall just as Hattie was carrying a leathery leg of lamb into the dining room. Margot would have preferred to take a plate in the kitchen, but Dick and Ramona and her parents were all seated at the dining room table. It seemed better to sit down and make the best of it.

"Have a good day, Margot?" her father asked.

"I did, Father, thanks."

Ramona said, "Are you really going to live over the garage?" Dick flashed her a look, but Margot smiled.

"It's better that way. So the telephone doesn't disturb you all at odd hours."

"It's just so strange," Ramona said. "I mean, servants' quarters—"

Dick blew out a breath, and snapped, "Leave it alone, Ramona. Margot has a right to live where she wants."

Ramona flushed, and Margot felt a flash of sympathy. "It's all right, Dick. Ramona's quite right. It's a bit unusual."

"Makes perfect sense," Dickson rumbled, and began to struggle with the carving knife and the overdone roast. Leona came in with a dish of watery mint sauce and passed it around. "I hear from Peretti you're going to assist him in the operating theater next week."

"Yes. He asked me yesterday."

"Good, good. Something interesting?"

Margot was about to answer, but caught herself. "I'll tell you about it sometime if you like, Father. Some other time." The glance Ramona gave her across the table was grateful, and almost sisterly. Margot smiled at her, and Ramona smiled prettily back.

Margot glanced at her mother, at the end of the table. She looked better than she had the day before. She had bathed, at least, and it looked as if Hattie had tried to help her with her hair. She wore powder, and lipstick, but beneath the cosmetics her face was pale and her eyes were hollow. She kept her eyes down as Dickson put meat on her plate and passed it.

With her eyes on her mother's still face, Margot said, "Have you set the date for the funeral, Father?" Dickson answered, explaining that it would happen the next week, that the interment would be at the new Evergreen Cemetery, and that Father McBride would officiate. Edith's features didn't change throughout his recitation. It was as if she hadn't heard the question.

Or didn't want to hear the answer.

It was strange to say good night to everyone, then make her way through the kitchen, out the back door, and across the yard to the garage. It was already dark, the autumn evenings beginning to close in. She switched on the bulb hanging in the stairwell, and climbed the stairs, hearing no sounds but the faint buzzing of electricity and the click of her heels on the treads.

She was startled, as she reached the top of the staircase, to see that a brand-new candlestick telephone rested on the kitchen counter next to the old hot plate. She smiled, and touched its black surface with her fingers, caressed the shining brass trim. This was her father's doing, of course. He hadn't mentioned it, but he must have arranged to have it installed while she was at the hospital. She wished she knew how to reach Frank. She would have liked to hear his voice, but he had been adamant. She had been allowed to doctor him once. No more.

She turned off the light over the stairs and went into the bedroom to undress in the dark. It was a clear night, and without the camellia blocking her window, she could lie in Blake's old fourposter bed and watch the stars until she fell asleep. It was comforting, somehow, to climb in between the fresh sheets, lay her head on the pillow, and think that the last person to sleep here had been Blake himself.

She gazed at the stars beyond her window, and thought about Preston, who had discovered what it was like to die. Margot had seen plenty of death, as any physician would, but though she had watched people breathe their last, seen their bodies go limp and empty, felt that absence in a room that only a death could create, it was still the final mystery, the one all of her science couldn't solve.

She rolled on her side. Only one way to find out, she thought wryly. And she wasn't ready for that for a long, long time. She yawned, and closed her eyes, warm, comfortable, deliciously drowsy.

When she startled awake, she had no idea how long she had been asleep. Clouds had rolled in to obscure the stars, and she could see only the faintest outline of the window. She sat up, pushing her tumbled hair away from her perspiring face. She shuddered, thinking of the nightmare that had disturbed her sleep, and glad it was over.

She had dreamed of Preston. In the dream he was a shadow figure, eerily silent, pursuing her through the corridors of Benedict Hall. She couldn't see his face, but she knew it was him. She fled from him, up to the third-floor servants' rooms, down to the basement laundry, around the long porch, through the shrubberies of the garden. He was so close behind her she thought she could feel his breath on her neck. She didn't know what weapon he might carry, but her back, in the dream, tingled with anticipation of whatever violence he intended.

In the dream, she reached the garage, and managed, barely, to lock the door before he could follow her inside. He still made no noise, but he hovered outside the garage, demanding she give in to him.

There was something he wanted. Something he believed she had.

The whole thing was irrational. Preston was gone. He couldn't hurt her anymore. The dream was no more than a remnant of the years of conflict and misery.

But somehow, still, she knew he wanted the sapphire.

Margot lay down again, and pulled the blankets up to her chin. She would not give in to such a pointless fancy. It was no less silly than Ramona and her fairies. Preston might have believed the stone had some sort of special power, but she was a scientist. She knew better.

Determinedly, she closed her eyes, and willed herself to go back to sleep. She had to get up early to be at the hospital. She needed her rest.

It was no use. The sapphire filled the little apartment with its presence, imagined or not. Margot berated herself for allowing an illogical idea to take hold of her—as it had her mother—but she couldn't banish it.

"Damn," she muttered, and threw back the covers.

She fumbled her way through the dim bedroom and the even darker kitchen. She opened the cupboard, and reached into the back for the coffee can, groping with her fingers. When she got hold of it, and pulled it to the front of the cupboard, she gasped, and nearly dropped it.

A second later she laughed. It was just a stone, after all. A big sapphire on an antique silver chain.

But when she had first looked into the old coffee can, she had seen—or thought she had—a blue glow coming from the stone, glimmering through the darkness where there was no light for it to reflect. Flickering, as if—

"Poppycock," Margot said aloud. She thumped the can onto the counter with unnecessary force. "It's a rock, and if it keeps me awake all night, so be it!"

She turned her back, and marched back to the bedroom. She got into bed, plumped her pillow, and pulled the covers over her head.

CHAPTER 22

The day of Frank's return to Seattle was glorious, brilliant with Indian summer sunshine. The cottonwoods along Aloha were shedding the yellow coins of their leaves, sending drifting veils of gold over the streets and lawns. Margot took the streetcar down Broadway, and walked to King Street Station. There she stood beneath the coffered ceiling, watching the reader board for the train's arrival time, pacing back and forth on the marble floor as the Northern Pacific train pulled in and the passengers began to disembark.

She caught sight of him as he made his way past the line of cars toward the station entrance. He wore his Stetson at a jaunty angle, and he carried a valise in one hand and—her heart leaped as she saw it—a newspaper in the other. In the other hand. Not really a hand, of course. It was artificial, a Carnes arm, the latest in prostheses. But that didn't matter. It didn't matter in the least. He was wearing it, using it, swinging his arms in the most natural way.

Margot's eyes filled with tears of relief. She pressed the heels of her hands to her cheeks, trying to stop them. He shouldn't see her crying, for heaven's sake. He should see her smiling, confident, as if she had always known it would work out.

He caught sight of her, and she saw his grin from beneath the shadow of his hat brim. She hurried to meet him as he came through the turnstile.

He didn't say a word when he reached her. He set his valise on the floor, and his newspaper on top of it, then took her in his arms and squeezed her so tightly she laughed. The artificial arm felt slightly stiff against her back, but she felt the flex of the wrist, the bend of the elbow, and her heart swelled with pride. She hugged him back, both arms around his neck, then kissed his ear, his cheek, and finally found his mouth.

When he released her at last, her tears had escaped despite her intentions, but it didn't seem to matter. He brushed them away with his right hand, smiling down at her. "Left hand is a bit hard for tears," he said. "But it works damned well for everything else." He held it up to demonstrate. The wrist rotated in a clockwise motion so the jointed fingers turned naturally toward him. When he straightened his arm, the wrist turned back. She ran her hand up his shoulder to feel the snug fit of the brace. "Officer's arm, they call it," he said with a chuckle. "Best of the lot."

"Oh, Frank," she said, through tremulous lips. "I'm just so— so *happy!*"

He took her in his arms again, oblivious to the people swirling past, jostling them. "Good," he said huskily. "That's good."

Frank had just completed a circuit of the building site, double-checking measurements before the concrete would be poured, when Margot came striding up Post Street. Her legs, long and slim, flashed beneath her skirt, and Frank remembered that her legs were the first thing he had noticed about Margot Benedict, before he had any idea who she was. Today she wore a small white straw hat and white cotton gloves. Her dress was low waisted and narrow, her hair bobbed to swing just below her earlobes.

"Who's that?" one of the workmen asked, leaning on his shovel.

"Dr. Benedict," Frank said.

The man gave a low whistle. "I never seen no doctor who looked like that!"

Frank chuckled, and went to meet her. When he told her what the workman had said, she laughed. "You should have seen what I put on first! I got dressed to dig in the dirt, but then Hattie wouldn't let me out of the house unless I changed. Hattie, who gave me such a look when I cut my hair and shortened my skirts! Now she says my young man shouldn't see me in a dowdy three-year-old dress."

She squeezed his fingers, and they walked together up the street to the site.

All the detritus from the fire had been cleared away. To Frank, the bare dirt seemed as full of possibilities as a freshly ploughed bed must seem to a gardener. He could see the new building in his mind as clearly as if he had sketched it in the air, the footings installed, the walls constructed and poured. He pointed here and there, telling Margot where her office would be, where the examining room and the waiting room would stand. In his plans, he had rotated the building so that the window of her office gave her a glimpse of the waters of the bay. The entrance to the building would be wider than it had been, with a short walk to the street. He planned a trellis to make it inviting.

"And I have a surprise," he said.

She smiled. "Show me."

He had wrapped it in a piece of canvas, and laid it ready for this morning. As he folded the material back, she exclaimed, "Frank! Where did you get it?"

"It was in the pile of things to be carted off." With pride, he handed it to her.

She took the sign, and ran a loving hand over its surface. M. BENEDICT, M. D., it proclaimed, in fresh red paint. The new varnish sparkled in the sunlight. "Oh, Frank! This is the nicest thing you could have done for me. Thank you so much."

"Glad you like it."

They stood together watching the concrete for the slab flow in a thick, gritty stream onto a neat layer of gravel that had been trucked in from the foothills. By the time the men started smoothing and detailing the slab, the sun was high overhead, and the heat had begun to rise. It was, Frank thought, a fine omen that there was no rain today. The concrete would cure perfectly.

The men wandered off with their lunch pails to find some shade. Frank was about to ask Margot if she wanted to go down the street to the café for some lunch when she released his arm, put her hand in her pocket, and stepped close to the smoothed wet concrete. He followed, wondering, and stood behind her as she crouched next to the northwest corner, where the anchor bolt showed above the level of the soil. He caught sight of the sapphire in her hand, gleaming blue in the sun. It was a beautiful thing, surely a valuable thing. And she was going to drop it into the wet cement.

He said, "Wait!"

She glanced at him over her shoulder. "Why? Do you want it?"

"Margo—a museum, or something—"

She held up the necklace, and the sapphire revolved slowly in the sunshine. "I don't think so," she murmured. "I know it's not scientific—but there's something strange about this stone. It has an effect on people, real or imagined, and I think it's better if it's hidden away." She grinned. "You'll think I'm becoming a spiritualist, I suppose."

Frank crouched, too, his bent knee touching her shoulder. "The thing scared Carter."

"Preston seemed to think it had some sort of power, but then, my brother wasn't really sane. Mother is sane, of course, but she'd had a lot of sedation. That might account for her obsessing over it. Everything can be explained in a logical way."

"But?"

She turned her face up to the sunshine, closing her eyes, drawing a deep breath. "It's a feeling. It's like—like when I know

what's wrong with a patient before I really have enough information to make a diagnosis."

"Instinct."

"Yes." She made a rueful face. "Many of my colleagues don't
believe in instinct, of course. They want facts. Evidence."

"But you—"

"I prefer facts, believe me. But when instinct is what there is . . ."

"Margot." He touched her shoulder with the fabricated fingers
of his left hand. "Do what you want with it."

She nodded. She held the stone out on its chain, then released
it so it dropped into the wet cement, chain and stone lying on the
surface in a little crater of gray paste. With her finger, she pushed
it beneath the surface. He reached down to help her, pressing
down the links of the chain until the whole thing disappeared.
He got up, and went to the pile of tools at one side of the foundation to find a trowel. He carried it back, and smoothed the surface of the wet cement.

When they stood up, there was no sign they had disturbed the
slab at all. Margot sighed. "It will be safe there," she said, "for a
very long time."

Frank encircled her with his arm, and bent to kiss her cheek.
"Too bad, though," he said softly, his lips right beside her ear. "It
could have helped buy our house."

He felt the tremor that ran through her, and heard her sudden
intake of breath. She said in a dry whisper, "What? What did you
say?"

He held her close to him, his cheek against her sun-warmed
hair. "Our house," he repeated. "When we're married."

She drew back, and her chin lifted in that challenging way he
had come to recognize. "Frank Parrish," she said sharply. "Is that
a proposal?"

He held his ground against her level gaze, but it wasn't easy,
and thinking that made him smile. "Cowboy proposal, I guess."
Her lips parted, but she didn't speak. He released her, and stood
back a little. "Margot—are you surprised?"

"I—" Her chin dropped, and she bit her lip. "I just thought—

it was so nice, being together. Having each other. I didn't think beyond that."

"But it's natural," he said awkwardly. "A man and a girl. The next step."

Her expression was one of confusion, even fear. He wanted to pull her against him, to kiss away her doubts, but he made himself stand still. She said, "Frank—I'm going to want to practice. To go on being a doctor."

"Why wouldn't you?"

She stared at him, her lips parted, her cheeks flushed. "My mother would be so relieved someone wanted me. She would say that now I should settle down. Give up all this foolishness."

"And *my* mother," he said, in as steady a voice as he could manage, "would call that a terrible waste."

"I want to meet her, Frank."

"She wants to meet you."

"Even if . . ." Margot's voice trailed off. She turned her head away from him, gazing out to the west, where the waters of Puget Sound sparkled bravely in the cool sunlight. "I just never thought I would be . . . a wife, I suppose. Someone's wife, like someone's house or someone's automobile. It has always seemed so—constricting."

"I don't want to constrict you."

"I don't know if you could help it."

"But you—you do want to be with me?"

She turned swiftly back to him. "Oh, yes! I want to be with you!" She moved close to him, pressing her cheek to his chest, pushing her little hat askew. "Frank, there are so many things that change when a woman marries. It's not the same for a man."

"What's not the same?"

"A woman is expected to change her name."

It was his turn to hesitate, to gaze out toward the water in search of answers. He said, searching for the right words, "I'd like you to have my name, but if you don't want to take it—" He broke off.

She pulled back, and looked up at him as she straightened her hat. "I love you," she blurted in a rush. "I'm ruining this, I know, but—I warned you I'm not like other women!"

Relieved, he grinned at her. "I don't want other women."

"You really don't mind if I—" Her voice broke, and he saw that her eyes shone with sudden, surprised tears. "If I go on being—me?"

"Margot!" He gripped her hands, one in his good, flesh right hand, the other in his careful, stiff, but working left. "Sweetheart! I wouldn't want you any other way!"

"It doesn't seem possible." Her chin thrust forward, even as one of the tears trembled on her eyelashes and escaped down her cheek. "But I'm so glad, Frank! You're just—you're the most wonderful man!"

At this he burst into laughter. He put his arm around her to guide her away from the building site and down toward the Public Market. "I want to buy you flowers," he said. "And try to propose properly." He squeezed her against him. "But only if you promise to say yes."

She flashed him a sidelong look. "We'll see," she said, but she was smiling, and she pressed herself close to his side, their steps matching as they walked. "We'll just see."

ACKNOWLEDGMENTS

The year 1920 seems in many ways a very long time ago, while in others it feels like yesterday. Medicine and fashion and technology were on the brink of great change, but had not yet stepped over that threshold. I'm deeply indebted to the following for helping me find what I needed to understand my characters and their period: Dean Crosgrove, P.A.C.; Nancy Crosgrove, R.N.; Phyllis Hollenbeck, M.D., author of *Sacred Trust;* Becky Kyle, medical librarian; John Little, Assistant Curator of the Museum of Flight, Seattle; the librarians of the King County Library System, who so tirelessly search for answers to even the most arcane questions; Hepzibah, a reference specialist in the Special Collections Division at the University of Washington Libraries; and Donald J. Ostrand of the Vintage Telephone Equipment Museum of Seattle.

Heartfelt thanks go to my first reader, Zack Marley. The fine writers Brenda Cooper and Cat Rambo provided discerning and incisive critiques. The Tahuya Writers group—Brian Bek, Jeralee Chapman, Niven Marquis, Dave Newton, and Catherine Whitehead—provided critical ears and emotional support.

A special note of thanks is due to my agent, Peter Rubie, and my editor, Audrey LaFehr: Thank you both for your encouragement and advice. This project wouldn't exist without your help.

Readers are invited to visit www.catecampbell.net to read more about *Benedict Hall* and the 1920s.

BENEDICT HALL

Cate Campbell

About This Guide

The suggested questions are included
to enhance your group's reading of
Cate Campbell's *Benedict Hall*.

Discussion Questions

1. The period following World War I, which ended in 1918, was one of social upheaval. In what ways do the different members of the Benedict family model the changes in society?

2. Margot Benedict faces strong opposition to her struggle for equal opportunities in a male-dominated field, and is working in a time of diminishing numbers of women physicians. Why do you think there is so much resistance to her efforts and those of other women of the day?

3. Do you think professional women face similar obstacles in the present day? What choices do women have now that they lacked in the 1920s?

4. Dickson Benedict and his daughter have spirited arguments over social issues. Do you think Dickson takes opposing views from Margot because he believes them, or purely for the sake of the debate?

5. Fashions for women changed much more swiftly in the 1920s than ever before in western history. Why do you think that was the case? What do shorter hemlines, bobbed hair, discarded corsets, and even the use of cosmetics tell us about how the role of women in society was changing?

6. Preston Benedict is convinced that the sapphire he stole in Jerusalem imbues him with special powers. Do you think his conviction is what creates that power? Do you think his belief speaks to the state of his sanity?

7. Abraham Blake was born free, although his parents were slaves, set free only by the Emancipation Proclamation. He is grateful to Dickson Benedict for his place in Bene-

dict Hall, but do you think he is still, in essence, an indentured servant? Was there any other choice for him?

8. Edith Benedict is a product of her time, a woman accustomed to comfort and wealth and assured of her social role. Her daughter, Margot, grew up with the same advantages. In what ways are these two women different? Are there any similarities between them?

9. Margot Benedict is practicing medicine nearly a decade before the advent of antibiotics. Are you surprised, reading the novel, at the level of medical sophistication being practiced in her day? Are there elements of Margot's medical practice that remain unchanged almost a century later?

10. Toward the end of the novel, Ramona Benedict reveals her own special talent for fashion, and helps her sister-in-law to choose clothes that flatter her instead of making her look like the dowdy lady doctor, as she did in the *Times* photograph. Do you think that Ramona and Margot, two such different women, have discovered a basis for friendship?